LINDSAY BUROKER

STAR KINGDOM

GATE QUEST

BOOK FIVE

Gate Quest

Star Kingdom

by Lindsay Buroker

Copyright © Lindsay Buroker 2019

ACKNOWLEDGMENTS

Thank you, good reader, for continuing on with my Star Kingdom series. I'm having fun writing these characters, and I hope you are enjoying spending time with them. Many thanks, also, to my editor, Shelley Holloway, and my beta readers: Rue Silver, Cindy Wilkinson, and Sarah Engelke.

CHAPTER 1

QIN PUSHED AGAINST THE FLOOR, HER GENETICALLY ENGINEERED muscles straining, but the metal netting didn't budge. She had a feeling she was wrapped up in one of the ridiculously strong alloys used to build space elevators. Worse, the net seemed to have a computer intelligence that knew precisely where and when to tighten to restrict her movements.

It had taken a half hour of panting and flexing to wiggle her arms around so she could press her palms against the sticky, stained metal floor. But all that effort was for naught. She couldn't push her cheek more than an inch off the floor, much less work her body free.

"What's the matter, Three?" one of her two captors caroled. "Not as strong as you thought?"

"Maybe she hasn't kept up with her training, and her muscles have gone mushy," the other said.

"Mushy? I think you mean they could have atrophied." Qin doubted the goons had ever opened a book or knew what the word meant. "And they haven't. Why don't you let me go, and I'll demonstrate how effective they are?"

"Nah, we like looking at them through that net. Kind of sexy."

"Don't talk to those idiots," Bonita said—she was on the floor on the other side of a bed, under an identical net. Their captors had dragged them into a space-station hostel that rented rooms by the hour and, judging by the grime and the rumpled comforter, didn't clean them between uses. Or at all. "Associating with them might make you dumber."

"Nobody asked you, Granny." One man prowled toward Bonita, his rifle in hand, his body protected by combat armor.

Not that their captors had needed armor. Qin, her stomach growling and whining pitifully, had allowed herself to walk right into that back-alley trap. She'd known there were people looking for them, and she'd still let herself be caught. She was ashamed and felt awful since Bonita was stuck here with her. There was nobody back on the *Stellar Dragon* to mount a rescue, not unless Viggo sent his cadre of robot vacuums out. They might improve the cleanliness of the room but would do nothing to free Qin and Bonita.

"I don't have children," Bonita informed them.

"What?"

"No kids. Without kids, you can't have grandkids and ergo can't be a grandmother."

"Ergo?" a new voice asked. "Atrophied? Such words. I had no idea bounty hunters were so erudite."

"Suck yourself, Toes," Bonita said.

"That's more what I'd expect." The new speaker strolled in, also wearing combat armor, though his helmet was off and tucked under one arm, revealing tattoos of barbed-wire daggers on his cheeks, a studded dog collar around his muscular neck, and the two thin braids dangling from his otherwise trimmed gray beard. They swayed against his chest plate as he walked.

Qin wanted to yank on them and drag him under one of his own nets.

"So glad we're not disappointing you," Bonita said.

While the men were focused on Bonita, Qin tried to think of a way she could barter for their freedom. Or at least *Bonita's* freedom. These brutish representatives from the Drucker pirates didn't want her captain. They only wanted Qin.

"Toes—or do you prefer Johnny?" Qin had listened to Bonita banter with Johnny Twelve Toes on the way to Death Knell Station, but she hadn't spoken to him herself.

"I've learned to let six-foot-two, genetically engineered cat women call me whatever they like," Johnny said.

"Asshole has a nice ring," Bonita said.

"Now, you're just being crude. Don't disappoint me, Laser. I was quite delighted by you during our earlier talks."

"I'm so pleased."

"Johnny," Qin said, "you've got us. Good job setting up that trap. I didn't even smell your people coming—the armor, I guess. But you don't need my captain. You just need me. You can drag me back to your ship in this net, but I'll fight you the whole way. Unless you let her go. Then I'll walk with you without trying to escape."

"*Qin*," Bonita whispered harshly. "Don't make that deal."

"There will be no deals, I'm afraid," Johnny said. "I'm taking you both back to our warship. Captain Laser has attempted to double-cross the Drucker family. The brothers don't allow such things to go unpunished." He turned toward the other two men. "Bandit, Snaggle, I need you two to run an errand. I've just learned the dockmaster isn't willing to let our shuttle fly away unless we pay a ridiculously hefty fine. That's what we get for coming to a station run by enemies. Go to their office and flex a little muscle, will you? Let them know we'll pay the standard fee but not a dollar more."

"You sure we got to do that so soon, boss? Couldn't we have a little fun with the Qin first? She's getting me excited with all that straining down there. And there's that nice bed right there."

Qin gritted her teeth, flooded with memories of the times the pirates had come to her and her sisters and used them for sex. Letting them do so had been one of her duties since she'd been twelve and removed from the laboratory where she and her sisters had been raised. Bought and paid for by the Druckers. Maybe she'd been foolish to believe she could ever be anything but their slave for the rest of her life.

"We're not taking that net off her," Johnny said.

"Maybe we could just… go through the holes."

His buddy snorted. "You are an idiot, Snaggle."

"Screw you."

"I'm not wearing a net—you still interested?"

"No wonder you wanted your freedom," Bonita muttered to Qin.

"Yeah." A lump of sadness swelled in her throat. It had been more than six months since she'd escaped and started working for Bonita. Long enough to taste freedom and know how precious it was—to learn how much she didn't want to give it up.

"Go deal with the dock authority," Johnny said. "Both of you. If we're late getting back to the warship, the Druckers won't leave you with a dick to use."

The two men tramped out, leaving Qin and Bonita alone in the room with Johnny.

Qin liked that the odds had become better, but Johnny had already proven himself intelligent by seeing through their ruse and capturing them. She would have preferred that he'd gone and left the other two. Qin and Bonita might have been able to trick *them*.

Johnny pulled a chair over to Bonita's side and sat down. With the bed in the way, Qin couldn't see either of them now, but her enhanced ears and nostrils told her much. In the quiet room, she could even hear their heartbeats. Bonita's was surprisingly slow and steady, given the situation. Johnny's was a little faster, and he smelled of sweat. Faint thumps sounded as one of his knees bounced up and down, the heel of his boot bumping the floor. Was he nervous? That surprised her.

"I lied," Johnny said.

Bonita snorted. "Hear the shock in my voice."

"I *am* willing to deal. But we don't have much time."

"Let me out of this net, and I'll consider listening to you without interjecting snide comments."

"Really?" he asked. "I wouldn't have guessed that was possible."

"I have amazing self-control."

"I'd tell you that was getting me excited, but I don't want you to think I'm the sexual deviant Snaggle is."

"Too late."

Rustling sounded, followed by a click and a snap.

Qin gaped. Had he freed her?

Not that Johnny would feel threatened by Bonita. She was an excellent sharpshooter, but she didn't have a weapon. Not unless she could get Johnny's rifle away from him...

"Free me, too, please," Qin said as politely as she could manage. "I also won't make snide comments."

"I don't think your freedom would be conducive to my health," Johnny said.

"What?" Bonita asked. "Are you afraid she'd cut off your extra toes? Don't you want to see what it's like to go through life with a normal number?"

"I think you'll be more amenable to my proposition," Johnny said, "if there aren't bloody gouges in my feet."

"I'm completely indifferent to your feet."

"Are you? They seem to have nestled into a nook in your mind."

"Nestled into a nook?" Bonita snorted. "What kind of pirate are you?"

"That's what I want to discuss with you. I'm not a pirate." Johnny lowered his voice. "I'm Bjarke, a knight from the Star Kingdom who was sent to spy on the Druckers almost a year ago. I'm one of two of Jager's spies in System Cerberus keeping an eye on the pirate families here to make sure neither the Miners' Union nor some other government with a militia pays them to become a threat to the Kingdom."

Qin was skeptical, but it was such a bizarre story to come out of a pirate's mouth that she didn't immediately scoff.

Bonita, however, scoffed. Loudly. "I was just on Odin. None of the knights we saw had tattoos muddying up their good looks."

"I'd like to think the tattoos enhance my looks," Johnny said, "but they are temporary. The man whose name I took had them. I had to look as much like him as possible so the Druckers wouldn't be suspicious when I applied for a job. Technically, I let them kidnap me and convince me that it would be good for my health and career to become their accountant. Apparently, good bookkeepers are hard to come by in this system."

"Let's pretend I believe you," Bonita said. "What's your proposition?"

"I recently received new orders to head to System Hydra and Tiamat Station to help with a mess over there. I could steal a shuttle and get to the gate on my own, but it would be ideal if I left in such a way that I could come back to the Druckers later without suspicion. Which is why I'd like you to use your wit, and your hulking sidekick there, to overcome me, kidnap me, and take me off on your ship to sell to the highest bidder."

Bonita digested that for a few seconds. Qin didn't know what to think, but it sounded like he was willing to let them escape… as long as they took him with them. Was that really true? Or was this some new trap? She didn't believe he was a knight. *Asger* was a knight. Noble, respectful, brave, and unmarred by ugly tattoos or dog collars. She missed him.

"Highest bidder?" Bonita asked. "You think the Druckers will believe someone is willing to bid money for you?"

"If nothing else, my organs are in excellent shape. There's a market for authentic ones rather than cybernetic replacements." Johnny's chair creaked as he leaned back in it. "I thought about staging my death, but you know how difficult that is to make plausible."

Qin couldn't see the wryness on his face, but she could hear it in his voice.

"I'm starting to hate you," Bonita said.

"No, you're not. I'm handsome, witty, and delightful."

"Make that delusional."

"I need your decision quickly. We don't have much time before those two get back. I'll pay you ten thousand crowns for a ride to System Hydra—two thousand now and eight thousand once we get there—and you can either drop me off at Tiamat Station or transfer me to the warship *Osprey*. And I need you to say, if the pirates comm you, that you kidnapped me. Maybe you can say there's a bounty on my head. That's more believable than a sudden interest in selling my organs, I suppose."

"A bounty where? I'm sure they have access to the same job boards that I do."

"I can have the Kingdom issue something."

"If you're really a knight, why can't you have the Kingdom rescue you?"

"They're not here, and you are."

Bonita sighed. "Qin, what do you think?"

"That if he frees us and we can get to the *Dragon*, I'm willing to fly along with him. Or help you put him in the brig."

"Yeah," Bonita said. "That's the deal, Toes. We'll take you to Hydra, but you ride in a cell. And then we comm the Kingdom warship and see if they really want you."

"I assure you Captain Ishii will be pleased to have a knight offering his services."

The last Qin had heard, Captain Ishii already *had* a knight offering his services. Asger.

"Uh huh," Bonita said. "Why don't I trust you?"

"Because your life dealing with criminals and deadbeats has left you cynical and suspicious of everyone?"

"That must be it. Let Qin go."

Johnny walked around the bed to crouch beside Qin. "May I have your word, Qin Liangyu Three, that you won't attack me? As I mentioned, we're short on time, and we need to use it to artfully arrange the room to make my kidnapping look plausible."

"I won't attack you unless my captain tells me to."

"So my fate is in her hands? How fitting." He tapped a key fob, and the net went limp. Another tap, and it rolled itself into a ball that he stuck in his helmet.

Qin stood up, stretched her muscles, and faced Bonita. She raised her eyebrows, silently asking if Bonita believed anything Johnny was saying.

Bonita shook her head slowly. No.

On the Kingdom warship *Osprey*, heading from Tiamat Station to Xolas Moon, Kim waved at the door chime outside Casmir's cabin. The door opened almost immediately.

She was on the verge of pointing out that a man with a bounty on his head shouldn't open his door without checking to see who was on the other side, but Zee, the six-and-a-half-foot-tall tarry black crusher, loomed inside like a wall of death.

"Greetings, Kim Sato," Zee said. "It is delightful to see you today."

Maybe less a wall of death and just a wall.

"Thank you," Kim said. "It's, uh, good to see you too."

Casmir had programmed the crusher to protect her as well as himself, which had been handy on numerous occasions, but Kim still wasn't that comfortable around him. She certainly didn't share Casmir's feeling of warmth toward Zee, who happened to look like the crushers that had tried to kill them back on Odin. But Casmir felt warmth toward all robots, sentient and not. A couple of days ago, he'd been lamenting parting ways with Viggo and his vacuums. It had taken a few seconds for him to remember to also lament parting ways with Qin and Bonita.

"Please enter." Zee stepped aside. "Will you speak with Casmir Dabrowski? I have observed that he has been moody and withdrawn since leaving Tiamat Station."

"I'm not moody," came Casmir's voice from the desk around the corner. "I'm contemplative. And you're only noticing my silence because you're missing Tork."

"There is no reason why I would miss an inferior android."

"He stayed up all night playing network games with you."

"Androids and crushers do not sleep, so staying up all night is not an inconvenience. And I am a pleasure to game with."

Kim eyed Zee as she stepped into the cabin. "Casmir, your crusher has developed even more personality since I last saw him."

"You keep saying that as if it were a bug rather than a feature."

"You noticed."

At least Zee's personality didn't suggest he was inclined to quash humanity and take over the Twelve Systems. Overly clever AIs made some people nervous, since they *had* once revolted and headed off to claim Verloren Moon in System Cerberus for themselves. They'd stayed there—so far—instead of branching out to conquer any human governments, but there were rules and limitations against developing free-thinking computers now. Casmir might get in trouble if someone back home figured out how intelligent his crushers were. Not that he wasn't already in trouble for a great many other things.

"Have you been writing heartfelt apologies to King Jager?" Kim waved at the glowing light of the display at the desk where he sat. The rest of the room was dim, save for a soft red light beside the bed, since the night cycle had started on the *Osprey*.

"No. Should I be?"

"You were singlehandedly responsible for putting a new president into power on Tiamat Station, one who told the Kingdom to stuff it."

"It wasn't singlehanded. Asger was there. And so was Zee."

"I'm sure Zee masterminded everything."

"You were there too."

"Not in the control center when all the banter with the pirates was going on."

Casmir's usually expressive face grew closed at the mention of *pirates*, and Kim regretted mentioning them. It wasn't as if they had been paragons of humanity, but even she would have felt morally squeamish had she been the one to kill the power to all of their ships, an act that had allowed the four Kingdom warships to swoop in and annihilate them. Per Ambassador Romano's orders, from what she'd heard. Even Captain Ishii had appeared glum at the role he'd played in slaying thousands of helpless people.

"President Nguyen hasn't said she *won't* negotiate with the Kingdom," Casmir said. "Just that she wants me to be there if she does."

"Which definitely won't draw Jager's attention to you. Again."

Casmir spread a helpless hand. "Even if I sent a letter of abject apology, I'm sure he wouldn't read it. I'm just a peon."

"Not quite." Kim sat on the end of the bed. From there, she could see the text and photos glowing on his display. Ah, he'd been researching his progenitor, Admiral Tariq Mikita. It was about time. "Find anything interesting?"

"Some pictures that look startlingly like me. Something between me and Rache, actually."

Rache.

Her stomach did a little flipflop at his name, and she remembered him standing in his airlock, telling her how Jager had masterminded his kidnapping and the brutal death of his fiancée. Even after ten years, his eyes had been haunted with pain. She understood now why Rache loathed King Jager and wanted to make his life miserable. She was surprised Rache hadn't assassinated the man, since it seemed like someone with his talents and resources could pull that off, but maybe he wanted Jager to suffer, to feel emasculated by loss after loss…

"See here?" Casmir pointed at a photograph. "Mikita looks kind of hard and intense like Rache is, but then in this picture, he's smiling and seems… maybe not as goofy as me but approachable. It probably depended on whether he was on his way to conquer a system or if he'd just conquered it." Casmir's lips twisted with wry uncertainty.

Kim deduced that he hadn't yet decided if having been cloned from the legendary admiral was a good thing or not. "Maybe he was determined when he was thinking up ways to win Princess Sofia's love and smiling after she sent him a note about how charming his robots were."

"I'm sure *that* didn't happen. There's nothing about an interest in robotics in his record here. Just military strategies and tactics." Casmir brought a thoughtful finger to his chin. "Do I look determined when I'm thinking up ways to win Princess Oku's interest?"

"More frenetic and scheming."

"Oh. Is there any chance women like that in a man?"

Since Kim was horrible at lying, she avoided answering. "I'm going to send you some of the work I've been doing for her on bee bacteria these last two days."

His eyebrow twitch said he had noticed that she'd avoided the question, but he nodded and leaned forward, letting himself be diverted since this was also about Princess Oku.

"I heard we're only a couple of hours from reaching Xolas Moon's orbit," Kim said, "so you probably won't have time to work on anything, but I had an idea where you might come in."

"With bee bacteria?"

"With robot bees. I can improve the health of some regular bees with a custom strain of beneficial bacteria, and I think that will allow them to survive more easily in the atypical environment of a rotating space habitat, and also compensate for the strange anomalies of gravity created through its spin. But from the research I've done, they rely on magnetoreceptors in their abdomens to navigate by the magnetic field on Odin—and other similar planets. The magnetic fields on space habitats aren't as strong. I think that stressor may be a large part of what's been causing the deaths of the experimental bees in space. They're struggling to find their way home after gathering pollen. I was thinking, since bees are such social insects, that maybe putting some robotic guide bees into their swarm and having them programmed with routes to and from gathering areas might help the biological bees find their way back to their hives."

"Oh!" Casmir sat forward, eagerness in his eyes. "I already designed robot bees."

"Yes, you showed Oku. She mentioned it."

"She did? You've spoken to her?" He touched his chest and smiled hopefully. "About my bees?"

"We—" The door chimed, and Kim broke off.

Casmir hesitated, then waved for Zee to answer it.

"I'll send her my thoughts on the project," Kim finished as the door slid open. "And we can run some experiments when we're done with our mission here." She smiled, trying not to let any bleakness into her smile, though she worried that their *mission* would not be easy.

They had to use submarines to retrieve an ancient wormhole gate from an astroshaman base believed to be in the sea under the ice of Xolas Moon. The astroshamans had the advantage of this being their home base and their home system, and they also had greater technology and likely had greater numbers of people on their side. Further, the submarines the Fleet had acquired weren't designed for military use. They were for civilians wishing to tour the water worlds of the system and had been rented from Tiamat Station. To top it off, Rache and his mercenaries were also after the gate and had chosen the best submarines before the Fleet ever got there.

No reasons to feel daunted, none at all.

"Let me in," a male voice growled from the corridor.

"This is the private cabin of Casmir Dabrowski," Zee informed the speaker—Kim wasn't sure who it was, since she couldn't see around the massive crusher. "Hostile visitors are not permitted in."

"I'm not hostile. I'm an ambassador. I'm diplomatic."

The clipped tone sounded plenty hostile to Kim, and she grimaced at the identification. Ambassador Romano had given the order— supposedly delivered by Jager, but who knew?—to have all those pirates killed. After he had possibly made a deal to convince those pirates to come in the first place, to harry the station and make the citizens eager for the protection of the Kingdom. He hadn't confessed to that, but Kim had heard the hypothesis from numerous people.

"If you leave your cabin number or a comm ident where you can be reached, I will let Casmir Dabrowski know to visit you during daylight hours."

"You'll wake his ass up so we can visit *now*." Romano raised his voice. "Dabrowski, are you *sleeping* in there? I will, as the king's specially appointed agent on this ship, speak with you. *Tonight*."

"Such a polite specially appointed agent," Kim murmured.

Casmir rolled his eyes. "If he's not armed, you can let him in, Zee."

"His clothing may hide weapons," Zee stated. "I need to search him physically to know if he's armed. Shall I do so?"

"No!" Romano roared.

A wicked glint entered Casmir's eyes.

Kim shook her head and raised a hand in warning.

"If he truly wishes to speak with me," Casmir said, "I'm sure he won't object to a quick pat-down. After all, someone on this very ship tried to assassinate me just a few weeks ago. As a reasonable man, he will understand my need for precaution."

"I have been instructed to search you for weapons," Zee informed Romano.

"Maybe he'll go away," Casmir mouthed to Kim.

Kim rubbed her face. Her affable robotics professor roommate who could make friends with anyone had an alarming knack for making enemies out of people with the power to ruin his life.

"Fine," Romano growled.

"Damn." Casmir turned off the display, hiding his research.

Kim believed that Royal Intelligence knew all about Casmir's origins, and figured they'd likely told the ambassador, but she could see why Casmir wouldn't want the man to know what he was up to. The photographs alone promised that the entries on Admiral Mikita here in System Hydra were much different from the ones in the Kingdom, where a giant hero of a man had been inserted into the history texts. Whoever the real face had belonged to, he looked nothing like five-foot-seven seizure-prone Casmir.

"He is unarmed," Zee announced.

A red-faced, scowling Romano walked into the cabin and straight up to Casmir without glancing at Kim. Casmir rose and forced a smile.

"Welcome, Ambassador," he said as Romano, who towered several inches above him, prodded a finger into his chest, which Casmir ignored. "Thank you so much for enduring my security ministrations—you can't be too careful when there's a bounty on your head, you know. I don't suppose you know anything about that? I've been terribly confused about why some prince from the Miners' Union would want me dead. Is it true that he has a home here in System Hydra? I was reading about him earlier, and it said his main residence and operations are in System Stymphalia."

By taking control of the conversation first, Casmir seemed to throw off Romano, who answered instead of leading with whatever had been on the tip of his tongue.

Albeit, it wasn't a flattering answer. "I don't know where he lives, but I'm sure lots of people who've met you want you dead."

"If that's true, that's disturbing. Can I get you something to drink? I was able to acquire grape and cherry fizzop on Tiamat Station."

Romano's eyes narrowed. "From *President* Nguyen, by chance?"

"Ah, she may have been the one to know of a beverage provider who hadn't been looted."

"Neither the king nor I are pleased with the role you played on Tiamat. You are not to comm that *president*—a former secretary of education running a huge space station with a population of millions, dear *God*—or send text messages to her, or stand on the hull of the ship and use signal flags in her direction." Romano prodded him in the chest again. "Do you understand?"

"Certainly, Ambassador. I'm only here to help Captain Ishii find the gate. Which, lucky for him, I did." Casmir smiled brightly.

"We'll see if it's actually down there," Romano growled. "You better hope it is. More than your career rides on you making the king happy."

With that ominous threat delivered, Romano stalked toward the door. Zee was still near the threshold, and Romano bumped him with his shoulder. Zee didn't budge, so Romano wobbled into the wall. He cursed and stalked out, muttering about the universe going to robots.

"You need to work on your relationship with him," Kim said.

"This is the first time we've even spoken to each other face to face."

"Yes, and in case you didn't notice, it didn't go well." Kim was sure Casmir hadn't missed that unveiled threat about more than his career being at stake. He loved his parents and would worry about his actions affecting them negatively. Since the Dabrowskis lived fewer than ten miles from Drachen Castle and Royal Intelligence Headquarters, they would be easy targets for the king's minions.

"I did notice, but I'm not sure how to fix it except by doing what Jager sent me to do, help pinpoint the location of the gate." He shrugged.

As he'd said, he'd already made his best guess, and Ishii and his marines were either going to find it under the ice down there or not.

"If you disable the gate's security measures, the ones that make it ooze deadly pseudo radiation any time someone without immunity gets close, that might make Jager and everyone who has to deal with it happy."

She'd already suggested that to him—and to Captain Ishii. Since he had immunity, he was the logical one to take on the task, but she didn't know if he was capable of it. He was a genius when it came to robotics, but whatever technology had been used to build the wormhole gates was far beyond what humanity—at least the humanity residing in the Twelve Systems—knew and understood.

"If that's what they're expecting of me, I better finish the crash course I started on gate theory instead of researching Mikita or working on Oku's robot bees." He waved to the computer display, though he looked glum. Or daunted. Or both.

"Just be glad your three-hundred-year-old genes didn't get the modification that protects people born today from the Great Plague, since you'll have the opportunity to *try* to deactivate the gate defenses without dying a not-so-slow death."

"Rache will be able to try too. If he gets there first."

"He probably will. They got a head start, right? You'll just have to be smarter and know more than he does."

"Be smarter than my clone? Right, no problem there."

"He doesn't have an advanced degree in robotics. His specialty is in making people dead." Kim grimaced, wishing that wasn't the truth, that Rache hadn't felt compelled to become the killer he was today.

"So naturally, he's exactly the man I should want to compete against in a quest."

Kim thought about mentioning that she had received a message from Yas Peshlakai, Rache's doctor, asking if she knew of any bacteria that might affect people who were modified with cybernetic implants.

She'd given him a terse answer, since it would have felt like a betrayal to the Kingdom to help Rache beat her own people to the gate, but there were two species of bacteria that had come to mind. They were both known to feed not on the implants themselves, which were fairly indestructible, but on the synthetic myelin sheath material typically used on the cyberware that wired the implants into the human nervous system. It could be debilitating on someone with a lot of implants, requiring a return to a surgeon to have everything rewired. A couple of years earlier, her corporation had created a bacteriophage that could destroy the invasive bacteria in an infected person, which was the main reason for her familiarity with the subject.

Inspired by Yas's query, she'd hunted through the bacteria she'd brought along on this trip and found that she had a strain of one of the known offenders. She had agar plates growing more in the sickbay lab now and planned to tinker to see if she could modify them to act more quickly once they infected an astroshaman, perhaps after delivery by a fast-acting inhalant. But *anyone* with cybernetic implants would be affected, so she didn't know how effective a weapon it would make. Further, anyone inside combat armor would be protected from an inhalant.

Kim decided not to mention her work to Casmir, since she feared nothing would come of it, but he did look like he needed moral support.

She gave him a pat on the shoulder, wondering if she would ever stop feeling awkward at such gestures. "You'll do fine, Casmir. You're crafty. I've never seen you fail to achieve something you truly wanted."

Kim just wished Casmir truly wanted to make King Jager happy. He seemed far more interested in making the Twelve Systems a better place. Which was admirable... but might get him killed.

CHAPTER 2

IR WILLIAM ASGER STOOD IN THE BRIEFING ROOM off the bridge, the doors closed so he could take the comm that had come in from his superiors at Prester Court in private. He ignored a message from his agent that had also arrived, saying he'd gotten Asger a modeling deal to promote children's sporting equipment, though a bleak sarcastic part of him admitted that at least he'd have a backup job if he was kicked out of the knighthood.

But he didn't *want* to be kicked out. He wanted to do the right thing, as he believed he had on Tiamat Station, and he wanted his superiors to understand that it was the right thing. And to praise him instead of berating him.

Judging by the exasperated expression that appeared on Sir Baron Farley's face when it came up on the vid, praise wasn't what would come out of his mouth. Even knowing it was a recording, Asger braced himself.

"Asger, what the hell are you doing over there?" were the first words out of Farley's wide mouth. As his lips reared back in displeasure, white teeth flashed like a wolf's fangs. "You were supposed to save the existing president, not put a new one on the throne."

Asger supposed his boss wouldn't appreciate a correction that presidents had normal seats, rather than thrones.

"Chronis was already dead when I got there," he muttered, even though there was no point in replying to a recording. He would have to think about how best to phrase a response to record and send back.

"You haven't done one thing right this year," Farley went on. "Why can't I depend on you? You passed all the exams, you swore the oath, and your IQ tests assure me you aren't an idiot. Why are you making such idiotic choices? Chief Superintendent Van Dijk from Royal Intelligence was in here this morning, demanding to know why I sent someone so young on this mission. You better make sure Captain Ishii gets that gate for the Kingdom, or don't bother coming home. We'll have to ask you to ship your pertundo and your armor back in a crate and resign."

Asger hung his head, tears pricking at his eyes. He was glad it was a recording and that Farley couldn't see his reaction.

Frustration accounted for the tears as much as sadness, because he didn't think he'd done anything wrong. Oh, he shouldn't have helped Casmir back on that cargo ship in System Lion, but it wasn't as if he could have known Casmir wouldn't turn the gate over to the military. Asger couldn't have foreseen any of this trouble. And he believed they'd helped a good person take charge of Tiamat Station. He would have protected Chronis if he'd arrived in time, but he had the niggling suspicion that, no matter what King Jager wanted, Nguyen was better for Tiamat Station and its people. And it wasn't as if she'd said no to an alliance with the Kingdom. Just that she insisted Casmir be involved in the negotiations.

"And that's part of what's irking them, I'm sure," Asger muttered.

But he'd helped get rid of the terrorist outpost on Odin. Maybe he hadn't gone in personally with Casmir and Rache—he'd *wanted* to— but he'd helped Qin clean up those combat robots outside and make sure the way was clear when the Kingdom Guard arrived. Why couldn't he get any credit for that? Surely, they weren't giving it to Rache or Qin, even though Qin deserved it.

Qin.

He closed his eyes. What was she doing? He'd sent a note a week or two earlier, jokingly asking if she'd found any trees in System Cerberus, but he'd mostly wanted to know if she was all right. The last he'd heard, she had been going off with Bonita to try to get that bounty off her head and make the Drucker pirates forget about her. It was a job for a fleet, not two people, and he felt guilty that he couldn't have gone to help.

When he'd first met Qin, he'd mistaken her for an enemy and treated her poorly, so that didn't help with his sense of guilt. As he'd gotten to know her, he'd realized she was a sweet girl—woman—under the fur and fangs, and he'd also seen how she was treated by the average human, especially the average Kingdom human. Somewhere along the way, his feelings had changed, and now he wanted to protect her. Maybe that was silly since she didn't need protecting, not in the physical sense, but she needed… someone to make the universe a more accepting place for her.

Maybe he should have mentioned that to her instead of teasing her about trees, but jokes made him feel safer, less vulnerable. He wasn't ready to contemplate the meaning of his feelings. There was too much else to worry about now.

Shaking his head, Asger walked out. He would record a response for Farley before he headed down to the moon. He needed to let his frustration and temper ebb first.

As he stepped onto the bridge, the first thing he heard was Ishii growling at someone.

"Where in all the dark matter did all these *ships* come from?" Ishii was sitting in his command chair, which looked far more like a throne than anything President Nguyen would get, and wasn't addressing any specific bridge officer stationed around him.

Asger looked at the forward display for evidence of these ships, but all he saw was the curving white-gray horizon of Xolas Moon. The *Osprey* and the other three Kingdom warships had reached it and taken up orbits.

Ishii was scowling at his handheld tablet rather than the forward display.

"The ones approaching Tiamat Station, sir?" an officer asked.

"No, the ones flying up my ass."

Someone sniggered.

Asger walked up to his chair, wanting to see the tablet.

Ishii glanced up at him. The fingers of his free hand were curled into a fist. "I'm struggling to maintain my military professionalism this week."

"Do you not usually discuss your ass with your officers?"

"I try to only share my ass troubles with Dr. Sikou."

"She's a lucky woman."

"It's what she spent all those years in medical school for." Ishii tilted the tablet so Asger could see it.

Ishii had also been annoyed with Asger after the gate had gone missing, but they'd been through a couple of sticky situations since then—and shared sake in his quarters twice—so he'd been treating Asger more like a confidant lately.

The tablet's display showed a dozen dots—ships—flying toward Tiamat Station, all less than a day out. There was also a column of ident codes and a summary of each of the spacecraft. They were from different governments around the system, most from universities rather than militaries.

"At least they're not pirates," Asger said.

"I'd rather deal with pirates," Ishii grumbled. "You're allowed to *shoot* them."

"It doesn't look like they're heading here." Asger waved at the icy white moon on the display. "Maybe we won't have to deal with them."

"They're close enough to see us on their scanners and wonder what four Kingdom ships are doing hugging up to their barren and supposedly uninhabited moon."

"True."

"Ambassador Romano has already bribed a few government officials not to notice us."

"Is that what he's here for," Asger murmured.

Ishii gave him a dark look. "That was *supposed* to be all."

"Sir?" the officer who'd spoken before asked. "I've got some intel on them. It seems that President Nguyen sent out invitations to all the governments in the system. She wants to put together an alliance and is hosting a meeting."

"Damn, she moves fast, doesn't she?" Ishii pushed a hand through his short black hair. "How long has she officially been in office? Two days?"

"About that, sir."

Ishii looked up at Asger. "You know what kind of alliance she'll want to put together, right?"

Lunar wing moths fluttered in Asger's stomach. "One designed to keep the Kingdom out of the system?"

If that was the end result of Nguyen's new rule, Asger could see why Jager and Royal Intelligence would be annoyed. Was he deluding himself about the role he'd played? Had he truly done the *wrong* thing? There'd been so few other options…

"That's my guess," Ishii said. "Which would mean she was just saying what we wanted to hear, and that she never had any intention of negotiating a treaty with us, whether Dabrowski shows up at the table or not."

"There's a ship hailing us, sir," the comm officer said.

"One of the ones heading to this *meeting*?" Ishii curled a lip.

"No. This is a big mining ship that someone fortified with a lot of weapons. It's been in the system longer than we have—it was lurking in the asteroids of the outer belt when we first came in. Now, it's heading our way."

"The system is getting extra popular, isn't it?"

The officer didn't answer, but someone brought up a visual of the ship on the forward display. It was long, rectangular, and large enough to spin and provide gravity for its crew. Rail guns, sun destroyers, and cannons were mounted on all of its sides.

"That looks more like a pirate ship than a mining ship," Asger said.

"No kidding. Tibbs, tell Colonel Jeppesen to get his marine teams together and have our engineers finish prepping the subs. All these ships are making me nervous. I want our people in the water and to find that gate yesterday."

"Yes, sir."

"Do we answer the hail, sir?" the comm officer asked.

"You get an ident on that ship?" Ishii asked.

"Uh, not a real one. We're reading it as a mining ship from the Songtham family, but they were usurped by the Dubashis ten years ago and don't legally own any ships in their own name anymore."

"Let's see what they have to say." Ishii waved at the display.

A bald, pale-skinned man with freckles and a red mustache appeared, then bowed deeply. "Did I get it right? My bow? That's how they do it in the Kingdom, isn't it?"

"That's how we do it." Ishii didn't bow back. He identified himself and said, "Who are you?"

"Captain Cullen. I have a proposition for you, *Osprey*."

"What do you and that large ship do for a living, Captain Cullen?" Ishii asked.

"Exploratory mining, of course."

"With railguns and sun destroyers?"

"Sometimes asteroids put up a fight." Cullen smiled easily.

"Uh huh. What's your proposition?"

"We've learned through various channels that you have a Professor Casmir Dabrowski on board. Is that correct?"

Asger rocked back. This wasn't about that bounty again, was it?

He made a note to ask Farley if the knights or Royal Intelligence knew why a Miners' Union family was gunning for Casmir. Farley might not tell him even if he knew, but Asger felt compelled to look out for his friend.

"What do you want with him?" Ishii asked without admitting they had him.

The lift doors opened, and Ambassador Romano walked onto the bridge. Ishii, focused on the display, didn't seem to see him.

"We could use a roboticist," Cullen said. "We have a large number of mining robots on board, and many are on the fritz. We're willing to offer five thousand Union dollars."

"You want to *buy* a human being?" Ishii gaped at him.

"Yes, that's legal in several systems."

"Not this one, and not in the Kingdom either. Dabrowski is a Kingdom subject."

The ambassador, eyeing the cheeky Captain Cullen curiously, came to stand next to Asger and Ishii.

"Let's not quibble, *Osprey*," Cullen said. "The rules are flexible in the space between habitats and planets. I'll go as high as seven thousand, and I'll also give you some information that I recently purchased. Invaluable information, especially to someone like yourself."

"I'm sure. Dabrowski isn't—"

"What information?" Romano interrupted.

Ishii shot him a glare and muted the comm. "It's not Kingdom policy to negotiate with pirates or traffickers of human slaves."

"Do we have proof that this man is either?" Romano asked.

"He's as much as admitted it."

"Hm, nonetheless, it would behoove you to gather as much intelligence as possible."

Ishii continued to glare for several seconds—he didn't look like he appreciated having some civilian attaché on his ship and interfering with his command. Asger didn't blame him. He half-expected Ishii to ask one of his men, or even Asger, to tote the ambassador off the bridge, but Romano had made it clear that he was good buddies with the king, so he expected preferential treatment.

Ishii un-muted the comm. "What information are you offering, Captain?"

Cullen smiled broadly, as if the trap he'd laid had sprung in front of his eyes. Asger was positive that nothing good would come from talking to this guy.

"It turns out that an associate of mine was on Tiamat Station during the upheaval a few days ago. I believe your warships were also there but weren't invited to dock."

"So?"

"So that's unfortunate, because you might have been able to do what my brazen associate was able to do."

"And that was?" Ishii's fingers were curled into fists again. Unfortunate that one couldn't send punches through a video channel.

"She noticed that a couple of shuttles owned by Captain Tenebris Rache, the infamous mercenary, came in to dock. She, being an entrepreneurial gatherer and seller of information, sent a drone out to watch his crew. It was, unfortunately, spotted and shot down, but not before she learned they were skulking around the station and stealing submarines of all things. Can you imagine?"

"No."

"No? Are you sure? I can't help but notice your little fleet is orbiting a moon with an ocean under the ice. What an odd place to visit."

Ishii looked at Romano, not muting the comm. "This is a waste of time. This buffoon doesn't have any information we don't already know."

"Ah, but wait." Cullen lifted his hand. "There's more. While Rache's people were stealing these submarines, my brazen friend programmed another drone, a small and less noticeable one. She sent it into one of his shuttles when the hatch was opened, had it place a locator beacon on board, and then zip out. His men were too busy to notice. She then sold me the frequency of the locator beacon in case I wished to find the shuttle once it was back aboard Rache's ship, the *Fedallah*, which has, I believe, slydar coating that makes it difficult for your people to track."

"For *anyone* to track," Ishii said.

"Anyone who doesn't have the frequency of the locator beacon." Cullen smiled.

"Which you'll give to us, along with seven thousand dollars, for Dabrowski?" Romano asked.

"Yes, it's a fabulous deal. Especially considering I had to pay ten thousand for the frequency. She's a shrewd negotiator, my contact."

"But you'd be turning Dabrowski over to Prince Dubashi," Ishii said, "who wants him dead, and is paying fifty thousand Union dollars to the person who makes that happen."

"*Is* he?" Cullen's mouth opened, and he touched his hand to his cheek. "How *interesting*. I, of course, need him to fix robots on my ship, so I can't take advantage of that."

"Uh huh. We're not interested. Don't comm us again." Ishii made a throat-cutting motion to his officer, and the face on the display disappeared.

Ambassador Romano frowned. "You should have kept him talking and learned as much as you could."

"We did. He wants Dabrowski to sell to the prince, and the odds of him having anything to track Rache are close to zero."

"I wouldn't be so sure," Romano said. "He knew what was going on in that station, and there's no way he should have unless someone inside reported to him."

"For all we know, the whole story is on the news network by now."

"It's not, sir," the bridge intelligence officer offered. "We've been monitoring all of the media outlets. Tiamat Station has recently started broadcasting again, after a hiatus of several days, but they're saying nothing of what happened, only that control has been re-established and it's safe to visit. There's nothing out there to suggest Rache is even in the system, not on the public channels."

The look Ishii shot him didn't appear that appreciative, and the officer turned back to his station.

Romano opened his mouth, but Ishii spoke first. "We don't deal with pirates, criminals, or other miscreants, Ambassador. I'm sure you're familiar with Kingdom policy. We also don't sell our subjects to slavers or bounty hunters to gain intel."

"I wasn't suggesting that," Romano said dryly, "just that we should have milked this contact for all we could. If we could get that frequency, it could be invaluable. Rache is our biggest competitor for the gate, after the astroshamans themselves."

Ishii rose from his seat. "You don't have to tell me that. That's why we're getting our teams together right away. We'll beat him down there. Even if we don't, he has one ship, and we have four."

"Superior numbers have rarely resulted in the Kingdom defeating him," Romano pointed out. "And we managed to acquire only an equal number of submarines."

Judging by Ishii's clenched jaw and the muscle ticking in his cheek, he knew that and didn't appreciate being reminded of it. "We'll handle it, Ambassador. In the meantime, I would appreciate it if you would return to your quarters and leave the bridge to military personnel."

Asger thought Romano might argue, but he merely clasped his hands behind his back and walked away with a bland, "As you wish, Captain."

Asger frowned after him, finding that easy acquiescence unsettling.

"What a pain in the ass," Ishii said after the lift doors closed. He didn't bother to lower his voice.

Asger wondered how their conversation had gone when Romano had given the order to obliterate the defenseless pirate ships.

"Given your problems in that area today, you better make an appointment to see Dr. Sikou." Asger smiled, hoping to lighten Ishii's mood, though his own mood was bleak. "Maybe she has a helpful cream she can offer you."

"Funny. If you don't make it as a knight, you can get a comedy gig at a nightclub."

"That wouldn't be necessary. My agent has a new modeling job lined up for me when I get home."

"Your face going to be on more tubes of underwear?"

Damn, was there anybody who hadn't seen that?

"Baseball bats and zero-g rackets actually."

"You're moving up in the universe." Ishii headed to one of his stations to check on an officer.

"If only that were true," Asger muttered, not wanting to contemplate the possibility that he might truly be kicked out of the knighthood and would have to fall back on modeling and competitive bodybuilding.

What would his father say about that? Not that he'd seen the man or even heard from him in over a year. His father had made it clear when he hadn't shown up for Asger's graduation ceremony that he didn't care about him. Someday, he'd learn how to keep the sarcastic jerk from taking up space in his mind.

"Someday," he sighed, heading for the lift so he could warn Casmir that bounty hunters were still looking for him.

Dr. Yas Peshlakai reported to the largest shuttle bay on the *Fedallah,* not because Captain Rache had ordered it but because Chief Jess Khonsari had requested it.

He stepped into a cacophony of controlled chaos. The entire engineering department was there, preparing six long, white and blue submarines for their deployment. Names on the sides such as *Tiamat Tours: Bubbles 3* were a reminder that they hadn't been built to go into battle. The engineers were affixing torpedo launchers to the hulls, but Yas didn't envy the teams that would go down. The submarines seemed paltry devices for attacking a high-tech base full of who knew how many human and robot defenders.

Cranes and heavy machinery that Yas couldn't name had been brought out of storage and assembled, presumably to lower the submarines into the ocean. He remembered the fissure that Rache's team had explored—and he also remembered the drones that had zipped out of it and attacked them. What would be waiting to defend the ocean entrance this time?

"Over here, Doc." Jess waved to him.

Pain furrowed her brow, and she lacked her usual smile. He'd brought his medical kit, assuming someone was injured—nobody requested his presence otherwise—and he hurried over.

"What is it Je— Chief?"

"You can call me Jess. It's fine." She smiled briefly, but it appeared forced. "Especially now. I heard you found your parents and that the sleazy usurper who killed your former president got hanged by his own people. That means you're not a criminal anymore, right?"

Yas eyed the submarines. "I suppose that depends on the various systems' treatment of men who *aid* criminals."

Jess also looked at the submarines. "We're not doing crime. We're collecting an artifact from people who stole it. Though I'm upset that it's the astroshamans. I still wish... well, I told you what I wish."

Yes, she'd expressed interest in their religion and those who left their human bodies behind to live entirely as machines. Maybe she thought that would be a way to escape the pain she dealt with from being a human with so many cybernetic parts. Or just from being a human.

"You did." Yas tried to keep any judgment out of his voice, and he didn't let himself point out that if she'd only come to sickbay and let him help, they might be able to find a better way to deal with her pain. One that didn't mean giving up her humanity. "Is someone injured?"

He didn't see anyone clutching an arm or sitting out of work.

"I've got a headache and need something strong. The first of the Kingdom ships is now orbiting around the moon, with the rest almost here, and the captain wanted these subs ready to go three hours ago. He's not happy that we're behind, but it's not like spaceships are designed to drop off submarines. Yes, the moon's gravity is low enough that we can fly down to the surface and back without the assistance of a launch loop, but you can't just hover over a crack in the ice and shove them out the door."

Yas was sure his face grew green as he imagined being inside a submarine shoved out the *door* from hundreds of feet up.

"They're designed to withstand the pressure of hundreds of meters of water overhead, but they're not indestructible. We'll get 'em in and out, but it's a lot of work. But, Doc." Jess patted his shoulder and turned it into a squeeze, a somewhat desperate squeeze. "I've got pickaxes trying to bore out the soft tissue in my skull. I need something. I already tried... other medications."

"The trylochanix?"

She met his eyes warily. She'd slipped into sickbay recently and liberated more doses from the medical cabinet with a lock that it turned out engineers could thwart. "Yeah."

"If you use the same medication constantly, the body becomes inured to it. It's better to switch it up." Or go off it altogether, he thought, and try something less addictive. "After it's been a while since you've been exposed to it, you'll regain your sensitivity. Caffeine works the same way. At first, it's a noticeable stimulant, but then you need larger and larger doses to achieve the same effect. After a while—"

"*Pickaxes*, Doc." Jess released his shoulder to point at her skull. "What about this face I'm making—" she grimaced deeply, "—suggested I wanted to hear a medical lecture?"

"I thought you might find the explanation useful in making drug choices in the future."

"Nope." She glanced toward the doorway out of the shuttle bay, though it was closed. "I just got a message from the captain. He's on his way. Gimme something good. Please." She opened her palm and wriggled her fingers.

Yas sighed and chose a painkiller that operated on different receptors than her trylochanix. He slid an ampule into his jet injector, positive she wanted something fast-acting.

"If you come to sickbay for your physical and let me run a DNA test," he said quietly, "we can come up with something optimal for you."

"I thought, from the fact that you've scheduled three physicals for me and I haven't shown up for any of them, you might have given up."

"Not at all. Corporal Chains has now not shown up for five physicals."

"Mercenaries are stubborn."

"I've noticed."

"How many has Rache not shown up for?"

"When I tried to schedule him for one, he hacked into the scheduling system and had it play a clip from a cartoon vid where a pack of wolves chase down a doctor and devour him. I *think* it was a joke, but there's a nugget of truth in all jokes, right?"

"In the good ones." She grinned at him, the furrows in her brow already less pronounced as the drug took effect. "Aren't you glad I just don't show up?"

"No. I'm sad that you don't show up." Yas smiled, even though it was the truth. He was still trying to be careful not to apply pressure, since he kept thinking that she would see the light on her own and come see him. But would she have to hit the bottom first? He knew he could keep her from dealing with so much pain, but... maybe more pain was what it would take.

"Because you're a doctor and can't stand it when patients don't comply with your wishes? Or because you want an excuse to fondle my lady bits?"

Ugh, he wasn't doing a good job of hiding his attraction to her. "I only fondle my patients after hours." He winced. That hadn't come out right. He was bad at jokes. Why did he try them? "I mean, I don't fondle my patients. That gets you written up by the medical board and kicked out of your profession."

"Probably not here. Especially since none of your patients show up to be fondled." Jess winked. "Uh oh, gotta run."

She raced toward one of the cranes, grabbing a toolbox as she went.

Yas looked to the door and wasn't surprised to find Rache walking in. He wore his black combat armor and his equally black hood and mask. He carried his helmet in his hand and wore a lumpy pack and two rifles on straps on his back.

"Khonsari," he barked, though he walked toward Yas.

"We're almost ready, sir," Jess called from the crane. "Fly on down to wherever you're dropping these hounds off. We can deploy them now, and I'll work on the system for getting them back on board while the teams are away."

Rache must have sent an order up to his pilot on the bridge, for the deck rumbled and the noise of the engines shifted. The *Fedallah* was heading down to the moon.

"It's good that you're here, Doctor," Rache said, walking up.

"Do you also have a headache?" Yas waved his injector.

"No. What I have is a need for a trained surgeon to go along on this mission to fix up anyone who's injured during the fighting."

Yas lowered his arm. "Oh."

"Don't worry. I'm going too. I'll throw myself in front of any torpedoes heading your way."

"Are the odds good that a mercenary in combat armor would keep a torpedo from blowing away what's behind him?"

"Oh, probably not."

"So we'll get to die together in a frozen hell under miles of ice?"

"It'll be a bonding experience."

"Like bonding our exploded particles together in a lumpy mass of blood and bone?"

"You're starting to sound like a mercenary, Peshlakai." Rache sounded like he was grinning.

"Now you're just being insulting."

"Captain." The giant-hat-wearing intelligence officer, Amergin, trotted into the shuttle bay. He waved a tablet. "I've got something interesting you might want to see before you go down."

Rache waved him over. "Show me."

Yas knew he should go pack for his impending submarine experience—or impending doom, as his mind wanted to call it—but Rache didn't move away from him as Amergin approached. Curious what the *something interesting* was, Yas watched as the tablet display flared to life.

"I've been working on disassembling the latest Kingdom encryption keys so I can snag copies of their communications for us, but this wasn't even encrypted." Amergin tilted the tablet toward them as a bald man's face came up, a red mustache dangling around a smarmy smile.

"That's Red Dog Cullen, a bounty hunter," Rache said. "His stolen and refurbished, as he calls it, ship is in the system. I saw it on the scans earlier."

"Yes, it is. And guess who he's talking to?" Amergin asked.

"The Kingdom?"

"One of the king's ambassadors who's on the *Osprey* right now." Amergin waved at the tablet, and the video played.

"Captain Ishii," Cullen said, "I'm delighted you reconsidered and opened communications with me. I haven't yet sold that frequency to anyone else."

"My name is Ambassador Romano," a cool voice said, the screen splitting to show a heavy-jowled face opposite the bounty hunter. "All further correspondence will go through me, not the captain."

"I'll talk to whoever wants to pay me. And give me Dabrowski."

Rache dropped his chin to his fist, but the mask, as always, hid his facial expression.

Yas was startled to hear some random bounty hunter bringing up the robotics professor, but Dabrowski's fingers had been all over the rise of the new Tiamat Station president, so maybe it wasn't surprising. Or maybe it had something to do with him working with Rache? If their king had learned of that, the professor could be in trouble.

"Do you actually want him?" Romano asked. "Or do you just want him dead?"

"Prince Dubashi wants him dead but also wants to see the body for proof that he's gone, so I need him. Or his corpse. In such a way that it's recognizable."

"I see. That may be difficult, but if you're still willing to give me the frequency of the locator that your contact put on one of Rache's shuttles…"

Rache jerked his hand down, and his chin came up. "What?"

"I can probably make sure Dabrowski doesn't come back from his mission," Romano finished.

"I won't give you the frequency until I have him," Cullen said.

"That's not acceptable. We need it now so we can find Rache's ship and ensure he doesn't get in the way of our mission."

"What is your mission, Ambassador?" Cullen drawled. "You know the entire system has noticed your little fleet and is mighty curious why it's orbiting a barren moon, right?"

"That's none of your concern. Send me the frequency, and you have my word that you can have Casmir Dabrowski's body once the mission is over. But you must agree to send it now."

"Are you in such a hurry to do battle with Rache's warship? The mercenary is wily."

"We'll handle him. Do you agree or not?"

Cullen tapped his chin with a single long finger. "I agree, but if I don't receive Dabrowski, alive or dead, within the week… Well, I'm taking *someone's* dead body to Dubashi." He stared pointedly into the camera.

Romano didn't appear concerned by the threat. "A week should be fine. I'll transfer the money now. Don't comm the ship again, except with the frequency, which you'll send directly to me."

"Needy, aren't you?"

"Yes, I am. Out."

The display went dark.

"Chief Khonsari," Rache called.

"We're ready to go, boss!" Jess jumped out of the crane and waved for a couple of her men to clamber down from the submarine they'd been hooking up.

"Good, but I have another task for you. It seems one of our shuttles that visited Tiamat Station may have picked up a tracking device."

"Nasty when that happens."

"Yes. Find it and destroy it."

"You got it, Captain." She saluted him and jogged off.

She was so much perkier and more vibrant than when Yas came in. He wished it was due to a love-induced release of endorphins at his presence rather than the drug he'd pumped into her system.

"What happens if our guys can't find it, sir?" Amergin asked.

"Then we'll have to launch the shuttles so they can't be used to drag down the *Fedallah*. I don't want our bridge crew battling four Kingdom warships while I'm miles under the ice."

Neither did Yas. He couldn't help but imagine a scenario where they were down there in submarines, the *Fedallah* was destroyed, and there was nobody to retrieve them.

CHAPTER 3

CASMIR'S MOOD WAS IMPROVING. HE WAS LYING ON the deck of his cabin with his hands folded behind his head as he watched and re-watched a video that had arrived the last time a courier ship gated into the system. It was from Princess Oku.

The video started with her hound Chasca rolling on her back in the manicured grass outside of the greenhouse in Drachen Castle's courtyard. Then Oku had walked inside and recorded soil, seeds, and sprouts in varying degrees of growth on a workbench while explaining her current project. She was working on hybridizing strains of a cereal grain that grew well on the system's space habitats and stations, hoping to increase yields.

Casmir found this glimpse of normal life back on Odin refreshing. Nobody was dying. Nobody was getting ready to invade anybody else's base. It was idyllic.

And so was Oku. Since she was the one recording the video, there weren't any images of her face, but he enjoyed hearing her voice, and he caught a few glimpses of her hands patting soil into pots, dirt under her finely trimmed nails. He grinned, still tickled that his princess wandered around in sandals with grass between her toes and thought nothing of dirtying her hands.

Not *his* princess. He shouldn't think of her like that. She was Princess Oku, who happened to have sent him a message that had nothing to do with her bee project and hadn't requested anything from him. She'd sent it just because. And he was delighted.

When it started playing for the sixth time, starting with the rolling hound again, he considered what kind of response he might send. He would prefer to share something cute rather than anything about all the death he'd seen on Tiamat Station—or the death that had occurred outside of it.

"Zee, I don't suppose you'd like to roll on the deck on your back and playfully wriggle your arms and legs in the air?"

Zee, who was standing in his usual guard spot by the door, looked down at him without commenting.

"I'll take that for a no."

"You are lying on the deck. I was debating if you had a seizure. I've observed that this can happen without thrashing and flailing, and that atypical words sometimes come out of your mouth afterward."

"That's all true, though I think it's more that the typical words just get a little slurred. I did not, however, have a seizure. The deck looked comfortable. Princess Oku sent me a video of her dog rolling on the grass. Crushers, of course, are far more intelligent and sophisticated than dogs, so I didn't truly expect you to roll around on your back."

"Also, there is no grass here."

"Which is the main reason you're not entertaining the idea."

"It is approximately .13 percent of the reason."

Casmir grinned. "That's a higher percentage than I would have guessed."

A new message came in, this one local and therefore present time.

Professor Dabrowski, scrolled President Nguyen's text. *Are you available to speak for a few minutes?*

Greetings, President Nguyen. I'm trying unsuccessfully to get Zee to roll around on the deck for my love letter, but otherwise, I'm not busy. Other than all the gate research he'd been doing, and the scanner he was trying to put together to read the pseudo radiation, but he couldn't mention those things to the leader of a foreign government who was probably wondering why the Kingdom warships were still in her system.

He would have to be careful with what he said, since he felt like he'd come to know Nguyen in the short time he'd been on Tiamat Station, and he wasn't good at keeping things back from people that he liked. Or from loathsome enemies. He needed to learn more restraint.

Zee? Wasn't that the large naked black robot trailing you around?

He's a little more sophisticated than a robot, but he is large. And naked. Kim hasn't yet convinced me to buy him a pink bow tie.

Is she the one who'll be the recipient of your love letter?

No, that's— someone else.

Someone who appreciates your robot's antics?

I do hope so. What can I help you with, ma'am? Is Tork doing well? Did he get a chance to explore your telescope?

He's fixing it right now, as there was some damage during our civil war. He seems well, though, and says it will give him an opportunity to make improvements. As for myself, I've called representatives from all of the governments in the system to Tiamat Station to discuss issues that face us.

Casmir wondered if the *Osprey* and the other three Kingdom warships loitering only a couple of days from her station were considered the "issues."

Many of them want to know why your fleet is skulking around Xolas Moon. Her dryness came through even with text only, and he had the answer to his question. *We can't believe that you've been invited down to visit the astroshaman base that nobody is supposed to know about. They're supremely unwelcoming to visitors without cybernetic implants.*

It's not my fleet, ma'am. Casmir wasn't surprised that she knew about the astroshamans since the moon was so close to Tiamat Station, but he dared not speak of it, since it tied into the real reason the Fleet was here. *I am merely a civilian advisor.*

Of course, I believe that.

Casmir scratched his jaw, not certain what to say. What did she *think* he was?

I assume you won't tell me what your fleet is up to, Nguyen continued, *and that's not why I sent a message. I wanted to ask if you'd be available to return to the station to help negotiate, as a neutral third party.*

Er, neutral in what manner?

I'm proposing that we unite the system to better face any threats that may come in the future. Not under one government but in a solid alliance that shares people and resources with each other as needed.

That seems logical. Casmir wondered how she could consider him neutral, when he was a part of the largest threat she likely had in mind. *But I'm not at liberty to leave the* Osprey—*technically, I wasn't at liberty to do so last time either. The Kingdom Fleet gets huffy if its civilian advisors wander off.*

Are you sure? I could send a ship to pick you up.

And spy on what we're doing on the moon?

Of course not. But don't be surprised if the ship has a lot of portholes. And scanners. You might recall that I'm an academic. We're a curious sort.

I know that well, ma'am. Perhaps after the mission, I'll have the freedom to come and go as I please. As soon as he mentally typed the words, he doubted the likelihood of them. *But I don't have any negotiating or diplomacy experience, so I don't feel qualified to help with your goal.*

Are you sure? You managed to get me to like you even though I was slung over your knight's shoulder.

I've heard from some women that Asger's shoulder is an appealing place to be.

It's more likely that you heard that from him.

That is possible, Casmir agreed.

I have a tremendous amount of work to do, so I'll sign off, but if you change your mind and come, it's possible the alliance will be more open to future negotiations with the Kingdom. Right now, they're all against having anything to do with Jager—and some of them are talking about putting together a force to drive your warships out of the system. But you might be able to charm them and convince them otherwise.

Are you positive *you didn't find Asger's shoulder appealing? You seem to be remembering our time together as better than it was.*

Just keep it in mind. I'm a historian, and I know your Kingdom was different three hundred years ago—your Admiral Mikita is remembered here as an honorable warrior and the rulers of that time as fair—but most people only go by memories of what happened after the rebellions started. The Kingdom was under different rulers by then, and they got ugly when systems wanted to leave. Very ugly. That's what most people remember.

Casmir stared at the ceiling. Did she *know* he'd been cloned from Mikita? Or was it simply chance that she'd brought him up?

She was, he recalled, an archaeologist, but it sounded like she had a solid background in more recent history. She'd done a double-take when she first met him. Had she seen enough photos of Mikita to notice the similarity?

I will keep it in mind. Thank you. Casmir rubbed his face, wondering if he should share the information she'd given him with Ishii. Ambassador Romano might make more sense—if he weren't an ass. President Nguyen was saying that the Kingdom had a chance to have a presence here, if not an outright alliance, if they—Casmir—showed up for their big meeting and spoke convincingly on their behalf.

But could he do that? Put effort into trying to help Jager extend his reach? If anything, he worried that Jager wasn't good for the Kingdom—or the rest of the systems. As much as he loved his home and his homeland, since all this had started, he'd been thinking about how it needed to change. Maybe it didn't need to become as progressive and liberal as so many of the other governments, but more open-mindedness would serve its subjects well.

If Jager got the gate, succeeded in replicating it and placing new gates in other star systems, he or his descendants would be the ones to call the shots about where humanity went in the future. Casmir feared that would make the Kingdom more powerful and allow it to be more insular and unyielding. If any other governments wanted to use those gates, they would have to play by the Kingdom rules.

There's something else, ma'am, he added, knowing he had to be careful with what he said.

He wanted to do the right thing, but with his parents and friends back on Odin, he feared the repercussions of openly defying Jager. But he also feared the repercussions of Jager getting the gate for himself. Casmir had suggested to Kim that the ideal scenario for humanity in general would be to give pieces of the gate to whoever was interested in studying it. He still thought that was logical and egalitarian. Unfortunately, he was positive Jager would see it as treason.

He could encrypt what he sent, but that would only make some communications officer monitoring the ship's communications traffic suspicious. And if the officer couldn't crack the code, he would call up Lieutenant Grunburg, who would handle it without trouble.

Yes? Nguyen prompted.

Casmir shook his head sadly. He was too much the coward to defy Jager outright when the future was such an unknown. He couldn't be sure that Jager's possession of the gate would change the course of humanity and give the Kingdom more power. For all he knew, even the brightest engineers on Odin wouldn't be able to replicate the gate. Or Rache would get it first and sell it to someone else. Or throw it into a sun to make sure nobody got it.

I don't know how to say this without sounding condescending, but I'm pleased that you were elected. You seem very proactive toward making the system better for your people and others who inhabit it. I do hope to have the opportunity to help you further one day. It wasn't what he'd had on his mind, but he did mean the words, and it made him realize he hadn't congratulated her.

Thank you, Professor. Would you still feel that way if I admitted that I'm as nervous as a cat picking a path across cracked ice and terrified that I'm going to screw up?

Absolutely. I feel that way all the time.

Oh good.

She signed off, and he smiled, though he wished he'd had the chutzpah to tell her to give notice to all of those ships that they should send archaeological teams backed by military vessels to Xolas Moon to demand a piece of the gate. They could work together and blockade the working gate out of the system to ensure the Kingdom Fleet couldn't leave unless it shared.

Treason, his mind whispered, and he was both glad and ashamed that he hadn't sent a message to her.

But what if Jager, who was already irritated with him, decided to ostracize him anyway? He might regret that he'd stood meekly by as the Fleet extracted the gate and took it home.

"When did life get so complicated, Zee?"

"What are you referencing, Casmir Dabrowski? You are lying on the deck and looking at the ceiling."

"Yes, complicatedly." Casmir smiled slightly. "I suppose if everything goes wonky, President Nguyen would let us move to Tiamat Station." He tried not to think about how he would then never see Princess Oku again.

"Tiamat Station is the home of Tork-57 now."

"Yes. I'm sure he wouldn't mind sharing it with you."

"Of course not. He has no one else who can challenge him at network games. He was modified to be intellectually superior to most androids. But not to a crusher."

"Naturally not."

"I have been contemplating my existence since we left the station." Zee left his guard post by the door to look down at Casmir.

"Oh? What have you come up with?"

"I believe you should make another crusher. Not one of those mindless killers from the batch you made for the military."

Casmir raised his eyebrows but didn't point out that he'd made only a very few modifications to Zee. If the others were mindless killers, it was because the soldiers who gave them orders were making them so. A sad thought.

"You should make another that is similar to but not identical to me, so that we may discuss and contemplate our existences together."

"Zee, do you want a *mate*?"

"It is possible that word applies."

Casmir knew he'd made Zee with the ability to learn and adapt, but he hadn't expected him to develop human feelings or the desire for companionship. Huh.

"I could do that. Not *here*." Casmir waved to indicate the warship. "I'd need raw materials and a metallurgy shop at least equal to that on Forseti Station, but if we survive this mission and go back to Odin, I ought to be able to gain access to such."

Maybe the prison that Jager threw him in after finding out about his duplicity would have a nice shop.

"Excellent," Zee said. "In the meantime, I will continue to play games and exchange witty barbs with the inferior android Tork."

A realization slammed into Casmir, and he forgot to breathe. Was this a conduit through which he could get a message to Nguyen? One those comm officers might not think to watch for?

"Have you remained in contact with him?" he asked carefully.

"I have. You sleep so many hours of the day, Casmir Dabrowski. This time is not stimulating for me."

"I'd say it isn't for me, either, but last night I dreamed about…" An image of Oku popped into his mind, her eyes glinting with humor, her mouth smiling. "Uhm, never mind. You wouldn't be interested in that."

"Likely not," Zee said, as if he knew exactly what Casmir had meant.

Casmir hoped that didn't mean he'd been talking in his sleep.

He lowered his voice to ask his next question, even though he doubted he would be overheard. He'd checked his cabin for bugs in the past, found a monitoring device, and carefully removed it and stuck it behind the toilet in the lavatory—he now kept the door shut when he wasn't using it. "Would you be able to send a message to President Nguyen for me? Through Tork? One that the comm officers on this ship wouldn't be able to intercept? Or wouldn't be able to decrypt if they *did* intercept it?"

"Certainly. It would be a simple matter to hide a message within a move for a game."

"Excellent. Thank you. I'm going to send you something to transmit." Casmir broke out in a sweat, even though he was still lying on the deck, barely moving a muscle. He could still get caught, but the risk should be much lower. Making sure this technology would be available to everyone was worth that small risk.

"I am prepared."

As soon as Casmir sent it, a soft beep sounded, and Ishii spoke through the cabin's speaker.

"Dabrowski, come down to Bay Three."

Casmir's left eye blinked twice. Ishii couldn't know. There was no way. Not that soon. Not at all.

"Now?" His voice squeaked on the word.

Damn it, Ishii *would* know if he acted suspiciously. He could drag Casmir to sickbay and question him under a truth drug that he wasn't allergic to. They wouldn't need to crack any codes.

"No, I want you to stop by Sato's lab and make lattes for the crew on your way."

Something about Ishii's typical sarcasm was comforting. Maybe because it was exactly that. Typical.

"Uh, really?"

"No, not really. Get your ass down here. And bring all your gear and medications."

"Am I going somewhere?"

"Yes."

The speaker clicked off.

"That sounds ominous, Zee." Casmir pushed himself to his feet. The only place he could imagine being sent was in one of those submarines down to the well-guarded astroshaman base.

"Have no fear, Casmir Dabrowski. I am programmed to protect you."

"Can you protect me from drowning?" he asked glumly, already starting to panic at the idea of being cooped up in a submarine.

Zee hesitated before answering, which was unusual for him. "I am familiar with cardiopulmonary resuscitation and mouth-to-mouth resuscitation. I do not have lungs of my own or a need for oxygen unless I engage the metabolic process with which I convert inorganic material into usable energy, but it is possible I could create and fill air sacs within myself to deliver the necessary oxygen."

"I'll keep that in mind when our sub is sinking. Thank you."

Qin eyed the crowd as they entered the busiest part of Death Knell Station, expecting Johnny's comrades—or at least the two minions he'd sent on that fool's errand—to jump out at them.

"Explain to me again why I have to wear a pillowcase on my head?" Johnny murmured as they passed through the crowded concourse. He still wore his armor, but Bonita had taken his helmet and rifle. Qin toted a duffel bag that he'd grabbed out of the hostel room, and after a quick search, Bonita had decided it could come along.

Qin thought a more thorough search would have been in order—all Bonita had done was dig in enough to see that it was mostly full of clothing—but Bonita didn't seem to care what he brought with him, as long as he didn't have access to it.

Nobody batted an eye at Johnny walking between two women with his head covered and weapons pointed at him. Qin doubted anyone on Death Knell Station cared about kidnappings. When the *Stellar Dragon* flew out of dock, and the pilot aboard the Druckers' shuttle noticed, that was when things might get tricky. He'd only had those two thugs with him for the ambush, and they were hopefully still dealing with the dock authority, but Qin assumed the six men who'd come to the alley for her supposed handoff were on board now.

"So people can't identify you," Bonita said.

"I *want* them to know you're kidnapping me."

"I'm sure your people can figure it out from your armor, but if I were truly kidnapping you out from under their noses, I wouldn't be brazen about it. I'm just sad that our freezer case was blown up so I can't stuff you into that. You'd look good with frozen steaks covering your face."

"Better than I look with a pillowcase over my head?"

"Maybe about the same. Either way, I wouldn't have to look at those garish tattoos."

"Which I informed you were temporary. I'm shocked you don't believe me and aren't waiting in eager anticipation to see my handsome face after I have them removed."

"I don't believe much of what you're saying." Bonita tilted her head toward a couple of security robots, presumably for Qin's benefit rather than Johnny's, since he couldn't see them.

Qin nodded once and kept an eye on them. They, like all the humans wandering around, appeared indifferent to their trio.

"You wound me, Laser. I thought we'd established a rapport. But if that were true, you wouldn't be suffocating me with this pillowcase."

"You'd be talking less if you were truly suffocating."

"True. It's more the odor that makes me feel that I might pass out. They don't wash the bedding in those rooms after they're used."

"You picked the place."

"Because higher-end hostels would think it alarming if a group of men carried two women rolled in nets into their establishments."

"I'm troubled that there are *any* hostels where that's not considered alarming."

"Well, this is System Cerberus."

As they walked on board the *Dragon*, Bonita gripping Johnny's arm from the side and Qin pressing her Brockinger anti-tank gun into his spine from behind, Viggo's voice boomed from the speakers in the cargo hold.

"At long last, my fearless crew has returned."

"Is that your ship's AI?" Johnny asked.

"Viggo," Bonita said.

"He seems perky."

"He's been lonely without anyone but his vacuums to talk to."

"This is not untrue," Viggo said, "but I also have news for you."

Bonita held up a finger. "Save it until we park our prisoner."

"Are you truly going to put me in a cell?" Johnny asked.

"With great enthusiasm, yes." Bonita smiled, and Qin sensed that she enjoyed the banter.

Qin trusted Bonita to remain the experienced professional in charge, but she was a little concerned that her captain would develop feelings for their fast-talking guest. Qin didn't believe that he was a knight—he was far too different from Asger and from all the knights she'd read about in legends. Even if he truly was a spy, wouldn't he have dropped the cocky pirate act by now?

Bonita walked with Qin to the single cell near engineering, and they steered Johnny into it. He went in without a fight, pulling off the pillowcase as soon as his hands were free.

As Qin hit the controls to bring down the bars and secure him, she braced herself for a snarky comment—or a plea to give him the freedom of the ship. Bonita was also waiting, her eyebrows raised as if she expected something similar. Or maybe she was anticipating more snark.

"Let me know if you need any help with the shuttle," Johnny said. "There are eight men in it, and they're expecting me and those other two to return with you. It's possible my colleagues won't care that you kidnapped me, but I do good bookkeeping work for the Druckers, so they'll find it inconvenient if they have to find somebody new."

"Meaning it's possible we'll be chased all the way to the gate?" Bonita asked.

"Yes. You'll want to leave right away and accelerate hard."

"Thanks for the tip. I was thinking of stopping for ice cream and lattes and to get my nails done to match Qin's."

Johnny looked at Qin's claws. Bonita had painted them a few days earlier, so they didn't need a manicure. Qin had bedazzled them herself, and even though she didn't trust Johnny, she couldn't resist the urge to extend them and show them off.

"In length?" Johnny asked. "Or the amount of glitter stuck to them?"

"Maybe both. You can contemplate it while you're down here alone." Bonita waved for Qin to follow her and turned off the lights on the way out.

"Excellent," Johnny called after them. "It'll be easier for me to fantasize about your nails in the dark."

Qin would have ignored him, but Bonita called back, "My *nails* aren't what's going to keep you entertained in that cell for a week."

"You're not going to have sex with him, are you, Captain?" Qin asked as they crossed the cargo hold toward the ladder that led up to the cabins, lounge, mess hall, and navigation.

"Probably not."

"*Probably*? You don't really believe he's a knight, do you?"

"No, but snarky, handsome younger men are my type." Bonita sighed. "Which *definitely* means I should avoid him. Since I've been married to my type three times, and I've told you how well that's worked out."

"Yes. Many times. You've also told me that men are evil and not to be trusted."

"I stand by that. That's why I would only sleep with him, not marry him."

"That comforts me less than you might think."

Bonita clapped her on the shoulder, then climbed up the two levels to navigation. Qin hoped she was only joking.

Several of the round robot vacuums were whirring along the deck and climbing the bulkheads on the top level of the ship. One vroomed along upside down on the ceiling, and two more were in navigation when they stepped in.

"The ship is sparkling, Viggo," Bonita said.

"*Thank* you for noticing."

"Keep an eye on our prisoner, will you? If he starts muttering to himself or opening a channel to his people on some comm designed to look like a piece of hair, I want to know about it."

"And do you also want to know if he strips out of his armor and starts fantasizing about you vigorously?" Viggo must have been listening when they'd been dropping him off.

"I'm not going to say yes with young Qin here listening, but I think we both know the answer to that."

Qin blinked. "I'm not unfamiliar with sex, Captain."

"I know."

"I'm just disturbed that you seem to be attracted to him."

"I know that too. Don't worry. My libido isn't what it once was. I'm sure I can keep my flagging hormones in check for the trip to System Hydra."

Qin wasn't sure she believed her.

"System Hydra?" Viggo asked. "I was just going to tell you about the goings on there."

"What goings on?"

"A courier ship came through the gate a few hours ago and transmitted news updates from around the Twelve Systems. Tiamat Station in System Hydra recently underwent a civil war in which its president was killed and replaced, via a vote from the citizens, by the secretary of education."

Bonita grunted. "So? What's that have to do with us?"

She sat in the pilot's pod and started the undocking procedure.

"Casmir was there, and there are rumors that he helped the new president gain power, against the Kingdom's wishes."

"That seems implausible."

"The rumors also say he took over all the robots on the station and sent a computer virus to a bunch of pirates to deactivate their ships."

"That sounds more like him."

"Isn't that where Johnny wants us to take him?" Qin asked. "Tiamat Station?"

"Shit, you're right." Bonita turned and squinted at her. "You say this news just came into the system, Viggo?"

"Approximately 2.4 hours ago."

"He must have heard about the trouble before it was officially announced. You don't think he's telling the truth, do you?"

Qin wasn't sure if the question was for her or Viggo, but she shook her head. "Maybe if there's some turmoil there, he or the Druckers as a whole want to take advantage of it somehow."

"Why would they care about a space station? Or do you think..." Bonita rolled her eyes ceilingward. "It's that damn gate. It's got to be. Whatever Casmir was doing at that station, it has to be related to the gate quest. That's what the Kingdom ships dragged him off for."

Qin nodded. If the Druckers had heard about the gate, she had no trouble imagining them trying to get their hands on it. The pirate brothers didn't have the technological resources to reverse engineer it, nor did they have any interest in archaeology, as far as she knew, but they would know how valuable it was. They might want to get it to sell it to the highest bidder. Maybe they wanted to send Johnny ahead, with allies of Casmir and the others, to gain information.

Bonita waved her banking chip over a scanner to send the docking fee to the station, then activated the thrusters to take them out into space.

"Are we going to help Casmir?" Viggo sounded hopeful. The vacuum sucking microscopic dirt from the ceiling seams paused, as if it was also waiting for an answer.

"Normally, I would say no," Bonita said.

"But you agree that he's a friend and needs our help?" Viggo asked.

"It didn't sound like, from your news, that Casmir needs help. But Toes said he'd pay us ten thousand crowns to take him there, so we're going."

"*Toes?*" Viggo asked.

"His name is Johnny Twelve Toes," Qin explained.

"He doesn't sound like as appealing a passenger as Casmir," Viggo said.

"I'm sorry I can't always bring you roboticists to caress your vacuums, Viggo." Bonita held up her finger. "Hold on. Let me check my bank account to see if he actually transferred the first two thousand."

"If he didn't, can we ditch him and go help our friends without any pirate spies aboard?" This time, Qin was the one to sound hopeful, and she knew it.

The comm panel beeped.

"It's the Druckers' shuttle. They're demanding to speak with us. They're still docked, but..." Bonita leaned over to look at the scanner display and tap a button. "They're powering up their engines."

"If this is all a ruse, won't they let us leave with Johnny?" Qin refused to call him Toes.

"The only way to find out is to leave." Bonita tapped her embedded chip. "My account shows the transfer. He actually paid us. Huh."

"Of course he paid if he wishes you to take him on a spy mission," Viggo said.

The *Dragon* pulled farther away from the station, and Bonita pointed the nose toward the gate, which was many long hours away. If the Druckers wanted to make a problem, they could. In addition to that shuttle, they had a warship that was in orbit around a nearby moon and was capable of intercepting them.

"That shuttle is comming again," Viggo said. "Incessantly."

"Don't answer."

"It hasn't pulled out yet. It looks like the docking clamps are holding it there."

"Good," Bonita said.

Qin watched the various displays on the control console, but mostly, she was thinking that Johnny had a lot of sway if he'd engineered a way to detain the Druckers' shuttle. Bonita's friends, the Amigos, ran the station and were enemies of the pirate family. They shouldn't have even talked with him.

Johnny was not one to be underestimated, even if he was in a dark cell.

"We are on course for the gate, and then to Tiamat Station," Viggo informed them after several minutes.

The shuttle was still stuck at the station. Qin let out a slow breath, though she didn't know if she should be relieved.

"He requested Tiamat Station or the *Osprey*," Bonita said. "We'll see which is closest when we get to System Hydra."

"The Kingdom warship the *Osprey?*" Viggo asked. "That's the vessel that delivered doctors to the *Machu Picchu*. It may also be the warship that Casmir is on."

"You may get your vacuums caressed after all."

"I hope this *Toes* does not have nefarious intent," Viggo said.

Qin hoped that too.

Bonita gripped her chin. "We'll keep him in his cell and let the warship know we have him as soon as we're in the system, instead of letting him try to sneak onto their ship or whatever he has in mind. Maybe they'll reward us for turning over a pirate who seems to have access to intelligence reports from around the systems. We could get paid twice. That's always a good thing."

Qin couldn't share her enthusiasm. She worried that Johnny was up to something horrible, and that they would inadvertently help him achieve it.

CHAPTER 4

CASMIR WALKED INTO ONE OF THE *OSPREY'S* TWO cavernous shuttle bays with Zee trailing after him. The shuttles had been lifted up to the ceiling on harnesses, and the deck space was now dominated by submarines. He wasn't surprised to see Ishii in the middle of the bay, barking orders. He *was* surprised that Kim stood near the door, two cases stacked next to her, with a glower that she zapped Casmir with when he entered.

"They're making you go too?" he guessed as Zee walked over to the submarines, either to look for threats to Casmir or because of a newfound interest in aquatic craft.

"If by *they*, you mean Ishii, then yes. Or are you suggesting the nebulous behind-the-scenes players that influence him?"

"I'm not sure Romano and Jager are that nebulous."

Ishii saw them talking, issued a few more orders to his men, and stalked over.

"Hello, Sora," Casmir said cheerfully, deciding not to mention that Ishii looked amazingly grumpy, considering the mission hadn't started yet. Shouldn't that degree of dyspepsia be reserved for after things started to go wrong? Of course, it was possible Ishii believed things had started going wrong back at Tiamat Station. Or as soon as Casmir arrived on his ship. "Are you coming with us?"

"No."

"Are you going to explain why we're going?" Casmir pointed to himself and Kim. He understood that Kim had told Ishii he might be able to deactivate the gate, but he'd envisioned that happening after the marines went in and defeated the astroshamans and pulled it out from under the ice. "I thought I was only here to locate the gate and that Kim was here to help heal people who get irradiated. She's also working on a very important project for the crown. I believe Princess Oku would be most displeased if Kim were killed on this mission before finishing her work."

"But after is acceptable?" Kim murmured.

"I'm not sure how strongly she feels about you. Perhaps we could all get together for pizza and fizzop when we get back and have a nice get-to-know-you session."

"I'm sure those are the kinds of delights that entice royalty to visit your home."

"Do you think she'd come to the house?" Casmir imagined Oku, and however many bodyguards accompanied her wherever she went, going up to use the bathroom and seeing his Robot Remstar shampoo on the tub ledge.

"I'm sending you to shut you up and get you off my ship," Ishii growled.

Kim turned her narrow-eyed glower onto him.

Casmir blinked. "That can't be true. You've barely been around to hear us speak these past three days."

Ishii sighed. "No, it's not true. I don't want to send Scholar Sato at all, but I need my best people to go because this isn't going to be an easy mission. You'll go in the rearmost submarine—both of you—with the marines and my combat officers going well ahead of you to deal with the astroshamans. They'll secure the base, and *then* your pilot will take you in. You'll find the gate, Dabrowski will figure out a way to nullify its radiation-spitting nozzles or whatever it has, and Scholar Sato will be there to help with any bacterial or radiation emergencies."

"I'm willing to attempt that, but I have to warn you that this isn't my area of expertise. You're basically sending in a plumber to fix a spaceship drive." Casmir tapped his tool satchel. "I may end up just whacking it with a wrench."

"I doubt that," Ishii said, "but it is possible that we've got another civilian expert coming to help you. He hasn't arrived in the system yet, and we can't delay the mission, not with Rache sniffing around down there, but I'll let you know if he arrives in time to help. We'll leave a submarine here, just in case."

"An expert who's immune to the gate?" Kim asked.

"Yes. In the meantime…" Ishii leaned over and patted Casmir's tool satchel. "Do your best with your wrench banging."

"Right." Casmir smiled again, telling himself this would be a grand adventure, not another opportunity for burdening his parents with the need to arrange his funeral. "I'll do my best. You say we get the sturdiest and most fortified submarine since we're more fragile souls than your marines?"

Kim's eyebrow twitched. Maybe he shouldn't have called her fragile. *She* didn't have to worry about seizures.

Ishii snorted and pointed. "You get that one."

Casmir eyed the long craft closest to them. "Is that a duck painted on the side?"

"You know very well that they're from private companies on that station," Ishii said. "They're not military grade."

"The *Waddler*," Casmir read the name on the side. "Ah, yes, I'm sure it's very fortified and sturdy."

He accessed his chip to see what depth the submarines could withstand, but their ratings were based on the gravity of the water-world planets, not this largely unexplored moon. He also checked to see if a galaxy suit such as he was now wearing could withstand much water pressure, because his panic-prone mind could easily envision the *Waddler* springing a leak and the crew—and innocent civilian advisors—having to abandon ship. Unfortunately, the SmartWeave fabric was designed for the vacuum of space rather than the intense pressure of aquatic depths. It could keep him warm in the ocean, but deep dives would be out of the question. Hard-shelled combat armor, he noticed, fared better.

"The lead teams are going in the *Sea Otter*, the *Pufferfish*, *Bubbles 1, Bubbles 2,* and *Bubbles 4*," Ishii said.

"Names sure to drive fear into the astroshamans' hearts."

"We think Rache got *Bubbles 3*."

"I believe he's secure enough in his nefariousness that he won't worry about riding in a submarine with a wimpy name," Casmir said. "Can we borrow some combat armor?"

"What for? You're not going into battle."

"Because combat armor has a crush depth of over a thousand meters on *Odin*. It'll be even better here. And, uh, a galaxy suit can withstand significantly fewer PSIs."

Kim eyed him, and he expected her to tease him for being fatalistic, but she said, "I'll take a set too."

Ishii grunted. "If I give you suits of armor, you're not going to puke in them, are you, Dabrowski?"

Casmir looked at Kim. "Why did he state my name specifically?"

"It's a mystery," she said.

"Do you get seasick?" Ishii asked.

"I may not in a submarine. I don't have any experience with them. But as for boats in general... I once took a passenger ferry to a chess camp on Urin Island just outside of Zamek, and it didn't go well for my stomach. There were no vomit bags, but I didn't want to make a mess, just as I wouldn't make a mess inside your armor, so I used my duffel." Casmir scratched his jaw, grimacing as he remembered that summer. "Unfortunately, word got out, and nobody wanted to play with my chess pieces the whole time I was there."

"You're all the varieties of special in one gift box, aren't you?"

"My parents have always assured me of that," Casmir said.

Ishii waved over a soldier and ordered him to get two suits of armor.

"I'm sure you won't need the armor," Ishii told them, looking more at Kim than Casmir. Which was ironic since Kim was largely unflappable and probably thought a submarine ride in an under-ice sea on a distant moon sounded like a great adventure that she could one day write about. "I've got teams cleaning and inspecting the submarines right now. There won't be any mechanical difficulties. I'll also make sure there are several marines riding along with you to keep you safe."

"Oh good," Casmir said. "I get along swimmingly with large, beefy men who can break me with their pinkies."

"Just don't puke in their duffel bags and you'll be fine."

"Uhm, sir?" a young officer said from the open hatch of a submarine. There was an odd note to his voice.

"What?"

"Maybe you should see this."

Ishii grunted and headed toward the *Waddler*.

"Maybe we should request another sub," Casmir said.

"They already loaded most of my equipment into that one," Kim said.

Casmir looked at the two cases next to her. "So you're packing light?"

"I don't know what we'll encounter down there. I want to be prepared. I'm *not* pleased about going."

"You're not? I thought you would believe it a great adventure."

"The submarine ride? Probably. Cozying up to pieces of that gate again? No."

"Technically, the gate pieces were already gone when you were down in that wreck, weren't they?"

"And the lingering pseudo radiation still almost killed us all."

"Oh, right."

"Do you know what they say about being exposed to deadly radiation twice in the same year?"

"No."

"Don't do it."

"Wise advice."

"I'm sorry I got you volunteered against your wishes for this, but I hope you can deactivate it."

"Me too." Casmir imagined himself being pushed into some undersea ice cave at the end of a very long pole as the rest of Ishii's people waited outside.

"I'm beginning to wish I'd taken your suggestion to let myself be kidnapped by Rache so I could spy on him."

"Spy on him? I thought you promised to read a book and discuss sentient bacteria with him."

"As a way to get close while spying."

"I'm now imagining you explaining that setup to Royal Intelligence."

He'd meant it as a joke, but a sad wistful expression crossed Kim's usually stoic face.

Casmir wondered if it was wrong of him to hope that Rache outsmarted the Kingdom teams, made it to the base first, and dealt with the gate himself. After all, he was also immune. Maybe *he* could figure out how to deactivate it. Or, if all he wanted was to keep Jager from getting it, maybe he could dump it into the deepest part of that ocean down where no submarine could reach it.

Unfortunately, Rache hadn't said that was what he wanted to do, so Casmir couldn't let himself wish for him to get there first. He wanted to believe that Rache wasn't pure evil, especially since Kim had been flirting with him of late, but he thought Rache was capable of doing *something* evil just to spite Jager.

Zee returned to them. He hadn't gone into the submarines, but he'd inspected the *Waddler* from the outside. "This craft is approximately thirty years old and may not be in optimal operating condition, but I did not detect any weaknesses in the hull."

"I'm glad we're getting the combat armor," Casmir told Kim.

But she wasn't looking at him. She pointed at the *Waddler*. "Is that a body?"

Ishii had climbed out ahead of a team that was extracting a blue-haired woman wearing riotous green and yellow clothing. That definitely wasn't one of the crew. She wasn't moving.

"Maybe she's sleeping?" Casmir hoped so.

But it had been three days since the *Osprey* had procured the submarines from the station and departed. That would have been one long nap.

"Take her to sickbay for Dr. Sikou to autopsy and ID," Ishii said.

Kim stepped to the side of the doorway so she wouldn't be in the way. Casmir stepped *far* to the side.

"It's probably someone who died in the fighting on the station," Kim said.

Casmir remembered the bodies they'd passed in the corridors there and started to nod but paused. "And then stuffed herself into the back of a submarine?"

"Maybe she was injured and crawled in to hide. Or someone killed her and stuck the body in there to hide the evidence." Kim twitched a shoulder, not appearing worried about it.

Casmir would have been less worried if that wasn't the submarine *he* was supposed to ride in. A body might leave behind germs or bacteria or… bad mojo.

"Which sub is ours?" Asger asked, walking into the bay with a bag, a rifle, his pertundo, and wearing his silver liquid armor, his blond-brown hair tumbling about his shoulders as if someone had styled it for a photo shoot.

"The one they took that body out of." Kim pointed, then waved him to the side.

"Uh." Asger joined her and Casmir as the crewmen removing the body approached the exit.

They were carrying her facedown, which revealed a dagger sticking out of her back. A dagger that, judging by all the blood and the holes in her shirt, had been stabbed into her at least ten times before being left.

"Dear God," Asger murmured.

"I don't think that autopsy is going to be necessary," Casmir said bleakly as Ishii rejoined their group. He murmured a quick prayer for the poor dead woman.

"It's standard operating procedure," Ishii said. "The cleaning crews will disinfect the area where she was found."

"That's good, but… could we ride in *that* submarine?" Casmir pointed to one on the opposite side of the bay from the *Waddler.* As a robotics professor with an advanced degree, he was far too educated and intelligent to genuinely believe in *bad mojo*, but it didn't hurt to be safe.

"Sorry, the combat teams already have their gear packed into the other subs."

"Damn."

"Why did it take so long to find the body?" Kim was looking toward the exit, though the crew had already disappeared into the corridor with the woman.

"It—she—was wedged into a luggage compartment," Ishii said. "It must have been hell on that station. I guess I can't be surprised. I saw the photo of Chronis with a rope around his neck." He shook his head and walked toward the exit. "Once the cleaning crew finishes, pack your gear inside. You're leaving as soon as possible. Rache is probably already down there somewhere. We have to catch up with him."

Casmir gazed numbly at the submarine. There had been bodies on Tiamat Station and plenty of signs of violence, but he hadn't seen anything *that* violent. He hadn't gone opening luggage compartments on his trip through the station, but still…

"At the risk of sounding like a pansy," he said, "does anyone else have a bad feeling about this?"

"Yes," Kim and Asger said together.

Yas gripped the armrests of his seat in the submarine as it was lowered into a hole in the ice, swaying on the long chain hanging from the *Fedallah.* He would have felt much more secure in one of the ship's pods, the smart sides cupping him gently, protecting his spine and organs from the travails of space travel. Instead, he had a narrow band across his waist, cupholders, and children's magazines about undersea adventures stuck in a rack on the seatback in front of him.

He wished Jess had come along on the mission, but her engineering assistant had been sent instead, a brooding man in combat armor who sat across the aisle from Yas. Rache was somewhere up front, talking to whatever pilot he'd decided had the skills to navigate underwater as well as in space.

Five other submarines had already been lowered and released into the dark, deep hole in the ice. It wasn't the same fissure that Rache's team had explored on their first visit to the moon. He'd sent two of his shuttles down before the Kingdom ships had arrived in orbit to use sustained blasts from their weapons to melt an entry point in a spot where the ice was only hundreds of meters thick instead of kilometers, the theory being that the astroshamans and their robotic security drones wouldn't see them coming if they entered hundreds of kilometers away and sneaked in under the ice.

Yas thought Rache might be underestimating the astroshamans. It seemed far more likely that they knew exactly what was going on, both down on their moon and up in orbit. Maybe in the rest of the system too.

"One of the Kingdom warships is heading this way," the comm officer reported.

"This way?" Rache asked. "To the hole *we* drilled?"

"Maybe, sir. Or they may have detected the *Fedallah* hovering over it. It's easier to detect the ship, even with the slydar hull camouflage, down on a planet or moon, since it's affected by air currents and creates shadows."

Yas leaned out into the aisle. "Did you ever find that locator beacon, Captain?"

"We did, yes. And we fired it far away from the moon with a railgun before dropping out of orbit. It doesn't look like that fooled the Kingdom." Rache waved to his pilot. "Just get us in the water. I'll order the *Fedallah* back up into orbit as soon as all of our subs are in. Then she can play cat-and-mouse with the Kingdom fleet while we handle things down here."

Yas hoped that cat-and-mouse game wouldn't result in anyone being hurt while he was gone. But what if there had been more than one locator beacon? He thought of Jess, still up there on the ship, and the handful of other mercenaries that he spoke to now and then. There were a few decent sorts up there. Some of them even came to the appointments he made for them.

The submarine rocked as it splashed down, and Yas's hands tightened around the armrests.

Rache slid into the seat beside him, not bothering to belt himself in. Maybe his cybernetic upgrades caused him to be less worried about being hurled into the air and cracking his head on the ceiling. Yas should consider getting some.

"We're descending now," the pilot said. "The *Fedallah* has released us and is heading out, shooting off in the opposite direction of the incoming warship."

"Good," Rache said.

"Uh, sir? Someone is comming us. It looks like a channel that the submarines use to talk to each other, but it's not coming from any of our people."

Rache snorted. "It's probably a Kingdom officer. This is what happens when you all shop at the same submarine store."

"Do you want me to reply, sir?"

"No. Just slide us under the ice and head for the power generator we detected on our scouting mission. Run scans and see if you can pinpoint the base itself along the way."

"Yes, sir."

"Mind if I try to listen in on the channel chatter of their subs, sir?" the comm officer asked.

"Not at all," Rache said. "That's why I brought you, even though you've got the combat prowess of a three-legged hedgehog."

"Your sense of humor is coming out more of late, sir. You know that?"

"I'm working on self-improvement."

Yas wondered if Rache's flirtations with Kim Sato had anything to do with his lighter mood of late. Or maybe he was simply excited to go on a dangerous mission.

Some people found such things exhilarating. Others squeezed the stuffing out of their armrests.

"Did you know," Yas said, eyeing the dark water outside his porthole, "that the hedgehog is one of four mammals brought from Old Earth with a nicotinic acetylcholine receptor that protects against snake venom?"

"Did you study them in your toxicology classes?"

"I studied their receptors. They were quite fine."

Yas grimaced, waiting for Rache to ask him about the poison he'd been tasked with making… and hadn't. He hadn't been able to think of something that would affect astroshamans without being a threat to every human being around. He'd been desperate enough to send a message to Kim Sato to see if she knew of any bacteria that might work. Her reply had been professional but terse, and he suspected it was because they were in competition for the gate.

That bothered Yas, because he didn't want to see her as an enemy or a competitor. It also bothered Yas that he hadn't come up with a solution. He couldn't help but feel he'd failed Rache in this.

Surprisingly, given the opening, Rache didn't bring up poisons. He leaned a casual elbow on his armrest and gripped his chin. "I was hoping we'd have an advantage over the Kingdom submarines and could get to the base ahead of them, since we were here before to scout, but now I'm wondering if we should let them go in first and take the brunt of the astroshamans' ire, while we try to find a back door to slide through."

"Scouting?" Yas asked. "Is that what you were doing when those drones popped out of the water and started shooting at you?"

"More or less."

"Will we be able to hide from the Kingdom subs down here? Or can they all track each other?" Yas waved toward the small navigation cabin up front. If all of the submarines could speak to each other on the same comm channel, maybe they all kept track of each other automatically.

"There *were* trackers, but Chief Khonsari took them out."

"We've descended to six hundred meters, sir," the pilot said, "and are successfully traveling along under the ice behind our other five submarines."

A faint groan came from the hull.

Yas's eyes widened in alarm. "How deep can these subs go before, uhm…"

"They collapse under the pressure?" Rache asked. "Very deep here. Don't worry."

"Not even about those groans?"

"If you're concerned, perhaps you can enjoy that children's adventure magazine there."

"I already looked at it. The advertisements want to sell me a lovely vacation to Balneario del Mar. Which sounds appealing right now. Do I have any leave coming up? We haven't discussed how mercenaries get vacations."

"That's because you didn't sign a typical contract. That would have been your opportunity to negotiate for perks."

"It was hard to negotiate for perks from under your table while people were shooting at me."

"You'll know to arrange for a better environment when it's time for you to decide if you want to reenlist."

"Definitely," Yas said.

"The Kingdom subs are in the water behind us, sir," the pilot reported.

"I still can't believe they used our hole," Rache muttered. "I was hoping they'd be lured in by that big fissure and that the astroshaman drones would pepper them with fire."

"You should have left a few candy bars on the ice to lure them down. From what I've observed of the dietary preferences of your men, that might have worked. Assuming soldiers are much the same around the Twelve Systems."

"Maybe so."

"I'm picking up some of their chatter," the comm officer said as they sailed along under the ice, the water pitch black outside beyond the submarine's running lights. "I think they know we're listening, or at least that it's a possibility. They're not saying anything about tactics, but I did get that they've got five subs that are going ahead to look for the base—and us if we get in their way—and one that's going to wait back near the hole in the ice until the gate has been located. Something about their civilian advisors being on board."

Rache straightened in his seat. "Advisors? It was plural?"

"Yes, sir."

"That might be Kim and Casmir." Rache looked at Yas. "I can see why they might have brought Casmir to deal with the systems' preeminent machine-integrated society, but why would Kim be on board? Because they think they'll need her bacteria or expertise in dealing with that radiation? But wouldn't they have inoculated all their people before sending them in to potentially get near the gate? The same as we did?"

"I inoculated everyone," Yas pointed out, "and you still brought me."

"Because you're a doctor, not because you're a medical researcher."

"The bacteria would only buy us time; they don't convey immunity."

"Hm." Rache leaned back in his seat. "I suppose it doesn't matter if she's along. Casmir is who I was thinking of kidnapping."

Yas blinked. "*Kidnapping?* When did that become part of the plan?"

"Recently. I wasn't sure if it would be a possibility, but since they're following us, it may be feasible, especially if there will only be one sub to deal with. I wasn't sure they would bring Casmir, but I would far prefer to have his robotics expertise along when we walk up to the gate. We have the same problem that the Kingdom does, that we can't take that gate on board the *Fedallah* while it's oozing that radiation." Rache lowered his voice. "As far as I know, only Casmir and I are immune to its effects. I'm not sure if he knows much about the gate tech, but I know even less."

"And would he appreciate being kidnapped by you?"

"No, but I could get him to work for me anyway. Especially if I show him a certain video. I'm more concerned about kidnapping Kim for a second time if she's with him."

"Yes, you probably shouldn't do that repeatedly to a woman you're romantically interested in."

Rache gave him a long look, and Yas decided he shouldn't bring up such things when his men might overhear. Just because Rache had been in a good mood since leaving the station didn't erase what he was or what he had been for the last ten years.

Yas lifted an apologetic hand.

"We'll risk it," Rache said. "Maybe I can convince her it's for her good too. I'm arrogant enough to believe our team is superior to those Kingdom schlubs and that the odds of surviving this mission are going to be better with us."

Yas didn't want another glare so he didn't point out that the sentiment *was* arrogant. Besides, since he was stuck here, he hoped it was true.

"Maybe you can take him without her," Yas suggested. "Are there airlocks somewhere on the submarines?"

Rache nodded. "On the port side back there. They're designed to let divers go in and out." He spoke up for the comm officer. "Rasher, tell four of our other subs to continue on and search for the base. Order the *Reef Darter* to hang back with us. Chung, find us a hiding spot where we can wait while the majority of the Kingdom subs slide past, ideally a nook in the ice where their sonar wouldn't catch us."

"We getting rid of the competition early?" the pilot asked.

"Even better. We're going to kidnap their civilian advisors." Rache leaned out into the aisle and looked forward and back at the armored fighters also buckled into the rows of seats. "You gents interested in a warmup raid?"

Several grunts and *yes, sirs* came back.

Though one cheeky mercenary asked, "There combat bonuses, sir?"

"That's how you negotiate for perks," Rache told Yas.

"I'll keep that in mind."

CHAPTER 5

KIM SAT BUCKLED IN A SEAT BY A porthole as the submarine descended through a deep hole in the ice toward the dark water far below, water that never saw the sun's influence. Not that such an influence would have mattered much. This moon was far enough away from Hydra's sun that days on the surface were no brighter than twilight back on Odin.

A twinge of homesickness went through her at the thought of the planet, the capital city, her lab, and her house that she'd once again left. The squirrels were doubtless confused at the sporadic delivery of their peanuts this year.

The submarine wobbled as the pilot bumped the icy wall surrounding them, and she grimaced, hoping that didn't mean he would prove a poor navigator down here. The man had probably only flown spaceships. Kim couldn't imagine that submarines were similar.

She shifted her weight, the toe of her heavy boot bumping the bag at her feet. She jerked back in alarm before remembering that she'd placed her vials in a sturdy case inside the bag, so they wouldn't be easily broken. Still, she felt like a hulking dinosaur in the combat armor Casmir had finagled for them, and she could imagine the boot going right through the case if she accidentally kicked it. She'd already broken her armrest, thanks to whatever servos and gizmos inside added strength to her natural movements.

"No, no," came Casmir's voice from farther up the aisle as Kim bent to tuck her sack safely under her seat. "You can't get the bonus that way. You have to blow up the mushroom and *then* kill the ogre."

"You sure?" a baritone voice replied. "I got sprayed with mushroom acid last time and died."

"After you plant your explosive, make sure to dart back behind a tree, just like when you blew up the boss on the previous level."

"I'll give it a try."

"Good. I'm going to my seat. Let me know if there are any more power glitches."

Kim leaned past the empty seat next to her—Casmir had only spent thirty seconds in it so far—in time to see him pat a burly soldier on the armored shoulder.

"Will do," the man said, a pair of virtual reality glasses hooked over his ears. His legs were propped on the seat in front of him, and he appeared ready for a long trip.

Casmir moved back down the aisle toward Kim, but he paused at each row of seats to offer a hand and a bow to the soldiers. To each one, he said a variation of, "Thank you for volunteering for this mission. I have faith that you'll keep us all alive and we'll succeed."

Most of the men appeared bemused, though they all accepted the handshake. A couple of them said, "You're welcome, Professor."

Kim didn't know if they had truly volunteered or simply been assigned.

Asger sat across the aisle from Casmir's empty seat, and he had his chin clasped in his hand, his elbow on the armrest as he watched the spectacle. When Casmir reached them, he grinned and offered Asger his hand.

"I didn't volunteer," Asger said preemptively, though he accepted the handclasp. "I tried to get myself assigned to the main incursion team so I could hew down astroshamans like bamboo in a canebrake."

"Does that mean your mission is no longer to keep me alive?" Casmir touched his hand to his chest. "I'm distressed."

"It's possible the queen still wants that, but I haven't heard from her in a while. My recent orders from Sir Baron Farley—my boss—made it clear that I'm to help Ishii get the gate without screwing up again."

"You haven't screwed up, and I'll be certain to tell King Jager that while his minions are holding me upside down over a vat of boiling sap just before dipping me in to be flayed alive." Casmir smiled and pantomimed something that looked more like a hanging than an upside-down flaying.

"Your last words will be to praise me?"

"Yes, of course. What else would I talk about? I mean, my father would be disappointed in me if I didn't also work in *A Song of Ascent*, but I see Jager as someone who would make speeches about betrayals and punishments as he was killing a man, so there ought to be time for both."

"Are you sure you wouldn't devote your dying words to talking about robots?" Kim asked.

"As long as I've had time to update my will to make sure Zee is taken care of—" Casmir gave a thumbs up to the back where Zee stood instead of sitting, "—I can give my last breath to Asger."

"I'm honored," Asger said. "But I suggest we all work to get the gate and drop it in the middle of Jager's throne room. Thus to avoid flaying."

Casmir hesitated before nodding and smiling again. "Yes, let's do that."

He slid in beside Kim, arranged his tool satchel in his lap, and fastened the seatbelt.

"What was that all about?" She'd caught that hesitation, and it concerned her. What plots had he put into place now?

"Corporal Carvalho's virtual-reality glasses weren't working, and I tightened a connector to fix the power hiccup." He patted his tool satchel. He'd brought that but not any weapons. Once again.

Kim had asked for and been given a stunner. She'd been tempted to request a rifle, but she was ambivalent about using deadly force on the astroshamans when, as far as she knew, their only crime was removing an artifact from System Lion. Admittedly, Kyla Moonrazor had programmed that virus and tried to kill everyone on the *Osprey*, but the rest of the people in the base here might be innocent of even the theft.

"So you took the moment to thank everyone? You looked like someone running for political office."

"I know they were disgruntled about getting stuck with us civilian advisors bringing up the rear. Most of them were arguing to be sent in first." Casmir shuddered at the idea. "I thought a little gratitude might help them feel better about being with us. *We* have the most important part of the mission, after all."

"Speak for yourself. I'm here for decoration."

"Is that what's in the bag under your seat?" Casmir pointed. "Decorations? Rosh Hashanah is coming up. Maybe you could drape garlands around the astroshaman base."

"That's not a big Shinto holiday." Kim didn't know yet if her concoction would do anything useful, so she hadn't mentioned the vials to anyone. There hadn't been time for tests. Still, if they *did* work, Casmir might be able to jigger up a delivery mechanism that would allow them to be fired across a distance. "They're vials of a bacteria-enriched liquid that will turn into a gaseous compound that, if inhaled, should debilitate people with a lot of cybernetic implants. The bacteria feed on the lipids used in the artificial nerves that tie the implants into the human nervous system. Everything with cyborgs is synthetic except that special lipid compound, which is almost always the first choice in cyborg surgeries, because the human body recognizes them as natural parts of the nervous system rather than foreign materials. But a couple of species of bacteria *love* them. I've attempted to speed up their metabolism so they work far more quickly than in nature."

Casmir's eyes widened. "What happens to the people that are infected?"

"Their human parts will be fine, but their cyberware will melt down, and they'll lose access to any implants or synthetic limbs they have."

"Or synthetic organs?"

"If they've had such replacements done." Kim spread a hand. "Yes, people could die, but you may have noticed that all of these marines are carrying deadly weapons. Their plan seems to be: kill anyone who stands in their way. Maybe my bacteria, *if* they work, will spare lives. Most people affected will simply be incapacitated in some way."

Casmir gazed glumly at her.

"I'm sorry." Kim knew that whatever feelings of ambivalence she had for this mission, they were probably amplified for him. Not only was he more likely than she to have compassion for his enemies, but he probably blamed himself for their current situation with the gate. She offered a smile. "Is it too late to say that yes, I have holiday decorations in my bag?"

He returned the smile. It didn't reach his eyes, but he was willing to go along with the stab at humor. "Does that mean you should have worn makeup?"

"What?"

"You said you're here for decoration. Maybe you should have dressed up. It's too bad Qin and Bonita aren't here. They could do your nails for you. Maybe braid some ribbons into your hair. I saw Qin do that to herself once. Little purple ribbons with sparkles."

"I'm thinking of punching you."

"That won't be effective while I'm wearing this." Casmir rapped his knuckles on his chest plate.

"You're not wearing your helmet. I can punch you in the face."

"Drat." Casmir looked toward the porthole, though there was nothing to see but the blackness of the ocean. They were moving horizontally, so they had to be under the ice now, but the submarine's running lights didn't reveal it. "Do you think Rache is ahead of us? Nobody's telling us anything, but that hole we were lowered through wasn't natural."

"I noticed."

"It looked like it was very recent."

Kim nodded.

"We saw evidence that Rache's ship did that," Asger said from across the aisle. He was more in the loop than they were. "And the scanners on the *Osprey* picked up energy signatures identical to those our submarines put out before they disappeared under the ice. They were hoping to catch the *Fedallah* itself, but the warship must have cleared the area as soon as it dropped off the subs."

"Did the scanners sense anything *under* the ice?" Casmir asked.

Asger shook his head. "Nothing. The ice is thick enough to thwart scanner signals—*any* type of signal—and it may have been doctored up by the astroshamans to be even more effective at that. Right now, we don't even have any proof that the base is down here."

Casmir nodded, as if he'd known this, or guessed at it already. "I assumed Rache was down here. I'm just wondering if he's up ahead or if he's hiding under the ice somewhere and waiting for *us* to go in first?"

"Is that what you would do?" Asger asked.

"I think I would have sent automated submarines or aquatic drones to spy on the base to come up with more of a plan before tossing some of my best men into tin cans that the astroshamans will see coming from hundreds of miles away."

Asger opened his mouth, closed it again, then finally said, "We don't have any aquatic drones. We were limited by what we could rent from the station. I don't think the tour operators typically have to recon their destinations before arriving to show people octopuses, sharks, and zekzeki."

"I could have *made* aquatic drones." Casmir poked himself in the chest. "All Ishii would have had to do was ask."

"In three days? From parts scrounged from around the ship?" Asger raised his eyebrows skeptically, then looked into Casmir's face—Casmir appeared confused by the doubt—and said, "Never mind. Now I wish Ishii *had* consulted you about this. Though he's in a rush, so there might not have been time for preliminary scouting. He wants us to beat Rache there."

Casmir leaned back in his seat.

"You should have made drones anyway," Kim said quietly.

"You're right, but it didn't occur to me until now, to be honest. For the last three days, I've been under the assumption that I would be twiddling my thumbs in my cabin while this mission was going on, and that they'd only bring me down at the end to deactivate the gate. I *did* get a detector made that I believe will read the pseudo radiation. I haven't tested it yet."

"It's hard to get things tested when you're in a rush." Kim understood perfectly.

"Yeah. I also would have been more motivated to help the marines with their mission if Ishii was ever enthusiastic about my suggestions. I feel like I'm banging my forehead against a wall whenever I talk to people in charge of these military endeavors. I had much better luck convincing my superiors at the university of things."

"Maybe the Fleet officers sense that you're not as dedicated as they are to the outcome they desire."

Casmir waved his hand. She didn't know if it was in agreement, dismissal, or vague acknowledgment.

Kim lowered her voice even further. "You don't have any surprises planned that I should know about, do you?"

"Not me. I have no idea what surprises the astroshamans have in mind."

She wasn't sure she believed him, but she leaned back in her seat to settle in for the ride. Before she could open an e-book to read on her contact display, a message came in from Casmir.

I guess it's unlikely that the ship can monitor our communications through the ice, so let me confess to you. I doubt it'll affect anything we do down here, but I did send President Nguyen a note, via Tork, via Zee, to tell her colleagues—did you know she was an archaeologist before she got into politics?—about the gate and that I thought it might be better for everybody if ships came and everybody snagged a piece of the gate for themselves before the Fleet could make off with it.

"Casmir," Kim groaned aloud, dropping her face into her palm.

Asger, not privy to the text message, looked over at them. "Do women usually groan your name at random, Casmir?"

"Oh yes," Casmir said. "I star in many women's fantasies. It's extremely puzzling that I don't get propositioned daily by people wanting to take my photo for underwear ads."

Asger squinted at him, and Kim vowed to keep further responses silent. Asger could become a problem if he realized Casmir was working at odds with his goals.

"You have to get an agent if you want that," Asger said.

"Will you introduce me to yours?" Casmir asked.

"No."

"That's disappointing." Casmir drummed his fingers on his tool satchel and gazed up at the rivets in the blue ceiling, or maybe the large whale painted between them.

When Asger looked away, Casmir texted Kim again. *The entire system is already suspicious about our little fleet of warships. Nguyen asked me what we were up to. She already knew about the astroshaman base.* He twitched a shoulder in a small shrug.

You should have left her guessing, Kim replied. *What if dozens of ships show up while we're down here? You might be starting a war.*

We're here in someone else's system with military ships, and I'm pretty sure nobody asked permission before showing up. If there's a war, it'll be because we instigated it. If Jager had honorable intentions, he would have asked the governments for permission to come retrieve the stolen artifact, but you know he didn't.

I don't know that, and neither do you.

There was that hand wave again. This time, it was definitely dismissive. Maybe he *did* know Jager's plans. They'd chatted in the castle dungeon, after all, and Casmir was better at reading people than she was. Still...

It's not that I think your desire to share the gate with all of humanity is a bad idea—it's probably the morally ideal one. My concern is that you're picking fights with Jager, and he's the most powerful man in the Kingdom. What you should have done was help him get the gate, so he has no reason to question your loyalties, and then address the Senate at one of its quarterly meetings. You can be persuasive when you want to be—I've seen you pitching rich executives for donations for fundraisers for your department—especially when you really believe in what you're saying. You might have been able to convince them that letting other governments come research the gate would be in the best interests of the Kingdom.

Casmir's face scrunched up with skepticism. *First off, I'm not noble, so I couldn't have gotten in to address the Senate—*

I'm positive that if you came out with whose genes you share, they would have let you in. You technically are *noble, right?*

I don't think it would have been that easy. I also think Jager wants to keep the gate a secret and would have me shot if I spoke of it to the Senate or anyone else.

He'll have you shot anyway when he finds out you told the universe about the gate.

I'm rather hoping he won't find out. That's why I had Zee send the message to Tork, tucked in between the network game moves they zip back and forth to each other. I could even say, if someone linked it back to me, that Zee had acted on his own, or that someone had bugged him. Casmir's eyes gleamed as he manufactured the scenario in his mind.

Kim resisted the urge to roll her own eyes. *Zee is more loyal to you than any human bodyguard ever would be. Nobody would believe he was working for someone else. He'd do anything for you.*

Not anything. You should have seen the look he gave me when I asked if he would wiggle around on the deck like a dog rolling in the grass.

I'm not going to ask why *you requested that.*

I thought Oku might think it was cute.

I didn't ask.

I know, but you're looking at me like I'm strange. I thought I would assuage your concerns.

I'm not assuaged by anything coming out of your mouth. Your chip.

Not anything? Damn. But we're still best friends, right? He offered a lopsided smile.

Kim sighed. *Yes.*

"It worked," the baritone-voiced soldier blurted. "Professor, I got the bonus. I'm on the next level. This is going to be my highest score ever. You're brilliant. Thank you. That tip isn't even on any of the network walkthroughs."

"You're welcome," Casmir replied. He whispered to Kim, "A student told me about it. I've only played the game three times."

Kim shook her head. He was delusional if he didn't think he could go before the Senate and sway them. Though maybe he was right that Jager would continue to keep the gate a secret after the military had secured it, until some future decade when they'd managed to create more gates and were ready to deploy them.

"We may have a problem, sir," someone spoke quietly from the front. Was that the pilot? "There are two submarines approaching. And I don't think they're ours."

"They're not responding to comms," someone else said.

Kim glanced out the porthole again. The submarines' running lights flicked off, as if the pilots hoped that would hide them. She was sure the submarines had sonar or some other means of detecting each other down here.

"Evasive maneuvers," the commander ordered. "*Now.*"

Something clanged off the submarine, and Kim gripped the armrests. Silence fell for several seconds, and then a muffled boom reached her ears. A pressure wave slammed into the craft, rocking it violently.

"Torpedo," someone barked.

"Astroshamans?" Casmir asked, though he was shaking his head, as if he already knew that wasn't the answer.

"Rache," Kim said with certainty, her stomach sinking.

"That bastard," Asger growled, coming to the same conclusion. "After we *worked* with him. Helped his man find his family."

What was Rache *doing*? Why pick a fight now and with their rearmost submarine? Why wouldn't he do as Asger and Casmir had discussed—let the Kingdom go in first and deal with the brunt of the astroshamans' defenses?

"Return fire," the commander ordered.

A *thwump* reverberated through the deck.

"Helmets on," the commander called back. "Get ready in case they try to board us."

With an angry snarl, Asger unfurled his helmet, snapping it into place, and sprang from his seat with his pertundo in his hands. Other armored men jumped into the aisle, some rushing toward an airlock in the back.

Casmir leaned closer to Kim, as if he worried he might be clubbed by their own team. As a rifle butt came perilously close to his head, Kim decided that was a possibility.

But one man patted him on the head as he passed. "Don't worry, Professor." It was the game player, his virtual-reality glasses replaced by his helmet. "We'll protect you."

"Good," Casmir said as gloved fingers mussed his hair. "Thank you."

Greetings, Scholar Sato, a text appeared on her contact, the sender identified as Rache. *Are you, by chance, aboard that submarine?*

The pilot wheeled their craft to the side, barely evading a torpedo jetting their way. But the pressure wave still caught them, the force trying to knock Kim's teeth out of her jaw.

The submarine you're attacking? she replied, imagining a punch slamming into his jaw and hoping her chip found a way to convey that. *Yes, I am.*

Excellent. I did hope to see you again.

See me! You're trying to blow us up.

Simply disable you, actually. Is Casmir also with you?

Realizing she shouldn't give him any intel, she didn't reply. The submarine recovered and returned fire again, more *thwumps* reverberating through the craft. It felt like the torpedoes were launching from under the deck, though she knew Ishii's engineers had done a crude retrofit and attached them to the sides of the hull.

"We almost got one of them," the pilot said. "They'll at least feel that. These things are as maneuverable as tubs, but at least they're in the same boat. Literally."

"Almost isn't good enough. Hit the bastards, and *destroy* them." A thump sounded as the commander slammed a fist onto a comm panel and asked the rest of the Kingdom subs to come back and help.

I'll take your loyal silence for a yes, Rache messaged. *Which means his crusher is also there, I suppose. My men and I are here to rescue you, so if there's anything you can do to make that easier on us, I'd appreciate it.*

Rescue us! You mean kidnap us?

Certainly not. I'll explain in full once we've acquired you.

You've already acquired me once, and I didn't appreciate it the first time.

Casmir groaned as the pilot put the submarine through maneuvers that made even Kim's sturdy stomach writhe.

Not at all? I thought we had some delightful banter. Perhaps you could forward my request to Casmir—he's never given me permission to contact him chip-to-chip—as I imagine he could disable that submarine in a less destructive manner than I.

Not from a seat in the back row, Kim replied before realizing she'd just confirmed Casmir was here. Not that it mattered. She was sure Rache knew. And she was doubly sure he wanted Casmir to help him disable the gate defenses. Why else would Rache snatch him?

I'll be shocked if he can't disable it from the lav. Now, if you'll forward this to him and get his help, I'll be so grateful to you that I'll rub your feet. In case that delightful offer isn't enough to sway you, then I will point out that I have two submarines to your one, and that the rest of your team is nearly twenty minutes away now. That's plenty of time for my men to force their way on, capture your sub, kill all of the Kingdom soldiers in there, and collect you.

If you kill anybody, I'll shoot you myself. Kim glowered down at her stunner, now regretting that she hadn't requested a rifle.

That's no way to get a foot rub. Relay my message to him, please. We'll try to do this without killing anyone, but that'll be much easier if we have an ally within.

I'm not your ally. Not now.

I'm distressed by that. Tell Casmir, anyway, please. Also, if you could ask him to have his crusher need to conveniently take a piss while we're boarding, that would help.

Kim looked at the looming marines ready to fight, all armored and all armed. Casmir hadn't put his helmet on yet, and neither had she, but they would have to, and then hide under the seats if they didn't want to be killed.

She groped for a way to get that lunatic Rache to change his mind— just when she'd started to think he was a decent man when Jager's men weren't in his sights, he pulled this?—but the only thing that came to mind was that she and Casmir could volunteer to go over there to avoid a bloodbath. Would the commander even consider that?

Flustered, Kim forwarded the entire message string to Casmir.

He read it in a second and gaped at her. *Rescue us? What is he talking about?*

You know as much as I do. What should we do?

Casmir was the schemer. He would come up with something that would spare lives. She hoped.

Do you trust him? He gazed intently into her eyes, all seriousness for once.

No! I mean, I don't know. I'd like to, but this is ludicrous.

Casmir bit his lip, then dug into his tool satchel with one hand and thumbed open an outlet in the armrest with the other. It looked like something to plug headphones into, but he jammed an adapter and a cable into it and popped open a device that was wirelessly linked to his chip. Commands in a programming language scrolled by, and what looked like a schematic of the submarine flashed on the tiny display.

Casmir paused whatever he was doing and glanced toward the porthole. The submarine wheeled again to evade an attack, but the torpedo still exploded nearby. Their craft pitched sideways in a roll that would have hurled Kim from her seat if not for the belt. Asger grunted as he almost landed in Casmir's lap. He gripped the seat backs and righted himself the best he could. The submarine was slow to recover, and the deck seemed to be tilted to one side.

A command flashed on Casmir's little device. He had the screen tilted toward her and away from any of the soldiers who might witness it—away from Asger.

An instant later, the lights inside went out. Everywhere. Pitch blackness engulfed the submarine. The thrum of the engine disappeared.

The pilot swore vehemently. "Main power went out."

"No shit," the commander said. "Find auxiliary power."

"I don't know if there is any."

"Find it anyway."

"Are we going to sink?" a soldier's concerned query sounded.

Nobody answered him.

A crackle came over a poor-quality comm speaker—or maybe one running on a weak battery backup.

"Greetings, *Waddler*. This is Captain Tenebris Rache on the lethal *Bubbles 3*. I've neutralized your submarine, and I intend to personally lead a boarding party to kidnap your civilian advisors, Casmir Dabrowski and Kim Sato."

Zee strode up the aisle to stand next to Casmir's seat. Asger snarled something inaudible. Kim glanced at him, surprised he was purely angry instead of suspicious at the conveniently timed power outage. Maybe that would come later when he'd had time to think about the moment.

The marines also issued defiant snarls. Casmir's new gaming friend swore he wouldn't let the filthy bastard touch their professor.

"You can save yourself the loss of lives," Rache went on, "which my well-trained and cybernetically enhanced men *will* otherwise take, by handing over the prisoners without a fight. Put them in diving suits and shove them out your airlock. We'll come collect them. If you don't do this voluntarily—" Rache's dry tone switched to one of icy cold, "—we will gladly come aboard and kill every man who's sworn to do Jager's bidding. The end is inevitable. You have two minutes to decide. We have you surrounded."

Casmir disconnected his device and bowed his head. Probably wondering if he'd done the right thing. Kim had no idea. Rache sounded like he relished the idea of killing the Kingdom soldiers.

"We're not giving up anyone," the commander said after a long pause. Kim wondered if he'd been thinking about it. "We only have to hold them off until the rest of our subs get here. Prepare to fight, men."

An eager roar tore from a dozen throats. Kim closed her eyes, imagining those throats all slit, their armor peeled open, and the soldiers dead.

"I am prepared to defend you, Kim Sato and Casmir Dabrowski," Zee announced from the aisle.

"Good," Casmir said. "Thank you, Zee."

I'm a little skeptical he can force his way on and win, especially with Asger and Zee helping these guys, but, Kim... Casmir found her arm in the dark and patted it. *If anyone dies, and I'm sure they will in a fight, I'll blame myself.*

I know. I think we have to surrender ourselves to him and trust that...

He wants to rescue us? Casmir texted.

Kim didn't need light to know his eyebrows were raised skeptically. *Trust that we can get away or figure out how to report his movements back to our people. Does it even matter if he gets the gate first when you've got Nguyen's allies coming to fight whoever pulls it out of the water?*

If she tells people about it, they'll send science vessels, not warships. Casmir released her arm.

She sensed him standing up, and she realized he was about to do exactly what she'd been suggesting. If the commander reported that Casmir had volunteered to go, Jager might be suspicious of him. He already had reasons to mistrust Casmir. And so did Ishii. Even Asger did. But Kim didn't think anyone except Casmir knew she had feelings for Rache—or she had until he'd pulled this idiotic move.

She lurched to her feet and spoke before Casmir. "Commander, let us go. It's better than people being killed in a huge fight. If he wants us, it's for our science and engineering knowledge. He won't kill us, and maybe we can get away, or even find an opportunity to transmit information back to you on what his team is doing."

"We don't hand people over to enemies of the Kingdom to become hostages," the commander said coolly. "We're especially not giving that animal a *woman*."

Kim cursed under her breath. Of all the things for the guy to get uppity about, he was worried about her sex?

The speaker crackled.

"Thirty seconds, Commander," Rache said. "Are you sending them over?"

"No," the commander snarled to the comm as Kim yelled, "Yes."

"She's right," Casmir said. "You need all your men to fight the astroshamans. This isn't worth people dying over. I'll take my crusher along to protect us, just in case. And Sir Asger."

Silence filled the cabin, and in the dark, Kim had no idea what Asger's reaction was.

"Sir Knight?" the commander said, sounding less certain now.

Asger didn't reply right away.

Kim wondered if Casmir would message him and urge him to go along with it.

"He may shoot you as soon as you're on board," the commander pointed out. "He only asked for our advisors."

"We won't let him," Casmir said. "If he wants our help, he'll leave Asger be."

"You won't really give him your help, will you?"

Kim was surprised the commander was entertaining this. Maybe he truly didn't want to fight Rache's enhanced mercenaries. Or he agreed that they needed all of their men for the assault on the astroshamans.

"I'll lead him to think we will," Casmir said. "Because we're so scared that we'll do anything he says. But we'll figure something out."

"I'll go with them and keep them safe," Asger finally said. "They're right. It's better than a fight when they have twice our numbers."

"Commander?" Rache prompted.

"We agree to your terms," the officer bit out.

CHAPTER 6

THE WARM, SPICY SCENT OF *POZOLE ROJO* WAFTED through the corridors of the *Stellar Dragon*.

Qin's stomach rumbled, and she allowed herself to be deterred from her mission to learn everything she could about Johnny, and she headed for the lounge. Before they'd left System Cerberus, she'd carefully gone through his pack, but she'd found little more than clothing, a couple of DEW-Tek pistols and smoke bombs and grenades. A few types of hard currency had been stuffed into an inside pouch, but there hadn't been any identification or any hints to who he truly was.

Since then, she'd poked around on the network, hoping to find his name in an article or on a roster of Kingdom knights. But she wasn't sure how to spell it, as the name he'd given hadn't been one she was familiar with, and she also hadn't found lists of knights in the databases for either System Cerberus or System Hydra. The Kingdom probably kept that information private.

On the kitchen side of the lounge, Bonita was stirring her stewpot. Freshly fried tortilla chips filled a basket on the counter next to a couple of sauces and sliced cabbage and radish.

Qin's stomach rumbled again, and she headed to grab the bowls from the cabinet and help set their little table. They'd come out of the wormhole gate and into System Hydra that morning and were accelerating toward Tiamat Station three days away, so they had enough gravity to dine in comfort.

"Grab a bowl for Toes," Bonita said.

"You didn't invite him to dinner, did you?" Qin glanced around the lounge in alarm, though she would have seen and smelled him if he'd been in there.

"No, but prisoners like it if you feed them. And he's a *paying* prisoner, so I might even bring him seconds."

"Are you going to comm the *Osprey* and see if they really want him?" Qin asked.

"I hailed them when we first entered the system. Their comm officer couldn't be bothered to answer, so I left a message, and they haven't gotten back to me yet. If they don't want our help, I'm not going to force it on them. Or force him on them. He also said we could drop him off at Tiamat Station. That would give us an opportunity to get supplies—my fresh vegetable offerings are limited, as you can see—and the opportunity to have nothing to do with the Kingdom."

"Bonita," Viggo chided, "shouldn't we make another attempt to communicate? I'd like to find out if Casmir is on that ship before we decide to have nothing to do with it."

"You can send messages to his chip if you've been missing him. I don't see any reason to cozy up to a Kingdom warship that isn't interested in us."

"He can't repair X-17's faulty nozzle over his chip. That requires hands-on work."

"I agree that we should try again," Qin said. "So we can find out if the Kingdom knows who Johnny is. Maybe there's a reward for turning in someone impersonating a knight."

Bonita looked up from her pot. "Did you find evidence to prove that's what he's doing? Besides the supposedly removable tattoos?"

"I didn't find anything but clothes and weapons in his bag, but if he really was a knight, wouldn't he have a pertundo? Like Asger?"

Asger. A little zing went through her as she imagined his face in her mind.

He'd sent a message sometime in the last week, but courier ships didn't risk visiting System Cerberus that often, so she'd only received it that morning when they entered Hydra. He'd asked how she was doing on her quest with the pirates and if she'd found any trees to hug. He'd also said he was tied up with work for his superiors, but that if she needed help, she should let him know, and he would try to find an opportunity to take leave.

She'd appreciated the note, the fact that he'd been wondering enough about her to write. It meant something. She wasn't sure what, but it at least meant he considered her a friend, didn't it?

Casmir had sent a couple of messages, too, both to her and Bonita, and more openly expressed concern at their silence, but that seemed more the norm from him. He probably checked up on all of his friends and relatives regularly. He wasn't stoic and distant like Asger. Asger's note had seemed... special.

"Even when the shafts on those are collapsed, they'd still be large to stick in your luggage," Bonita said, and Qin pulled her mind back to pertundos, not certain knights. "And if the Druckers searched his stuff and found one, that would have made it hard for him to spy on them."

"Do you *believe* he's a knight?" Qin hadn't seen Bonita going down to the cell except to take meals, so she had relaxed her concern that Bonita might do something unwise—like take Johnny up to her cabin for a romp between the sheets.

"No, but I'm not sure we can condemn him based on the lack of a purple cloak and an axe."

"It's more of a halberd."

Bonita waved a dismissive hand.

"There's a ship dead ahead on our course, Bonita," Viggo said. "It's showing signs of weapons damage, and there are breaches in its hull. It does still have power and is issuing a distress call."

"I'm sure there are a lot of ships in this system that can help it," Bonita said. "Especially this close to the gate."

"They may not have much time. It's a ship we're familiar with."

"Not the *Osprey*?" Qin asked.

"No," Viggo said. "It's the *Machu Picchu*."

Qin frowned, trying to place the familiar name.

"The research ship where you went for treatment after you were exposed to the gate on the cargo ship, Qin," Viggo added.

"Oh, right." Qin tapped a nail to her chin. Even though Kim had been the one to give her treatment, it had been using the ship's equipment, which left her feeling indebted and inclined to help the crew.

"Huh." Bonita set her spoon aside and put the lid on her pot. "What's it doing in this system? That was a Kingdom ship, wasn't it?"

"Registered to one of the universities on Odin, yes," Viggo said. "Perhaps if we answer their distress call we can find out."

"If the *Osprey* is in the system, *it* can help the ship."

Qin frowned. Even though she knew they had to be careful out in space by themselves, especially since the *Dragon* was ostensibly a freighter with only a single railgun mounted on the top, she didn't like the idea of abandoning people who might need help. If they were on a research ship, they were likely civilian scientists, not pirates or criminals who'd gotten themselves into trouble.

"We are nearby," Viggo said.

"Is there a reason you're eager to help out and potentially risk ourselves?" Bonita asked.

Viggo hesitated. "I believe it's what Casmir would do."

Bonita dropped her face into her hand.

Qin smiled faintly. "Casmir has made quite an impression on Viggo."

"We're making a new rule going forward, Qin." Bonita lowered her hand. "No more mechanics, roboticists, or engineers are allowed as passengers."

"Because they're a bad influence on Viggo?"

"Because Viggo falls in *love* with them."

"Really, Bonita." Viggo sniffed impressively well for someone with no nostrils. "I'm not in love, but since we will likely meet Casmir again, I would like to act honorably and help those from his world. Then he'll be more inclined to—"

"Adjust the nozzles on your vacuums?" Bonita cut in.

"Certainly."

Bonita waved her spoon at her pot, then handed the utensil to Qin. "Don't let this burn."

"Where are you going?" Qin asked as she headed out.

"To alter course to check on the damaged ship."

"You're a good woman, Captain," Qin called after her.

"A good woman who's probably walking into a trap that'll get us all killed." Bonita disappeared down the corridor.

"A slightly bitter and jaded woman but a good one," Qin said.

"She has informed me on more than one occasion," Viggo said, "that tendencies toward skepticism, pessimism, and disbelief help keep one alive longer."

"Oh?" Qin sampled the *pozole rojo*, the two kinds of chiles dancing on her taste buds. "That sounds verbose for her."

"It's possible she used a shorter idiom in her native tongue to convey the point. It involved avoiding getting one's testicles cut off."

"That sounds more like her."

"Yes."

Asger stood in the airlock with Casmir, Kim, and Zee, water filling the chamber and their armored shoulders mashed together in the tight space. A bag Kim had slung over her shoulder clunked him in the side of the helmet. It had something hard in it. He hoped that meant she and Casmir had a plan. When they'd spoken, Asger had been about to agree with the marines that they should fight to keep the damn mercenaries from forcing their way aboard their submarine.

Then Casmir had sent a single one-line message. *Go along with it. It's better than people dying here.*

He had the niggling suspicion that Casmir knew more than he should about what Rache wanted, but he wouldn't speak of it while they were still on board. Not that it was likely there was any recording equipment active at the moment. The power was still out in the submarine, and they'd had to open the airlock hatch and order the chamber to fill using manual levers and latches.

Asger had his helmet lamp activated, opting for that over the night-vision option, and a narrow beam of light ameliorated the darkness in the chamber. It was enough for Asger to make out his comrades and see Zee blending in with the shadows.

He was waterproof, presumably, but could he swim? He had to weigh almost as much as solid metal.

If Asger hadn't practiced swimming in combat armor during his training, he would also be worried about its extra weight, but the built-in air tank and air in the helmet and small gaps of the interior kept it from sinking. It was more likely that he would have to exert effort to keep from floating up rather than staying level.

"Comm check," Asger said quietly, setting up a channel for their group and inviting Kim and Casmir onto it.

"We hear you," Casmir said.

"Yes," Kim added.

But chip-to-chip would be better, I think, Casmir texted him, looping Kim in. *There will be records of anything we say in our armor.*

And we're going to say things that we don't want a record of? Asger replied through his chip.

I think that's a given.

Have you been in contact with Rache? Once the chamber was full of water, Asger spun the outer hatch wheel to open it manually. The blue and yellow paint of Rache's sub was visible thirty or forty meters away—its running lights were on.

Kim was the one to answer. *He messaged me and told me he's rescuing us.*

From our own people? Oh, I bet. I assume he wants Casmir to deactivate the gate and is bullshitting about the rest.

We'll find out.

Asger started to go out first, but Casmir stopped him before he could push out into an ocean that was darker than space, except for the dim lighting along the exterior of the other vessel. Absolutely no light filtered down through the thick ice above.

Let me go first, Casmir messaged. *They won't shoot me or Kim.*

Asger's training to defend those weaker than himself made him want to protest, but Casmir had a point. All Rache wanted was Kim and Casmir. Asger and Zee were crashing the party.

Still, he couldn't bring himself to hide behind anyone. He went out at the same time as Casmir. He pushed off, as he would do if he were leaving the airlock of a warship, but the water outside was vastly different from the frozen vacuum of space—or even the lake he'd practiced in back on Odin.

The seams of his armor groaned at the pressure, and an alarm flashed on his heads-up display. But as he'd guessed, he started floating upward. He paddled hard, angling himself downward and toward the other submarine. Since he didn't think his jet boots would work underwater, he didn't try to activate them. Fins would have been better.

The hatch in the side of Rache's submarine opened slowly. Two men in black armor waited inside the airlock.

A dark figure moved next to Asger, on the side opposite of Casmir, and he jerked, envisioning some massive sea creature swooping in to attack.

But it was Zee, kicking and swimming hard, his arms flailing to keep his heavy body from sinking. As Asger watched, he re-formed his arms into something more akin to fins, his legs into great flippers. Once he made the adjustment, he zipped ahead, not caring if he arrived first and the mercenaries fired at him. Maybe he *wanted* that.

Fortunately, the two mercenaries hadn't brought out rifles or pistols. Maybe they hadn't known if their weapons would work underwater. Asger didn't know, either, but he was sure his pertundo would work fine, the cleaving halberd head and spike, if not the technological energy component.

He landed in the airlock behind Zee. Casmir and Kim reached the submarine, but there wasn't room for anyone else inside. They found nearby handholds, but Casmir waved for Asger to trade positions with him.

Asger debated. He would rather go inside, face the mercenaries, and make sure it was safe before Casmir and Kim came in, but Rache and his people hated the Kingdom and had killed knights before—Asger gritted his teeth as he remembered hearing about the incidents in the news and the discussion around Prester Court when he'd still been a squire. The mercenaries might take him down if Casmir didn't go in first and deliver his threat to not help unless they let Asger live.

He reluctantly pushed himself back outside, making room for Casmir and Kim to squeeze in behind Zee and the two mercenaries.

The hatch closed, leaving Asger hanging on to the hull, his legs floating upward behind him. He swallowed uneasily, feeling alone and vulnerable. He reminded himself that if the hatch didn't open again after the airlock cycled, he could go back to the other submarine if he must. But leaving Casmir and Kim to Rache's devices would be another failure.

He leaned his helmet against the hull, telling himself this wasn't the time to dwell on how often he'd been applying that word to himself of late. Casmir might argue otherwise, but he was in trouble with the king too. Winning Casmir's favor wouldn't do anything for Asger's career. It might continue to hurt it.

"Did you take your seizure medication this morning?" Kim's voice came over their shared channel.

"Yes, Mom," Casmir said. "If I hadn't, it would be a little late to do so anyway."

Were they still in the airlock?

"Did you bring it along with you for your kidnapping?"

"I thought it was a rescue."

"We'll see."

"Yes, I did. In my tool satchel. Which that hulking man with the metal thorns implanted in his cheeks just took away. Hm."

"They're taking my vials too," Kim muttered.

"Maybe they'll accidentally break them open and incapacitate themselves," Casmir whispered even more quietly.

Asger wondered what concoction Kim had made.

"They're all wearing full armor. That makes them safe from airborne particles—and bacteria."

"Ah, so we have to convince them to strip naked first?" Casmir asked.

"Just removing their helmets would do."

"I forgot," Casmir said, "you don't get excited by naked men."

"If *you* do, Prin— any women you're thinking of dating might be disappointed."

Asger frowned at that slip. That hadn't been about Princess *Oku*, had it? Surely, Casmir couldn't imagine he had a chance with royalty. Beautiful and serene royalty, at that.

How odd that Asger had almost forgotten about Oku lately. He'd been thinking more about Qin. But not romantically, he assured himself. Oku was the kind of woman men dreamed of. Qin was just… a good friend. That was all.

The hatch opened, and Asger berated himself for his drifting thoughts. He swam into the empty water-filled airlock.

"You two all right?" he asked quietly, hoping the mercenaries cycled the airlock and let him in. They might find this a handy brig to store him in.

"Many large armed men are pointing their rifles at us," Casmir said.

"Actually, they're pointing them at Zee," Kim said. "And gaping as his fins turn back into arms and legs."

Casmir and Kim fell silent, and Asger worried. He shifted his weight impatiently as the hatch closed behind him and the water drained out. He'd put his pertundo in its holder for the swim across, but he drew it now. Just in case.

It was dark in the airlock, and when the inner hatch opened and light flooded in, he squinted. His headlamp turned off automatically.

"We taking their weapons, boss?" someone asked as Asger stepped out into the divers' prep area, his boots landing on damp perforated rubber mats.

"I don't have any weapons." Casmir lifted his hands, gauntleted fingers spread.

An armored merc was searching through his tool satchel as water dripped from it. Asger thought of the gauges and electronic devices he'd seen Casmir use and hoped they were in waterproof cases inside.

Kim's bag had already disappeared, and she wore an irritated expression behind her faceplate. Her arms were crossed over her chest. A stunner was attached to her utility belt, but she didn't reach for it.

"Not if they remove their helmets and make it easy for us to stun them," Rache's voice came from the front of the submarine.

"Isn't that an appealing suggestion." Kim sent a dark look in his direction.

The deck rumbled as engines came to life, and Asger sensed movement. He couldn't see a porthole from where he stood, but he knew they were sailing away from the Kingdom submarine.

The clock on his helmet display said the rest of their allies had to be ten minutes away, if they were on the way at all. He wasn't sure. Maybe they'd considered their part of the mission too important to come back, and that was why the commander had decided he was willing to cooperate.

The mercenaries parted, and an armored man shorter than the others walked forward, his helmet off, but his black mask and hood hiding his features. Rache bowed to Kim and Casmir, glanced at Zee, and ignored Asger.

"If you'll follow me to the office in the back," Rache told Casmir, "I'll show you how I'm rescuing you instead of kidnapping you."

"Are you sure you know the different meanings of those words?" Casmir asked. "Because this feels like a kidnapping." He turned to Kim. "Doesn't it feel like a kidnapping to you?"

Kim sighed.

"If you wish me to attack these men and attempt to take over the vessel to ensure your safety, Kim Sato and Casmir Dabrowski, I am prepared." Zee wasn't taller than all of the mercenaries, but he exuded an ominous presence with his solid, nearly indestructible build. "Simply give the order."

Rache didn't look alarmed. He pointed past Asger toward whatever cabin he'd mentioned.

"Can *I* give the order?" Asger muttered.

"No," Zee said. "Casmir Dabrowski has not programmed me to accept orders from anyone else other than Kim Sato."

A familiar man leaned out of an open hatchway behind a couple of mercenaries. Dr. Yas Peshlakai. He was holding Kim's bag and watching the goings on curiously. Unlike the mercenaries, he wasn't in armor.

Rache pushed Casmir to the side and walked into the short back corridor, a few hatches lining the bulkhead. "This way."

"I expected we'd spend more time bantering first," Casmir said.

"Guess he's in a hurry." Kim was the first one to follow Rache.

Several of the mercenaries eyed Asger's pertundo, but to his surprise, nobody tried to take it. The man who'd been searching Casmir's satchel withdrew a chocolate bar, then handed it back to him.

"Rache." Casmir slung the satchel over his shoulder and followed Kim. "One of your fearless mercenaries just stole my emergency rations."

Asger had the urge to spring at the man and protect Casmir's belongings, but the thief withdrew behind a wall of his comrades. One of them eyed the chocolate bar like a starving wolf. Asger supposed it was silly to hope they would all get in a fight over it, kill each other, and Asger could take over the submarine.

"Emergency rations? That looked like a candy bar." Rache entered a hatchway just before engineering.

"Actually, it's a Cosmic Crater Deluxe, far superior to some generic sweet."

"Maybe he'll give it back if you help us with the gate."

"That seems unlikely. He's opened the wrapper and is sniffing it now."

Two men followed Asger, rifles pointed at his back, as he entered the cabin behind Kim and Casmir. There were posters all over the bulkheads, promising good deals to those who booked tours four months in advance.

Rache waved to a tablet on a desk but didn't sit in the chair. "I have something to show you, Casmir. Asger, close the hatch."

"Sir?" one of the mercs behind them asked. "You don't want some of us in there with you?"

"I'll call you if I need you, Chains." Rache waved toward Asger.

Asger was happy to slam the hatch shut in front of the mercenaries' faces. And he felt better being alone in the cabin with Zee, Casmir, and Kim. Even though Rache was armored, he didn't have an obvious weapon, and it crossed Asger's mind that he and Zee could overpower him and hold him hostage. Maybe force the rest of the mercenaries to take a trip out that airlock hatch.

"Zee and I could take him," Asger whispered into his helmet's comm pickup.

"I want to see how he rescued us first," Casmir whispered back.

Asger clenched his fist but didn't push.

Rache waved for the tablet to play a video and slid it across the desk toward Casmir and Kim. Asger, taller than both, had no trouble seeing it.

Thoughts of commandeering the submarine slipped from his mind as Ambassador Romano's face came up side by side with that Captain Cullen who'd tried to barter with Ishii for Casmir. To repair his robots, he'd said.

Cullen didn't keep up the pretense with Romano, and Asger's mouth dropped open as the video played and Romano callously bartered for Casmir's life.

"We already found and neutralized the locator beacon," Rache said when the video was done.

"Oh, good," Casmir said. "Because that's the thing I was most concerned about."

"I just want you to know that Jager's puppy was going to sell you out—sell your *life*—to some scummy bounty hunter for nothing." Rache rested a hand on his chest. "I *am* rescuing you."

Kim had removed her helmet to watch the video. She said nothing but raised her eyebrows, not appearing impressed.

Rache looked at her. "I'll admit nobody was talking about killing you, but I thought you might be caught in the crossfire as some suborned thug took shots at Casmir."

"So I should consider myself preemptively rescued?" It was hard to tell if she was joking or if she was still angry.

The latter, Asger hoped.

"I believe so," Rache said.

"Who was he going to get to shoot me?" Casmir flipped his helmet back and scrubbed at his already tousled dark hair. It was damp with sweat, which was surprising since the swim over hadn't been that laborious or long. Maybe he was more nervous than he sounded. "How many suborn-able men does Ishii have on his ship? And is that a word?"

"No," Kim said at the same time as Rache.

Kim added, "A man who believed he was working for the ambassador—and through him Jager—might not consider himself suborned. He might think he was doing the right thing for the crown. Either that, or Romano was going to pay someone from the kitchen.

We already know they're motivated by money. At least that way, you'd know him by the choice of assassination weapon."

"Right. I wouldn't have needed to be rescued." Casmir looked at Rache. "I would have just avoided the man swinging a whisk."

"I envisioned a meat cleaver," Kim said.

"That's gory," Casmir said.

"Sorry."

Asger looked at Zee, the only other person—if one could call him that—not bantering casually in front of the enemy who'd captured them. The only other *sane* person in the cabin.

Asger knew they had all dined together at that apartment in the capital, but that didn't mean they should trust Rache. He'd sounded bloodthirsty when he'd spoken about how his enhanced men would destroy anyone who'd sworn an oath to Jager. That, along with knowing about all the crimes he'd committed over the years—all the people he'd *murdered*—made Asger want to slam the blade of his pertundo through that helmet and mask.

"Where are you taking us, oh noble rescuer?" Kim asked Rache.

"To the astroshaman base," Rache said, "to get the gate while your people are distracting the defenders."

"I believe their plan is to sneak in while *your* people are distracting the defenders," Casmir said.

"You did arrive first with the submarines you stole instead of renting," Asger said. "That means your people are in the lead."

"That's what you think." Rache bowed slightly to Kim, then walked out.

He shut the hatch behind him, leaving their group alone. The lock clicked. Alone and imprisoned.

"I don't like that man," Asger announced, not caring if the cabin was bugged.

"What are your feelings on Ambassador Romano?" Casmir asked.

"I don't like him either. When I joined the knighthood, I thought I'd be surrounded by and working for noble and honorable people. Casmir, why does everybody want you dead? Is it just because of your genes?"

"I don't know." Casmir looked bleakly at Kim, but she wasn't saying much. She mostly looked irked, not at Casmir but at Rache, if her glare toward the closed hatch was any indicator.

"How would a Miners' Union prince even know about your genes?" Asger added.

"I don't know that, either, though I did find some photos of Admiral Mikita here in System Hydra. The resemblance is clear. I think President Nguyen recognized me right away."

"Going from thinking you resemble him to assuming you're his clone is a stretch." Asger kicked the desk, annoyed that Casmir was in danger and annoyed that they were in Rache's clutches.

He wasn't positive they'd made the right decision in handing over Casmir and Kim instead of fighting for them. What if they—what if *he*—inadvertently helped Rache acquire the gate instead of the Kingdom? Asger was already at risk of being kicked out of the knighthood. At this rate, he would end up with a bounty on his head.

"Perhaps it is I that this prince fears," Zee said, "and he is targeting Casmir Dabrowski so he cannot build me a mate. Who would be equally fearsome."

Asger stared at the crusher. So did Kim. Casmir only smiled, though it was a wan smile. Sweat dampened his forehead. That couldn't still be from the swim, could it?

"I am attempting to use levity to lessen the human tension in the room," Zee stated. "I have observed that Casmir Dabrowski does this often, to varying degrees of success."

"Are you rubbing off on your crusher, Casmir?" Asger asked.

"Like a fungal infection," Kim said.

"Ouch." Casmir touched his hand to his chest. "Shouldn't you save your vitriol for the man who kidnapped you twice in the same year?"

"I've got plenty stored up for him."

"Why did he kidnap you?" Asger asked her. "I could see him wanting Casmir, but doesn't he already have your bacteria?"

"Yes." Kim shrugged. "I'll be sure to ask him when I'm unleashing my vitriol."

"Shall I let him know you want to see him alone?" Asger pointed his thumb at the hatch.

"We don't need to be alone for it."

The hatch opened, and Asger expected Rache—who else would be brave enough to come in and engage with a vitriolic woman?—but it was the mercenary doctor, Yas.

"Uhm, hello." He lifted a tentative hand. A mercenary loomed in the corridor behind him. "Scholar Sato? I apologize that you've been brought here against your wishes again—I can say I had nothing to do with the idea this time—but as long as you're here, I wondered if we could talk about what's in your case."

"Do I get to charge an hourly consulting fee?" Her expression was flat, and it was hard to tell if she was joking.

"Certainly. Bill it to Rache."

She snorted. "Fine. Come in."

"Actually, I've got them laid out in sickbay."

"These subs have sickbays?" Kim asked. "I didn't notice that on ours."

"There's a chair in a cubby with a first-aid kit strapped to the wall. I just set up a small folding table."

Kim grumbled something under her breath and walked toward the hatchway.

Zee stepped toward the hatch ahead of her, and Yas lurched backward, bumping into the chest of the mercenary behind him.

"Do you need me to accompany you and protect you, Kim Sato?" Zee asked.

"Uh, he won't fit in the sickbay," Yas said.

"I don't think I need protection from Dr. Peshlakai," Kim said.

"What about the heinous and nefarious Tenebris Rache?" Zee asked.

Kim raised her eyebrows at Casmir. "Did you program him to use those adjectives?"

"No," Casmir said. "Zee is a superior individual, capable of making his own judgments about human beings."

"Did you program him with Kingdom newsfeeds?"

"I have been watching Kingdom dramas," Zee informed them. "And also reading fictional narratives that Tork suggested about astroshamans. We are attempting to learn to better understand humanity through the art that it creates."

"Rache stars in dramas?" Casmir looked puzzled. Or maybe envious.

"Tenebris Rache is the villain in no fewer than three recently produced fictional narratives," Zee said.

"The heinous and nefarious villain?" Kim asked, her face still difficult to read.

"Indeed so."

"I'll risk it. You better stay here with Casmir, Zee." Kim waved back to her friend. "He looks wan."

Zee strode to Casmir's side and slung an arm around his shoulder. "I am prepared to assist if he has a seizure or other medical malady."

"I'm fine, but thanks." Casmir patted the tarry black arm. "Just hot. Why is this sub so much warmer than the other one?"

Asger frowned. "It's not."

Kim waved Asger to the door before heading out after Yas. "I don't have network access anymore." She waved at her temple. "Are you able to contact the ship or anyone on the other subs?"

Asger shook his head. He'd had access when they'd been near the entrance into the ocean, but he suspected they'd moved too far away from it and the ice was blocking satellite signals.

"Damn. I wish I'd thought to ask earlier for a report."

"A report on what?"

Kim glanced at Casmir, but he wasn't watching them. He was teaching Zee how to make the Kingdom's three-fingered let's-be-friends-instead-of-enemies gesture.

"I want to know what the autopsy on that woman's body revealed," Kim whispered, her comm channel off so Casmir wouldn't overhear.

"I'm sure it will be confirmed that she was stabbed." Asger wasn't sure why this was a secret, but he also lowered his voice and turned off the comm. "I saw the knife in her back."

"I did, too, but you don't need to stab someone twelve times and stuff them in a luggage compartment if all you want to do is kill them."

"I assumed the murderer was a very angry person."

"I didn't think much of it at the time, but I'm starting to wonder if the murderer was a very scared person."

A chill went through Asger. He hadn't observed that Kim was the type to give in to melodrama. "Why?"

Kim glanced over her shoulder at Casmir again. "Just a hunch."

"Scholar Sato?" Yas poked his head back inside.

"Yes, I'm coming."

Asger frowned after her as she walked out. The last thing they needed was *another* problem.

CHAPTER 7

I T WAS THE MIDDLE OF THE NIGHT SHIP'S time when the *Dragon* drew close to the *Machu Picchu*.

When they were half an hour away, the alarm Qin had set went off, and she dressed and headed up to navigation. She thought about donning her armor, but she didn't yet know if Bonita would send her aboard. It had been an automated distress call, so it was possible nobody was left alive over there. But the *Dragon* ought to be close enough now for the scanners to determine that.

Qin was surprised that Bonita wasn't in navigation. The forward display was zoomed in on the damaged research vessel.

"Bonita went down to the cell," Viggo informed her as Qin slid into the co-pilot's pod to check the scanners.

"To talk to the prisoner?" Qin supposed he was technically a passenger, not a prisoner, but since he was locked up for the trip, she was inclined to think of him as the latter. "Or, uhm, do something else with him?"

"The bars remain in place with Bonita on the outside and Johnny Twelve Toes on the inside."

"That doesn't entirely answer my question." Qin imagined Bonita being experienced enough with sex to come up with creative ways to engage in the various acts through bars.

"She is questioning him to determine if he knows anything about the *Machu Picchu* or what a Kingdom research vessel is doing in this system," Viggo said dryly.

"Oh, good."

"They discussed sex earlier. And whether extra toes offer any advantages during coitus."

"Ew." Qin leaned an elbow on the console to peruse the results of the scan. "Does he actually have extra toes?"

"If he's taken off his boots at all during the trip, it was while the lights were off. I do have night-vision capabilities of a sort, but they are limited to areas of the ship where I can employ heat sensors. That cell is not such a place."

"So some things remain a mystery even to the sentient ship who sees all in his domain?"

"Indeed so."

Qin chewed on her lip. "They took a *lot* of damage."

It was definitely from weapons fire, not an explosion caused by a malfunction. One of the rings that assisted with the big ship's spin gravity had been blown half off, the hull was scoured black in numerous places with large pieces of plating missing. A great gaping hole exposed several decks on the starboard side. The thrusters were offline, but it looked like the engine that powered the environmental systems was still online. The ship wasn't spinning, so there wouldn't be any gravity over there, but there was heat and air. And there was life.

"It looks like at least four life signs, maybe more," she said.

"I've picked out six while I've been watching. A couple are in engineering, and the heat from the engine interferes with the readings."

"Have they tried to comm us?"

"No, they're still issuing the distress call, but that appears to be coming from an auxiliary comm system rather than the main one on the bridge. I don't read power from the bridge or the deck below."

"So it's a real mess over there." Qin tapped the scanner display, picking out airlocks on either side of the ship. One was close enough to the damaged area that it might be too warped to dock with, but the other one hadn't been hit. "Have you tried to comm them?"

"Bonita did when she was up here. There was no answer."

"Probably nobody in that auxiliary comm cabin to hear it. They may be hiding. Or trying to repair their ship."

"That's what I surmise. I—"

Their comm panel lit up, and Viggo paused.

"Is that them? Should I answer it?" Qin frowned at the display. The hail wasn't coming from the *Machu Picchu* but from another ship about four hours away.

"I'm not the captain. You don't have to ask *me*."

"But you're more than a hundred years old and wise."

Qin hesitated, not sure if she should answer or not. This wasn't System Cerberus, but that didn't mean that everyone who wanted to talk would be friendly. She pinged the ship first and tried to get an ident.

"Nobody has called me that before," Viggo said.

"Not even Casmir?"

"No, but we've spent so little time together. Perhaps he would eventually."

"I'm sure of it."

The ident came back as a freighter called the *Maze Runner*. The name sounded familiar. Qin didn't think she'd run into it in the months she'd traveled with Bonita, but it was possible the Druckers had dealt with it in her years working for them.

"It's a smuggler," Viggo said. "That ship is in our database under Captain Amazing. We've encountered him before."

"Captain *Amazing*?"

"Presumably, he named himself. If all is the same as it was two years ago, he is a smuggler and opportunist with a crew of at least twenty, and they've got a lot of hidden weapons on the hull of the ship, even though it's designed to look like they don't. It's registered out of Cerberus."

"I think I'll *not* answer the comm then."

"I'll let Bonita know there's an old friend who wants to talk to her."

"*Is* he an old friend?"

"They've exchanged gunfire a couple of times. When last they met, she gouged a hole in the side of his temple."

"So they're close to each other."

"Their DEW-Tek bolts have been close to each other."

Qin definitely wasn't answering the comm. But the caller was insistent. The comm kept pinging until Bonita clomped out of the ladder well and into navigation.

"It's Captain Amazing," Viggo informed her.

"What's he doing in a respectable system?"

"He seems eager to tell you."

Bonita settled into her pod and accepted the comm.

"Back off, Lopez," a male voice ordered. "We've already laid a salvager's claim on that ship."

"You can't claim a ship from halfway across the system, you idiot," Bonita said.

"Screw you. We're two hours away."

Bonita glanced at the long-range scanner display. "It looks more like four."

"If you're there trying to steal our salvage when we get there, we'll blow your decrepit garbage scow out of the sky."

"Decrepit! Garbage scow!" Viggo's voice thundered from the speakers. Somewhere, vacuums vroomed like air bikes revving up for a race.

"You're offending my ship," Bonita said blandly.

Qin rotated her ears away from the hatchway and the roar of the vacuums. She was tempted to grab a couple of cotton balls, but she didn't want to miss any of this. Her blood warmed as she imagined going into battle with this Captain Amazing.

"Your ship can suck my cock. If you take *anything* off our salvage, I'll blow you all the way back to the gate. This isn't like Port Blanco. You can't shoot at me from behind a crate. We've got you outgunned a thousand times."

"Yeah, yeah, you're tougher than a black hole. We're just going to rescue the crew. The crew that might object to you salvaging their ship while they're on board it."

"Unfortunately, as I'll report to the authorities, the crew's not going to have made it. Their comm is down. They're not telling anyone otherwise. If you don't want the same report to be filed on you and your noisy garbage scow, you'll be long gone by the time we get there."

The channel went dead.

"Bonita," Viggo said, "I want to order more weapons and hull armoring for the *Dragon* so we don't have to kowtow to criminals like that."

"As soon as we get you paid off with the bank, we can add all the upgrades you want. In the meantime, we're not kowtowing."

"We're still going to rescue the crew, right, Captain?" Qin rose to her feet. "I'll go get my armor on. We've got time."

"Yeah, go get dressed. Viggo, where in the system is that Kingdom ship? The *Osprey*."

"Orbiting Xolas Moon approximately one day away. Two other Kingdom warships are with them, and another one is flying from the moon toward the gate, but it's not much closer. This is the same small fleet that left Odin when we did."

"Let's send them a message. They might be too far away to have heard the research vessel's distress call, but they should send some help if they know smugglers are trying to salvage one of their ships."

Qin was on her way down the ladder, but she heard Viggo's reply.

"Even if they divert that closest ship, it won't get here in time to stop the *Maze Runner.*"

"I'm hoping that some threats from the Kingdom will be enough," Bonita said.

"In this system, I doubt it."

Qin hopped into her cabin and grabbed her armor and her anti-tank gun. *She* would be enough. Maybe not to keep the ship from being illegally salvaged, but she could rescue the crew and be back in under three hours.

Assuming they didn't see her cat's ears and fur through her helmet and run off and hide. It *was* a Kingdom crew. She frowned, worried about the possibility, especially since Bonita would need to stay on the *Dragon.* She couldn't go to another ship when an enemy was coming.

"I'll rescue them, whether they agree to come along or not," Qin muttered.

Casmir checked the settings for his combat armor, wondering why it wasn't doing a good job of keeping the temperature at an optimal point for his body. The SmartWeave of a galaxy suit always did, and he'd assumed this would be superior. If combat armor could handle an icy ocean or the even icier dominion of space, why would it have trouble maintaining an accurate temperature in a climate-controlled submarine?

He tugged at the hard collar, tempted to remove more than his helmet. What would Rache and his mercenaries think if he wandered around naked? Not that he had wandering in mind. He felt more like lying down for a nap. Why couldn't Rache have locked them in a bedroom rather than an office?

"You doing all right, Casmir?" Asger had his hands clasped behind his back and was pacing, as he had been for the last hour.

"Fine. I'm just warm. And thirsty." Casmir looked around but didn't see any water. "Aren't kidnappers supposed to provide beverages for their hostages? If that's not covered in the Intersystem War Treaty, it definitely should be."

"I think it is mentioned in the humane conditions chapter."

"I knew it."

"According to my sensors," Zee said from the spot he'd taken up next to the locked hatch, "your body temperature is elevated."

"I have a fever?" Casmir plastered a hand to his forehead and groaned. "I'm sick? I don't mean to kvetch, but this isn't fair, Asger. I can't be sick now. There's too much to do."

Asger stopped pacing and stared at him. He glanced at the hatch—Kim still hadn't come back—and then stared at Casmir some more.

"Are you just now noticing how radiant and appealing I am?" Casmir scratched an itch on his cheek. His skin felt rough, as if he'd been hugging a cat or some other animal he was allergic to.

"Something like that," Asger murmured, though his eyes appeared more worried than amused.

He probably didn't want to get sick from whatever bug Casmir had caught. Unfortunately, they were stuck together in this cabin.

"Sorry," Casmir said. "I'll try not to breathe on you."

Asger started to say something, but the hatch opened. Rache leaned his head in and looked right at Zee, as if waiting to see if he would attack before committing himself to entering.

Zee gazed back indifferently. Casmir had told him only to pursue his usual bodyguard duties here, not to be aggressive with anyone. Even if Rache might deserve some aggression—Casmir didn't believe his *rescue* had been anything more than an excuse to snag him for his knowledge—Kim could give him that when he inevitably spoke to her. Probably in front of all of his men, because Casmir doubted Kim would allow Rache to talk to her alone in an airlock after this stunt. At least, that was his hope.

"Let's have a chat, Casmir," Rache said.

"What's the matter? Are you lonely with only the company of your stolid and unimaginative mercenaries?" Casmir's eye blinked. Would he ever stop feeling nervous around Rache?

"They have excellent imaginations. Just a minute ago, Corporal Chains was regaling the others with amusing stories of sexual conquests that were obviously made up."

"I bet."

Rache crooked a finger. "Come."

He walked out of the cabin without waiting to see if Casmir actually did. Asger rolled his eyes.

Casmir was tempted to stay where he was, but he was curious if there was any sign yet of the astroshaman base. He was also curious if Rache had a better plan than the Kingdom submarines did—insofar as Casmir had been informed. Ishii and the marines had all been tight-lipped when he'd asked how they planned to defeat the technologically superior astroshamans. Casmir hoped it involved more than rowing up in their tourist submarines and spitting torpedoes.

"Breathe on *him* when you're out there," Asger said as Casmir passed.

Casmir snapped his fingers and pointed at him. "An excellent plan. I shall endeavor to do so."

Asger clapped him on the back. Zee followed him into the corridor.

Rows of men in the seats looked curiously at them. Casmir wondered if any of them had compared voices and noticed that he and Rache had very similar ones. Admittedly, Rache's had that snooty nobleman's accent that the upper class favored. The byproduct of growing up in a castle, no doubt.

Rache was up front at an open hatch that led into the navigation center.

"Mind if I get a drink first?" Casmir pointed his thumb over his shoulder to where the supplies had been stored on the other sub. "I'd do advanced calculus for an orange fizzop right now."

Rache's masked face gazed back at him. Casmir had no idea if it was a glare or not. Maybe he shouldn't be flippant with all the mercenaries watching. Rache probably put up a tough front for them. Not that it was a front, exactly. The dramas didn't paint him as heinous and nefarious for no reason.

"You do advanced calculus for fun, Casmir," came Kim's voice from a little nook with an open door. The minuscule sickbay.

"Yeah, but I don't show my work. I'd show my work for an orange fizzop. Even a raspberry one, and I hate raspberry. I'm dehydrated."

"And caffeinated fizzy soda water is exactly what's recommended for that," she said with her typical dryness.

"Is it? As a medical professional, you would know. Excellent. I'm relieved."

Rache was still staring back at him. Maybe Casmir was failing in his attempt not to be flippant.

"There's water in the supply cabin," Rache said coolly. "Get what you need and come up here so I can question you." Yup, he was definitely going with the tough merc captain persona. He sounded menacing enough that Casmir worried Rache had some of the truth drug he was allergic to up there. Or maybe a nice set of pliers for removing fingernails.

Casmir found the supply cabin and tanks of water along with crates of Insta-Beefsta-Meals, the labels on the side promising they provided all the carbohydrates, fats, protein, and micronutrients that one needed in a day. If that was what the mercenaries ate, he didn't need to worry about assassinations from kitchen staff.

Hopeful for something better, Casmir opened the other nearby hatches. He found another supply cabin, storage for diving gear, and a cabin with a bunk and a desk inside. The captain's quarters? Or maybe *tour operator* was the proper name.

He opened a cabinet and found a mini fridge. A combination lock secured it. Did that mean there was something worth finding inside?

Casmir went back to the cabin where Asger waited, retrieved his tool satchel, and returned to the fridge. Zee plodded along after him without judgment. Casmir would definitely build Zee a mate one day, as soon as he had the time and resources. If his crusher wanted a friend of his own kind, Casmir would oblige.

Trying to work quickly, lest Rache have a reason to come back and hoist him over his cybernetically enhanced shoulder, Casmir removed the lock-cracking device he'd brought, anticipating he might need to do such things in the base. He frowned at the dampness of his satchel, but he'd had the foresight to put anything that could be damaged by moisture into airtight baggies.

Fortunately, his device thwarted the simple fridge lock with ease. The astroshaman doors would likely prove more difficult.

"Consider that a warmup, my friend," he said as he carefully returned the device to its bag.

"Were you speaking to your tool, Casmir Dabrowski?" Zee asked.

"Yes, I was."

"It is not sentient."

"One never knows when simple tools will gain intelligence and the power to take over the universe. I figure it's not a bad idea to treat them well. Especially if the tool delivered something good."

Had it? Casmir wrapped his fingers around the fridge handle, telling himself it was only his fever that made him hope with such longing for something good.

"Are you pausing for dramatic flair?" Zee asked.

"Absolutely." Casmir pulled open the door... and nearly fell over with delight.

Twelve bottles of chilled strawberry fizzop gleamed from the shelves. There was also a half-used carton of creamer that he would tell Kim about, in case she wanted to hunt around for a coffee pot. But he ignored that and gathered the bottles in his arms.

"Are you going to consume all of them?" Zee asked.

"As thirsty as I am, I think I could, but no. I'll share."

Casmir pushed himself to his feet with his bounty gathered in his arms, but he realized he would drop them if he tried to walk.

"Allow me to assist you," Zee said and formed his arms into something resembling a wine rack.

"You're an excellent crusher, Zee." Casmir slid most of the bottles into the slots he'd created.

"I know this."

"Your future mate will be pleased by how humble you are."

"I am certain it will not be difficult for you to create a mate that will be pleased with me."

Casmir walked up to the main passenger cabin, throwing a wink at Kim as he passed her. She was hunkered over a desk opposite Dr. Peshlakai, a bunch of vials lying out on it—and also what looked like a disassembled tranquilizer gun.

Though he was curious, Casmir knew Rache was waiting, so he kept going. He handed a bottle to the grim-faced mercenary who was keeping an eye on Asger's hatch and probably also making sure Casmir didn't sabotage the submarine. The man had a face that was a third fur, a third metal parts, and a third tattoos, and his mouth had been reshaped into something akin to a wolf's snout with leering fangs that no doubt dripped saliva when he got hungry. Casmir expected a snarl and a refusal of the drink, but the merc blinked in surprise and accepted it.

"Anyone else thirsty?" Casmir handed out bottles as he continued to the front.

Rache leaned out of the navigation cabin. "What are you *doing*, Dabrowski?"

"Attempting to buy the love of your mercenaries in case I ever run for office."

"Very few of them are Kingdom subjects."

"At the rate I'm going, I'll be running in whatever space station, habitat, or moon colony accepts refugees that Jager has exiled."

"Thank you," a man with pointy metal teeth said, accepting one of the cool bottles. He had a lisp, but the words sounded sincere.

"You're welcome," Casmir said.

"We haven't had leave for a while or the opportunity to purchase luxury items."

"You should definitely take that grievance up with management."

"Dabrowski," Rache said, "if you suborn my mercs, I'm going to kick your ass."

Casmir, saving the last two cherished fizzops, stepped into the small navigation compartment. Rache slammed the hatch shut behind him.

Ignoring his brusqueness, Casmir pointed at the view of black nothingness above the bank of instruments and gauges. It was an actual porthole rather than a display screen.

"I was expecting something grander and maybe some exotic sea life. The underwater aquarium in Zamek City has lots of colorful coral and seaweed and rocks with octopuses and fish and native orchastas swimming around in it. That's really disappointing. I hope you're not charging a lot for this tour."

"Will you sit down and be serious for five minutes?" Rache pointed to the empty seat.

Only then did Casmir realize that there wasn't a pilot. Was Rache qualified to steer this thing?

"That's a long time." Casmir offered him a fizzop. "Drink?"

"I don't consume sugar."

"That explains *so* much." Casmir sank into the seat, uncorked the top, and took a refreshing sip. Strawberry wasn't as good as orange, but it was still one of the better flavors, and he enjoyed its bubbly fruity freshness as it slid over his tongue.

"You look like shit considering how perky you are."

"I'm not perky. I think I have a fever. Asger told me to breathe on you."

"I see I won his adulation on Tiamat Station."

"You have to fight a few battles with him before he warms up to you." Casmir wiped his brow and studied the gauges. There wasn't anything to see through the porthole, but maybe the scanners were decent. "Any sign of the base yet?"

"No. We've been able to ping the router and power source that we located on our scouting mission, but the base isn't registering yet on our scanners or the limited sonar that came with the sub."

Casmir sat up. When had Rache had time for a scouting mission? That implied they'd gotten here first—but he couldn't have traveled from Tiamat Station much faster than the Kingdom ships. Or had Rache been here before? Had he figured out that this was where High Shaman Moonrazor had taken the gate before Casmir had? If so, Casmir found that disgruntling. Maybe a little annoying.

But he made himself issue a grunt of polite inquiry. If Rache was volunteering information, he should listen.

"They may have a way to camouflage it," Rache said. "Something akin to our slydar. I suppose they could even be using slydar. It's designed for space, but it could work down here. They may also be using the natural terrain, such as it is."

Rache pointed to a display where a sonar device was mapping the ice ceiling a hundred meters over their heads. It appeared to have interesting variations, almost like the ceiling of a cave.

Casmir tried to think what the underside of an iceberg looked like back on Odin, but his science knowledge failed him. There hadn't been icebergs in the aquarium.

"Let's talk about the gate," Rache said.

Casmir eyed him sidelong. "I see. Now that you've so heroically rescued me, I'm supposed to spill all my secrets."

"Do you *have* any secrets?"

"Not related to the gate. I know some of the unpublished cheat codes for *Death and Dungeons Six* since one of my students is on the development team." Casmir smiled, but he couldn't help but feel a twinge of longing for his old life, his colleagues and friends back home.

His students, some of whom would have graduated by now. Did they already have jobs? Were they searching and missing him because he wasn't there to provide well-deserved references?

Rache gave him a flat unfriendly look—somehow, Casmir knew it even with the mask hiding his face.

He sighed and said, "I've been looking at some of the studies various research teams have done on the ones that are networked and operational, but as I'm sure you know, there are ships guarding them all to make sure the Gate Accord is enforced. Nobody's allowed to remove any panels or poke around, lest we, in our ignorance, break something and cut one of the systems off from the other eleven. Or even bring down the whole gate network and isolate everyone."

"Yes, I know that."

"Since the gate was completely disassembled in that cargo ship and presumably in the original wreck on Skadi Moon, I'm guessing that each individual piece has this defensive mechanism built in, but if they're linked or there's one master controller…" Casmir rubbed his eyes. They were dry and gritty. "I'm basically hoping for enlightenment when I get there."

Rache issued something between a grunt and a snort. Either way, it didn't sound impressed.

"*If* we get there. Do you have a plan to ensure we will? Do you know about Kyla Moonrazor? I'm a little concerned about running into her. She sounded smarter than me."

"I've heard of her. She's one of the astroshaman cult leaders. And she shows her work when she does advanced calculus."

"I *knew* she was a genius."

Casmir waited, hoping for more information. They had lost the network signal at some point, so he couldn't send Rache's plans back to Ishii's submarine commanders, but maybe that would change later.

He *would* like to share some intelligence. He worried it would end up looking bad if one of the marines thought that he and Kim had seemed eager to join Rache's team. Royal Intelligence already seemed to believe Casmir wasn't as antagonistic toward Rache as he should be. He well remembered his chat with Lieutenant Meister in the gym on the *Osprey.* And then there was Ambassador Romano. What did he know? Why would he be willing to throw away Casmir's life for some locator-beacon frequency?

"Do you know anything about Ambassador Romano?" Casmir realized he had a resource here, if Rache would be willing to talk.

"What do you want to know?"

Casmir wasn't sure if that was a yes but... "For starters, why he wants me dead."

Rache tapped a couple of displays, cycling through readings of the surrounding terrain, the ice above and who knew how many miles of ocean that existed above the crust of the moon. "If I had to guess, it's less that he actively wants you dead and more that you annoyed him, so he'd be willing to give you up to gain something important."

"Such as you?"

"If he destroyed me and my ship and could brag about it to Jager, it might gain him something."

"Is he hungry to gain... things?" Casmir didn't know what ambassadors craved. More than cold orange fizzop, he supposed.

"Yes. He's a bastard of Baron Abbatelli but older than his legitimate sons. I haven't kept up on court gossip, mind you, but his mother was the publicly acknowledged mistress of the baron for more than twenty years. Romano has always been vocal about his right to part of the family estate and to be named one of the baron's heirs. If he'd gone into military service and become an officer of renown, the Senate probably would have ruled in his favor, but he doesn't have a heart for stabbing people in the front—only the back. So, diplomacy. He hopes to distinguish himself and be granted a title."

"So it's more that he wants *you* dead than me? I wish that were more heartening than it is."

"I doubt he knows who you are. Romano may believe he's Jager's trusted lackey, and he may have some authority over Ishii's mission, but I'm sure he doesn't get regular updates from Royal Intelligence."

Who you are. Casmir still thought it strange that his genes, copied from some centuries-dead man, could cause him to be a target. Or for people to believe he could do miraculous things.

"Should I tell him I'm Mikita's clone?" Casmir wondered aloud. "Assuming we survive this and I see him again."

"If we survive this and you see him again, you should punch him."

"Do you think I could take him? He has a few inches on me, but I'm younger and spryer."

"Could you punch someone without having a seizure?"

"Probably. Unless I thought about the possible ramifications of it for hours beforehand and worked myself up into a panicked state."

Rache looked at him. "I'm concerned that you're our best bet for outfoxing Moonrazor and deactivating the gate's defenses. She's brilliant."

"I knew you knew more about her than you were letting on."

"I'm hoping she already deactivated the gate so that her people wouldn't die from exposure, but it's possible everybody in that base is a robot."

"Dear God, I hope so." Casmir planted a hand on his chest.

"You're a weird kid, Casmir."

"I think I'm older than you. If Kim's ideas are true." He remembered Kim's reasoning that he'd been born first, and that Jager, disappointed with all of Casmir's genetic issues, arranged for Rache to be cooked up.

"That doesn't negate my statement." Rache glanced over his shoulder, though the hatch was still closed.

Uh oh, maybe Casmir shouldn't have mentioned Kim. Maybe Rache was thinking about her. Casmir didn't want to encourage that. Nor did he want to encourage some conversation where Rache asked him advice on how to get Kim to say yes to a date.

"Is she angry with me over this?" Rache waved at Casmir, then vaguely back toward the rest of the submarine.

Damn. Too late.

"You kidnapping us? Yes."

"I rescued you."

"Maybe me," Casmir said, though he wasn't convinced he'd been in danger, "but was any threat made to Kim?"

"Not that I saw, but it seemed like it would be better to keep you two together."

Casmir thought that sounded like an excuse. Rache could have easily asked the marines to punt Casmir out the airlock without mentioning her at all.

"You may have noticed that she's an independent person. Independent people don't like having their options taken away from them and being forced into a certain course of action. She's already irked with Royal Intelligence for deciding she should come on this mission instead of returning to her work back home. Even though she's getting paid a reasonable salary and gets more perks than I do aboard the ship."

"I can understand valuing freedom and not wanting to have your future chosen for you," Rache said quietly.

Right, he'd presumably known all along that Jager was having him raised and groomed for a certain fate. At the least, he would have known he was expected to become a knight.

"I don't want to take away her choices. This was just..." Rache flexed a hand.

"Extenuating circumstances?"

"Exactly."

"Are you sure?" Casmir also thought Rache might have used that message as an excuse to get him on his side. Though to what end, he didn't know. Something more than the gate?

"Mm."

"That was vague."

"Yeah. Do you think she'll forgive me?" Rache looked at him.

Casmir wanted to hide under the console. Or run fleeing from navigation. How had he ended up as an advice giver or intermediary between these two? He didn't even *want* them to be a two.

"Kim is complicated," Casmir said, hoping Rache would drop it.

"And you're simple?"

"Oh, I'm the definition of simple. If I like a girl, she's going to know it when I babble incessantly to her about how neat my robots are until she runs away fleeing."

"I think that's the definition of simpleton, not simple."

"Is it? Words are deceptively complicated." Looking for a way to change the subject, Casmir asked, "What are you going to do if you get the gate before the Kingdom does?"

He doubted Rache would answer, but he would like to know. That would help him figure out how hard he should work to keep Rache from his goal. And how heavily he should be breathing on him to get him sick.

Casmir grimaced and wiped his hot brow. He definitely had a fever, damn it. Had he picked up something on the station? Probably. It wasn't as if *he* had an enhanced immune system. Unfortunately.

"Isn't it enough to want to keep Jager from getting it?" Rache asked.

"No."

"Ah."

A few silent seconds passed before Casmir realized he wasn't going to get a real answer.

"Look," he said in a reasonable tone, "you've got some subs, the Kingdom has some subs, but *all* of them have cartoon ducks and whales on the sides. As it stands, the astroshamans are going to laugh when we show up."

"We added torpedo launchers under the ducks," Rache said.

"Yes, so did we, but you've heard rumors of what the astroshamans have. That cargo ship had enhancements we'd never heard of. And Tork had enhancements too."

"What did?"

"Not what—who. Tork-57. The android that was following me around on Tiamat Station. Never mind." Casmir waved to dismiss the tangent. "My point is that both sides are in over their heads."

"Technically true, since we all have hundreds of meters of ice and water above us."

"You know what I mean. We're outmatched. But if we work together, we'll have a better chance of getting past their defenses. And we might surprise them. Who would think that the heinous and nefarious Tenebris Rache would ever work with his most loathed enemy, the Kingdom?"

"Heinous and nefarious?"

"Zee's words, not mine. He's been watching dramas produced in the Kingdom. Apparently, you're the villain in at least three of them."

"The things I miss out on by not visiting my home system more often," Rache murmured.

He sounded more muted than sarcastic. He couldn't possibly be surprised that he was perceived that way, could he?

Casmir shook his head. That wasn't important now.

"What do you think?" he prompted.

"I will not work with the Kingdom to help Jager get the gate. You know that. I've told you that every time you've asked about it."

"What if Jager didn't get the gate?" Casmir asked.

Rache snorted.

Casmir spread a hand, utterly serious. He hadn't told anybody but Kim about his stunt with Zee and Tork, but it wasn't as if he had to worry about Rache comming Jager or even Ishii or Romano to rat him out. He had a feeling the secret would come out eventually one way or another, regardless. If anything came of his suggestion to Nguyen. It was possible nothing would.

Rache glanced at his face and then turned back for a longer look. "You're not— No, I can't believe someone with strawberry-colored lips is masterminding an insurrection."

"Not an insurrection. Dear God, my parents live scant miles from the castle. No insurrections on Kingdom territory, please. But... sometimes, it's better for humanity if one man's goals and ambitions don't come to pass."

"What are you proposing, hypothetical quasher of royal ambitions?"

"That all of humanity have access to the gate. Or anyone who wants to study it."

"All of humanity isn't here to fight for access to it."

Yet, Casmir thought.

"Does that matter? The best engineers and archaeologists from all of the systems should be able to access it and help better our collective understanding of it. And then, we should all have a say about where future gates are placed, assuming we can use this one to build new ones, so humanity can explore the stars together."

"I should have known better than to kidnap an idealist."

"Well, Kim balances me out. Maybe she'll rant at you about logic and human inadequacies later."

"I'll look forward to it." Rache leaned forward to look more closely at one of the scanners. There was a blip on it that hadn't been there before. "Even if all of humanity, as you call it, showed up, there's only one gate. It has to be stored somewhere."

"The last time I saw the gate, it was in five hundred pieces. Enough for every government in the Twelve Systems to have one."

"You're a loon. And so is whoever is in charge of this submarine." Rache planted his finger on the blip.

"Not one of your people?"

"No, my people aren't loons. It's the Kingdom submarine we rescued you from."

"The good old *Waddler*. Maybe the commander got through to Captain Ishii, and he ordered them to rescue us back."

"Whoever named these boats was also a loon."

"You're a judgmental mercenary," Casmir observed.

"They're speeding up and coming straight toward us." Rache opened the hatch and called back to his men. "Hocking, get up here. You're back to piloting so I can man the torpedoes."

"What am I doing?" Casmir wondered if he should try to comm whoever that was to try to stop a fight before it started. The whole reason he'd volunteered to swim over here was to avoid a bloodbath.

"Go take a nap. You look like crap stuck in a space toilet that won't flush."

"Flattering. Do you want me to talk to the commander?"

"No."

"Right." Casmir vacated his seat as Rache's pilot squeezed in, thumping him on the shoulder on the way past. He was one of the men Casmir had given a fizzop.

"Trouble, boss?"

"Yes."

The hatch clanged shut, almost hitting Casmir in the butt. He headed back to check on Kim, wobbling as the submarine took its first evasive maneuvers. The first twinge of nausea assailed his stomach.

He paused when he reached sickbay, wondering if he should drop himself off as a potential patient. Kim and Yas were still working on their project.

"What's going on?" Kim asked.

"The *Waddler* is chasing us. At least, there was only one blip. I suppose more could be coming." Casmir shrugged.

"Why can't these idiots focus on the astroshamans? That Moonrazor will fall over laughing if we blow each other up before we get anywhere near her base."

"That's what I told Rache. By the way, he would love for you to share your opinions on the illogical nature of humans later."

"Gladly."

A *thwump* sounded. A torpedo firing. Casmir went to find a seat to buckle himself into. He feared his day was about to get worse.

CHAPTER 8

QIN PUSHED HERSELF DOWN THE LADDER WELL, SEALING her magnetic boots to the deck when she reached the bottom. They had reached the *Machu Picchu* and were linking up to its airlock hatch. Neither vessel had any semblance of gravity now that they were stopped, so Qin could only walk as fast as she could lock one boot and then the next to the deck, but she moved as quickly as possible across the cargo hold toward the airlock hatch.

Since they didn't have much time before Captain Amazing showed up, she wouldn't waste it. But she slowed her pace when she saw Bonita waiting there… with Johnny.

He wasn't armed, armored, or even wearing a galaxy suit, save for a pair of magnetic boots, but the way he leaned against the hull by the airlock made it look like he was going. Or like he *thought* he was going. Qin would take one of Viggo's vacuums before the lying pirate accountant.

"Your fearsome cat woman is scowling at me, Laser," Johnny drawled, his arms folded over his chest.

"She probably doesn't recognize you without the bag on your head."

"Shall I don it again? Perhaps it'll confuse the wounded scientists, and they'll be less likely to shoot."

"Your Kingdom accent and unfurry face is supposed to convince them not to shoot."

Johnny raised his eyebrows as he stroked the several days' worth of beard that had grown while he'd been in the cell. Bonita had brought him food and water, but nothing as dangerous as a razor or even beard-removal gel, which, according to space legends, had been used on occasion to eat through jail bars.

"Your accent then," Bonita amended.

"Captain, he's not going with me," Qin protested, still scowling at Johnny. When he turned his raised eyebrows toward her, she told him straight out, "You're not coming with me."

"I believe your lovely lady captain is in charge, Ms. Qin. She said I could go if I didn't make trouble and was able to charm any women over there."

"I said convince them not to shoot Qin, not charm them," Bonita said.

"Qin is fearsome. A great deal of charming will be required."

"They're probably injured and will be happy if anyone carries them off that ship," Qin said. "Captain, we can't trust this man. You should put him back in his box."

Johnny lifted a finger. "Might I remind you that I hired you for passage *after* releasing you from a troublesome predicament on Death Knell Station? Paying passengers aren't usually kept in cells—or boxes. I believe I've been quite amiable and polite by not complaining about my meager accommodations."

"Meager?" Bonita asked. "You've been getting the same food we eat."

"Which has actually been quite excellent." He bowed deeply to her, sweeping his hand from the spot where a pertundo would hang if he truly were the knight he claimed to be. "I thank you for that. I was referring specifically to the cell with its lack of a bed, blankets, or even a porthole, not to mention its insulation that keeps me from accessing the network with my chip." He waved toward his temple.

"That's not insulation," Bonita said. "The fusion reactor is right behind that cell, and its radiation interferes with signals."

"While unraveling the DNA in my sperm, I imagine."

"Surely, you're not worried about siring children at your advanced age."

"My age is still healthy and virile, thank you. Or it was until I was nestled up to your reactor for a week."

Qin cleared her throat. These two were a disaster waiting to happen. If this was representative of the kinds of men Bonita liked and married, it was no wonder her previous relationships had all crashed and burned.

"Yes, yes, we're all hooked up." Bonita waved at the airlock hatch. "You can go over any time. Qin, I know you don't trust Toes. Neither do I. But he's agreed to go without a suit or a weapon."

"I didn't agree to the latter," he said. "You were simply unwilling to give me the ones in my bag."

"Your bag is full of grenades and DEW-Tek pistols. Why ever would I refuse to give them to you?"

"There could be threats over there," Johnny said. "*Someone* beat the electrical sockets out of that ship, right? What if they boarded afterward and didn't leave? What if you're reading them and not the original crew?"

"Qin will protect you."

This time, Qin raised *her* eyebrows.

"I'm not positive I believe that," Johnny said. "She's oozing menace toward me. I can feel it from here."

"Nah, that's the aftereffects of the reactor making your pores tingle. Qin is honorable and doesn't have a menacing bone in her body."

Qin lifted her chin, pleased by the praise, even if it came while these two were slinging sarcasm at each other. She believed that Bonita thought it was true.

"If it'll make you be quiet, I'll give you a weapon. Wait here." Bonita raised a finger, then strode across the hold, not toward the armory but toward the ladder and her quarters on the deck above.

Even though Qin was worried about Johnny, she couldn't help but smile. It was good to see her captain navigating the ladders without pain instead of grimacing at every bending of her knee.

Bonita returned with a case that had a stunner etched on the top. "This was a gift from a collector, but I'm going to let you use it because I think you'll look good with it."

Qin had never seen the case before and didn't know what to expect.

"I look good with *all* weapons." Johnny smiled.

Bonita flipped open the case. Johnny's smile faltered. It was a stunner, but it was pink with pale blue highlights and a gold trigger.

"It's a Lady Shufflebottom," Bonita said. "They're quite expensive and valued by many princesses in the Miners' Union, I'm told."

"Snufflebottom?" Johnny asked skeptically.

"Shufflebottom."

"What's the difference?"

"If you want a weapon…"

"Fine." Johnny withdrew the pink stunner from the case.

It was smaller than typical, which was especially noticeable in his grip. Qin doubted she could have held it in her large hand and pulled the trigger.

"I'm ready," he said.

Bonita nodded at Qin. "You're in charge. Get in, find the injured people, tell them we're heading to Tiamat Station, and offer them a ride and medical supplies. Keep your helmet on so your... catness isn't so obvious."

Qin twitched a pointed ear.

"Yes, that catness right there. Also, it might not hurt to let them know that smugglers are coming and would prefer there weren't witnesses to their salvage activities."

"Yes, Captain." Qin frowned at Johnny, but Bonita was her captain and in charge. If she thought he should go, Qin would accept it as a challenge.

Maybe he would try to betray her, and she would be within her rights to beat him up and leave him locked in a freezer. Did research vessels have freezers? She hoped so.

She stepped into the airlock, hoping Johnny would be too busy sneering at the pink stunner to join her, but he pulled himself in beside her. The inner hatch closed, and seconds oozed past as the chamber matched itself to what waited on the other side.

Her sensitive nose wrinkled. It wasn't his fault, since he'd been locked in his cell, but she could tell Johnny hadn't washed for some time. He smelled of body odor and his most recent meal. Oddly, it reminded her of the scents of Odin and the park she'd visited there. If he had been gone for a year, he shouldn't carry any lingering odors from the planet, but maybe he had some cologne that he'd used days earlier that captured the scent of the trees there.

When the hatch opened, she caught herself thinking wistfully of that park and the trees she'd romped through. Forcing herself to focus on the present, Qin put her helmet up. Viggo had said the other ship's environmental systems were working and that there was air, but there might be other threats waiting.

She crossed into the other ship's airlock and found the interior hatch leading into the *Machu Picchu* locked. She wasn't surprised, since they had been attacked. She'd brought a blowtorch along.

But before she could fire it up, Johnny leaned forward, flipped open a panel under the lock screen, and pressed his palm to it for a scan.

Qin snorted, certain an Odin university research ship wouldn't recognize him, whether he had a Kingdom accent or not, but it beeped an affirmative, and the hatch unsealed. Johnny bowed to her and stuck out a hand, but she wasn't sure if he was inviting her to go first or offering to go first himself.

"You've been on this ship before?" Qin brushed past him and stepped into a cargo hold full of crates and long rectangular freight boxes.

The cargo was all strapped down, and nothing appeared damaged by the attack or the slip into zero-g, at least nothing here. The lighting was poor, with only auxiliary strips along the deck leading to the main exit from the hold.

"No." Johnny stepped out after her.

"Then why does your hand open the door?"

"It's magical, just like the rest of me."

She frowned back at him, but she had no intention of engaging in silly banter. There were people here to save.

"From Viggo's scans, most of the people were in sickbay, but some were also in engineering. The bridge didn't appear to have power—or life." Qin headed for the main exit on the far side, the readings on her helmet display verifying that the ship still had air and heat. Just not gravity.

"Enemies may have targeted the bridge and engineering specifically," Johnny said.

"Yeah." Qin looked around as they walked, expecting to find bodies. The six life forms Viggo's scanners had detected seemed far too few for a ship this size.

"Do you want to split up?" Johnny asked. "You can go to sickbay and carry out any injured people there, and I can go to—"

"No."

"Why not? It's a big ship and it doesn't sound like we have much time."

"Because I don't trust you." Qin walked into the corridor and headed for lifts at the end. Since she'd been to sickbay before and knew where it was, she would take them there first.

Johnny surprised her by not responding with a quip or protest. Through her rear helmet cam, she could see him watching their surroundings attentively, the pink stunner in his hand.

Normally, she wouldn't have trusted him at her back with a weapon, but a stunner wouldn't do anything to her combat armor. At the lift, the control panel didn't respond. A light glowed red, but nothing else happened when she waved and tapped at it.

"I don't suppose your magical hand has a way to override that?" Qin pointed at the doors. "We need to go three levels up."

Johnny prodded the panel and nothing happened. "It's not locked; it's broken."

"I'm not sure where the ladder wells are. I was only here once briefly."

Johnny tilted his head, his eyes glazing as he accessed his chip.

A thrum echoed through the ship, followed by a *bom bom bom* that was as much sound as reverberation. A few more lights came on in the corridor, and she felt a weird lurch in her gut. It took her a moment to realize that gravity had returned. Whoever was working in engineering must have restored power to the spin drive. Maybe full lights and power to the lift would return soon.

"Sorry." Johnny shook his head. "This system doesn't have Kingdom ships in its public databases. I could have found the schematics if we were in System Lion."

Qin waved at the panel again, in case power had returned to it, but nothing happened. She shrugged and planted her hands on either side of the gap and pushed.

The doors groaned and slid open to reveal a dark empty shaft.

"Your hands may be more magical than mine," Johnny said.

She leaned into the shaft and looked up and down, her night vision kicking in.

"The car is down there." She pointed. "We'll climb."

"Gravity just came back on. You may have noticed."

"So? It's only half gravity."

"Is there a ladder in there?"

"There's a vertical rail." Qin slithered into the shaft and gripped one of two rails running up opposite sides. They were narrow and only raised an inch from the surface, but her fingers had the strength to pull up her bodyweight, especially in partial gravity.

"Ah, yes." Johnny leaned in after she made room. "The ladder for those with so much upper body and finger strength that they sneer disdainfully at rungs."

"I assume that's you. Since you're magical."

"I suppose my ego is going to demand that I *ensure* it's me." A grunt sounded from below as he maneuvered himself into the shaft. His voice far more strained, he added, "I thought I'd gotten to the age where my ego wouldn't get me in trouble as often."

Qin passed two sets of closed doors and paused at the next set, hoping she remembered correctly and didn't end up climbing them into a closet. She also hoped the power didn't come on without warning, sending the car upward to squash them.

Johnny grunted and cursed his way up the shaft, but he did come climbing after her. She could have offered to carry him—if he came from the Kingdom, she doubted he had any genetic amplifications to his muscles—but she doubted he and his ego would permit it.

As it was, she struggled to brace herself horizontally, legs splayed between walls, so she could find the leverage to force the doors open. It was much harder from that position, and blood rushed to her face. She slipped once, her efforts too much for the magnetic soles to stay planted, and a noise of wary uncertainty came from Johnny.

"I won't fall on you," she promised, trying the doors again.

"Good. Thank you. I can't help but wonder if someone noticed us about to climb the elevator shaft and started up gravity just to hinder us."

"I'm hoping the only people here want to be rescued by us, not hinder us." She finally succeeded in shoving the doors open, then pulled herself through, almost stepping on a woman crumpled on the deck.

Qin swallowed, checking for enemies before crouching to check for a pulse. She didn't find one. The woman had died in her galaxy suit, but her helmet hadn't been on, and her face was burned beyond recognition. Scorch marks covered the walls, and if Qin hadn't been wearing her own helmet, she would have smelled the acrid remains of a fire. Some of the ceiling material had warped and melted into uneven waves.

Johnny scrambled out of the shaft behind her, and with thoughts of enemies fresh in her mind, Qin started to jerk her weapon toward him before catching herself.

He lifted his hands, eyeing her warily. "I'm on your side, remember?"

"Are you?" Qin shifted the weapon away from him and stepped past the body.

"I'm exactly what I told you I am."

"The second time or the first?"

"Would a pirate accountant have a palm print that opens Kingdom locks?"

"That might not be your own palm. Maybe you stole the prints of the guy whose name you took." Qin grimaced as they passed another burned body, this one charred all over.

"The spy's lament. Even when you tell the truth, you're mistrusted."

They turned down a corridor that was even more damaged than the first but thankfully devoid of bodies. Qin worried about what they would find in sickbay. More people dead than alive?

"How do you know Sir William Asger?" Johnny asked quietly.

Qin almost tripped. "What?"

"Laser showed me his calendar and implied he'd been a passenger." His tone turned dry. "I suppose it's possible she was lying and that she'd picked it up at a gift shop."

"It's none of your business, and this isn't the time to discuss it."

"As you wish."

Again, she was surprised when he didn't give a snarky response. She was also surprised he remembered Asger's name, even if Bonita had mentioned it at some point. Had she?

As they approached the double doors to sickbay, she sent a message to Bonita. *Captain, did you ever tell Johnny Asger's name? Because he just asked about him.*

I showed him your calendar, came Bonita's prompt response—she was probably monitoring their progress from navigation on the *Dragon.*

Apparently, it made an impression on him.

I don't think I ever shared Asger's name. He must have looked it up.

Based on what? An image search? If you just showed him the calendar over the comm, it would have taken a lot of work to snag an image file out of that, and would Asger's face even come up on a search outside of System Lion?

Is he giving you reasons to be suspicious of him? Bonita asked.

Well, he's not being sarcastic with me.

That is suspicious.

Qin couldn't tell if she was joking or not.

They reached the doors, but they didn't open. The fire hadn't damaged them or the surrounding wall, and Johnny stepped up next to her to try his palm on the panel.

"Wait." She caught his wrist. "In case it works, stand over there." She waved to the side of the door so he wouldn't be an easy target.

"Right. I'm not armored, am I?" He almost sounded surprised. Maybe accountants got into more fights than one would think. Pirate accountants.

He stepped to the side and palmed the lock. The doors slid open.

Qin caught movement and sprang to the other side as crimson DEW-Tek bolts streaked out of the dim interior. She'd glimpsed two people crouched behind exam tables.

"I'm Qin from the *Stellar Dragon*," she called as more bolts streaked out. "A civilian freighter." No need to mention Bonita's bounty-hunting tendencies. "We heard your distress call and came to help."

A few more bolts sizzled out, slamming into the charred walls farther down the corridor. Qin braced herself to run in and disarm the people—she'd seen enough to know they wore galaxy suits, not combat armor—but she would prefer not to risk hurting anyone.

"Hold on," someone whispered, Qin's keen ears catching it. "Lieutenant Schneider *did* send out a distress call."

"It could be those asshole pirates back to finish us off."

"We're from the Kingdom," Johnny called, emphasizing that arrogant-sounding nobleman's accent. "At least *I* am."

"And who are you?" a woman called.

"Sir Bjarke Asger."

Qin gaped at him. *Asger?*

When he'd given them his first name back at the station, she had assumed it was his surname. She squinted at his jawline, currently in profile, and tried to decide if he looked like Asger, *her* Asger.

The tattoos were distracting, and Johnny—it was hard to think of him by another name—was paler, like he hadn't been on a planet and exposed to sunlight in a long time. His hair was paler, too, but it was shot with gray, so maybe that was natural. They *did* have similar strong jaws, broad shoulders, and well-defined facial features.

"Show me your pertundo," the woman demanded.

"I don't have it. I've been undercover of late."

The woman snorted. "Sure you have."

"I'd be happy to show you other things of mine that are more permanently attached, but it's possible they'd attest only to my health and fitness and not my nobility."

Ugh, maybe he *was* related to the Asger she knew. William. Qin would have guessed that an older version of Asger would be more mature, but maybe not.

Someone else murmured, another woman.

"Ladies," Johnny—Bjarke—whoever—said. "If you send out distress calls and greet your rescuers like this, people won't come to rescue you more than once." He spoke in a friendly and soothing tone, if an arrogant one.

Qin held her tongue to see if his accent would be more likely to make the women relax than hers. There was also the matter of her fur and fangs that tended to distress people, especially Kingdom people.

"Throw down your weapons and come in," the first speaker said. "Then we can talk."

"Very well, but I do urge you to chat quickly. A salvage ship is on the way, and they've already warned us that they'll fire on our ship if we don't get away from here.

"Salvage!" the second speaker cried. "First someone kills the captain and first officer and deliberately wrecks almost all of our equipment, and now someone else is here to salvage the ship? We were supposed to be protected. This is an outrage! Captain Konig was supposed to bring his ship to escort us, not tell us to meet him at that moon. An outrage, I tell you. I hope the entire bill for repairs and replacement goes to him."

"Are you going in?" Qin asked Johnny. Since she was armored, she should go first, but if his face kept them from firing…

"I don't know. I think they could slay me with their eyes right now." He did toss his pink stunner through the doorway.

As it clattered across the deck, the women's conversation paused.

"Is that a gun or a toy?" one whispered.

"I'm told it's a Lady Shufflebottom," Johnny said.

"That's what you traded your pertundo for? What did you go undercover as? A male prostitute?"

"It's a long story." Johnny didn't sound that offended at the implication. Maybe he *had* gone undercover as a prostitute before.

Fearing they were wasting time, Qin pushed her big Brockinger anti-tank gun across the sickbay deck, then walked in after it with her hands up, facing the women still crouched behind the exam table. They both had pistols pointed toward her chest.

"I'm Qin. Do you have injured? What are your names?" Qin glanced toward protected rooms in the back—her ears caught someone moving back there. "Our ship, the *Stellar Dragon*, is attached to your port airlock."

They looked from the big gun to her and back to the gun. Maybe *she* should have thrown out a pink stunner.

"We have injured, yes. I'm Scholar Ito, and this is Dr. Kagawa. But Scholars Beaumont and Kelsey-Sato are in charge. They're in engineering with Wagner and Mazur. We'll have to ask them about leaving. Especially if there's a salvage ship on the way—damn it, we are *not* salvage."

"Scholar Kelsey-Sato, the archaeologist?" Qin asked. "I know her daughter, and I met her briefly on this ship back at Skadi Moon."

"You do?" The woman squinted at her. "What color is her hair?"

"Her hair? Uh, brown and monkey-colored."

Ito snorted. "Yeah."

Qin realized it had been a test.

"Give me a moment." Ito turned away and pulled out a comm unit and whispered into it. The words weren't meant for Qin's ears, but she heard them anyway, "Scholars, can you two come up here? We have visitors. They want to help us. One says she knows Kim."

"We're more rescuers than visitors," Johnny said, also catching the whispers. "Do you have injured people we can move to our ship? Your sickbay appears damaged." His gaze flicked toward scorched walls and equipment that had been destroyed not by fire but by weapons blasts. Strewn pieces were scattered across the deck.

"It's extremely damaged, due to pirates blowing everything to bits," the doctor snarled.

"Why did they do that?" This wasn't Qin's fight, but she couldn't help but wonder why the ship had been targeted. Because it was a Kingdom vessel outside of their system?

"They didn't say, but we're here for important research. We got permission from two of the governments in Hydra to come study the Heimdall Twist Quasar, which is most visible from this system."

"A quasar?" Qin had assumed they were here for the same reason as the Kingdom ships, to find that gate and study it. But maybe that was still top-secret, and this was their cover story.

"Indeed. It's been quite active of late."

"What was the name of the ship that attacked you?" Johnny asked.

"The *Roundabout*," Ito said. "It looked like a mining ship. We realized too late that it was retrofitted with all manner of weapons. Weapons that tore into us and caused significant damage. Scholar Kelsey-Sato thinks they wanted to attack the Kingdom warships but didn't dare go into battle against their equals—or betters—so they took their aggressions out on us. But if that's true, why did they send a team over to blow up all of our research equipment and kill so many of the crew?"

"The *Roundabout* is a pirate ship with loose ties to Prince Dubashi in the Miners' Union." Johnny gripped his chin. "The last I heard, Dubashi opposes King Jager's desires to expand and is willing to act against him, but not openly. He's hired people that can't easily be tied to him. Some say he's even hired the mercenary Rache." Johnny glanced at Qin.

That made her uneasy. How much did Johnny know about Bonita and Qin's adventures of late? He couldn't know that they'd all worked together with Rache against those terrorists on Odin, could he?

Johnny headed back to look in the rooms where Qin had heard people. "We need to clear everyone out of here, unless you're close to getting your engines back online and can escape the smugglers."

As he spoke, Qin heard faint footsteps in the corridor and turned.

"We're not," a new voice said, a man rounding a corner with Kim's monkey-android mother standing thigh-high at his side.

The speaker wore spectacles and a rumpled green-plaid suit with white shirttails hanging out. His eyes had a mechanical cast to them, and Qin's first thought was that they were cybernetic replacements, but her helmet display informed her that neither Scholar Sato nor the man had heat signatures. He had to also be an android.

"We're not leaving and letting those *people*—" his lip curled in a human sneer, "—come salvage a ship worth tens of millions of crowns for parts."

"Professor Beaumont," Ito said. "We have injured and—"

"Yes, I know." He—Beaumont—adjusted his glasses. "If the captain of the freighter is willing to take them to the nearest station for medical assistance and protection, we should transfer them. But everyone else who's able to remain and can handle a weapon should stay to defend the ship." His gaze fell to the Brockinger and the stunner, lingering on the latter. "That will not be sufficient against criminals."

"Tell me about it," Johnny said dryly.

"I've sent a communication to Captain Konig of the *Eagle*," Beaumont said, "and his ship is already on the way. It *should* have been at the gate when we entered the system, waiting to escort us, but I understand the Kingdom is playing hide-and-seek with a mercenary ship around Xolas Moon. Konig estimates he'll be here within sixteen hours."

"The salvage crew will be here within two," Johnny said.

"So we only need to hold the ship for fourteen hours. Excellent. This can be done."

"We didn't hold it last time," Ito snapped.

Scholar Kelsey-Sato's tail twitched during the conversation, but she didn't disagree with her chatty colleague. She looked curiously toward Qin, but Qin couldn't tell if there was recognition on that furry monkey face.

"Last time," Beaumont said, "the pirates caught us off-guard and boarded with a party of more than fifty armored men."

"Last time, *we* had armored men and women. Who are now dead. Nobody left alive and uninjured is a combatant."

"We had only a dozen people trained in firearms to defend the ship," Beaumont said. "If the university—and King Jager—had known we were going into a system of such unrest, we should have been given far more. I will be having words with the board when we get back."

"Which you'll only survive to do if we leave the ship and get passage to a station where we can arrange transport home. Don't think your android circuits make you immune to pirates with rifles."

"They do make me sturdy."

"Which is why you hid with the rest of us civilians when the boarding party came."

"I hid because of the top-secret knowledge stored up here." Beaumont pointed to the side of his head. "It will be imperative when the military recovers—"

Ito hissed loudly to interrupt him and waved at Qin and Johnny. "Your maps of the Heimdall Twist Quasar aren't as important as you think."

Qin thought about pointing out that she knew about the gate, but she didn't know if Johnny did. Did any of this even matter right now?

She looked back and forth between the arguing people, aware of seconds ticking past. Two hours was not much time, and they had even less than that if they wanted to get away before Captain Amazing took pot shots at the *Dragon*. Qin would be willing to attempt to hold the *Machu Picchu* from within against a boarding party, if she heard a good reason, and if Bonita agreed, but she was skeptical about either happening. With the ship already so damaged, did it matter if a salvage crew came on? As it was, they would likely be disappointed with the offerings.

"Who are you?" Johnny asked the android. "Just a professor?"

Qin guessed he was another loaded droid, like Scholar Kelsey-Sato. He also had a Kingdom accent. Everyone here did.

"Professor Beaumont is in charge of the civilian team and the science mission," Ito told Johnny. "We lost the captain, first mate, and most of the crew, so he's more or less in charge of the entire ship now."

"Who are *you*?" Beaumont looked Johnny up and down disdainfully.

"Sir Bjarke Asger." Johnny bowed. "Undercover and using feminine weapons this week."

"Vilmar's son?"

Johnny blinked. "Yes. You knew my father?"

"Knew? Has he passed on?"

"A few years ago."

"He was so young."

"He was ninety when he died."

"So young. He was a student of mine. He should have uploaded his mind. He was an excellent scientist, for a noble."

"I remember him as being eccentric and dragging us on trips to all the ruin sites on Odin."

Qin cleared her throat. Another time, she would find it interesting to learn more about Asger's family, perhaps *after* they'd all gotten away from the impending danger.

"My captain says she's leaving before the smugglers come, and anyone who wants a ride needs to get aboard now." Even though Bonita hadn't said that, Qin was certain she would agree if asked. "We've only got a single railgun on our freighter."

"Take the injured and anyone who won't fight," Beaumont said. "I will defend the ship until our backup arrives." He looked down at Scholar Kelsey-Sato. "You, my lady—" he bowed, his voice turning less stiff and more friendly, "—should leave on the freighter, since Jager doesn't know you're aboard. He'd be certain to discover it if you were rescued by a Kingdom warship and given passage."

"I'm a Kingdom subject," Kelsey-Sato said. "And I've been assigned to this ship for months. He shouldn't object to my presence."

"You know he finds it disconcerting that you have acquaintances all over the Twelve Systems and have published as many papers abroad as at home."

Qin shrugged and walked back to the sickbay rooms. If she started carrying people off, that should move things along.

She was tempted to hoist the rest of the people over her shoulders and carry them off too. Why couldn't they temporarily take refuge on the *Dragon*? Once the warship arrived and scared off the salvagers, they could come back.

Qin found numerous corpses, a living-but-sedated burned man, and a woman with a broken leg who was trying to program nanites and fit a grav-crutch to herself. Qin lifted the man, since he would be least likely to object, and gently laid him over her broad shoulder.

"I'm here to rescue you," she told the woman, bracing herself for a protest.

She dropped the medical equipment and flopped back in a chair. "I'm ready to be rescued."

She let Qin hoist her over her other shoulder without protest. The load was awkward, but between her strength and what the armor added, she could bear it easily enough.

As Qin walked back out, she found Beaumont standing in front of Johnny. "I implore you, Sir Knight, help us defend this ship. As my young colleague has pointed out—" he pointed to Scholar Ito, "—none of us are trained as combatants. But there are files on the computers here that cannot be allowed to fall into the hands of thugs from another system. It's everything our people know about…" He glanced at Qin. "Quasars."

Qin rolled her eyes. "I've probably known about the newly discovered ancient gate longer than you have."

At this point, Qin didn't care if Johnny knew or not. Besides, Beaumont seemed to believe his claim of knighthood and was about to share everything with him. She just hoped Johnny was who he said he was and wasn't gathering intel for someone else.

Beaumont stared at Qin for a second, then twitched a dismissive shoulder and focused on Johnny. "You must help us until the Kingdom warship arrives. Those hooligans cannot be allowed to get their hands on our databases. We're fortunate they weren't all destroyed in the first attack—thank the builders for redundancy. We have constructed a magnetic field around a protected area in one of the cargo bays to transport a certain archaeological find if it is discovered, as we hope it is. Unlike the warships, the *Machu Picchu* isn't crewed by hundreds of people who are susceptible to space radiation of all sorts."

"Especially now," Ito muttered.

Qin started to walk past Johnny with her injured people, but she paused when he spoke.

"I understand. I'll stay and do my best to defend the ship." Johnny looked at Qin, and she thought he might ask her to help, too, but all he did was give her a nod when he saw her carrying the injured and say, "Tell Laser, will you? That I must regretfully depart from her ship, her fine food, and her less-fine cell. And if she would see fit to send over my bag with the weapons in it, I would appreciate it."

"I'll tell her."

Qin walked out, not sure if Bonita would be pleased or disappointed, and also not sure if leaving Johnny here was a good idea. What if he wasn't who he claimed he was, and he was still working for the Druckers? Or some other nefarious organization?

CHAPTER 9

THE SUBMARINE SHUDDERED, AND KIM GRIPPED THE EDGE of the small table in sickbay. Her vials rattled in the open case.

"They're firing at us!" a mercenary blurted, his nose pressed to a porthole.

"Good deduction, genius," his seat mate replied. "Next, see if you can figure out who my real father is, will you?"

"We'll have to wait to try loading them." Yas closed the case and shifted the now-converted, thanks to an engineering assistant, tranquilizer gun off the table. "I thank you for these."

"I didn't agree to give them to you," Kim said. "Your mercenaries confiscated them, much like Casmir's candy bar."

"They're not *my* mercenaries. I'm not sure they're even technically my patients. They don't show up for appointments and only call for me when they're grievously wounded. But in case Rache asks, how quickly will the bacteria affect the cyborgs, once they've been inhaled?"

"I don't know. My new strain hasn't been tested. I tried to make the bacteria work much more quickly than usual, but..." Kim shrugged and leaned out the hatchway to check on Casmir. She was worried about him. She'd lost track of how long they had been making their way under the ice, but it felt more like days than hours. If they had to return the same way, they could be stuck down here for a long time, and Casmir might get a lot sicker.

"And everyone with cybernetic implants will be affected, right?" Yas asked.

"If they inhale the gas, yes."

"You, Casmir, and I may be the only ones in these submarines without implants."

"And Asger," Kim said. "Knights don't usually get cybernetic enhancements. They've got a pseudo religion that espouses purity of the human form."

"Great. I'll just give him the tranquilizer gun—the *vial* gun. I'm sure Rache will approve."

The submarine rose sharply, bubbles spewing past a nearby porthole, and the deck rocked. A low groan came from Casmir, who'd belted himself into a rear seat and had a hand clasped to his stomach.

So far, the maneuvers hadn't been that drastic, so Kim didn't know if motion sickness was affecting him or if it had more to do with whatever was causing his fever.

"If you could get Rache to work with the Kingdom people, you could give *them* the gun. They won't have cybernetic enhancements either."

"You'd have to be the one to talk him into that," Yas said, "but I don't think even you have the power to sway him to work with Kingdom troops. Besides, they would be quick to use the vials on Rache and his people. He'll know that."

Kim shook her head, both at the idea that she had any power over Rache and at the likelihood of the two teams working together.

"They're all armored," Kim said. "We'll have to hope the astroshamans aren't, or the bacteria won't get through."

She didn't know if astroshamans wandered around in combat armor at home or not, but they would know visitors were coming and would be prepared.

"There's probably not time to come up with anything else," Yas said. "At least Jess isn't down here. She has a lot of cybernetic implants, so I wouldn't want to risk her being affected. She has… enough problems as it is."

"She's the one with the trylochanix addiction, right?" Kim remembered the woman going through withdrawal symptoms in addition to all the damage done by the pseudo radiation.

"Yes."

The submarine lurched, and Kim tumbled forward, ramming her gut against the table. Elsewhere, something toppled with a metallic clang.

"Dabrowski, Kim," Rache barked from the navigation hatchway. "Come talk to your people."

"Please," Kim growled, pushing herself upright.

She strode up the aisle, pausing to put a hand on Casmir's shoulder. He was struggling to unfasten his belt and had already filled a vomit bag. "Stay. I'll talk to whoever that is."

He slumped back, relief flashing in his eyes. "Let me know if you need me to…" His cheeks puffed outward.

"Puke on Rache? I'll definitely tell the Kingdom commander that option is on the table."

She made a stay-there motion with her hand and jogged to the front. Their submarine fired a trio of torpedoes. How many had the various teams brought? She envisioned them pulling up to the astroshaman base with nothing left but submarine-tour pamphlets to hurl at their enemies.

"It's not like maneuvering a fighter," the pilot growled as Kim stepped into the hatchway.

"You're doing well," Rache said. "We got them twice. If they're not insane, they'll give up and back off."

"We sure about their sanity, sir?"

"Not after that message, no." Rache saw Kim and pointed at the comm. "Talk to them and let them know you're alive. They are under the assumption that we've killed you, Asger, and Casmir. No mention of the crusher. They may not value him as much."

"Please," she reminded him and waved for him to open the comm.

"*Please* talk to them and help us save your lives."

"It doesn't count if it's laced with sarcasm." Kim stepped up to his side, feeling claustrophobic between the two armored men, and having the sudden urge to escape the sub and all of these people. All these stupid people who kept attacking each other over some artifact that might or might not change anything in the universe.

Rache pointed at the comm. The channel was open.

"This is Scholar Kim Sato," she said, "requesting to speak with the commander of whichever sub is attacking this one."

"The *Waddler*," Rache supplied.

"You expect me to believe that, Rache?" came the commander's voice over the comm. "You either recorded that earlier or are using a voice synth to make it sound like her."

"He's firing again," the pilot whispered, turning them as quickly as the ponderous submarine would comply.

"I'm sure you can ask her some questions that only she would know to verify that it's her," Rache said.

Kim shook her head. Rache knew her better than anyone left on the Kingdom submarine did. What would the commander ask her?

"Or I can get Casmir up here," Rache said, "and he can vomit in your ear as proof that it's him."

"Please don't," the pilot murmured, resting a protective hand over the instruments.

"You want a video?" Rache asked. "You're risking killing your own people."

"Even if they *were* alive," the commander said, "they'd be working for you now. Suborned or drugged and no longer on our side. We're wise to you, criminal."

The channel cut out.

"The hell with him," Rache said. "Take us around, Hocking. We're blowing them out of the water."

Kim rubbed her face. The commander hadn't sounded rational. Was it possible he was the man—or one of several men—that Ambassador Romano had gotten to and bribed or threatened to make sure Casmir didn't make it back? Speaking of people who'd been suborned…

"Wait." Kim held up a hand, but she wasn't sure Rache saw it. He had his face pressed against some scope, his thumb on the trigger of an improvised weapons station that his people had created. She gripped his shoulder so he wouldn't ignore her. "Comm one of the other Kingdom sub commanders. If Romano bribed the one that's chasing us, we just have to get someone with more rank to order him to stand down."

Rache looked at her hand. Thinking it presumptuous of her to touch him and give him orders with his pilot sitting next to them? Too bad.

She shook his shoulder. She would have squeezed it, but he wore his armor, making that type of gesture pointless. As it was, he probably didn't feel her grip.

"Do it. This is all too stupid for words. You're wasting your torpedoes and so are they, at the least. You may be wasting lives you'll need to get your prize."

The pilot glanced over, raising his eyebrows at her hand on Rache's shoulder, but he didn't say anything.

Rache tapped the comm panel, bringing up a map with other blips—it looked like his other subs and all the Kingdom subs except for this one were in clumps still heading toward the believed location of the base. He tapped the one in the lead.

"Kingdom submarine," he said, "this is Rache. Is there a reason why the wayward commander of your *Waddler* is trying to blow us up when we have Sato, Dabrowski, and Asger aboard? Do these people have no value to you? We only need them for a short time—I didn't need Asger at all—and then they will be returned whole and healthy."

A long moment passed, and Kim wondered if the new commander had even accepted the comm.

"We haven't been tortured yet," Kim added, in case he'd also come to believe that they were dead.

A woman answered—the single female submarine commander among the group. "Yet?"

"I don't know what the future holds," Kim said. "Rache is a notorious hater of the Kingdom and its subjects." She kept herself from pointing out his inability to say *please* as a further failure. This wasn't the time for humor—or anything that would lead the Kingdom to think that she and Rache were... She didn't know what. Not on the same side, but not necessarily on sides as opposing as they should be.

She tugged at her ponytail, worried she didn't sound authentic even though she was telling the truth. There was a subtle lie in her words, a distancing of herself from Rache that seemed inaccurate and a lie. She didn't know what he was to her, but it wasn't some distant villain.

"Commander Birken said he saw a body being jettisoned," the woman said.

Rache shook his head but didn't say anything. Even if the commander had lied, his fellow officers wouldn't believe Rache over their colleague.

"Is Dabrowski still alive?" the female commander asked. "And Asger?"

"Yes," Kim said, "for now."

"Birken must have been mistaken. Let me call him off."

The channel closed.

"Let's see if that idiot can accept orders from a woman," Rache said.

"Couldn't you?" Kim lowered her hand.

"I don't take orders from anyone. The perk of being in command of your own ship."

Kim noticed the *Waddler* in Rache's sights—thanks to the pilot's maneuvering, they had ended up chasing it instead of the other way around—but he didn't fire.

Unfortunately, his pilot noticed it too. They could see the glow of the other submarine's running lights in the dark water ahead.

"You've got them lined up for a killing shot, sir?" the pilot asked. "It doesn't matter what these Kingdom schlubs chat about then. We'll just take that sub out, right? Here, I'll get us closer."

Rache, gazing at the submarine in the sights for the torpedo launcher, seemed to be considering that very thing.

Kim sought something she could say that would get him to spare those men's lives. Even if the commander had been bought off by Romano, all the marines riding along knew nothing about it. Those men didn't deserve to die, and there was nothing to be gained from killing them. She thought of Casmir's new gaming friend and opened her mouth.

"Let's see what he does," Rache said first.

"Sir?" The pilot stared at him.

The submarine ahead veered off in another direction, toward the rest of the Kingdom vessels.

Rache waited to make sure it didn't turn again, then removed his finger from the trigger. "Return to our previous course, Hocking."

"But... those are Kingdom troops sailing those subs, sir. You hate the Kingdom." The pilot glanced at Kim.

She couldn't tell if he was looking at her for confirmation or if he suspected her of influencing Rache. Probably in a way the mercenary did not approve of.

"Yes, I do," Rache agreed. "But we need as much cannon fodder down here as possible to keep the astroshamans distracted while we move in."

"But they attacked us, and you've always retaliated. Won't they continue to be a threat?"

"Do not question me further, Lieutenant." Rache's tone was icy, and he stared at the man. "It is not your position to do so."

"Er, sorry, sir."

Rache jerked a thumb toward the hatch. "Return to the passenger cabin. I will pilot the craft for now."

The pilot hurried to unfasten his harness and stand up. Kim shifted to the side to let him pass, but he paused.

"What about her, sir?"

"What about her?" Rache's tone was still icy.

"Do you want me to take her back there too?"

"No. I will question her."

"Oh. Yes, sir."

The pilot slunk out, shutting the hatch behind him.

"Thank you," Kim said quietly.

"For promising to question you? You don't even know what that will involve yet."

"For not obliterating that submarine. And I know what kinds of questions you ask me. Unfortunately, I've only had a chance to read up to seventy-five percent in your book."

He snorted but didn't deny that he'd had literary questions in mind.

It seemed strange given how little time they had spent together, but she trusted that he wouldn't do anything to hurt her. Even if she was irked with the kidnapping, she'd had time to cool off. She didn't appreciate his approach to *rescuing* Casmir, such as it was, but they now knew that there was a genuine threat down here. At least to Casmir. But being the person sitting next to Casmir could have also gotten her killed.

"Only seventy-five percent?" Rache shifted the submarine to a new course. "It's been three days. I'd thought such an intelligent lady as yourself would be done by now."

"I've been working on a project for Princess Oku. I also didn't expect to see you again so soon. Every time we part ways, I'm reasonably certain there's no logical reason I'll run into you again. Yet you're becoming a more predictable fixture in my life than Salad Saturdays."

"You should sound delighted, not perplexed, about seeing me frequently. What are Salad Saturdays?"

"Casmir usually goes over to his parents' for the Sabbath, and I'm recovering from an arduous work week, so I don't bother cooking. For lunch, I walk to the Garden Gate on campus where an actual human chef makes these amazing custom salads with more than a hundred ingredients to pick from and fantastic dressings that they mix on the spot."

"I've never heard anyone sound so excited about salads."

"I always hated them as a kid. Until I was ten, I liked and was willing to eat... about three foods that were good for me. And all manner of junk food and sweets. It wasn't until I saw the effects of high-sugar diets on intestinal bacteria that I realized I would be better off consuming fewer sweets and more fiber."

"You realized this at ten."

"At eight, truth be told. But I was stubborn, and it took me a while to come around to the idea."

"By ten you were wiser."

"Naturally. It got easier when I started at the university and found the Garden Gate. Their dressings and the ability to pick all the good toppings while avoiding suspicious vegetables made me a fan."

"And what are suspicious vegetables?" Rache sounded amused by this conversation.

She wasn't sure if she should also find it amusing or if she should punch him.

"Anything that takes too long to chew or has a weird texture or strong taste. There are even more suspicious seafoods." She curled a lip at memories of her father's attempts to get her to like various rubbery or slimy—sometimes rubbery *and* slimy—seafood offerings over the years. Her brothers had always been willing to chomp down anything placed in front of them. As usual, she was the odd one in the family. She had no idea if her android-body-inhabiting mother had ever been like her when it came to food.

"You'll have to make me a list of what's allowed at dinner."

"Why, are you going to cook for me?"

"If we survive this, certainly."

"*Can* you cook?" Kim thought of the picture she'd seen of the young nobleman David Lichtenberg with a haughty tilt to his chin as he held his air-bike helmet under one arm. He hadn't looked like someone who'd ever had to prepare his own meals.

"I can find a video demonstration with a recipe and follow the steps. Though your palate sounds like it may throw a few more obstacles than usual in the path."

"Yes, you'll have to apply filters to your recipe search. It'll add at least five seconds. I'll have to ooze gratefulness when I sit down to the meal."

Rache laughed, then glanced at the hatch and cut himself short. Nefarious villains probably weren't supposed to laugh when they were questioning prisoners. Not with amusement. Perhaps with maniacal glee.

She smiled, feeling pleased that she'd prompted the response.

"Do you know why I like you, Kim?" he asked quietly.

No, she thought promptly and lost her smile, worried this was about to go to some serious romantic place that she wasn't ready to visit. Especially not *now,* when they were on their way to infiltrate an enemy base. She needed her adventures to end for a time and for her life to return to normal before she could analyze how she felt. And act on those feelings.

Which wasn't logical because, as she'd already admitted, he could never be a part of her normal life. He could never return to Odin, not for more than a visit, and even then, he would have to hide from the Kingdom Guard the whole time.

Rache looked back at her—she was still standing near the hatch while he sat in the pilot's seat, checking gauges and monitoring their path.

"Because of my perky exuberance, I assume," she said, the first thing that came to mind.

"You have an impressive deadpan delivery on lines like that."

On *most* lines. She had never been good at showing a lot of emotion or gesticulating passionately. Whenever she'd tried, usually because some acquaintance had been teasing her about sounding like an android, she had always felt like an actor putting on a show. It was exhausting.

Kim shrugged, feeling a familiar self-consciousness that she'd never quite grown out of, despite all her accomplishments in her field.

"It's because I knew from day one that I didn't have to worry about you seducing me." He sounded like he was smiling behind his mask.

Kim relaxed. It didn't sound like this was going to be the serious talk about romantic feelings that she'd feared.

"You do not have to worry about that," she agreed. "The first few times we met, I wanted to punch you."

"When did you stop feeling that way?"

"I didn't."

He snorted.

"I was almost there, and then you kidnapped me again."

"Damn. Does it help if I say I only wanted to kidnap Casmir and that you just happened to be on the same sub?"

"No, I don't like it when villains kidnap my friends either."

"I can see it's going to be an uphill battle to win your love."

Hearing the word love made her uneasy again, so she switched subjects. "You've alluded to people trying to seduce you and kill you before."

"Yeah."

He didn't continue, so she thought that was as much as he would admit. She wouldn't pry and ask for more. It wasn't like his life was any of her business. He'd already shared more of it than she'd expected, including the reason why he hated Jager so much.

"There's an energy beacon ahead. Maybe a buoy is the more accurate term. I think it's anchored in place." Rache tapped a couple of instruments. A hint of excitement entered his voice as he added, "We might have reached a monitoring perimeter that the astroshamans have in place."

"Do you want me to go back there and send your pilot up?"

"No. I don't need him yet. And he doesn't tell me stories about salads."

"A lack you didn't realize you had in your life."

"Not until recently, no." He looked back at her, not a glance but a long look.

"If you're gazing affectionately at me, let me know so I can modulate my facial expression appropriately. The mask makes it impossible to tell."

"It might be worth taking it off to see this modulation."

"I might even offer to hold your hand."

Rache tore his hood and mask off in a split second and held out his palm.

This time, she laughed. She kept it soft, positive there were no circumstances in which prisoners were supposed to chuckle during an interrogation. And she clasped his hand. He wasn't wearing his gauntlets, so she felt the calloused warmth of his palm.

"That came off far more quickly than I would have expected," she said.

The corners of his mouth quirked upward in a hesitant smile. He did not have laugh or crinkle lines around his mouth or eyes, like Casmir was starting to get, and the smile seemed foreign to him, or maybe something he hadn't done for a long time. That made her sad, and she touched the side of his face.

"It's not like the armor. That takes far more of a commitment." He rubbed his thumb against the back of her hand, and it wasn't... unpleasant.

Maybe it was even nice, she admitted somewhat reluctantly. Better than the urgent groping and grabbing that she remembered from her peer-pressure-induced experimentation with sex in school. She still couldn't imagine liking it, but maybe some touching wouldn't be so bad. With someone who understood that she wasn't that into it. But would he? Normal people with normal sexual urges never seemed to grasp that some people were different and weren't going to change because they met some romance-novel stud with all the right moves.

He was very still and watching her, and she wondered what he was thinking. She'd forgotten how intense his eyes were.

Maybe he guessed that his gaze was disconcerting, for he tilted his head forward, looking down at the deck. She shifted her fingers to his dark brown hair. It was soft, despite a short military cut that made it stick up and made his face seem more angular than it was.

"There have been a few assassins sent by Royal Intelligence," Rache said. "I usually ferreted them out—I've gotten good at self-preservation—and dealt with them."

She swallowed, not wanting to deliberate on what *dealt with them* meant.

"But there was one, toward the end of Chief Superintendent Bernard's time heading the office, that he and Jager probably picked together." His voice turned hard even though his touch on her hand remained gentle, and he didn't pull away from her stroking his hair. "A beautiful woman, the most dangerous kind, of course. She was trained to be a spy and an assassin, and her weapons skills were excellent. I know because when she applied for a position with my mercenaries, I tested her myself. I thought it might be a trap of some kind, but her background files had been forged exquisitely. I didn't have Amergin running my intelligence department then, or maybe he would have sniffed out the inconsistencies, but she appeared to have been born in a system far, far from the Kingdom, and she had an accent that backed that up, and she'd been a bounty hunter for years... It doesn't matter. We'll say the setup was good and leave it at that."

He paused, and she asked, "She tried to kill you?"

"Eventually. The seduction part happened first, though I admit, she didn't have to try that hard. It had been more than five years since Thea's death. I hadn't been entirely chaste, but never anything serious. I knew it would be a mistake to have a relationship with a subordinate in any case, but after a few months and a few battles, it seemed she was a real part of the crew and admittedly someone I liked, even though she never brought up salads."

He looked up, his forehead creased.

Was he worried she would be offended if he spoke of past lovers and caring for them? She found herself more curious about him and what drove him than upset that he'd loved other women before. And she still wasn't sure she wanted him to love *her*. Because then, she would have to love him, and that would have been complicated even if he weren't a hated criminal of the crown.

"I've heard bounty hunters aren't overly concerned with the health of their intestinal microflora," she said, because it seemed like she should say something. As soon as the words came out, she feared they were wrong, that this was the time for a concerned nod rather than a joke.

But one corner of his mouth twitched upward. "Nor spies nor assassins."

"A strange group of people."

"No doubt."

He lowered his head again. "Anyway, we eventually had a physical relationship. I knew it wasn't smart, and that the men would talk, but I'd been alone for a long time." He shrugged a shoulder.

You've been alone for a long time again, Kim thought.

"She didn't try to assassinate me *right* away," Rache said. "I would have been more ready for it then. It was some weeks before she tried to poison my food. And, when that was a miss, tried to stab me in bed while I was sleeping. It wouldn't have seemed like so much of a betrayal if she hadn't— Well, she made me care. And think... Oh, it doesn't matter now, I suppose. I've just come to realize that someone like me doesn't get to have a normal life, relationships. I guess I knew that from the beginning, when I chose revenge instead of running away to start a new life somewhere. But I couldn't imagine not retaliating. *Someone* had to—I'm not the only person Jager has screwed. I'm just the one who was his own creation, the one most appropriate to kill Frankenstein."

Kim lowered her hand. She had asked him about this, so she couldn't begrudge him sharing his story, but she'd been more comfortable when it had been about his past rather than his need for revenge. "I assume you recall that the monster killed everyone around Frankenstein but not him."

She didn't doubt that he'd read the Old Earth classic.

"Yes, Frankenstein was trying to destroy his creation when he fell into the arctic ocean and later died of pneumonia, and the monster went off to commit suicide. And Ahab never killed the whale. He was caught in the harpoon line and dragged to his death. Revenge never works out the way literary heroes plan, does it?" Rache lifted his head, showing a lopsided smile.

There was no joy or pleasure in it. As poor as Kim was at reading facial expression, she could guess that it was partially wry and partially fatalistic.

"I've thought about assassinating him," Rache said bluntly. "In the beginning, that was why I got all the enhancements. So my odds would be better of getting past castle security and to him, so I could do to him what his femme fatale later tried to do to me. But with all these literary examples guiding me, I can't help but fear I'd get myself killed before killing him. I'd be willing to trade my life for his, but the thought of dying before completing the mission…"

He looked toward the dark, lifeless water outside, an ocean devoid of even bacteria, from what the network entry on the moon said. "I've gone off to fearlessly risk my life for other missions. I'm not sure why I have such a hang-up about risking my life to get to him. I've told myself that it's enough to torment him, to take away his resources and his ships, to make him hate the sound of the name Tenebris Rache. But that's a justification, and I know it. The Twelve Systems would be a better place if he were dead. But I'd have to hope someone would come along and assassinate Jorg too. He's too much of a spoiled snot to be left in charge of a marble collection, much less billions of lives. Why does history keep repeating itself, Kim? Hereditary rule, democracy, socialism, capitalism… For thousands of years, we've kept trying them on and they've kept failing us, but we continue to default to one or another, and we can't figure out a system of governing ourselves that really works."

"Maybe because we keep trying to found our civilizations on the logical and rational, and forget that we evolved from animals and are dominated by emotions and instincts, whether we want to accept it or not." She spread her hand, not sure how to address his concerns and fears, and feeling strange that he was confessing so much to her. This was what she got for not being a seductress and putting him on edge. Instead, she'd become the confidante for a man she shouldn't have anything to do with.

"*You* don't seem to be. If you're ever ruled by your emotions, it would shock me."

"They're there. I'm poor at demonstrating them, but I feel—"

A beep came from the control panel, and Kim fell silent as Rache turned to it.

He sighed.

"What is it?" she asked.

"The *Waddler* destroyed that buoy."

"Which will alert the astroshamans that we're coming for them?"

"I'm sure they already knew, but this is like flicking their noses and then trying to sneak up from straight in front of them. I'd hoped they would expect us to go in through the crevice where we encountered their drones last week." Rache rose to his feet and grabbed his hood and mask. "I need to talk to Casmir and give him his assignment."

"More than deactivating the gate's defenses?"

"We have to *get* to the gate first." He faced her before donning the mask. "Thank you for the therapy session." The lopsided smile returned. "And for fondling my head. If you would like anything of yours fondled, let me know. I believe in fair trades with the opposite sex."

"That's egalitarian of you."

He bowed his head, then put his mask on and walked out.

Kim gazed at the dark waters ahead, wondering what was waiting for them and if any of them would survive this.

CHAPTER 10

H E'S *WHO?*" BONITA GAPED.

"He says he's Sir Bjarke Asger, which I assume would make him *our* Asger's father." Qin blushed a little at calling William Asger hers. Or theirs. It wasn't as if she would likely see him again.

"Bjarke. What the hell does that mean?"

Qin shrugged. "What does Johnny mean?"

They were on the *Dragon*'s middle deck, having put the injured people in the ship's small sickbay and given bunks and cabins to the others. Fortunately, the woman with the broken leg was a medical researcher with hospital experience, and she'd volunteered to tend to the burned man. The refugees were all quiet and subdued—so few of their comrades had survived.

"He asked if he could have his bag of weapons back," Qin added.

"What, so he can stay there by himself and fight Captain Amazing's entire crew?"

"Scholars Kelsey-Sato and Beaumont are staying aboard the *Machu Picchu* with him. But I'm not sure if they know how to use weapons. They're both loaded droids. And academics."

"Kelsey-Sato? That's Kim Sato's mother, isn't it? The monkey woman? I'm sure she'll scare off the enemy when she hoots and fluffs up her fur."

As someone with fur of her own she could fluff up, Qin declined to comment.

"They'll all get themselves killed." Bonita shook her head. "Viggo, how long do we have until Captain Amazing gets here?"

"A little over an hour and a half. Scholar Kelsey-Sato wandered into the cargo hold, found a stunner in our armory, and wandered back to the other ship."

"If Sato thinks that's going to do anything to armored men, she's not as smart as you'd expect for a Scholar So-and-so," Bonita said. "And is anyone else here confused? Now we have two Scholar Satos and two Sir Asgers. We'll have to use nicknames. Johnny can continue to be Toes, and this Scholar Sato can be Furry Sato."

Qin raised her eyebrows. "It's Kelsey-Sato."

"That's a mouthful."

"And Furry Sato isn't?"

"Good point. Viggo, next time someone wanders into the armory, you should deter him or her. It's not a library. Random people don't get to check out weapons."

"I assumed we were considering her an ally," he said. "I did speak with her."

"About how we don't run a library?"

"I gave her the specs on my engines and also told her about my vacuums. She looked at one curiously."

"More likely, she almost tripped over one." Bonita waved for Qin to follow her and headed to the storage cabinet where she'd stuffed Johnny's duffel.

Qin imagined her tossing it through the airlock tube, disconnecting the freighter, and taking off.

Which was fine. They'd done their duty in answering the distress call and taking the injured people aboard, but Qin couldn't help but feel they were leaving Johnny to die and the androids to be destroyed. Even if Johnny was a knight, he couldn't fight off a boarding party all on his own. Not against a crew as large as Amazing had, men who would be armed and armored. Johnny didn't even have a galaxy suit, much less armor of his own.

"Do you think we should help them defend against the smugglers?" Qin asked as Bonita pulled the duffel out and hoisted it onto her shoulder.

"Not with my ship. Absolutely not."

"You could take the *Dragon* someplace safe and leave me to either help Johnny or club him over the head if he's lying and plans to betray Kelsey-Sato and Beaumont."

Bonita sighed and dropped the bag to look at her. "Qin, your noble streak is wonderful, and it's good that you want to help people, but this is so far from being our fight that it might as well be taking place in another galaxy. You could be hurt or killed if you battle those men, and there's not even any reason to. There's a Kingdom warship coming, right?"

"Yes, but it won't arrive until twelve hours after the smugglers get here, men who could be in and out, killing everyone and taking everything, in that time."

"All the warship will have to do is yell some threatening comm messages to them to get them to knock it off. Nobody wants to risk the Kingdom's ire."

"Are you sure, Captain? This isn't their system, and someone already *did* risk their ire to attack their research ship."

Bonita took a deep breath. "Qin, it's not our fight. I've already snubbed Captain Amazing twice when we were competing for the same bounties. If I annoy him again, he might make it his life's mission to hunt me down."

"I'm not asking *you* to stay and help, Captain. You have to get these people to safety. I'm asking if *I* should stay to help Johnny—Bjarke—Toes—whoever." Qin shrugged.

"Toes. I told you, we're using nicknames to keep these people straight."

Qin refused to call Kim's mother Furry Sato.

"If you stay behind, and you're lucky enough to survive, you'll end up getting picked up by that Kingdom ship. Assuming they don't hang you out to get sucked into the nearest black hole. I can't stick around for Amazing to shoot at, especially not now that I'm obligated to take these refugees to a station."

"I know. I wouldn't expect you to. But if Johnny is who he says he is, he'll need help. If he's lying… I'd regret it if something happened to Kim's mother when I could have helped."

Bonita opened her mouth, but Viggo spoke first.

"There's a comm for you in navigation, Bonita."

"Is it anyone I'll want to talk to?" she asked.

"I'm unable to discern that with the information I currently have."

"I guess that means it's not Captain Amazing." Bonita climbed the ladder to the top level.

Qin, not done arguing her side, followed, though Bonita had raised a valid concern. Qin could risk her life helping the Kingdom people, as she had after that temple bombing in their capital, and the soldiers on that warship might still try to shoot her because she was genetically modified. Or a freak, as they would call her.

Johnny's face was on the display when they walked into navigation. Judging from the dim background behind him, computer panels dark aside from a few emergency indicators, he'd moved from sickbay to the bridge.

Bonita's grunt sounded more irritated than indicative of a desire to talk to him. "What do you want, Toes?"

He arched his eyebrows. "Did your helpful assistant not inform you that my full name had been revealed?"

"She did. Even if that's really your name, I've decided to continue calling you Johnny Twelve Toes to avoid confusion with the Sir Asger we already know."

"And here I thought my real name might intrigue you."

"Asger?"

"Bjarke. It means bear in the language of my ancestors."

"I'm indifferent to bears. They're not commonplace on spaceships or stations."

"Fortunate since they're powerful and ferocious. I will send you some video footage of the ones on Odin, should I survive the next day."

"I'll look forward to it. What do you want?"

"Other than my bag of weapons and underwear, which I assume you have no need of, I wish to inform you that I've transferred the remaining eight thousand crowns to your bank account." He bowed, his head dipping out of view, since whatever camera he was using didn't follow him. "I hope that our paths cross again one day and that I can show you why I'm called bear. Especially in bed."

He winked and closed the channel.

Bonita flopped into the pilot's pod and gripped her chin.

"I'll take his bag over," Qin said, "assuming you don't mean to deny him his underwear."

"I would never deny a man the insulation he uses to keep his grenades safe."

"You're talking about the smoke grenades in the bag, right?"

Bonita smirked, but it was fleeting. "I'm checking my bank account."

Qin paused, not sure if she was supposed to wait. If Johnny hadn't transferred the money, would Bonita want to withhold the bag?

"It's there. Plus five thousand more." Bonita made a fist and dropped it on the console, appearing far more irritated than pleased by this tip. "What'd he do that for? I didn't even take him all the way to Tiamat Station."

Qin didn't know what to say. If Johnny truly was the knight he said he was, and he belonged to the nobility and had an estate, maybe an extra five thousand meant little to him. If he wasn't who he said… why, indeed, would he have done that? To throw her off?

"Maybe we should put some of your leftover soup in a container for him so he has something to eat while he's fighting," Qin suggested. "And maybe I should take it over personally with extra weapons from the armory. And myself." She smiled, though she doubted this would have changed Bonita's stance on whether Qin should stay to help.

"Viggo?" Bonita asked, not looking at Qin. "You can fly yourself by yourself, right?"

"What an odd thing to ask. Of course I'm fully capable of flying myself. And requesting permission to dock at a station and transfer passengers. I'd have to tell the port authority to deduct the docking fee from your account, but that's also not a problem, since I often shop for new parts and make purchases using your banking information."

"No kidding."

It took Qin a moment to understand what they were talking about. "Captain, you're coming with me? To defend the research ship?"

"Someone with marksmanship skills has to keep you two from being overrun. For all we know, Bear over there might not be able to hit the broad side of a mining ship."

"From what I've read, knights go through extensive combat training and academic exams before they're granted knighthood. I'm guessing shooting is included."

"*I'm* guessing all they have to be able to do is cleave people's heads off with their big axes." Bonita pushed herself to her feet. "Come on. Let's check the armory." She waved at the bag Qin had been dragging around. "Take that. If Toes gets scared and has an accident, we want to make sure he has fresh underwear."

"I'm sure that doesn't happen to knights, Captain."

"You were sure they were all noble and defended a lady's honor, too, and Asger tried to kill you the first time you met. And Toes kidnapped us."

"Only after we deceived him." Qin didn't defend Asger, since he had been an ass the first few weeks she'd known him, but he'd changed once he'd gotten to know her. Now he was… a good fighting partner. Maybe a friend.

"Toes deserved deceiving. What a blockhead."

As Bonita headed for the ladder well, Qin smiled. Even though this wasn't likely a wise career move for either of them, she had seen Bonita's fine marksmanship on display numerous times and thought the odds would be better with her along. It might still only be three to twenty, or however many men Amazing brought over, but that was better than two to twenty.

Casmir sat in the last row of seats, alternating between trying to sleep and using his chip to check for the presence of nearby networks. It was likely they would be almost on top of the base before he detected anything, but he wanted as long as possible to study it and try to find a way in. He feared the astroshaman network would be much harder to access than Tiamat Station's had been, but he told himself not to psych himself out before he even tried. Just because Moonrazor was educated and intelligent didn't mean she'd been the one to set up the network.

Asger came and sat in the empty seat next to him. "You still look like hell. You should be napping."

"I've been trying. Sleep is elusive." Casmir waved to the water bottle he'd claimed. He'd finished his fizzop and switched to the more boring beverage, in case his body needed a more natural replenishment. He was sweating, fevered, and felt a little indignant that nobody else was, but since the troops had to fight the astroshamans, it would be better if they were in good form.

Assuming they did have to fight. Why was everyone so eager to start a war over this gate? And so certain that he was naive for wanting to share it with everyone? A crazy part of him wanted to try to contact Moonrazor and send her a message offering a trade. Maybe if she would be willing to give up half the gate, that would be enough for everyone who wanted one to have a piece to study.

"You need a woman to cuddle with you and take care of you," Asger suggested.

Casmir thought of Oku, weeks away, and wondered if she would cuddle a man and take care of him. Bring him comic books and fizzop when he was sick. Or did royalty pay the staff to handle that?

"Kim is the only woman on this sub," Casmir said. "My odds would be better of getting Zee to cuddle with me."

"I'm not going to argue against that. Besides…" Asger leaned into the aisle to look toward the closed hatch to navigation. "I think she may be cuddling Rache."

"Don't say that. I'm already nauseated. And I'm sure it's not true. She doesn't cuddle anyone."

"If you say so."

Casmir closed his eyes and checked for a network again. Anything was better than imagining Kim doing anything other than talking with Rache. Even private talks were worrisome. What if word got back home?

A network signal popped up on Casmir's chip. It disappeared as soon as it arrived, making him wonder if he'd imagined it, but it was more likely that they were coming into range.

"It would be *mishegas* to send a message to Moonrazor and try to make a deal with her, right?" Casmir had mentioned this back on the *Osprey*, but hadn't seriously entertained it. As the other people around the briefing table had suggested, it was unlikely any contact information for the astroshamans that he could dig up would get him a direct line to her.

"I don't think there's a deal you could offer her that Jager would approve of," Asger said.

"I don't know if you've noticed it, but I've been doing a lot of things Jager wouldn't approve of. So there's a precedent."

"I've noticed," Asger said glumly. "Which is why it's insane that I'm sitting next to you. I should be avoiding you like the plague."

"And here I've been polite and tried not to breathe in your direction."

The network signal popped up again. Casmir tried to hop on to it, found it secured, and started his hacking programs running. He'd downloaded a couple of new ones on the way to the moon, one supposedly coded by an astroshaman. Maybe it would have a good chance of getting onto a secure astroshaman network.

"Here comes the other bad influence in my life right now." Asger waved toward the aisle. "I can't tell if he looks freshly cuddled. Do you think he does that with the mask on?"

"Would you mind if we *didn't* contemplate my best friend cuddling heinous criminals?"

Rache arrived in time to hear that, resting a hand on the back of the seat ahead of Asger. "I need to talk to Dabrowski. Go polish your axe."

"It's a halberd," Asger said coolly.

"I know. Extendable up to eight feet, four-point-six pounds in weight, made of a reputedly indestructible alloy, and infused with chaotic crackle-energy, as the knight technical manual calls it. Go find a place to polish it."

Asger glared at Rache's masked face, but he must have remembered that he was surrounded by Rache's mercenaries, because his defiance didn't last.

He rose, saying, "I'll check on Kim to make sure she wasn't horribly maimed and scarred in the interrogation session you were supposedly running up there."

"It's possible she's both, though only emotionally. I was telling her about my past."

"I bet that's a fun tale."

"It's delightful. If you don't move, I'll share it with you, including the part where I started on the path toward becoming a heinous criminal by slaying an arrogant knight who wouldn't get out of my seat."

"I'm quivering with fear."

"Don't wet yourself. I want to get my damage deposit back on the sub."

"I'll fall on my own pertundo if you paid a single crown to rent these." Asger curled his lip in disgust and stepped into the aisle. "Let me know if he bothers you, Casmir. I'll come back and grind my halberd on his helmet."

Casmir waved away Asger. He was watching his programs at work, the data scrolling rapidly down his contact interface.

Asger bumped shoulders hard with Rache as he passed—Rache didn't budge, despite being much shorter. He barely reacted at all. He was looking at something farther back in the submarine.

"Do you want to threaten to grind something on me, too, or can I sit down?" Rache asked.

"Who are you talking to?" Casmir wondered if he could sling a leg into the empty seat and forbid anyone from sitting there.

"Your crusher is glaring at me."

"I have no need to sharpen anything," Zee stated from behind the passenger area. "I can easily create a sharp edge by manipulating my structure on the molecular level. Casmir Dabrowski will inform me if he wishes me to attack you, but I have observed that you have ceased to project a threatening body language with him."

"Don't announce that, eh? It's bad for my villainous image." Rache sat beside Casmir. "We're almost there."

"I know," Casmir said.

"I need you to—"

"I'm working on it." Casmir rubbed his gritty eyes, longing to be in his bed back home with his mother puttering around downstairs making chicken soup. She always swore it could cure any ailment. Maybe Oku would visit if he looked particularly pitiful and promised to let her dog sleep on his bed.

"Hacking into the network?"

"Seeing if it's possible, yes."

"Your eyes are glazed."

Casmir grimaced as an alarm bonged in his mind. He cut his chip off from the network, and errors of indignation popped up as the programs running informed him they'd lost connectivity.

"No kidding," he muttered to them and pulled up an antivirus program that he hoped was up to snuff.

He'd had Tork help modify it based on the code they'd used on Moonrazor's other virus. Would it be enough? He had it scan everything, and it spotted an intruder file lurking in a dark corner. He definitely hadn't downloaded that himself.

Aware of Rache looking at him, Casmir said, "The network tried to give me a virus for trying to get on it. Or simply for being here."

"One of the Kingdom subs destroyed a monitoring buoy on their perimeter. The astroshamans may not be happy with us."

"They may attack with more than viruses soon. Make sure the subs are running with their wireless receivers off, and everyone should take their chips offline. There's no connectivity with the system down here anyway. I'd close all of the subs' comms too."

"We need to be able to communicate with the rest of our team."

"They attacked us over the comm back in System Lion. It shut down the *Osprey*. Almost permanently." Casmir worried they would run into something equally dangerous here. There had to be a reason the inhabitants of System Hydra were aware this place existed but never came here to explore the moon's oceans.

"Right. I'll send some final orders and then have everyone turn off the comms. Let me know if you're able to get into the network.

Anything we could do to distract and harass Moonrazor's people would be useful."

"I know, I know."

Rache tilted his head. "You're much snippier than usual."

Casmir slumped in his seat. "I'm sorry. I'm not feeling well."

"Sir," came a call from navigation. "We've got some activity ahead."

Kim appeared in the aisle. Rache vacated his seat, heading toward the front, and she sat next to Casmir. She frowned and rested a hand on his forehead.

"I must look truly awful if you're touching me," he said.

She lowered her hand. "I composed a message to Dr. Sikou, asking about that stabbed body, but it won't go out unless we go under a shallow spot in the ice and get some connectivity with the ships up there."

"I just told Rache to order everyone to turn off their chips, so the astroshamans can't attack us that way. You should too."

She hesitated, then said, "All right." She was watching him, studying him.

Was he in more trouble than he thought? Dr. Sikou had been autopsying that body, the body that had been stabbed to death and stuffed in a compartment. He'd thought someone hadn't wanted it to be found so as to escape blame for the murder. But what if someone had locked it up for another reason?

Casmir scratched his chin. His skin was warm and dry. "You think the body was carrying a disease? Can bodies do that?"

"Maybe." There was that hesitation again. "There are a handful of viruses in the Twelve Systems that can infect humans and are virulent enough to continue living in and around a body for days after death. But we shouldn't be premature. It's possible you have a simple flu. I asked Yas to come check you out." She glanced back and lifted a hand. "I should have asked him earlier. He may have something that could help."

"Something superior to fizzop? Is there such a thing?" Casmir smiled, but it was a distracted smile. His antivirus program was munching on the intruder file. Soon, he could unlock his chip and try again to get on the network.

"Nothing as tasty, I'm certain." Kim rose, and Dr. Peshlakai took the empty seat.

Casmir hoped he didn't get all of his visiting seat mates sick.

"Mind if I take a blood sample?" Yas asked.

"Go for it. I'm not uppity and secretive about that like some people."

The submarine rose upward with a lurch and turned hard. Something bright skimmed past the window. An energy bolt? Casmir didn't know, but he grabbed his stomach as the craft swerved more than should have been possible for a long cylinder moving through water.

"I may have another kind of sample for you in a minute," he muttered.

"That's not necessary," Yas said. "You can keep that to yourself."

"If only I could."

Yas gave him an anti-nausea medication, took the blood sample, patted him on the shoulder, and left.

Kim returned to sit beside Casmir, pretending not to sneak worried glances at him. Dear God, what awful disease had he contracted? And was he in danger of giving it to everyone else in the submarine? Maybe he should have locked himself in one of those back cabins instead of sitting in the main compartment.

"Should I quarantine myself somewhere?" he whispered to Kim.

"It's probably too late for that if you're contagious."

He groaned. "I'm sorry. I wasn't thinking. Sorry."

"It's not your fault."

The thought of making everyone sick latched on to him like a tick, and he almost missed the notification that one of his programs had found an access code—if it could be called that. It was nothing like the typical numbers and letters and symbols massed together for passwords, and more of an equation to a complicated math problem relayed in binary. But his program sent the right answer, and he gained access.

Something struck the submarine, and curses and alarmed shouts came from the mercenaries.

"Got a leak!" someone shouted.

"Stick your tongue on it and stop it up," came a reply.

People shuffled around, and a banging started up that echoed in Casmir's skull. He wrapped his hands over his head and leaned his head forward, trying to ignore the maneuvers of the submarine and find out what he could access in the network that might give him some insight into what was going on around him.

"What's attacking us?" someone asked.

"Drones. You can see them out there."

"Send that knight outside with his axe to chop them down."

"It's a halberd," Asger grumbled.

Casmir found identifications on the network that might represent the drones, except there were a lot of them, and when he pulled up locations, they were forming a rough circle of more than fifty miles. An alarm was flashing for one, and it was reported as unavailable. Not drones, he realized. Those were the monitoring buoys, including the one the Kingdom commander had destroyed.

A *thwump* emanated through the submarine. Another torpedo launching.

Something slammed into the hull of their craft, the force knocking Casmir around in his seat.

"He's going to end up dying right here today," Kim muttered.

"Who?"

"Nobody."

"Nobody gets a gender? Interesting." Casmir couldn't find identifiers for the drones attacking their craft. "Weird, very weird," he muttered.

"Are you talking about genders or something else?"

He shook his head and pointed at the closest porthole. Another bright light flashed outside. It was pale green rather than the typical orange or red of DEW-Tek bolts. They had to be dealing with some special underwater weapon. Or were the drones themselves emitting light?

"Did that one have fins?" Kim squinted at the porthole.

"I... Oh, maybe that's it." Casmir unbuckled his belt, swaying before he caught himself on the seats, and pressed his nose to the porthole, hoping to see one again.

"What's it?" Kim asked.

"The torpedoes are missing them by a mile," someone groaned. "They're too small and too fast."

"Casmir Dabrowski," Zee said from the aisle as another *thwump* sounded, "we are threatened."

"Yes, we are," Casmir said.

The sound of water dripping came from somewhere inside the submarine. Another leak?

"Do you wish me to go outside of the submarine and combat these nemeses up close?"

"How's your swimming?"

Another drone zipped past. It did have fins. And it wasn't a drone at all, not in the mechanical sense. "No wonder. They're biological."

"Better," Zee said, "now that I've realized I can fill up bubbles of air within my body so that I do not sink."

"Go tell Rache," Casmir started to say, but Rache ran down the aisle, glancing at them as he passed.

"New plan," he said before disappearing into the back.

"Tell him we're being attacked by some sea creatures the astroshamans must have engineered, not drones," Casmir said.

"I will." Kim rose from her seat as they were struck again, the deck plating rattling underfoot. "He may have already figured it out."

"Good. I'll try to pinpoint the location of the base before someone realizes I'm on the network and kicks me off." Casmir closed his eyes, trying to concentrate—and not to hear the drip of water leaking in.

CHAPTER 11

THEY HAD LESS THAN AN HOUR UNTIL THE *Maze Runner* arrived—Viggo had confirmed that it was continuing on course and hadn't been deterred by the Kingdom warship also heading in this direction—when Qin and Bonita walked through the airlock tube and onto the *Machu Picchu*.

All of the scientists save for Professor Beaumont and Scholar Sato had transferred aboard the *Dragon*, and Viggo was speeding them toward Tiamat Station. Captain Amazing shouldn't guess that Qin and Bonita, both well-armed and armored, had stayed behind. He would only get readings for three people, and with luck, he would assume they were civilians without combat experience.

Qin lifted her chin. He would be in for a surprise.

A door opened as they walked across the ship's cargo hold, and Johnny walked in, his tattooed cheeks twitching in surprise.

"Your ship just left," he said.

"You're right," Bonita told Qin. "Knights are observant."

"I didn't say that," Qin replied. "I said they take academic tests and combat exams before getting their knighthood."

"Where they must learn to be observant."

"It *is* encouraged." Johnny's voice had turned dry, but it remained puzzled. He glanced at his duffel slung over Qin's shoulder. "All I thought I'd find down here was my underwear."

"I assumed from your flirtatious tone that you wanted me to deliver it personally." Bonita pulled a tied-up galaxy suit out from under her arm. "Along with this. Which may or may not fit. It's the largest one I had on the ship."

"I do appreciate you noticing and appreciating my substantial size." Johnny walked forward and caught the suit as she tossed it, more like one might hurl a grenade than gently lob a gift.

"I noticed it. Whether I appreciate it remains to be determined."

Johnny stopped in front of them—in front of Bonita, specifically, but he did nod politely at Qin. "I'm glad you brought this, but you shouldn't have stayed. I'm confused about why you would want to, to be frank. This is a Kingdom matter, and you're just a—"

"*Just?*" Bonita's eyebrows flew up. "I'm an excellent bounty hunter and skilled with my guns, as you'll see when that asshole captain comes over. Or, as is more likely, sends his minions in while he sits in his command chair on the bridge and sucks down his *saladitos.*"

"His what?"

"Dried plums."

Johnny's forehead furrowed.

"They're coated in chile and lime, and delicious when I make them. Qin, give the man his weapons. We need to decide where we're going to make a stand. Is there some area in particular that they'll angle for? Something beyond the usual engine and other salvageable ship parts that they'll target? I assume there's gold bullion in a vault somewhere since everybody is after this ship."

Johnny recovered and nodded. "Not gold bullion. All the data the Kingdom has on gate technology and everything they could dig up that might be pertinent to nullifying some defense system the gates can ooze." He glanced at Qin. "Professor Beaumont gave me some details. I haven't been in the loop for anything regarding the gate, so I'm playing catchup."

"I've had firsthand experience with it," Qin said.

"It's absolutely real then?"

"Yes. When I say firsthand experience, I should say only that I fought a battle on the cargo ship that eventually stole it from your system. I was there for less than an hour, and I wasn't in the hold where all the pieces were being stored, but it was long enough and close enough that I received deadly levels of the pseudo radiation it exudes. My genes are extra hardy at handling radiation, but that's typical space radiation. This was something different. Kim Sato treated me on this very ship."

Bonita waved away the discussion. "I doubt Captain Amazing is in anyone's loop, either, so he shouldn't have heard about any of that."

Qin wasn't so sure—the astroshamans knew about the gate, and many people in the Kingdom knew about it, so it seemed plausible that information could have leaked out—but maybe it didn't matter. All they had to do was defend the *Machu Picchu* long enough for the warship to get here.

"More likely, he wants the fancy medical and astronomical research equipment here," Bonita added. "It's a new ship—or it was. I seem to recall someone mentioning there's a lot of high-end stuff here."

"Much of it was damaged in the attack," Johnny said. "Beaumont said the pirates targeted it specifically when they boarded, either because *they* knew something or because an employer who hired them knew something. Someone didn't want this ship to reach the warships and help the Kingdom retrieve the gate and research it. I suppose the smugglers coming now might not know anything and only want it for salvage."

"Who is this Professor Beaumont? Should he have gone on the *Dragon*?" Bonita frowned.

"He's the one who insisted on staying and begged me to help," Johnny said.

"Begged?" Qin asked. "From what I saw, he just requested that you, a knight, assist him."

"His eyes were imploring."

"His android eyes."

"They can implore," Johnny said. "My point is that he stayed. He and Kelsey-Sato are down in engineering, reading technical manuals and trying to get more of the ship's systems back online. They would prefer it if the *Machu Picchu* could fly away before the smugglers arrive, and avoid another fight altogether."

"What's he a professor of?" Bonita asked.

"Archaeology, the same as Kelsey-Sato."

Bonita snorted. "Just the experts needed to repair engines. We're not going anywhere."

Johnny smiled slightly. "Probably not."

"It's too bad Casmir isn't around," Bonita said. "I would believe he could repair engines by reading technical manuals."

"What's *he* a professor of?"

"Robotics."

"That's probably closer to engines than archaeology."

"Yes," Bonita said. "It's doubtful this state-of-the-art ship has potsherds embedded in its parts."

"I knew you missed him," Viggo's voice came over Qin's helmet speaker. And also Bonita's, judging by the way she rolled her eyes behind her faceplate. "You tried to deny it," he added, "but Casmir is exceedingly handy to have around."

"Viggo," Bonita said, "Qin and I are maintaining an open channel with each other so we can discuss battle tactics, not so you can chime in about your fantasy lover."

"That's not fair, Bonita. I've been forced to listen to you and Johnny discuss his substantial size."

Qin expected Johnny to hear that and jump in, but all he said was, "As for your earlier question, I think we should lay a few booby traps in here and then set a trail of breadcrumbs. I would love to rid the galaxy of criminal salvage operators, but with our smaller numbers, the best we may be able to do is delay them. The longer we keep them winding around in a maze, the better."

"What kind of breadcrumbs does one use on smugglers?" Qin imagined a trail of physical Miners' Union dollars, or maybe valuable pieces from an engineering component, strategically placed to lure them to some desired locale.

"We might be able to close off bulkheads and light certain corridors over others to entice them along a certain route," Johnny said. "Or we can assume they'll head for the research laboratories to grab the mass spectrometers and other valuable science equipment."

"I've met Captain Amazing. I'm skeptical he knew what a mass spectrometer was *before* I shot him in the head and fried his brain cells."

"You've shot him before?" Johnny almost purred the words, as if he was proud of her for this.

"Actually, I only grazed his temple. Intentionally. At the time, I didn't know he would vex me further if he survived. I try not to murder people. My religion frowns upon it, and more importantly, you never know who has a lover or sibling who will make a career of hunting you down afterward."

"Not to mention the pesky legal repercussions," Johnny said.

"I've found lovers more problematic. Mine and other people's." Bonita pointed to the tops of the stacks of crates in the hold. "Given my perspective as a sharpshooter, these would be a good place to lay an ambush. I could be up there and have high ground and some cover. I brought my best rifle and Qin has her anti-tank gun—we've both got explosive rounds that will give even armored opponents trouble."

"They'll have explosives, too, I'm sure. If you're overcome, that's the only door out into a corridor, and it's exposed and out in the open." Johnny pointed at the exit.

"*Now.*" Bonita's eyes glinted. "Qin, want to help me rearrange some crates?"

"Does helping you mean I do the moving while you point to where they go?"

"I see you've been my employee long enough to know how things work." Bonita clapped her on the shoulder. "Don't worry. I just got some bonus money, so I'll make it worth your while."

"That's not necessary, Captain. Judging by the way your flirting is going—" Qin waved at Johnny, "—you may need your extra money to buy a larger bed."

"She noted my substantial size, too, I see," Johnny said.

"I hope not. She's too young and sweet for you." Bonita stalked off, looking at crates and the sight lines in the cargo hold.

"I'll help you move them," Johnny told Qin. "I'm not sure it's wise to attack a boarding party when they're expecting it, but I think the professor will be happy if we can keep them from getting into the rest of the ship and doing damage. More damage."

Qin nodded. "Do you think they'll run away when the warship gets close?"

"Let's hope so."

"Can I ask you something?" Qin hesitated, feeling strange about requesting a favor when she and Bonita had kept him locked up for the last week and she still wasn't sure if he was what he said he was.

"Yes." Johnny untied the galaxy suit and held it up to his body to check the size.

"Our ship is heading to Tiamat Station since that burned man was in bad shape. When the warship gets here, we'll need a ride there or somewhere where we can catch a ride there."

"Yes, I will too. This wasn't my original assignment, though it does look like it ties in."

"I'm sure they'll see the captain as normal, but I've had trouble in the past with Kingdom people thinking I'm... Well, they might refuse to take me."

He'd been pulling on the legs of the suit, but he paused to regard her. "Ah, yes. I've been out of System Lion for so much of my career now that I've stopped seeing modded people as anything odd. But we do have our ingrained prejudices, don't we?"

It seemed strange that the father might be more liberal and open-minded than the son. But she also knew Asger had her back these days and would shoo away any Kingdom soldiers or Guard officers who wanted to shoot her or lock her up. She still didn't know what to think about Johnny. She also didn't know if his own people would recognize him as the knight he said he was. Since she'd searched his bag, she knew there wasn't a purple cloak, liquid armor, or a pertundo in it. Did he have an ident and banking chip embedded in his fingers that would prove who he was? Or were those removed when someone went undercover?

"Toes," Bonita yelled from atop a crate she'd climbed—her knees were definitely better these days. "What'd you do with my Lady Shufflebottom?"

"What would I do with it? Rub it if you like."

"You know I'm talking about the stunner."

"Ah, of course. I believe Professor Beaumont is borrowing it. I'll be sure to retrieve it once we've annihilated the bad guys."

"Good. There's not much time. Let's get set up, everyone." Bonita waved at the tops of the crate stacks. "And someone tell that professor not to wander down here while we're fighting."

"Did she just take charge of my defense of the ship?" Johnny asked.

"I believe so, yes," Qin said. "She's a captain, you know."

"And has the nickname of Laser. I look forward to seeing if this is earned."

"It is. You'll see."

Johnny nodded and trotted off to find high ground of his own. Qin went to adjust the big crates to provide cover for the exit in case they needed to retreat.

It had been less than a week since Yas had briefly spoken to his parents and decided he was obligated to finish out the five years he'd promised to serve as Rache's doctor. He already regretted it.

How was he supposed to run a blood analysis in the crude sickbay of a submarine under attack and springing leaks?

The lights went out, and he groaned at this additional obstacle. Whoever was in navigation had stopped firing torpedoes. Either because they'd run out or they couldn't hit their targets.

As Yas stared at the glow of the display on his blood analyzer, he tried not to acknowledge the fear building in his chest. He tried not to think about how nobody would ever find them if their submarine went down here, about how the ocean was so deep that the vessel would implode after it fell to a certain depth and the pressure grew too great.

The result of the analysis popped up, and he swore as another reason to be afraid presented itself.

"Sir?" Yas had seen Rache run past sickbay a few seconds ago, and he leaned out.

Rache was in the corridor with Kim, tearing open ration packs and dumping gravy-slathered vat meat into a bag. Yas stared, too puzzled to speak. They filled the bag, cut a couple of holes in it, and Rache sprang into the airlock, slamming the hatch shut behind him.

Yas caught Kim's gaze. "What is he doing?"

"Hoping they're hungry," she said.

"The drones attacking us?"

"They're not drones. They're creatures."

"There's no life on Xolas Moon, not even bacterial."

"There are astroshamans and whatever life they created or brought with them."

Yas looked toward a porthole as something glowing green zipped past. "Oh, like guard dogs?"

"Guard fish, it seems. Or maybe more like guard sharks." Kim waved toward two mercenaries working to weld a leak. "Guard sharks that like the taste of submarine hulls."

Yas grimaced. "And Rache is going out there with them?"

He would be in his armor, but if those creatures could harm a submarine hull, would that be enough?

"Just to drop the bait, I think."

"Got a patch put in," one of the mercenaries yelled. "We're airtight again."

The submarine lurched, and a new seam split. Water dribbled in.

"Never mind."

Yas pushed a hand through his hair. This was madness.

Kim appeared far too calm for the situation. Her dark hair was back in a ponytail, and there wasn't a single strand out of place.

Her gaze fell to the analyzer. "Did you find anything?"

"Yes." Yas was reluctant to admit what. The last thing they needed was something else to worry about.

"Show me." Kim's eyes were intent.

Not curious, he thought. Maybe she already suspected.

He held out the display, knowing she would understand the finding by the scientific name that had popped up. "Do you know where he would have contracted it? Tiamat Station? It's not like mankind has eradicated it, but it's infrequent to find humans that are infected anymore."

Yas grimaced at the thought of the virus already having had several days to incubate in Casmir's system.

"We pulled a body out of one of the submarines before we left. A woman. I didn't see the face or I would have known right away."

Yas nodded. There were telltale splotches that appeared on the skin.

"The dead woman had been stabbed multiple times." Kim tugged at her ponytail, the first time she'd showed any nerves that he'd seen. "At first, I assumed it was a crime of violence, something to do with the rebellion."

"Someone must have recognized it and been terrified, thought killing her would stop it from infecting him or her." Yas shook his head. "They probably weren't in danger to start with. The only ones here who should be are Casmir and Rache."

Neither of whom Yas wanted to lose when the team was depending on them to outsmart the very smart astroshamans.

"There's not a cure, is there?" Kim asked. "Aside from the genetic modifications to a person's mitochondria?"

Yas shook his head. "A simpler cure eluded scientists two hundred years ago. That's why they were so desperate and made the genetic change—and why everyone rushed in for the treatment, even those in the gene-modification-hating Kingdom."

"And since that worked, and the change was hereditary, nobody's been that motivated to keep studying it to find a way to eradicate the virus." Kim shook her head.

Yas shrugged helplessly. She knew this information as well as he did. They had read the same articles. If anything, she probably knew more.

"Kim?" Casmir called back.

She leaned out of sickbay to look at him.

"Where'd Rache go?"

"He stepped out temporarily."

Yas didn't see Casmir mouth "stepped out" but imagined that he did.

"When you see him, tell him I've found the base."

"Good. I will." Kim leaned back into sickbay. "Do you have any drugs that might boost his immune system or at least act as a palliative to make him feel better until…" She flexed her hand. "We'll have to figure something out."

"Yes, I have both. And some people *did* survive." He smiled, hoping it was encouraging.

"Fewer than ten percent. It almost wiped out humanity. And those who survived were usually people in excellent health to start with."

"Casmir and Rache are in the prime of their lives."

She grimaced. "Casmir has a handful of health issues. I don't know if…" She swallowed, moisture gleaming in her eyes. "Just prepare anything you've got that will give him a good chance. I need to think about this."

Think about it? What did she think she could do? Concoct some bacteria to eat the virus? Or more likely a virophage. But thousands of smart people had tried that two hundred years before. Yas was sure there had been numerous advances since anyone had seriously tried, but what could she do down here? In a submarine in the middle of a forsaken ocean? A submarine under *attack*?

Although…

"Has the attack stopped?" Yas asked.

They hadn't been struck for several minutes. All he could hear were the grunts and clangs of the mercenaries working to patch the leaks.

Kim blinked and looked up—her mind had clearly been elsewhere. "I think so."

The inner airlock hatch squeaked as it opened. Rache, water dripping from his armor, stepped in and removed his helmet. The bag was gone.

"They're eating the stuff," Rache said, looking into sickbay. "I'm not sure how long it will keep them busy. If they come back, I want some poison to shove in the food." He looked expectantly at Yas.

"I didn't bring any poisons along. I wouldn't have the foggiest idea what would work on sea life imported from who knows where."

"Make some guesses, Doctor," Rache said. "The other submarines might be getting attacked too. I'm going to have to risk opening the comm to warn them. And until we locate the base—"

"Casmir found it." Kim pointed toward his seat. "I'm sure he can give your pilot directions."

"Good." Rache started toward him, but Yas leaned out and caught his wrist.

"Sir, wait. You need to see this." Yas held up the display and lowered his voice to say, "Casmir contracted the Great Plague. You may get it too."

Whatever Rache's reaction was, the mask hid it, and his tone was dry as he said, "I guess I should have been more concerned about him breathing on me."

CHAPTER 12

QIN CROUCHED ATOP A HIGH STACK OF CRATES, surveying the cargo hold from the position that Bonita had chosen for herself. At Qin's insistence—and Johnny had chimed in his agreement—Bonita was closest to the exit into the corridor, their escape route if they were overwhelmed and had to retreat.

Shortly, Qin would head over to the spot she'd chosen on the other side of the cargo hold, ensuring they had the most coverage possible for shooting at their enemies while staying out of each other's crossfire. Johnny had claimed a spot near the airlock hatch. They had also set traps on the deck.

Would Captain Amazing's men rush straight in and bumble into them? Or hurl out grenades or other projectiles first? They had to expect that the crew would defend the ship, but hopefully, they would be overly confident when they saw only three life signs aboard. The loaded droids wouldn't appear on any scans.

"Bonita," Viggo's voice came over their helmet comms. "My long-range scanners show that the *Maze Runner* has stopped near the undamaged airlock. I estimate they'll have their tube extended, locked on, and be ready to board within ten minutes."

"Thank you, Viggo."

"Captain Amazing commed the *Dragon* to threaten you. I answered and said you were too busy having vigorous sex with a passenger to reply in person."

"That seems as likely an excuse as any."

Johnny was walking over, and Qin wondered if he could hear Viggo's words.

"What did he say?" Bonita added.

"That old women having sex was gross."

"It most certainly is not, and I'm not old. I'm mature. But what I meant is did he sound suspicious?"

"Ah," Viggo said. "I don't believe so. There's no reason he would expect you to stay behind to defend another ship, right?"

"Right. Because there *is* no reason a sane captain would have done that." Bonita shook her head.

Qin raised her eyebrows, fearing she had regrets. She hoped Bonita wouldn't be hurt in this altercation. Or worse. Qin had never intended to talk her into helping.

"Do you have any unofficial updates to your will that you would like to make in case your plan doesn't work out?" Was Viggo thinking along the same lines?

They were probably being overly pessimistic. Qin *hoped* the would-be salvagers would back away when they realized they had a real fight on their hands. All they stood to gain was money, which wasn't a prize worth dying for.

"No, I'm not leaving you to Casmir," Bonita said, as if they'd had this conversation before. "Professors don't make enough money to pay the loans and taxes on spaceships."

"It is an unfortunate universe that we live in."

"Tell me about it."

"In any case, I shall wish you and Qin luck. Oh, and furthermore, you may wish to thoroughly embarrass and injure Captain Amazing, if you get the chance."

"Why?" Bonita asked. "Did he insult your vacuums or call you a garbage scow again?"

"He threatened to chase us down and blow us out of the stars if we took anything but people off the *Machu Picchu*. And *then* he called me a garbage scow."

"At least he didn't call you old."

"Which is ironic, since I'm far more mature than you."

"You're older. You're not more mature."

"We disagree," Viggo said. "Qin will have to be consulted for the tie-breaking vote."

Before Qin had to irk one of them with that vote, Johnny stopped at the base of the stack of crates and looked up at them.

"You're in my sights, Toes." Bonita tapped the rifle she'd set up, its tiny legs extended like a tripod for extra stability.

"So you won't miss seeing my handsome face."

"Is it somewhere under those ugly tattoos?"

"You don't think the daggers enhance my cheekbones?" Johnny touched one and raised his eyebrows. "The tattoo artist said they did."

"How much were you paying her?"

"She got a good tip."

"I bet."

Johnny lowered his hand, his face growing more serious. He looked at Qin, then Bonita, then opened his mouth, but the door slid aside before he spoke.

Beaumont and Kelsey-Sato walked in, making an odd couple even by galactic standards.

"The smugglers will be boarding any minute," Bonita said. "You two might want to hide in a storage locker together. On the other side of the ship. Assuming you're not here to fight."

Beaumont looked down at the pink Lady Shufflebottom and over at the comparatively drab stunner Kelsey-Sato had borrowed from the *Dragon's* armory. "No," he said, "that is not our intent. We merely wished to inform you that their ship is about to dock, but it sounds like you are aware of this."

"Yup," Bonita said.

"We also wish to thank you for helping us." Kelsey-Sato lifted one of her furred hands toward Johnny, but she also included Qin and Bonita with the gesture. "We are simple civilians working for the university, so we can't offer a reward, but I will be pleased to mention you in the acknowledgments of the book I'm putting together."

"What's the book on?" Johnny asked.

Qin wondered which name he would give her to use in those acknowledgments. Surely, no book had ever been dedicated to a Johnny Twelve Toes.

"It's a collection of numerous papers I've done on the gate network and the gates themselves," Kelsey-Sato said. "I hope to be able to update the material with new data soon."

"I've never been mentioned in a book," Bonita said.

"Nobody's written about the exploits of Laser Lopez?" Johnny asked.

"No."

"Maybe you should be giving passage to authors instead of roboticists," Kelsey-Sato said.

"I don't know," Bonita said. "I got new knees, thanks to Casmir."

"It would be helpful if he were here now," Kelsey-Sato said. "If we'd been able to get the drive engines back online, we could have flown away from these disreputable intruders."

A warning flash came from the panel next to the airlock. Another ship's tube was attaching.

"Positions," Bonita barked toward Qin and Johnny. "And a storage locker for you two." She pointed at Beaumont and Kelsey-Sato.

"Do you think she would be recommending such a location if we still had human bodies?" Beaumont asked Kelsey-Sato.

"I don't know. I was petite even when I was human." She guided him toward the exit.

"I was told I was chosen because my android body was considered an advantage for this mission. Storage lockers weren't mentioned."

They slipped off into the corridor, and the door slid shut on the rest of their conversation.

Qin hopped down, but Johnny lifted a hand. He hadn't yet headed for his chosen spot.

"Before this starts, I want to thank you both for coming to help. I wasn't expecting that." Johnny nodded at Qin and held Bonita's gaze longer. None of his usual sarcasm twisted his lips. "I hope you won't regret it."

"Me too." Bonita shooed him toward his spot.

Johnny smiled, bowed to her, and complied.

Qin ran to her chosen stack of crates, ensuring it was stable, then sprang twenty feet to the top. She dropped to her belly, one leg crooked, her elbows braced to hold up the rifle she'd chosen, and she sighted the airlock hatch.

She also shrugged her Brockinger off her back, but she wouldn't use the explosive rounds until their enemies were well inside. She didn't want to blow a hole in the hull and cause them all to be blown out into space. Besides, there were explosives planted on the deck below, charges designed to detonate upward without damaging what lay underneath.

The main lighting was still offline, but Johnny must have gained access to the auxiliary systems, because once he was in position, the emergency guidance lights along the deck disappeared, and it grew dark inside, the control panels by the doors shedding the only illumination.

Qin could still see. Anyone who entered in combat armor would have night vision and still be able to see until...

She drew a few smoke grenades out, ready to deploy them. Bonita and Johnny also had some. They'd raided the *Dragon's* armory so they could give these smugglers a hard time.

The airlock hatch whispered open, and Qin focused. At first, nobody came out. Then three canisters lofted into the hold.

Qin almost fired, but they weren't coming near any of them, and she recognized them as smoke grenades. They clattered to the deck, spewing their contents. It seemed everyone had the same idea.

Bonita snorted softly, the comm just picking it up.

Once the camouflage of smoke was provided, a team of twelve armored men raced into the cargo hold. Qin and Bonita calmly laid down fire.

The armored intruders weren't hurt, and indignant shouts of "Up there!" and "Ambush!" echoed through the hold.

While they were distracted firing upward, two men stepped on the explosives planted on the deck, the smoke having obscured them. Booms thundered from the walls, and a man screamed.

Qin, her heart hardened to these opportunists who were willing to kill a crew to salvage their ship, switched to her Brockinger. She fired at the men, knowing her explosive rounds would blow through their armor—and knock them across the hold.

Bonita fired relentlessly, sticking with her rifle, but she'd been the one to lay most of the charges on the deck, and even with the smoke, she found them with uncanny accuracy. The men stepped on some of them, but she detonated far more, her crimson DEW-Tek bolts slamming into them.

The chain of booms hurt Qin's sensitive ears, but she did her best to filter it out. Someone moved in the smoke below her crates, and she fired.

"Where's Toes?" Bonita growled, not stopping her own firing. "He shot twice and then disappeared."

All of Qin's fears that he meant to betray them reared up in her mind. She squinted into the gloom, looking for him, but someone sprang up out of the smoke toward her. The man's armor gave him the ability to reach the top of her stack of crates, but she shot before he reached her, a round slamming into his chest.

It ricocheted away before exploding, but the impact knocked him off his trajectory. She jumped to her feet and slammed a punch into him to ensure he wouldn't find purchase on her perch. The ship's gravity caught up with him and took him back toward the deck, but she'd been distracted momentarily. An explosion went off at the base of her crates.

What had been stable before bucked under her feet, and only through a gravity-defying dance of agility did she manage to snag her weapons before she tumbled off the side of the falling stack of crates.

For an instant, she had a view of the airlock tube, and she saw someone in a galaxy suit running down it toward the other ship. Johnny? Everyone else was armored.

Before she could warn Bonita or contemplate what his departure meant, the man she'd punched sprang out of the toppled crates. He was too close for her to bring her weapon to bear. He lunged at her, gauntleted fists leading.

Qin blocked the attacks with her rifle barrel, then growled and sprang at him. He tried to dodge out of the way but wasn't fast enough. She slammed her shoulder into him, knocking him back into the smoke.

Bonita, still safe on her perch, fired at him. He landed on one of the explosives that hadn't yet been detonated. It blew now, ripping his armor to pieces and sending shards tinkling all around the hold.

"Retreat!" someone cried. "There's a whole army here."

Several men stampeded out of the smoke and toward the airlock. But as they ran into the tube to escape back to their ship, an explosion flared orange, ripping the flexible passageway to shreds.

Armored men were blown out into space. Air and smoke from the hold whistled through the hatch.

At first, Qin assumed the ship's computer system would recognize the problem and close it automatically. But almost everything was offline. An alarm sounded, but the hatch remained opened.

"Qin, close that, will you?" Bonita barked. "We didn't bring oxygen tanks."

Qin was already on the move. "Yes, Captain."

She could feel the pull of the vacuum of space, threatening to draw her outside. Bits of broken crates and shards of armor clinked and clanked past as they hurtled through the hatchway.

Qin was surprised at how strong the pull was. She activated her magnetic boots to give her extra staying power as she ran, but she ended up almost flying to the hatch. She caught it, hooking her leg around it and yanking on it as she fought against the pull. Outside, the torn tube flapped as things struck it. The smuggler ship floated in space, fewer than ten meters away, but it had already closed its hatch. She had no idea what Johnny was doing over there.

Something careened past, clunking against her shoulder. Qin, with a snarl and a grunt, finished shutting the hatch. The pull disappeared, and the hold settled down, growing eerily quiet. Had all of their enemies been blown out into space? Or were some still alive and hiding, poised to shoot?

The smoke in the hold had all blown out, so the air—what remained of it—was clear. An alarm flashed, reporting that there wasn't enough oxygen left inside to breathe. Qin and Bonita would both have a few minutes of reserve air in their suits.

Qin wanted to slump against the hatch and recover for a few seconds, but she made herself push away and search for enemies. There weren't any bodies on the deck, either because they'd been blown out or the intruders had hidden. The crates that hadn't been damaged or knocked down from the explosives remained strapped to the deck and the walls, so that left numerous hiding spots.

"There's an armored guy in this corner back here who isn't moving." Bonita was kneeling atop her stack, peering around from her elevated position. "His armor is breached, so he may be dead. He's the only one I can see."

"I'm looking around," Qin replied quietly, prowling around the perimeter.

She always felt at a disadvantage when her nose was shut away behind a faceplate and she couldn't smell the scents around her. But no enemies sprang out at her. As she completed her circuit without hearing any scuffles or breathing or anything to suggest anyone other than she and Bonita remained in the hold, she came to a stop under her crates.

Bonita climbed down with her weapons slung over her shoulder. "Toes is gone?"

"I think I saw him run through the tube to the other ship. He was the only one I spotted wearing a galaxy suit."

"Before the explosion? Or after it?" Bonita's voice had a strange hitch to it. Concern?

For Johnny? Qin was more worried he was in the middle of betraying them and all that stuff about being Sir Bjarke Asger had been a lie.

"Before."

"Did he set it?" Bonita asked. "I didn't. Obviously. The tube wasn't attached yet when we were setting the charges."

"He might have dropped one as he ran through." Qin shrugged.

"To cut those guys off from their ship and keep them from escaping? Or to cut *us* off from him and leave us stranded here until the Kingdom warship arrives and its crew wonders if we were the saviors... or if we were behind the attack on the *Machu Picchu*?"

"I don't know."

Asger sat beside Casmir, watching out the nearest porthole.

Before, it had all been black out there. Now, a light blue glow brightened the water, and he could occasionally make out walls of ice and stalactites dangling down from above. The submarine was navigating through a tunnel toward what he'd heard, and hoped, was a back door. Asger had the sense of a massive complex with miles of tunnels embedded in or even carved into the bottom layer of the ice. Presumably, generators and a big environmental control system kept areas inside livable for the astroshamans who were still partially human.

But nobody was *telling* him anything. What he'd gathered had been from snippets of conversation between the mercenaries, and when the door to navigation was open, a few murmurs that slipped out from Rache and the pilot.

Asger knew that two more of Rache's submarines were coming this way and that the rest were trailing the Kingdom's team. *Stalking* the Kingdom's team, he feared. They had headed off in another direction, perhaps to the main entrance of the base. Asger didn't know how they'd found it, since Casmir had been the one to lead this submarine here, through some clues on the network he'd hacked into.

"You doing all right?" Asger asked Casmir.

He wasn't looking out the porthole or at anything. His chin was to his chest, his eyes closed, sweat gleaming on his forehead. Now and then, he wiped his brow or shifted in his seat, so Asger knew he wasn't sleeping, but his lack of interest in the changing surroundings was worrisome.

Casmir nodded and opened his eyes to look at him. "I'll be fine. I'm just trying to navigate the maze of their wireless network. It's unorthodox. I'm able to see that there are a lot of nodes on it, likely robots and androids and automated machinery inside the base, but I haven't been able to gain control of anything yet. I've spent most of my time trying to fend off attacks. There are these bots running around, attacking anything that isn't familiar. Namely me." A smile ghosted across his lips. "Are *you* all right? Nobody's picked any fights with you, have they? I'm sorry I haven't been paying much attention."

"You sound like you have enough to deal with especially when…" Asger started to point out that Casmir was clearly sick with something, but maybe he shouldn't mention that. He'd seen Yas and Kim trading whispers and looking Casmir's way with concerned expressions. Whatever he had, it was more than the flu. "Protecting me isn't your job," he finished instead.

"It seems like I should do my best to keep our kidnappers from harassing you when you only came along to help me."

Asger lowered his voice. "You just figure out how to give us an advantage so we can find the gate and get it away from the mercs and up to the surface where our ships can pick it up."

"That sounds more daunting than protecting you."

Before Asger could respond, Yas appeared at his shoulder with a jet injector. "I bring a gift," he said. "For Casmir."

Asger might have objected to the mercenary doctor injecting his friend with things, but Kim was at his side. She wouldn't let Yas give Casmir anything dangerous.

"A cold bottle of fizzop?" Casmir rubbed his eyes.

"An immune-system enhancer and a cellular energy booster."

"That doesn't sound very tasty."

"You don't have to ingest it." Yas leaned across Asger and pressed the injector to the side of Casmir's neck.

"Here." Kim handed him a cold bottle of water. "I put a packet of that electrolyte stuff you like in it."

Casmir accepted it but said, "Do you mean the electrolyte stuff you *think* I should like?"

"It's berry flavored. What's not to like?"

"It's unsweetened."

"Sugar doesn't need to lace *everything* you consume."

"Ugh, maybe you and Rache *are* right for each other."

Yas's eyebrows rose.

Kim frowned.

Asger shuddered. "Nobody's right for that man. He—"

Rache walked down the aisle and stopped to look at Asger. "I need to talk with you, knight." He jerked his thumb toward navigation and headed back that way without waiting for an answer.

"It's *Sir* Knight." Asger was inclined to ignore the command and stay in his seat.

But Yas squinted after Rache and then looked at Asger. "I think he's going to offer you a weapon to use against the astroshamans."

"Why me?"

"You're presumably not cybernetically enhanced," Yas said. "Is that true?"

"It's true. I don't *need* enhancements."

"Which you would know is true if you'd seen his calendars." Casmir patted him on the shoulder.

Asger frowned. He didn't want these grubby mercenaries knowing about his modeling work. Or Rache, dear God. He could imagine the snarky comments now.

"Will you go see what he wants, please?" Casmir lowered his voice. "Better to make him believe we're working with him for now, so he won't expect it later when we choose a moment to sneak off on our own."

"And return to the Kingdom subs?"

"And finish the mission while determining our own fate."

"You worry me, Casmir. For so many reasons."

Casmir smiled and gave him another pat. "You should go." He rested a hand on his midsection. "All this twisting around in these tunnels is unsettling my stomach further."

Asger lurched to his feet. "Seat's all yours," he told Kim and Yas, though he doubted anyone would sit in the potential line of fire, and headed up to navigation.

Rache had taken over the pilot's spot again, and he banged the hatch shut, trapping Asger alone inside with him. Rache wasn't wearing his helmet. It would be possible to strangle his vulnerable neck... if one were strong enough and quick enough. That would put an end to his murders of Kingdom subjects and his hobby of destroying Kingdom resources. Asger might get himself killed doing the deed, but maybe it would be worth it. A way to protect his friends and redeem himself to his superiors. If he killed the Kingdom's greatest enemy, nobody would question his worthiness to be a knight.

"If you don't stop staring at my neck and breathing hard," Rache said without looking back from the console, "I'm going to rethink my offer."

"What offer?" Asger crossed his arms over his chest and made himself look out the porthole.

The glowing pale blue light was brighter to the front, warming the icy walls comprising their tunnel. Asger jumped when he spotted machinery integrated into what looked to be a ceiling above them. A few black pillars dotted the route ahead, metal columns with glowing blue indicators—were they the source of the light?—that went from the top to an ice floor below them. They'd left the ocean and were completely within the ice now. Asger tried not to imagine pieces crumbling down to crush them.

"With Dr. Peshlakai's help, we've retrofitted a tranquilizer gun to shoot vials of a liquid that will break open and turn gaseous upon impact. You may be familiar with it since Kim was thoughtful enough to make it and bring it over."

Asger didn't know anything about it, but he didn't want to admit that Kim had confided more to the mercenaries than to him, so he grunted in response.

"It's designed to make a cyborg's cyberware break down," Rache said, "hopefully fast enough to have an effect in a battle."

"I'll take it and put it to use, if that's what you're offering."

Rache turned to look at him, which was disturbing since he was piloting them through the maze. "My people would also be susceptible. Our armor will protect us, but armor gets damaged. I need you to give me your word as a knight that you won't attack them. Or me."

Asger didn't bother hiding his grimace. He didn't want to give his word to Rache on anything. "Forever or just while we're infiltrating the base? I can't give my word not to attack you when we get to the gate—the Kingdom sent me to get that, not to help *you* get it."

"I want your word that you won't attack us with *our* weapon," Rache said.

"You just said Kim made it."

"We provided the gun."

"You're real criminal masterminds."

Rache looked at him for long seconds before saying, "Once we've defeated the astroshamans and claimed the gate, you and I can have another battle if you want."

Asger remembered their skirmish in the cargo hold of the astroshaman ship. He wouldn't have come out on top if Zee and Casmir hadn't helped, but his pride wouldn't let him back down from a challenge.

"I would *love* to battle you again, especially if it's to keep you busy while my colleagues are sneaking away with the gate."

"Your colleagues Kim and Casmir are going to carry the gate away? I don't think Casmir could carry the change in his pocket right now."

"You forgot about Zee."

Rache waved a dismissive hand and looked back long enough to adjust their path so they didn't run into one of those pillars. A line of little square lights flashed on and off as they sailed by. Asger hoped it wasn't an alarm, that their passage wasn't being tracked and transmitted to whatever headquarters existed inside.

"Give me your word or don't," Rache said. "I'd rather not take the weapon than give it to someone who will betray us."

Asger gritted his teeth. It wouldn't be a betrayal if he shot Rache. He would be doing the right thing. Giving his word, on the other hand, was like making a deal with the devil.

But he wanted any advantage he could get in dealing with what was ahead. "I promise I won't use your tranquilizer gun to shoot you or your people."

"Good." Rache seemed willing to accept his word. That was surprising. "Meet us at the airlock with your weapons and all your armor on in ten minutes. If nothing leaps out to attack the submarine, we'll head inside then."

"Head inside what?"

"*This.*"

Rache guided them around a corner, and the ice walls widened into an underwater harbor that was large enough to hold a hundred submarines like theirs. There wasn't anything that looked like a docking area, but two massive blue-black doors with more indicator lights were closed up ahead, suggesting an inner harbor beyond them.

"Those are big doors," he murmured. "Are we sure this is the *back* way?"

"Not entirely. When we were here last week, we located an underwater cable that goes into the base in another location about five miles away. We detected what we believe is a power station over there. The Kingdom submarines apparently detected it, too, because they headed that direction. Casmir is the one that found this back entrance through the network."

Asger gritted his teeth, frustrated that Casmir was helping the mercenaries instead of their own people. Not that he'd had a choice. It frustrated Asger further that there was no way to get a message to the Kingdom submarine commanders. Even if he took his chip online, the only network he could try to access was the astroshaman one, and from what he'd heard from Casmir, he'd get his chip fried even if he could get through the security to hop on.

As Rache turned their craft and entered the harbor, other vessels came into view to the left. At first, Asger thought they were the other borrowed tourism submarines, but these were made of the same black metal alloy as the pillars and the door, and their shapes reminded him more of jellyfish back on Odin than the long cylindrical submarines. Long limbs lined with fins dangled down from the dome-shaped bodies.

"No life readings," Rache murmured, "at least none that we can detect. Those vessels all appear to be powered down."

"Just parked there? I guess that means their crews are in the base."

"I expected no less." Rache waved at him again. "Go get ready."

Asger hadn't removed any of his armor except for his helmet since coming aboard—as if he'd be so insane as to make himself vulnerable around these men—so there wasn't much to *get ready*, but he headed back to check on the others. It occurred to him that Kim and Casmir shouldn't go along. There was no reason for Kim to go, and Casmir was too sick to infiltrate an enemy base and hunt through miles of corridors. Rache's people would have to come back and get him after they'd cleared the way and found the gate.

The idea of going off alone with these mercenaries didn't fill Asger with delight, but he would do it. And he would find his opportunity to take the prize for the Kingdom.

Asger paused near Casmir's seat—Yas was sitting next to him now, some diagnostic monitor hooked up to his arm—and eyed Zee, wondering if Casmir would be willing to send the crusher along to help him.

Before he could ask, Rache came up behind him.

Asger shifted to the side so the mercenary captain wouldn't be at his back. Maybe Rache was fantasizing just as much about strangling him. He hadn't seemed daunted by the idea of another skirmish.

"Casmir, where's your armor?" Rache asked. "You came aboard wearing some."

Casmir looked blearily at him, as if Rache were some desert mirage he was trying to figure out. "I was hot so I took it off. I left it…" The bleary expression shifted around the submarine. "Somewhere. Maybe in the refrigerator? I was wishing it would be cooler."

Asger gazed bleakly at Casmir. He sounded loopy. He ought to be sleeping, not infiltrating enemy networks.

"Why do you ask?" Kim leaned out of the sickbay compartment. "He can't go anywhere."

"He has to," Rache said. "He's going to have to deactivate the gate before we can take it anywhere."

"Why? You must have already accepted that we're all going to be exposed to the pseudo radiation again." Kim frowned darkly at him. "We'll have to head to Tiamat Station for medical treatment and hope they have everything we need."

"It would be preferable to deactivate the gate pieces *before* infecting everyone all over again. I'm assuming the astroshamans were smart enough to quarantine it. Either that, or this battle is going to be very easy since everyone will already be dead. But as soon as we remove it—"

"You were going to have to bring the pieces back out here to carry it out, right? I saw the chains and winch and everything you've got attached to the back."

"Yes. But we need him." Rache pointed at Casmir. "In addition to tinkering with the gate, he's our best bet for getting past whatever security system is in place. It hasn't escaped my notice that he's rather educated and bright when it comes to hacking."

"When it comes to *many* things." Kim lifted her chin. "Which is why he needs to stay here and rest until we get out of here and figure out how to help him recover. You *know* his life is at stake."

Asger jerked his head up. What?

He looked at Casmir. He'd assumed this was some flu or random space-station bug that was vexing him. Was Kim being melodramatic? Asger hadn't known her to be so before.

For the first time, he noticed splotches on Casmir's face and the backs of his hands. They were faint, but it had to represent the beginnings of a rash.

"I'll watch out for him," Rache said. "I'm not going to thrust him into any battles, but we need him or—"

"Or what? Some government leader who isn't you might get a wormhole gate? Who *cares*? You can go take your minions and break into Jager's secret vault and steal it later if you can't let your damn whale get away."

Now, Asger really didn't know what they were talking about. Most of the mercenaries were standing and staring at the arguers. Asger started to worry that Rache would snap at Kim out of some macho fear that he was being undermined in front of his men.

"This isn't about—" Rache started.

"It's *completely* about you."

"Uhm." Casmir raised a finger, but neither of them looked at him.

"It's about keeping my men alive while we complete a mission that is far more important than you seem to believe." Rache stepped toward her and reached for her arm.

Kim stepped back and jerked it away. "Don't touch me. And don't keep pretending you *rescued* us out of some altruistic act. All you wanted all along was to drag Casmir into that base to be your damn computer hacker. That message you intercepted just gave you a convenient excuse. A justification for kidnapping him."

"Let's talk about this in private." Rache's tone was flat and clipped, but he didn't reach for her again.

"I'm not letting you take him."

"Uhm." Casmir pushed himself to his feet this time before raising his finger. "If I could speak—"

"No," Kim and Rache snapped at him as one.

"Well, I'm going to do it anyway. Roboticists are recalcitrant, you may have heard." Casmir managed a wan smile. "I'll go along. Thank you, Kim, for trying to help me, but I'd rather be doing something to keep my mind off the thing you and Dr. Peshlakai have been very careful not to tell me."

Kim turned her frown onto him, but some of her anger faded. "Casmir… It would be better for your health if you rested and stayed quiet."

"I have not observed that Casmir Dabrowski is capable of resting *or* being quiet," Zee said, stepping up to peer at Casmir, "except during his nocturnal periods of unconsciousness."

"Sleep," Casmir murmured. "Humans call that sleep."

"Even then, he sometimes talks to himself of equations and ideas for homework problems to challenge students in his upcoming classes," Zee continued.

"Do I really?"

"Yes. Even though you are a poor rester, I believe you should heed Kim Sato's advice. My scanners show that your vital signs are subpar, with an elevated heart rate, poor heart rate variability, and a temperature of approximately one hundred and two degrees Fahrenheit, which is above the optimal human range."

"Thank you, Zee, but I'm going."

"Rest is the superior choice," Zee stated.

"See?" Kim said. "If you won't listen to me, maybe you'll listen to your crusher. Casmir, I'm serious. You need to stay here while these burly idiots—" she looked squarely at Rache, "—run off and play protagonists in some adventure novel."

"That sounds extremely boring. And if I go with Rache, I might get the chance to puke on him. That would be delightful, don't you think?"

"Yes," she said without hesitation.

"Really," Rache murmured.

"Let me find my armor." Casmir pushed himself into the aisle and wobbled lopsidedly toward the back.

Kim steadied him with a hand as he passed. She looked like she wanted to plant it on his chest and stop him, but she didn't. She glared at Rache, stalked into the office they'd first been put in, and closed the hatch behind her.

"Suit up," Rache barked to his men. "Get the explosives and all your weapons."

"Yes, sir." Their responses seemed more muted than usual.

Asger watched with new worry as Casmir disappeared into a cabin, looking for his armor. While the men scrambled to grab all their gear, Yas leaned his head out of sickbay, like a rabbit in a briar patch checking to see if the hunters had moved along and it was safe to come out.

Asger came up and gripped his arm before he could retreat again. "What's wrong with Casmir?"

"It's nothing you should need to worry yourself about."

"I'm worrying about *him*, not me."

Though Yas's statement promptly made him wonder if he should be worrying about everyone.

"I'm bound to keep the confidences of my patients," Yas said, "and I don't think anyone would be served by—"

"He's not your patient. He's my friend and the man your loathsome leader kidnapped." Asger kept himself from squeezing Yas's arm—he didn't want to be a bully about it—but it was hard.

Yas pressed his lips together in stubborn silence.

Asger growled and released him, then stalked into the office. Kim hadn't locked the hatch. When he opened it and strode in, she dropped into a defensive crouch with her fists up before realizing it wasn't Rache.

"What's wrong with Casmir?" Asger asked.

Kim lowered her fists, her shoulders slumping. "He's contracted the Great Plague."

"What? That shouldn't be poss—" Asger stopped, remembering the explanation he'd been given as to why Casmir was immune to the gate's defenses. "Oh, hell. There's no cure, is there?"

"No."

CHAPTER 13

THE SINGLE REMAINING ENEMY TURNED OUT TO BE dead, thanks to stepping on one of the explosives, so Qin and Bonita left the body for the Kingdom people to deal with when they arrived. Bonita found the controls for the cargo hold and activated the auxiliary lighting and was also able to get oxygen pumping back in. That was good since the exit into the corridor had locked itself during the breach. Qin knew she could force it open but didn't want to damage the *Machu Picchu* further if it wasn't necessary.

"I guess we should find the droid professors and report to them," Bonita said. "And then twiddle our thumbs until the Kingdom ship arrives and we have to explain this mess. I'd feel better about all this if it hadn't sounded like Kelsey-Sato was here in secret rather than as an authorized representative."

"They picked Professor Beaumont," Qin offered. "At least according to him."

"According to a quirky loaded droid we've only just met. I knew I'd regret coming over here."

"We weren't injured. Much." Qin rubbed her shoulder, a twinge of pain coming from something she'd twisted while falling off the crates. "And we thwarted the bad guys."

"In an ideal universe, we'd get a reward for that."

Bonita didn't mention that she'd never found the universe ideal. Qin knew her well enough that she didn't have to.

A *clang-clang-clang* came from the airlock hatch, and they both jumped.

Bonita swore and slung her rifle off her shoulder. "One of them must have used jet boots to get back over here."

"Does he know this is the ship where all the guns are?" Qin couldn't believe those men would try to come back here after they'd been routed. She dropped her Brockinger into her hands and strode to the hatch. "We're answering it, right?"

Bonita grunted. "I suppose. Answer it and then blow a hole in whoever's presuming to knock."

The panel on the wall showed that the outer hatch was operational and securely shut, and that the airlock was pressurized and not leaking air. All the damage had been to that tube.

After Qin unlocked the hatch, she jumped back, ready to shoot.

Johnny stood inside, a pistol pointed to the head of a sneering graying man that Qin didn't recognize. Captain Amazing? He wore armor, but his helmet was missing, so the pistol pressed against his thin hair. A small shuttle was docked behind them, so Qin could no longer see the *Maze Runner*. Was the other ship still out there?

"Mind if we come in?" Johnny asked brightly.

"Where did you *go*?" Bonita strode up and peered into the airlock, then jerked with surprise at the sight of them.

"To retrieve a gift for you, of course."

"A *gift*?" Bonita sneered to match the stranger's sneer. "That's not a gift. That's the wad of furry, linty crap that you throw out after Viggo's vacuums cough it up into the filter."

"I don't think she likes you," Johnny told his prisoner.

"Screw you," the man said. "And screw you too, Lopez."

"It's *Captain* Lopez, and I'd take Dagger-face there to bed before you."

"Ah," Johnny said, "you acknowledge that you *do* find my tattoos appealing. And that you're imagining me in bed."

"Don't flatter yourself." His prisoner glanced at him. "She's old and horny and desperate."

Johnny pushed him, and his head cracked against the side of the chamber. "Oops."

As Amazing, who did not look that amazing, winced, Johnny shoved him into the hold and stepped out behind him, keeping the pistol pointed at his head.

"I'm not sure about imagining you in bed," Bonita said, "but if you keep abusing my enemies, I might start to have warm fuzzy thoughts toward you."

"I would be honored, dear Laser. I'd bow to you, but my prisoner is in the way. We either need to find a cell to stick him in or stun him. I'd like to hand him over to the *Eagle* so he can explain why he thought pilfering goods from a Kingdom ship full of wounded people was a stellar idea."

"The professor took the stunner, remember?" Qin asked.

"Can't we just pummel him soundly in the head to knock him out?" Bonita waved at Amazing's face—he had an old scar at his temple, and Qin remembered her saying she'd shot him before. "I believe that's how they did it in the old pre-stunner days."

"I do appreciate a woman who has a place in her heart for brutality." Johnny winked.

Soft clangs sounded again, this time from the corridor side of the hold. The door slid open, and Kelsey-Sato and Beaumont peered around the jamb, his head up at human level, hers down at monkey level.

Amazing stiffened, as if he recognized them. There wasn't any reason he should if he'd only come for salvage. Could he have known about the gate and the data they carried?

"Maybe we should question him before brutalizing him," Qin said.

"At the same time works," Bonita said.

"I'm not telling you rejects from the gene bank anything."

"No need," Johnny said cheerfully. "When I couldn't find you right away—who knew a captain would hide in his cabin while his men were raiding another ship?—I had a chat with one of your officers. The squirrelly woman with diamonds drilled into her teeth. In truth, they may have been lesser gems that only look like diamonds. I didn't ask her about that. Only about what you were *really* doing here." Johnny's eyes narrowed, some of his affable nature fading.

"Roxy wouldn't have told you anything, not without a truth drug jacked into her veins." Amazing spoke belligerently, but Qin read a hint of uncertainty in his eyes.

"Oh, but she found me terribly charming and agreed that it would be worth speaking up if it meant you mysteriously disappeared into a Kingdom prison mine, along with most of the crew of your ship, and she was the only one left to claim ownership of the *Maze Runner*. It's registered in System Cerberus, I understand, and finders-keepers is how legal ownership is determined there."

Amazing clamped his mouth shut and glared. The scholars walked in, and he glared harder.

"What did the new owner of the *Maze Runner* say?" Bonita asked.

"That a certain mining ship failed to do a sufficient job of destroying the *Machu Picchu* here. Not only did they leave some of the crew alive, which was *not* the suggested course of action, but they failed to acquire an android with a database of important information in his memory." Johnny extended a hand toward Beaumont.

"Tsk, tsk." Beaumont shook his head.

"They did try to find us," Kelsey-Sato pointed out. "Well, not me, since they shouldn't have known I was here, but Beaumont. But we hid. I just wish the rest of the crew had hidden instead of trying to fight." Her tail twitched in what might have been agitation if she were a cat.

Qin wondered if it was strange that she was a touch envious of that tail. The scientists who'd mashed her genes together must not have thought a cat-woman warrior needed one.

"So Prince Dubashi tried again," Johnny continued.

"He's throwing money around left and right to get to Kingdom people, isn't he?" Bonita asked.

Kelsey-Sato tilted her head.

"He's got a fresh bounty on Casmir's head," Bonita explained.

"I must meet this Casmir that keeps getting mentioned," Beaumont said.

"He's a roboticist from Zamek City," Qin said. "I don't know why some Miners' Union prince would want him dead."

"I would think the prince would want him captured," Kelsey-Sato said. "For the same reason he wants Beaumont's memory. Casmir might be able to help whoever has him understand and deactivate the defenses of…" She glanced around. "The quasar."

Bonita rolled her eyes. Only Amazing looked confused. Maybe he had only been told to get the android, not what Beaumont's digital brain contained.

A soft ping sounded on Qin's comm helmet.

"Are you two still alive?" Viggo asked her and Bonita on the same channel.

"Yes," they said.

"Good. The *Eagle* has commed me and asked if I'm in contact with the *Machu Picchu*. Apparently, its comm is still down."

"Ship's comm down?" Bonita asked Kelsey-Sato and Beaumont.

"We've been trying to fix what we can," Kelsey-Sato said, "but having to hide frequently in storage closets tends to slow down repair times."

"Go ahead and tell us what they're saying, Viggo," Bonita said. "How far out are they? I'll take a look at the comm and see if I can figure out how to fix it."

"They asked what was going on and if I knew anything about it since I was just there. There may have been suspicion in the comm officer's tone. I look forward to you straightening it out so that Kingdom combat shuttles don't zip after the *Dragon*."

"Me? Toes here is going to straighten it out. He's a knight, remember."

Johnny raised his eyebrows. "I can only hear your half of that conversation."

"That's the important part," Bonita said.

"They say they'll be there in a few hours, and they want to speak with Professor Beaumont in person. And that if there's a knight there, they'll want to see him. It seems they have no knowledge of a knight on the *Machu Picchu*."

"I'm shocked," Bonita said.

Qin thought about pointing out that none of them were supposed to be on the *Machu Picchu*, at least not according to the plans they'd entered the system with, and it was only the distress call that had brought them here. But they could sort it all out later.

"Let's lock this prisoner up somewhere while we wait," Johnny said. "Is there a brig?"

"I know of some nice storage closets." Beaumont adjusted his glasses and smiled, like he would enjoy shoving someone else into one of his hiding spots.

"I guess that will do."

"*I'll* put him away." Bonita waved for Johnny to push Amazing toward her. "You two scholars can show me where, and then show me to the bridge so we can look at the comm."

Johnny hesitated to relinquish his prisoner. "He may make trouble for you."

Bonita walked up to Beaumont, took the pink Lady Shufflebottom from his hand, then stalked up to Amazing.

"Bitch," he snarled.

She shot him in the face. He crumpled, unconscious, and she slung him over her shoulder in a move that she wouldn't have tried a month earlier, even with her armor giving her legs extra strength and a bunch of support for her skeleton. Her knees wouldn't have allowed it. Qin smiled, pleased that she was feeling so much better.

Johnny stepped back, raising his hands, as if to hand off the mess to her—or in the hope that she wouldn't also shoot him.

Bonita walked out, waving for the scholars to come along.

"I am beginning to like that woman," Johnny stated, smiling fondly after her.

Qin looked at him but didn't comment, still skeptical that she should encourage a relationship. The fact that he'd come back made her feel better about him—maybe he *was* what he said—but with Bonita's three failed marriages, maybe it would be better for her to avoid men, especially snarky men. Johnny had more bite than Asger, and even if he hadn't been some spy always on one mission or another, Qin couldn't imagine him settling down with a woman long-term.

Though she supposed he must have if he was the father of Asger— *her* Asger. Was he? He hadn't said. He'd only asked about him.

Qin realized she didn't know Asger well enough to know if his father and mother were still around. She couldn't remember him ever speaking of either of them to her. What if his mother was back at home, waiting for her husband to return, and he was out here among the stars, flitting from one spy mission to another, flirting with strange women along the way?

"You don't approve?" Johnny was looking at her.

Qin wiped whatever expression had been on her face away and shrugged indifferently, even if she was anything but. "I watch out for my captain, the same as she watches out for me. You seem like trouble."

"Trouble? Me?" Johnny pressed a hand to his chest.

"You *did* kidnap us the first time we met."

"You were barely in that net for an hour. I don't think that counts as a legitimate kidnapping. I didn't even ransom you to anyone."

"You're really weird for a knight."

He flashed a grin. "Why do you think they keep sending me out of System Lion for missions?"

"You're not a good influence on other knights?"

"Oh, I'm not bad, I'm told. I had a squire once. He became quite the noble hero. Sir Zdrazil. Have you heard of him?"

Qin shook her head. "Until recently, I was never in System Lion."

"Right, you're one of the Druckers'... purchases."

"Yeah." At least he hadn't called her a freak. She squinted at him. "Are you Asger's father? William Asger?"

His face went from expressive and sarcastic to closed off. And he didn't answer right away.

She squinted even deeper and more suspiciously at him. What could be between him and Asger? Asger was brave and noble and a good fighter. Weren't those things knights were supposed to be?

"I am," he finally said.

"You don't get along with him?"

"You've seen that calendar?"

"Yes, he gave it to me."

Johnny snorted and rolled his eyes. "I can't believe he hasn't grown out of that. I guess it's better than the first batch of calendars he did. He was naked in all of the pictures for that one. It's *illegal* in the Kingdom to make pornographic material of an underage guy. He was sixteen then. He lied about his age so he could get an agent and get the deals. And why? To make money? No. The family has money, and he had an allowance. It was all ego. Or some desire to impress women or his friends. I don't know, but I had to beg and plead for him not to be kicked out of the squire program. And then I had to do it again when he passed his exams. There were questions of whether he should be allowed to become a knight, when he didn't seem to represent the ideals of honor and chivalry."

"Because he lets people take photos of him?" Since Qin had grown up in System Cerberus and been used as a sexual object by the pirates since she was twelve, she couldn't manage to sound properly affronted by the idea of nude calendars. And nobody was considered underage for anything there. Money trumped morality, and most of the denizens didn't have a moral code worth mentioning, anyway. It was only through reading books from elsewhere that she'd learned of such things.

"*Naked* photos. That get printed and distributed all over the system. Yes, he's an adult now and has a fake name tied to his modeling work, but it's not the image the Kingdom wants of its knights."

Qin eyed Johnny's barbed-wire dagger tattoos. She didn't say anything, but he must have guessed her thoughts.

"These—" he pointed to his inked cheeks and the studded dog collar around his neck, "—are because I had to fit in with the pirates. They are temporary. The fact that knights have a certain image and uniform makes it easier to go undercover without being suspected of being one."

"Ah."

Qin kept herself from making further judgments, even silently, but she thought of Asger speaking with her in the park that night, the dewy scent of trees and grass all around them, and how they'd run up together to help in the aftermath of the synagogue bombing. And how he'd stood by her side and kept his people from arresting her, even though they'd given him strange looks and probably doubted his sanity for vouching for a freak.

She agreed that the calendars—and the underwear—seemed like a silly part-time job for a knight who, as Johnny had pointed out, shouldn't need the money, but she doubted it was about money. Asger wasn't much older than she was, and she didn't feel all grown up yet, even if, in some ways, she'd never been allowed to be a child. Maybe he was still figuring himself out. Maybe he'd only wanted to put himself out there for attention. It didn't sound like his father had been home much. What of his mother? Was she alive?

Johnny must have decided their conversation was over, because he headed for the corridor. As Qin watched him go, she wondered if she should warn Asger about this. Did he know his father was now in the same system that he was? Would they end up being assigned to work together? Would that be as problematic as she feared it might?

CHAPTER 14

ASGER JOINED CASMIR, RACHE, AND ZEE IN THE airlock. All except the pilot, a fighter, and Kim and Yas had already exited. Asger expected Yas, as their doctor, to come along, but Rache had asked if he wanted to come, rather than ordering it, and Yas had pointed to the little sickbay in the submarine and said he would wait there. There were supposed to be a couple of combat medics among the mercenaries that were going.

Rache's other two submarines had found the underwater harbor and were spitting out more groups of his men. Asger would have felt better about this adventure if the Kingdom submarines were also in this part of the compound. He hated the idea of them inadvertently being used as cannon fodder.

Despite the glares Asger was shooting Rache, now that he knew how bad off Casmir was, Rache had given Asger the tranquilizer rifle he'd promised, with vials of Kim's concoction loaded into it instead of darts. He'd also allowed Asger to choose a shell gun from the stash of weapons in the submarine, so he had that in addition to his DEW-Tek rifle and pertundo. If one was going to storm an enemy base, one might as well be prepared.

Casmir had donned his armor, adding a supplemental air tank, as the others had done, and he gave a thumbs up when Asger looked at him, but he was far quieter than typical. Asger rested a hand on his shoulder as water filtered into the airlock.

Casmir patted his gauntlet and said, "I'm glad you're here, Asger. You're an amazing knight and a good friend. I'll tell your superiors that someday, if I live to see them." He chuckled.

Asger's throat swelled with emotion. He didn't think that was funny at all, but it touched him that Casmir was trying to bolster him instead of worrying about himself.

"Thank you," Asger said, his voice tight.

"I am also a good friend," Zee informed them, the water up to his chest. It seemed crushers were waterproof. "I will protect you on this mission, Casmir Dabrowski."

"Thank you," Casmir said. "You are indeed an excellent friend. Far beyond what your creator could have imagined."

"Yes," Zee said.

Casmir smiled.

"He's modest too," Asger said.

"Would you be modest if you were such a sublime creation?" Casmir asked.

Asger opened his mouth to reply, but Casmir held up a finger.

"Keeping in mind that I've seen your scantily-clad figure on underwear tubes."

"That doesn't bely my modesty."

"No? I would have thought one would have to have a reasonably high opinion of at least his exterior to have it plastered all over Zamek City."

"It's the interior I'm working on. And that underwear goes out all over the system, not just the capital on Odin."

"It's amazing that women don't rush up to you everywhere you go and ask for autographs." Casmir closed his eyes, as if the conversation was taking a lot out of him.

Asger hoped he wasn't engaging in it simply to take his mind off his illness. Or maybe he even felt the need to try to take Asger's mind off it.

"The pictures are on men's underwear tubes," Asger pointed out.

"But women are the ones that usually shop for men's underwear. As my mother will be quick to tell you."

"Maybe *boys'* underwear. If you ever get married, I hope you won't expect your wife to pick out your briefs."

A weird expression twisted Casmir's face, and he shook his head.

"I'm rescinding my offer of employment," Rache muttered. He was facing the exterior hatch, waiting with his back to them.

"What?" Asger was sure Rache had never made such an offer to him.

"I offered Casmir a job once. No, twice. I rescind the offer. I couldn't listen to this all day."

"I'm relieved he was wise enough to reject it." Asger shuddered at the idea of Casmir joining forces with Rache. The mercenary already had plenty of good men and a ship better than anything in the Kingdom fleet, as evinced by his ability to avoid getting caught again and again. He didn't need an elite roboticist with a knack for taking over computer networks.

"I still have a vain hope of being able to return to my old life." Casmir sounded sad, like he didn't think that would happen.

Asger felt that lump return to his throat. He didn't know if Casmir was worried about the illness—the Great Plague, damn it—or Jager, but Asger had to blink away moisture in his eyes at the idea that either would keep him from returning home.

Once the water filled the chamber, Rache opened the outer hatch, and the group swam out. Asger, worried the effort would tax Casmir too much, grabbed the back of his suit to help him along. Rache swam on his other side, keeping an eye on him.

Asger wished he could spit at the man, sure all that he cared about was keeping Casmir alive long enough to help his team get in.

The groups from the three submarines converged at the huge double doors that rose more than forty feet from the icy floor of the harbor to the black metal roof. The omnipresent pale blue light glinted off the mercenary team's dark armor and faceplates. Everybody locked their magnetic boots to the door while Rache and another man swam around to look for a control panel.

Asger glanced back toward the submarines and the mouth of the tunnel they had entered through, wondering if those creatures would return. He'd heard that the other submarines had also tossed food out to distract them and that it had worked, but eventually, the creatures would finish eating, wouldn't they?

"Everybody on the channel?" Rache asked over the comm.

He'd given Casmir and Asger the mercenaries' frequency. Casmir had muttered something about any kind of comm channel being unwise—he'd insisted the submarines keep their comms off except for emergencies—since the astroshamans liked to fling viruses around. But this couldn't be helped. They needed to be able to speak with each other.

Rache's men replied with obedient yeses. Asger grunted. Casmir mumbled something.

Asger was worried about him. His chin was down, face hidden. If he had a seizure in the water, how could they help him? Were the combat medics qualified to do so? Asger didn't know why Rache hadn't ordered Yas to come along. Because it would be too dangerous for a non-combatant? *Casmir* was a non-combatant. He wasn't even carrying a weapon, unless his tools counted.

"A bonus for anyone who figures out a way through this door without using explosives," Rache said.

"Without *explosives*, sir?" someone asked. "Where's the fun in that? I brought underwater explosives."

As other mercenaries chimed in with similar sentiments, Asger half walked with his magnetic boots and half paddled to the seam between the two doors. Rache and another man poked and prodded at a control panel.

Zee was standing on the bottom of the harbor, gazing up at them. Did he have the strength to force the huge doors open? He might not have heard the request since he wasn't wearing a helmet with speakers.

Asger thought he could force the blade of his pertundo into the seam, but he didn't know about using it to pry the massive doors apart. It would be like using a toothpick, however strong a toothpick, on a normal door. And what defenses might this place have? It seemed unwise to force anything when—

A rumble emanated from the doors, and they shifted ponderously aside. The mercenaries swam back, pointing their water-protected rifles at the widening gap.

"Who did that?" Rache lifted his hands from the control panel. The man next to him shook his helmeted head.

"Me," Casmir said. "Over the network. What kind of bonus do I get?"

"A pat on the back," Rache said.

"That's disappointing. I was at least hoping for a cookie."

"Your blood sugar level is still recovering from all that soda." Rache shined his helmet headlamp into the dark water beyond the doors.

"My blood sugar level is sublime," Casmir said, though he sounded like he had a headache—Asger doubted anything of his was sublime right now. "My body can handle a cookie and a fizzop in the same day."

Rache swam into the darkness, and more pale blue lights came on inside as he entered. It appeared to be an extension of the underwater harbor, with a couple more of the jellyfish-like ships inside.

"I'm reading a forcefield in there." Casmir grabbed the edge of the door and pulled himself through. "And I think, if this map can be trusted, a way out of the water and into some tunnels."

Asger shifted to stay near Casmir and go in ahead of him.

"The kind of forcefield you can lower with access to the network?" Rache asked.

"I'll try. I'm getting bombarded with bots hurling viruses and more blatant attacks at my chip. It's making it hard to do anything."

"I'll find you *two* cookies if you manage to get us in."

"We didn't bring any cookies, boss," someone whispered on the comm.

"We have the Protein Pucks."

"Those aren't sweet."

"They have chocolate chips."

"Those aren't chocolate, sir. I think they're dehydrated beef tendon bits."

"Oh."

Casmir looked over at Asger. "I didn't know getting kidnapped would be this bad."

"If we get out of here," Asger told him, "I'll buy you as many cookies as you want."

"Excellent. Thank you."

The group swam inward and upward, where they could see a docking area and a surface to the water, but the promised forcefield covered it. When someone's helmet bumped it, an electrical charge zapped him, and he gasped and jerked away.

"I can see something on the land up there," a man said.

Asger squinted through the transparent forcefield and the rippling surface of the water. He could make out a few dark blocky shapes but wasn't sure if they represented robotic threats or structures for storage or equipment.

"They're moving, whatever they are," another mercenary said.

Threats, it was.

"Shit," someone barked.

"Look out behind," Rache ordered.

Glowing creatures about three feet long zipped through the open doors toward them. They were the same entities that had attacked the submarine before.

Several of the mercenaries fired with their waterproof weapons. Zee pushed off the bottom, his arms turning into something akin to fins, and treaded water near Casmir.

Asger pulled out his pertundo as one of the drone-like creatures zipped toward him. It didn't have eyes, but a round fang-filled maw opened and closed with clear intent. Asger made sure he was blocking Casmir from the creature, then stabbed with the point of his pertundo.

The water made him slower than usual, and his aquatic enemy darted to the side, tentacles and fins giving it speed greater than he expected. It tried to get around Asger, as if it *knew* Casmir was the greater threat.

Asger lunged, stabbing again. "No, you don't, ugly."

This time, it was distracted, and he sank the point in deeply. The pertundo's electric energy flared to life, lightning bolts arcing around the tentacled body. For a moment, all of those tentacles went stiff. But then the creature grew limp, more like jelly than anything solid, and slid off the pertundo. It started swimming again.

Casmir swam back until he bumped into a pillar supporting the dock. The creature rushed after him—there was no question that he was the target. Two more angled in from the side. Zee lunged and rammed into one of them. Like Asger, Zee wasn't as agile in the water, but he managed to halt the creature's progress.

The two others slipped past. Asger roared, kicking and slashing. He would do more than stab them. He would cut them into dozens of pieces.

He cleaved the closest one in half an instant before it reached Casmir, who had only his armor for protection. Asger didn't know if that would be enough, but halving the thing seemed to kill it. He whirled toward the other as Zee ripped his foe into pieces.

A creature that Asger hadn't seen almost got to Casmir on the other side, but a mercenary darted in, stabbing it repeatedly with a dagger. He also held a pistol, but the blade seemed more effective. Was that Rache? He finished killing the creature and kicked it away.

Another enemy slithered past Zee and tried to get around Asger to Casmir again. Asger rammed his pertundo into it as Rache shot it and Casmir kicked it in the mouth. The creature was run through on the point of Asger's weapon, and he spun, hurling it as well as he could in the water. It flew past Zee, and Zee snatched it from its route and tore it into pieces with pincers he'd formed at the ends of his fin-arms.

Someone cursed. "It bit me!"

"Bite it back."

"Who's got the Protein Pucks now? Look out!"

DEW-Tek energy bolts flew through the water, striking targets, but they didn't do much damage. The creatures kept swimming toward the group.

"Stay in formation," Rache said calmly, "and out of each other's lines of fire. Casmir, when you're done playing soccer with these guys, the forcefield, if you please."

"*Soccer*? I was keeping that one from biting off my favorite parts."

"All your parts should be secure behind that armor. Forcefield."

"Tyrant," Casmir muttered.

One of the mercenaries produced some of the rations they'd brought along—the notorious Protein Pucks, perhaps—and unwrapped them and tried to throw them at the creatures. It was only partially effective. Asger faced two more that once again recognized Casmir as the greatest threat, to the base if not to their lives, and roared and attacked, refusing to let them through. Rache stayed close, also protecting Casmir, and he and Asger worked together to create a wall the creatures couldn't penetrate.

"The forcefield is down," Casmir said.

"Good," Rache said in the middle of a stab with his dagger—it wasn't the weapon a pertundo was, but blades were proving more effective than energy weapons on their gelatinous attackers. "Asger, get out and check for danger up above. Chains, Wu, you too."

"I'm not leaving Casmir," Asger said, even though Zee treaded beside Casmir and had proven himself as adept as any of them in the water.

"He's fine," Rache said. "He's got his crusher, and I'm right here."

Asger growled, not reassured, but if he got out, he could pull Casmir up on the dock. Even if there were further threats up there, it would be easier to fight on land. He hoped.

He pulled himself onto the dock and crouched, facing the blocky shapes he'd seen from below. They were robots on treads with more than a dozen flexible appendages, each with the muzzle of a weapon built into the end. Ten of the hulking defenders lined a beach made from ice, but none of them were moving.

Asger frowned suspiciously. They had been moving before. He was sure of it.

"There are robots up here, boss," a mercenary beside him said, "but they look like they're powered down now."

"That might change when we step onto their beach," the other mercenary said, "and interrupt their tanning session."

"Kind of hard to get a tan through a mile of ice."

Asger knelt at the end of the dock—it was made out of ice and metal but wasn't slippery. "Casmir, give me your hand." He could make out the top of Casmir's helmet through the water—and could also see more of those creatures darting through the doors. "I'll pull you up."

Casmir rose out of the water as if he were riding a geyser. Not a geyser, a crusher. Zee boosted him high, and Asger grabbed him and set him down on the deck.

The guardian robots still weren't moving. A few more mercenaries pushed themselves out of the water, but nobody encroached on the icy beach yet.

"Thank you for all the help," Casmir said as Zee popped out of the water, reshaping into a fully humanoid form next to him. "I'm trying not to feel like a useless invalid needing to be carried about, but it's not easy."

"Useless? You opened the doors and dropped the forcefield." Asger pointed at the massive inert robots. "And are you responsible for that?"

"Yes, but maybe not for long." Casmir winced, touching the side of his helmet near his temple. "More than the bots are aware of me now. I think Moonrazor is on the network, contemplating me. I'm trying to get her to contemplate all the ships in orbit instead, but the astroshamans know our teams are down here—and have for a while."

"Comforting."

The rest of the mercenaries gathered on the dock, making it tight. Rache strode onto the beach and up to one of the robots, and knocked on its metal treads.

"You could let that one go long enough for it to eat him," Asger muttered.

"Robots don't eat people," Casmir said.

"That would be most unappealing," Zee said. "Biological matter cannot be as efficiently processed for energy as inorganic material."

"Can it at least roll over him with those big treads?" Asger asked as Rache took out a handheld scanner.

"His armor would protect him from being crushed," Casmir said.

"Darn."

"I'd appreciate it if you two picked another channel to blather on if you're going to contemplate my death." Rache glared back at them, then walked toward one of two identical round tunnels that had been drilled into the ice. "I'm reading life forms in that section of the complex." He pointed off to the right. "And I'm reading the gate's unique signature in that half." He pointed to the left.

"Are we close enough that it might be affecting us with the pseudo radiation?" Asger asked.

"Yes." Rache headed down the tunnel toward the gate. "I was afraid of that."

A soft clank sounded as the *Eagle* docked to the airlock off the cargo hold in the *Machu Picchu*. The *Maze Runner* had skulked off hours earlier.

Qin hadn't left the area. She was resting and munching on *chicharrones* and vita-bars that she'd brought along while trying not to worry about her fate. She had helped the Kingdom scientists, so their military shouldn't hold a grudge against her, but since she needed a ride, she needed them to be willing to take her on board. She'd also done good deeds on Odin, but she didn't know if the soldiers on this warship would know of them. Or be able to look past her fur and fangs.

Bonita and Johnny walked in, Johnny carrying his prisoner over his shoulder, the man once again unconscious. Qin didn't know where Captain Amazing had been for the last few hours, or where Bonita and Johnny had been either. She hadn't wanted to bother them. Scholars Kelsey-Sato and Beaumont had been in and out of the hold, dragging in crates of equipment they wanted to take with them.

Qin wondered what would happen to the *Machu Picchu*. If they left it here, empty of a crew or guards, other salvage ships would be along. She also wondered what would happen with Johnny, who she would keep thinking of as Johnny until she knew for sure he was what and who he said he was. She was beginning to accept it—what stranger would tell stories of an underage Asger modeling for scandalous calendars?— but she struggled to think of him as a knight. After she'd read so many stories that featured heroic knights, first riding into battle on horses and later on air bikes and spaceships, protecting ladies' virtue and valiantly defeating enemies… it was hard to accept the tattooed, snarky man as a knight.

As Bonita walked toward her, Qin put away her food and rose to her feet, her weapons slung over her shoulder. Another clank emanated from the airlock chamber, and nerves tap-danced in her stomach.

"Now we find out if the Kingdom soldiers recognize their Kingdom knight, eh, Captain?" Qin said.

Bonita sniffed and looked at Johnny. "We will indeed. He doesn't seem nervous. He'd probably be wetting himself by now if he was a pirate or other hooligan and had to fake his way aboard."

"I think he's too cocky to wet himself."

Johnny walked to stand in front of the hatch with his prisoner.

It wasn't locked, so it flew open easily, and marines in combat armor tramped in with weapons. Qin tensed, her natural instinct to leap for cover and bring her own weapons to bear. But Bonita held out her open hands, and Qin made herself do the same.

"We've already ruthlessly taken care of the bad guys," Johnny drawled as the men fanned out, making sure the area was secure. "I'd offer you boys coffee and cookies, but the ship was damaged, and its mess isn't up to Fleet standards."

"Huh," Bonita said. "He's as irreverent with them as with me."

"I think he's irreverent with everyone." Qin had seen some of his serious side when he'd been talking about how disappointed he was in Asger's past conduct. She decided she preferred the snark.

A few men glanced at Johnny, but none responded. One murmured, "Secure," into his helmet comm, Qin's ears picking it up.

None of them pointed their weapons at Qin or Bonita, but Qin was keeping her helmet on. She doubted any of them had gotten a good look at her yet.

The marines waited in position until an officer with his helmet under his arm strode out of the airlock. He walked up to Johnny and bowed.

"Sir Asger. It's been too long."

Johnny dropped his unconscious prisoner to the deck and returned the bow. "Commander Berg. I'm relieved you recognize me. I was afraid I'd have a difficult time convincing your crew of my identity."

"You look disturbingly different from the last time we met. Dinner at Baron Farley's, wasn't it?"

"Yes. During which Sir Hayakawa attempted to convince Farley that seaweed and blowfish make a superior meal to goose and cranberry sauce."

"There was a memorable cook-off that night, yes." Berg's gaze shifted to the prisoner. "One of Dubashi's cronies?"

"I believe so. His first officer told some tales."

Captain Amazing, not as unconscious as Qin had thought, glared blearily up at them. "Lies. I'll want a lawyer before I talk to you people."

"I was thinking more of an interrogation chamber and a hefty course of a truth drug," Berg said.

Berg's gaze shifted toward the scholars, who'd waited to make sure nobody was shooting before coming up behind Johnny.

"Professor Beaumont?" Berg asked. "And, ah, droid?"

"Scholar Erin Kelsey-Sato." She flicked her tail.

"Oh, er, we weren't expecting you."

"Few ever are."

"Please come aboard." Berg bowed, though not as deeply as he had toward Johnny. "We have orders to take you directly to Xolas Moon where a team has already gone down to—" he glanced at Qin and Bonita, "—explore."

"I'm waiting for these people to realize we know more about what's going on than they do," Bonita muttered.

"Maybe it's safer if they don't know how much we know about their top-secret happenings," Qin murmured back.

"True."

Johnny extended a hand toward Qin and Bonita. "This is Captain Laser and her assistant Qin Liangyu. They're the crew of the *Stellar Dragon* and volunteered to help us repel the would-be salvagers. They need to be reunited with their freighter as soon as possible."

"We have to make the moon our priority," Berg said, "but we can either rendezvous with their ship afterward or drop them off at Tiamat Station."

"Yes, the moon is the priority." Kelsey-Sato trotted for the airlock. "Do hurry up. Before those buffoons get themselves into trouble."

Berg raised a finger, as if he might object to a monkey-droid charging onto his ship, but Professor Beaumont strode after her, and Berg lowered his hand. "Very well."

"Have your strapping young soldiers bring our equipment, please." Kelsey-Sato pointed at the crates she and Beaumont had hauled down.

"I'll get them," Qin volunteered, feeling useless and also like someone would be less inclined to peer through her faceplate if she was serving the scholars.

But as she strode forward, a couple of the "strapping young soldiers" did too. One glanced at her face and tripped, almost pitching into his comrade.

"What's wrong with you, Dopper?"

"That's a—" The soldier pointed at Qin. "A, uhm. She's got *fangs*, Sergeant."

Qin sighed and picked up two cases, hefting them over her shoulders. She decided not to comment and hoped the soldiers would leave her alone.

"Don't worry, men," Johnny drawled, walking over to pick up a crate. "I heard she hardly ever uses them in bed. Somewhat to the disappointment of her lovers."

"Love... lovers?" The soldier scrambled backward, almost tripping again. "*Human* lovers? But she's a freak, sir."

"She is not." Bonita strode up to stand beside Qin. "Scurry yourself back aboard your ship and go find an officer's ass to kiss."

"But—"

"You two," Berg barked from the airlock. "Leave the cases to them. Return to the ship."

Even though Qin was used to long stares and freak comments, she couldn't keep her cheeks from warming in embarrassment. She stared straight ahead as she carried the cases, hoping she and Bonita would be given a cabin and left alone for the rest of the trip. Already, she longed for the *Dragon* and her cabin decorated with unicorns, books, and other fun things that could make her forget about interacting with people and not fitting in.

Berg eyed Qin as she and Bonita passed, but he didn't say anything. Perhaps because Johnny wasn't far behind.

"I guess I have to stop calling him Johnny now," Qin muttered.

"You can if you want, but I'm not going to stop calling him Toes." Bonita walked beside her through the airlock tube.

"What if he doesn't turn out to have any extras?" Qin imagined the real Johnny Twelve Toes had been shoved out an airlock more than a year ago, so Bjarke Asger could take his identity.

"Then I'll be grievously disappointed."

"I didn't know mutants got you excited. Or is that why you took me on board?"

"I took you on board because you helped me collect a couple of bounties and didn't think it was weird that Viggo has his vacuums work to Old Earth operas."

"I did think that was weird. I just didn't say anything."

"Which is how I knew you would be a polite and obedient worker."
Bonita slapped her on the back.

"Thanks. I think."

Bjarke and Berg caught up to them in the warship's cargo hold, and
Berg waved for them to follow him.

"There are a lot of extra marines on board right now in case the
locals give us any trouble," Berg said, "so I can only spare two cabins
for your group and the scholars."

"That's fine." Bjarke winked back at Bonita. "We'll figure something out."

Qin held back a grimace. She hoped she would be able to room with
Bonita instead of strangers—or strange androids that probably stayed
up all night talking about *quasars*.

"You don't get to see me naked," Bonita said, "unless you show me
your toes first."

Berg stumbled. Their group certainly was unsettling the crew of the *Eagle*.

"My toes are legendary," Bjarke said toward Berg. "Women from
throughout the Twelve Systems want to see them."

"I don't want to know why."

"They're flexible and dexterous."

"Gross. You've been living too long with pirates, Sir Knight."

"Yes, so I've been told. Later, I'll go to your ship's church and pray
penitently for my soul."

"A good idea."

Bjarke winked back at Bonita again—without penitence.

"I'm not sure I believe *Asger* is the scandalous one in that family,"
Qin muttered.

"One wonders about his upbringing," Bonita said.

Qin didn't volunteer what she knew, since she didn't know if Asger
would appreciate the story of the calendar coming out. The *first* calendar.
She wondered if he would consider giving her a copy of that one. But
then she blushed. She shouldn't want to see him naked. It wasn't as if
a furred freak and a heroic knight of the Kingdom would ever have a
relationship beyond friendship. She should be happy that she had that
now, especially given how their first meeting had gone.

"I wonder if Asger will be at this moon we're going to," Qin
whispered to Bonita as their group approached a lift. "He mentioned
he'd gone with the warships to hunt for the gate."

"Probably so. What do you think will happen when this Asger and that Asger meet up?"

Qin looked up as Bjarke stepped into the lift with the commander and turned to face the doors.

"Bloodshed," Qin murmured.

"Truly?"

"Punching at the least."

"And here you're always lamenting that you don't have family. See how much trouble they are?" Bonita stepped in next to Bjarke and wriggled her eyebrows at him.

He couldn't have heard all of the conversation, but he'd heard her last line. "Did you just call me trouble?"

"Yes."

"That's apt." He slung an arm over her shoulders.

Since she was wearing armor, she couldn't have felt any enjoyment from the touch—she might not have felt the touch at all—but Bonita smirked and leaned against his side.

"My toes are eager to spring free from their cloistered confines," he told her.

Berg shot him a bewildered expression. Qin stepped farther away from them so that her shoulder pressed against the side of the lift.

"The confines of your boots?" Bonita looked down.

"Naturally."

"How long will it take us to get to Xolas Moon?" Beaumont asked, indifferent to toes and boots, or perhaps eager to change the topic.

Before Berg could answer, a comm chimed.

"Commander?" a female voice asked.

"I'm back on board, Captain," Berg responded.

"With Professor Beaumont?"

"Yes, ma'am."

"Good. We're boosting off to the moon now. There's been some trouble. The rest of the fleet needs us back there as soon as possible."

"Rache?" Berg asked, his voice hard.

Qin exchanged a long look with Bonita. What was the infamous mercenary up to in this system? Also trying to get the gate? Could she and Bonita end up in trouble yet if someone found out they'd worked with and even had dinner with him back on Odin?

"Among other things," the captain said grimly. "Xolas Moon has become an inordinately popular place."

"What does that mean?" Bonita wondered after the channel closed.

"That I may be busy soon," Bjarke said. "My toes may have to remain cloistered."

"Darn," Berg muttered.

CHAPTER 15

CASMIR STOICALLY RESISTED THE URGE TO ASK HOW much farther, mostly because he worried Zee or Asger would pick him up and carry him if he did. If he hadn't been surrounded by Rache and twenty-odd mercenaries, that might have been acceptable—his legs were rubbery and tired, and he was positive the endless ice tunnel they'd been walking through was uphill—but his ego demanded he attempt to keep ambulating of his own accord.

At least the floor was gritty, rather than slick, and the walking wasn't difficult. Several men could walk abreast in the tunnel. Of course, that meant that a vehicle or an army of huge robots could also appear out of nowhere and try to mow them down.

He was doing his best to keep an eye on the network, but there were hundreds, if not thousands, of nodes on there, and his attempts to pull up even a map had been met with resistance. It wasn't just that he was struggling to gain access to what he needed; there were bots and other threats roaming out there, constantly spotting his tiny little presence and attacking. He'd lost count of how many viruses they had tossed at his chip. If not for the antivirus program that he, Grunburg, and Tork had made to deal with Moonrazor's distinctive work back in System Lion, he was sure his chip would already have melted to mush in his head.

As it was, his brain throbbed. He didn't know if it was from the illness or all the effort he was expending, trying to monitor a dozen programs running at once and making adjustments as needed, but he wished he was at home curled up in bed. He would even settle for his bunk on Ishii's ship.

A shudder went through the floor, and the men ahead and behind jerked their weapons up as they peered into the darkness.

"Are those explosions?" someone asked.

"Yes. They're being set off on the other side of the base." Rache waved his scanner. "Either our men or the Kingdom men. Or both. I read hundreds of people in that direction."

"People or mech-heads?" someone asked.

"Both, I'm sure." Rache looked back at Asger, or maybe the special rifle he'd given him. So far, there hadn't been an opportunity to use it.

A loud snap erupted nearby, and even the hardened mercs jumped.

Casmir looked up. That hadn't been an explosion. It had been the ice above them. He remembered reading as a science-loving kid absorbing everything he could that ice snapped and cracked a lot in glaciers as they shifted. Hearing it overhead was ominous, especially since he knew how *much* ice was overhead.

"Keep walking," Rache said to his men.

He didn't sound concerned, but he rarely did. He would probably issue a calm, sarcastic observation as some enemy drove a dagger into his chest.

Sweat dribbled down the side of Casmir's face. He was thirsty, but he'd already consumed half of what was in the built-in reservoir in his armor, and he didn't know if the composition of the ice around them was drinkable.

He wished he could remove the combat armor. It was claustrophobic, with the insulating interior pressing against his body from all sides. If he thought about it too much, he would imagine it getting stuck on him and never being able to escape its enveloping clutches, and the claustrophobia would elevate into panic. He didn't need that here. He had too much else to worry about, too many *real* threats.

But he longed to take off his helmet to wipe his sweaty brow and rub his gritty eyes. His heads-up display promised the air was breathable if nippy at twenty degrees below zero, but he worried about attacks and figured he had better keep his head and everything else protected.

Rache fell back to walk at his side, waving Asger out of the way.

At first, Asger looked like he wouldn't oblige, but Casmir lifted a hand to let him know it was all right. He was a little surprised when it worked. It wasn't as if Asger was like Zee, programmed to protect him—and obey his orders.

"Are you wondering how you're going to get the gate pieces out when we find them?" Casmir asked, since he'd been wondering that off and on.

A few of the mercenaries were carrying large packs that had to hold more than supplies. Earlier, Casmir had assumed they were explosives or other weapons, but as they'd wound their way deeper into the ice base, another suspicion arose.

"I'll find a way," Rache said vaguely.

"You won't confide in me, eh? That's disappointing. Is it because you revoked your job offer?"

"Oh, that's not really revoked. I'd still hire you, especially now that I know you're even better than Amergin at getting into secure locations and disabling robot defenders." Rache looked over at him. "You just wouldn't be permitted to talk about silly topics."

"I couldn't talk about silly topics at *all*? If any of my previous employers had put that stipulation in my contract, I'd never have gotten a job."

"You can talk about them after-hours in your cabin, so long as I'm not there."

"That's very generous of you."

Rache thumped him on the back. "Yes."

Thanks to the armor, which made him more like a tank than his normal scrawny self, Casmir didn't pitch forward onto his nose from the friendly blow.

"Can you speak with anyone outside?" Rache waved upward toward the ice—or maybe the ships in orbit. "You're on the astroshaman network, right?"

"Sort of. I'm trying to make my presence very tiny and unnoticeable—though her bots are still finding me and attacking at irregular intervals." Even as he spoke, one of them darted in, reminding him of those biology vids they'd shown in school of sperm burrowing into an ovum, but these didn't want to make babies with him; they wanted to obliterate him, or at least scramble his chip beyond all use. He didn't *think* his biological body was at risk. Not from computer viruses. It had other problems to worry about. "I haven't tried to send any communications, since that would be akin to jumping up and down and waving flags."

"Could you send a quick one later if you have to? At that point, the astroshaman threat should be nullified."

"Possibly. Is that when you're going to want me to let your ship know where we are and that you're planning to take the gate pieces out through a hole in the ice instead of back the way we came?"

Rache looked sharply at him, and Casmir knew his guess was right. Those mercenaries likely carried the parts of some device that could be assembled to burn through however many hundreds of meters of ice were above them.

"Once we have the gate pieces, that's when I'll need to get the message out, yes." Rache hesitated, as if he wasn't sure he wanted to admit to the rest of his plan, but he shrugged and continued. "I may be able to get on the general system network once there's a large enough hole, and contact my ship directly, but it'll depend on where the *Fedallah* is and where the moon's satellites are."

"When we're ready to be valiantly rescued, I'll gladly use the astroshaman network to cry for help. Assuming I'm still alive and conscious and able to do so."

Casmir again resisted the urge to ask how much farther, mostly because he doubted Rache knew. His stomach was starting to feel queasy, and he worried he would have to puke, which he did not want to do with a helmet on. Ishii's admonition about throwing up in his borrowed armor came to mind.

Rache gazed at him. "Did they tell you what you have?"

"No."

"Do you know anyway?"

Casmir sighed. "Yes."

The Great Plague. If it had been some lesser calamity, Kim would have told him. If it had been something likely to make everyone around him sick, the crew would have been taking measures to quarantine him. Instead, everyone whose name he knew had come by to sit next to him at some point in that last hour. And Asger kept looking over at him like he might cry.

Casmir was touched that they cared, but he didn't want people to worry about him. He regretted that he'd contracted this and was now a burden on everyone, especially his friends. He didn't care that much about burdening the mercenaries. He felt guilty that he couldn't spend the mental energy to conjure wrenches to throw into Rache's plan.

"I'm not sure if I had it before," Rache said. "If not, I might look as bad as you before long."

"*That* bad? You must be terrified."

"Oh, I am. At least nobody would know if I got those little splotches." Rache waved to indicate his mask.

"You'd know. They itch. And they would get all gross under there from your sweat. Mask sweat. This is rarely mentioned in comic books about superheroes who wear masks, but it must be a thing."

"Mine is made from SmartWeave. It cools as needed."

"You might be all right then."

Casmir rested a hand on his stomach, not that he could even feel the touch through the armor, and willed it to stay calm. Maybe speaking wasn't a good idea. Still, he was curious about Rache's experience with the Plague. If he'd had it and survived it, was it possible Casmir could? Or had Rache only survived because of his clean genes and immune system enhancements?

"How can you not be sure if you had it? The Great Plague?"

"I remember getting horribly ill about a year after I left System Lion. I'd acquired my first ship and was recruiting mercenaries to get my army established. I was surrounded by experienced military officers who knew far more than I did. Many of them came from outfits where mutinies were common, and all you had to do was assassinate your captain to take his ship. I was trying to keep them together on a mission while not letting them notice that I was in a weakened state, but I had to disappear into my cabin for four days because I was puking and itching and itching while I puked."

Casmir's skin crawled in sympathy, and he reached up to scratch his cheek before he remembered the helmet. "What did your doctor say?"

"I didn't have a doctor yet. And I didn't want the men to know how bad off I was. I told them I was thinking deep tactical thoughts and would come out when I was ready to use my brilliance to pull off the mission."

"Did they believe that?"

"I don't know, but they left me alone. I survived, and we finished the mission."

"Because of brilliant tactical thoughts you had while sick?" Casmir doubted he could manage brilliant thoughts of any kind as long as he had this headache.

"More brute force and a little luck."

Another tremor shook the floor, and more snaps echoed from above. This time, Casmir heard an explosion, very faintly and muffled by distance and who knew how much intervening ice.

Rache looked at his scanner. "There's definitely a battle going on over there. It irks me not to be able to jump on the comm and get updates. I suppose I should be glad the enemy forces are occupied elsewhere."

An alarm pinged in Casmir's mind, and he turned his attention to his antivirus programs. One of the bots had altered its code and was coming in with a fresh attack. Grimacing, Casmir scrambled to combine his programs into a new defense that would keep it away.

"You said her before," Rache said. "Did you mean Moonrazor? Is she here? I have no way to tell if she's one of the ones battling the Kingdom over there."

Casmir held up a finger, needing his focus for this. A bead of sweat ran down his nose. He snarled and unclasped his helmet, risking a glacier falling on his head so he could wipe his face.

His programs wove together and repelled the new attack. He was about to turn off his chip, since they were just walking and hadn't encountered any physical threats since the harbor, but for the first time, a text message popped up on his contact.

Do not believe that I am unaware of your team or will let your incursion go unopposed.

Rache poked him.

"Yeah, her," Casmir said, remembering his question. "I've sensed her presence in the background, guiding the bots, and now... I think that's her speaking to me." The speaker hadn't asked for permission to establish contact, so she shouldn't have been able to send a message, but he wasn't surprised that she could.

"*Speaking* to you?"

Casmir waved to his chip and debated if he should answer or stay quiet. Earlier, he had contemplated trying to negotiate with her.

I deem the Kingdom the greater threat and am prioritizing dealing with them first, her message continued, *but I am aware that you forced open the doors to the emergency harbor and disabled my security robots. I do not know why you are working with those sleazy mercenaries, but it does not matter. You shall not steal the gate from my people.*

Uhm, you came into our system and stole the gate from us first. We are engaged in a perfectly legal retrieval operation. Casmir supposed there was nothing legal about Rache's retrieval attempt, since he was simply another opportunist attempting to snag the gate, but in the case of the Kingdom… *The gate ship crashed on a moon in System Lion, as I'm sure you haven't forgotten, so it was within Kingdom domain, and it had been found by our archaeologists.*

That ship crashed before the Kingdom ever existed. Just because your ancestors landed on Odin doesn't give you the right to the gate. Our ancestors created it together, using the advanced computer technology of the time, and it belongs to all of humankind, not backward shrubs from the Kingdom who consider it unholy to tinker with their genes. Half of them won't even chip themselves, so they wear glasses like dumb monkeys with tools.

Ignoring the insults to his people, Casmir latched on to what really mattered. *You believe the gate should belong to all of humanity? Anyone who wants to study it? I'm not opposed to this notion. But your actions don't jive with that. You're trying to keep it to yourselves. Wouldn't it be better to share it with all the Twelve Systems?*

That is not what your king wishes.

Yeah, but he's not here. I am. Let's negotiate. Is there anything you want that I can help you get in exchange for two-thirds of the gate? You could keep a third to study on your own.

Two-thirds! You have nothing and you think I'll negotiate with you?

Nothing? I have many things. Such as a fever, weary muscles, itchy skin, and achy joints that made him glad for the supportive framework of his leg armor, even if the suit as a whole was constricting. At least taking the helmet off had cured his head of being hot. His damp hair was freezing, and the frigid air burned as it went down his trachea, but he couldn't bring himself to put his helmet back on. *I don't suppose you'd be interested in some of my first-edition comics? There's one with an antihero that looks a bit like you. Mechofrez. Even though humanity doesn't trust her because of her machine bits, and she breaks the law and uses vigilante methods of pursuing justice, she regularly saves people from the villainous monsters sent by the super corporations trying to control the Twelve Systems. Have you heard of her? They're great comics.*

No. I would give you none of the gate, not even if you offered the most scintillating and tastiest data. We need it all.

Why is that? Didn't you say that it belonged to all of humanity? To study?

Casmir was aware of her prodding at his defenses as they spoke and realized that was the only reason she'd sent a message. To distract him.

He braced himself for another assault. He wasn't disappointed. His brain seemed to vibrate at the waves of attack bots battering the shores of his chip like a tsunami.

As he struggled to weave together defenses once again, scraping through his files for something new he could layer on that would further wall off his chip, the cold and the chatter of the mercenaries around him seemed to be too much, almost as much of an assault on his senses as the computerized attacks. He stopped walking, his vision warping around the edges as colored dots appeared, and he fought down panic—and what he feared was an incipient seizure. If he passed out, Moonrazor would have free rein to wreak havoc on his chip.

His breaths came in quick pants, and he focused on repelling her. Gradually, the tsunami weakened, pushed back beyond his mental breakwater. He forced himself to suck in cold shaky breaths, trying to slow his heart.

Is that little chip your only cybernetic part? You are impressive for a completely biological being.

Thanks. Casmir gripped his knees, focusing on the ground and willing his vision to normalize. *I wish more women told me that. You forgot to answer my question. If you believe all of humanity should have the right to study the gate, why hoard it for yourselves?*

We are not going to study it. We are going to use it.

"Casmir," Asger said, a hand resting on his shoulder. "Are you all right?"

Use it? How? It's only one gate. It would have to be taken to another system and tied into the existing network to be of any use. Which could potentially *disable* the existing network if anything went wrong. Casmir shuddered. *Do you know how to do that? You'd never get permission from the other governments to tinker with their gates.*

We do not need to ask for permission. We already have a ship ready to transport the gate as soon as we've proven it is viable. And we've taken control of the gate in System Stymphalia. If you irritate us, your prince will not make it back from his engagement ball.

"The astroshamans control the gate in System Stymphalia?" Casmir blurted aloud. "Has that been on the news and I've missed it or...?"

Rache looked back at Asger and then at Casmir. "The Miners' Union and the six major governments of that system have joint control of their gate. I haven't heard anything on the news or from my intel man about it." Rache squinted at Casmir. "She may be feeding you false information to throw you off. Why is she even talking to you?"

Good question. Why would Moonrazor volunteer information to him? Surely, not because he was asking nicely and had compared her to a comic book hero.

"Is the prince in System Stymphalia?" Casmir asked Asger.

"The last I heard, Jorg was heading off to meet a princess for a potential marriage his father is arranging for him," Asger said. "Her family is in that system. Why? Is Moonrazor threatening him?"

"Sort of. She says they control the gate to the system."

"Are you sure she's not just talking to you in order to locate you through the link?" Rache asked.

Casmir shook his head, then wished he hadn't, for his headache intensified. "She knows exactly where we are. She's prioritizing the Kingdom over some sleazy mercenaries. Her words."

"Tell her to come here and call me that to my face," Rache growled. "Or talk to my chip if she's too lazy."

"Keep your chip offline," Casmir said more sharply than he intended. But the fear that Moonrazor would attack someone else in the group who didn't have all the defensive programs downloaded and customized that he did sent fear rolling through him.

The chips couldn't be used to control people or anything that dastardly—the chips could only receive neural commands, not send them—but who knew what mayhem she could cause?

"We're all offline," Rache said. "Like you said in the sub. We're obedient mercs."

Asger snorted, then patted Casmir gently on the shoulder. "Put your helmet back on. You don't look well, and that air is too cold to breathe."

The air wasn't what was trying to put his brain on the fritz. As cold as it was, it was the only thing helping to clear his mind and cool down his fevered body.

They are simple compared to you, Moonrazor said, switching tactics when she didn't get a response about the prince. *You should accept cybernetic upgrades and improve your human body, or even leave it behind completely and upload your mind to an android form. I've read about you. I know you have health weaknesses.*

Casmir closed his eyes, trying not to find that chilling. He remembered the way Rache, after reading about him, had set up the perfect attack to trigger a seizure.

We have the means to do a number of surgeries here, she continued. *Agree to renounce the Kingdom and join us, and I'll give you a position of power among the astroshamans. You are already known by many of our people who watch the field of robotics. In time, they would be willing to follow you.*

Thanks, but I'm not looking to be followed, just to do the work I love. And I have a family back home. I can't leave to go to, ah, where did you say you would put the other gate? He tried to toss the inquiry in naturally.

I did not say. Her dryness came through even with the straight text message. *You will find out if you join us, because we will all travel there once the gate is installed. It is not so distant a star system that we will have to wait centuries for a ship to deliver it and set it up. Not that years matter much when you put aside your weak human biology and embrace the machine. Life can become eternal.*

But can you enjoy an orange fizzop?

You can't enjoy one of those if you're fully human. Dreadfully sweet.

Alas, I fear we have little in common, Moonrazor.

Do not dismiss my offer. I do not make it lightly. You can retain your human body and join our order. I have suffered no health issues yet, so I remain partially biological. It is simply that most see the wisdom of giving up their frailties or at least enhancing their bodies so those weaknesses are no longer an issue.

Casmir told himself it wasn't right to feel wistful at her words, to find them the tiniest bit enticing. Though in his current situation, he didn't think he could be blamed for it.

But he couldn't trust her. She was trying to keep him from disturbing her network and her facility, from helping the mercenaries take the gate. He shuddered at what she wanted to do with it, not only keeping others from studying it but using it in a way that might destroy the existing gate network. What if the astroshamans broke something when they tried to add a new node? What if the network went down forever, isolating humans in their own systems?

"Pick him up and carry him," Rache said, and Casmir realized they'd been discussing him. "We have to keep moving. The Kingdom schlubs won't keep our enemies distracted indefinitely."

"They're not schlubs," Asger said coolly.

"Pick him up anyway. You or Zee. I don't care, but we can't stay here."

Could you not rebuild the gate if we left you a third? Casmir knew that would take longer, and Moonrazor would find it unappealing, but he would be remiss if he didn't use this opportunity at communication to negotiate. *If you let us take two-thirds to share with others who wish to study it, I think I could get both the mercenaries and the Kingdom troops to leave your base alone. I know they're doing damage.*

Damage to a material place that will matter no longer once we are gone.

But you won't be able to leave for decades, right? The closest star system to Stymphalia is twenty years away with known spaceship-drive technology. You need a place to stay until then. Do you want to fight all of humanity because they're angry with you for stealing their gate? What if your robot ships arrive and install it, but there's nobody left to go through because humans rose up and annihilated astroshamans? Out of anger and fear and resentment?*

Casmir expected a flippant comment, since she had been indifferent to his words so far, but she did not answer right away.

Zee hefted him around the waist and slung Casmir over his shoulder. Casmir thought about protesting and saying he could walk, but he let himself go limp. There was so much else to concentrate on. As unmanly as it was, he let himself be carried.

That is a possibility, Moonrazor finally replied. *We will likely continue to have to find new hiding places. We have bases out at the edges of the systems already, far from the suns, where few but mining ships venture, but you are right that it is inconvenient to be hunted.*

Why choose to ostracize yourselves? Why leave the Twelve Systems? Is there not a place for you here where you can be happy?

You are naive.

If we've failed to accommodate you… Casmir wasn't sure what *we* he meant. The astroshamans didn't have a presence in the Kingdom, so he wasn't speaking of his own government, though surely their disapproving attitudes about core changes to humanity couldn't help anything. *Perhaps something could be done. Negotiations. Treaties. Just because you're choosing to make modifications to your bodies doesn't mean you're any less human. There should be a place for you here in the Twelve Systems.*

We are different. Humans don't like what's different. I think you know this. You are not like those around you.

It made him uncomfortable how well she seemed to know him. There shouldn't have been that much about him available on the System Hydra public network. Little more than a bio and some of the papers he'd published should have been transmitted beyond System Lion. Unless she had another source.

I am different, but I have a place where I belong. There are people who are comfortable enough in their own skins not to feel threatened by that which is different. Assuming different doesn't set itself up in the position of enemy.

Human beings are very good at creating *enemies,* Moonrazor replied, *whether different sets itself up to exist in that position or not. Different is always a target.*

If that's happened, let's change it. We can work at being more accepting of astroshamans, and perhaps some of your people could work at being benevolent ambassadors who help people realize you're not a threat. Newly appointed President Nguyen is hosting talks with government representatives from this system right now. If you went in peace to discuss finding a place where your people could be comfortable, they might be open to listening. I could go with you.

If he survived the Plague… and if Jager's minions didn't haul him back to Odin by his ear.

While your soldiers take the gate.

They're not my soldiers. They kidnapped me. Also, my desire is as I said, for the gate pieces to be divvied up among all who want to study them. The astroshamans could certainly keep a portion of them.

Generous of you.

Casmir exhaled slowly, struggling for patience—and an argument that would work—when he was hot and flushed and thirsty and sick with his head pounding.

Unfortunately, I doubt you have the power to make the deals you're proposing, she added. *Though I am beginning to wonder if you're responsible for the legion of ships now orbiting our moon.*

It's true that I don't have power—I am a simple robotics professor—but if you voluntarily surrendered the gate to share with others, except for a few pieces you could keep to study, the various governments would realize they owed their acquisition to you. I'm positive they would all prefer to have a piece of the gate, rather than see it leave our systems forever.

Perhaps, but if they are able to one day build their own gates, then our new system might simply turn into the next system humanity invades. We do not wish to be followed, Professor. We have tried to find a place here, and we are done trying. We are better than those who squabble like the apes they still are. We have risen above that. We seek to leave humanity behind when we go. To take all of those who embrace the next evolution and not to be pestered by the savage animals who do not. Further, it would take much longer if we had to build a new gate from scratch, using a single piece as a model. Each piece, as we have already learned, has a different function. They are not interchangeable, and they are not simple. To place this gate in another system would be a much shorter path to our goal. We already have a ship prepared and ready to start this mission.

A chill went through Casmir's fevered body, as he realized that time may not be on their side. Time *definitely* wasn't on his side.

Once all the astroshamans travel through the gate to our new chosen system, we will deactivate it once again, leaving humanity here to its own squabbles, and we will create our own civilization and never worry about irrational human beings again. I give you one last chance. Stop fighting me. Let us take care of these intruders—if there are some that are close to you that you want spared, I will allow it—and join us. Your family will be welcome to come. All those who embrace the astroshaman way are welcome. We care nothing of origins or color or language or religion, only that you agree that this is the logical next evolution for humanity and help us pursue it.

Another rumble went through the base, barely noticeable since Casmir wasn't standing on the floor now, but it spurred fresh cracks in the ice. Someone cursed as a fissure several inches wide opened in front of him. Other mercenaries hopped over it without a word.

"Let me know if you want your helmet, Casmir," Asger said quietly.

He was walking behind Zee, keeping an eye on them. On him.

"In a minute," Casmir murmured, his cheek pressed against Zee's cool back.

He was so hot, so miserable, that the temptation to put aside his human body for another alternative was real in that moment. A lot of the astroshamans did mind transfers into android bodies, so Moonrazor probably *did* have a workshop here capable of performing that operation.

He shouldn't trust her, but what if she meant what she was offering? What if this was a way to continue on, to live? In a sense. He would be like Kim's mother or Viggo. Alive but not human, not really. Not anymore.

He knew he'd lose much of what made him *him* if he put his consciousness into an android body, but what if he was about to lose all of that anyway? What if there was no cure to the Plague other than to have all of his mitochondria altered, something he highly doubted could be done on the *Osprey*, much less down here in the middle of nowhere. Would he survive the trip out of here and back to Tiamat Station?

If he did undergo the transformation, what would his parents say? What would his *rabbi* say? Casmir remembered a sermon from his childhood explicitly forbidding cybernetic enhancements for frivolous reasons, and this went far beyond *enhancements*. But prosthetic and cybernetic replacements for failing body parts were allowed. If it was clear he'd been dying, might replacing his entire body be permissible? Or would he live on in that form only to be a pariah in his own community?

Casmir knew he should be contemplating the larger picture—the gate and its impact on all of humanity—not just his own woes, but with his body making him miserable, it was hard to think about anything else but his illness. His impending death.

A tear leaked from his eye and froze on Zee's back.

Another explosion sounded in the distance.

Your decision? Moonrazor asked.

It occurred to him that if she was negotiating with him, it might be because she was worried. She might fear she didn't have the resources to fight off both parties.

He wasn't sure how to use that to his advantage, except to hint that he might be open to her offer. Maybe she would relax her guard and tell him more. The problem was that if he learned more, he might be more tempted.

Casmir licked his lips. *Can you create a loaded droid here? If I chose that fate?*

Yes. We do it often. Convince your people to stop bombing us to ensure our workshop isn't damaged.

Let me talk to my friend, he thought. *My very good friend. She is one of the people I would not wish to leave behind.*

That was true, but he highly doubted Kim would volunteer to become an astroshaman with him and fly off to another system. How would she get coffee beans for her espresso maker there?

Speak with whomever you wish. I am not stopping you.

No, but you and your bots have been attacking me.

We will give you a respite, so long as you don't take any more of my defenses offline. You truly are wasting your talent as a teacher.

Casmir found the comment puzzling. What better occupation could there be? All he said was, *I will only act to defend myself.*

So be it.

CHAPTER 16

KIM PACED THE AISLE OF THE SUBMARINE, WORRIED, angry, and feeling useless. She, Yas, the pilot, and a single mercenary were the only ones who'd been left behind. She kept glancing at the seat Casmir had vacated, angry with Rache for taking him, angry with Casmir for going, and more than the rest, angry with herself for throwing a hissy fit and staying in that office instead of hugging Casmir before he left and telling him to be careful.

She didn't *think* the disease would escalate so quickly that he would die before the team got back to the submarine, but they could die out there for all sorts of other reasons. The whole party could be wiped out by the astroshaman defenses before they made it fifty feet inside. And she would have let Casmir go without saying goodbye. And Rache… she didn't know how exactly she felt about him, especially since her anger was boiling over everything else right now, but she would also regret it if he died without her having said goodbye.

She even regretted not saying a farewell to Asger, who'd become something of a friend through their various sparring practices. They didn't have anything except their desire to stay fit in common, but she would be sad to lose him.

"Damn it, Yas," she said when her pacing took her by sickbay as he stepped out and she almost crashed into him.

He held his hands up. "Sorry."

"I'm not mad at you," she said, realizing she had sounded snippy about the near-bump. No, she was snippy about this whole situation.

"Are you sure? Because it sounds like you are." He smiled, but it was fleeting. He was probably worried too.

"I'm mad at *him*."

He lowered his hands. "I know. If it makes you feel better, he could also contract the Great Plague."

"That wouldn't make me feel better. I wouldn't wish that on anyone."

"Ah, I wasn't certain how much vitriol you felt toward him currently."

Kim shook her head. "He's probably already had it anyway."

"I don't know if that's true or not. He's one of *many* of my mercenaries who doesn't show up for physical exams, even when I request it."

"Are exams optional in mercenary outfits?"

"They're not supposed to be. I may have to talk to Rache about enforcing that."

Kim doubted a routine exam would have analyzed a person's various antibodies regardless. "It does seem like he would have gotten it before, since he's been traveling all over the Twelve Systems for the last ten years. It could have been a fluke that Casmir ran into it his first time out of System Lion, but the records tell us that it exists in pockets and does show up from time to time, occasionally finding someone descended from a nomad or rebel who didn't allow his or her mitochondria to be altered. Mitochondria are passed on through the mother, so it would depend on her ancestors."

Yas rubbed his chin. "I saw it in the hospitals of Tiamat Station a couple of times. Our station is such a hub that it gets traffic not only from all over System Hydra but from people coming to visit from other systems."

Kim paused to consider the ramifications of what she'd proposed. "If Rache has had it and survived it—it seems like all the immune amplifications he's done and his overall good health would have given him better odds than most—he would have antibodies against the virus and be immune to a reinfection, right?"

"I'd have to check the literature, which is unfortunately not available to me as long as we're buried down here without network access, but I believe that people who did survive rarely caught it again."

"Since he and Casmir are genetically almost the same, it might be possible to borrow some of Rache's antibodies and inject them into Casmir."

Yas nodded. "That might help him fight it off more quickly."

"Now I wish I'd asked Rache if he'd had it instead of yelling at him."

"You weren't yelling; you were talking sternly."

"That's how I yell." Kim went back to pacing. "You don't have a blood sample of his along, do you? I tested his mitochondria back on

Skadi Moon, and I tested him for a lot of diseases, but I don't think I looked for antibodies to the Great Plague. I got distracted by his unaltered mitochondria. And since hardly anyone gets the Great Plague anymore, at least in the Kingdom, why would you look for antibodies?"

"I don't have a blood sample. We could comm them and ask him to send a man back with one, but I don't have a laboratory here, so we might not be able to do anything."

"We'd have to get back to the *Osprey* and Dr. Sikou. Her labs are decent." Kim stopped pacing and looked through the open hatchway to navigation. The two mercenaries were seated up there.

"I doubt they're going to take us all the way back out and invite a Kingdom warship to come down and pluck us up," Yas said dryly.

"There's no point until we have the blood and find out if he had the Plague." If Kim *did* know and had the sample, she would do whatever it took to get it back to the lab on the *Osprey*. She could be working on that with Dr. Sikou instead of being useless down here. "I'm going to see if we can comm him."

She headed to navigation, wishing she had access to a network for chip-to-chip communication, so she could message Rache directly—and check in on Casmir.

The men eyed her warily when she stepped into the hatchway.

"I need to send a message to Rache." She waved at the comm. "Will you open the channel?"

"We have orders to keep the comm closed because those mech-heads are sending viruses."

"It would only take a minute. Not even that. You can close it down again afterward."

"Sorry, lady." The pilot smirked at her. "You'll have to wait until the captain gets back to tell him what a sexy stud he is."

"He's in danger of becoming a dead sexy stud."

She almost told them about the Plague but caught herself. Even if most people were immune to it, there was still a fear of it, memories of stories from long ago, along with a more real fear of current deadly diseases that were easily spread from person to person. She didn't want to say anything that would prompt them to get scared and take some stupid action, like leaving without Casmir.

"Yeah?" the pilot asked. "You going to yell at him about your sick friend again? I doubt any harpy's going to slay him with her hot breath."

Kim didn't reply. She already regretted that she'd argued with Rache in front of his men. It wasn't as if they were Kingdom soldiers, sworn to obey the king and those above them in their chain of command. It was surely only his reputation and the regular pay he gave them that kept them in line. Rache had deserved being yelled at, but not out in the open.

A faint shudder coursed through the submarine.

"Those creatures attacking again?" the other mercenary asked, tapping his gauntleted fingers on a rifle in his lap. "We're going to run out of rations to fling out to them."

"Maybe we can poison the next batch, but no, they're down on the bottom of the harbor eating some food the men threw out. It looks like…" The pilot leaned forward and checked his instruments. "We're nestled up to one of those pillars so we don't float away. I think the vibrations came to us through it."

Another faint shudder rattled the submarine.

"Our men must be using explosives." The mercenary sighed wistfully. "They've already seen more action in a few hours than we have all month. Why'd I have to stay behind?"

"To guard me and the doc. And the boss's harpy."

Kim closed her eyes. How did Rache manage to live among these people?

She was tempted to pull up the book he'd wanted to discuss and finish reading it, but she didn't think she could concentrate. She was worried about Casmir and wanted to find a way to help him. Rache would, she was certain, give her a blood sample, but not until he returned. Was there anything she could do from here to help them along on their mission?

Her gaze drifted toward the ceiling, and she wondered how much ice was above them. Enough to block communications with the orbiting ships and network signals from the moon's satellites. But it had to be possible to drill or use weapons to melt a hole in it—that was how they'd entered the ocean, after all.

"Sit down, woman," the pilot said. "You're not going anywhere and not doing anything. Might as well stop breathing all over our necks. Maybe the doc needs you to yell at him. He gets lonely."

"I'm sure he does," Kim murmured and headed back to her seat to mull over possibilities.

Kim, can you hear me?

She halted in the middle of the aisle, gripping the back of a seat. *Casmir? How are you contacting me? My chip is off.* She checked it and found it online, though the only network she could have accessed—the astroshaman one—was locked to her.

I know. I turned it back on remotely.

I didn't think that was possible.

I know your model and ident number. I'm sorry, but I needed to talk to you.

It's a good thing you're not a supervillain working for the other side.

Kim noticed the pilot frowning back at her, and she took a seat. They shouldn't be able to tell that she was using her chip to communicate, but she would prefer they not guess that she was doing something odd. It wasn't as if they trusted her. To them, she was a prisoner.

Funny you should bring that up. Moonrazor has asked me to give up my frail human body, transfer my consciousness to a droid, and join her side.

I can't believe you needed to message me to ask my opinion on that. Kim frowned.

I didn't. I need your opinion on something else.

Because you've already decided that Moonrazor is manipulating you and you'd be foolish to consider any offers she makes?

She's manipulating me? I was trying to manipulate her.

Don't. Women are better at that than men.

You never manipulate me. Do you?

No, but I'm not a good example of womendom.

You're a delightful example. But I do need an honest answer to my next question, please.

Kim closed her eyes, already suspecting what was on his mind. *Go ahead.*

I know I have the Great Plague, and I know it's bad because you didn't tell me. Am I right in that there isn't time to get me somewhere for the mitochondria modification?

She didn't want to hesitate, lest he think her evasive, but she carefully considered her answer, in case he truly *was* considering Moonrazor's offer. She didn't want to imagine his human body dying and leaving behind something akin to her mother. The distant mother who'd never known how to share feelings and likely no longer experienced anything beyond scientific curiosity. Computer-like scientific curiosity.

And that was a best-case scenario, if the transfer worked. It sometimes did not.

I'm not positive there's not *time,* Kim said. *It depends how quickly you finish up and get out of there so we can get you back to the* Osprey.

Does the ship have the capabilities to do the mod?

I don't think so. Tiamat Station should. We're going to have to head there anyway to help anyone who's exposed to the gate, so Ishii can't object to the trip.

I'd like to think he wouldn't anyway, but I suppose Ambassador Romano would. He'd want to flush me out the nearest airlock for some bounty hunter to pick up and deliver to that skanky prince.

We wouldn't allow that.

It's three days back to the station. Casmir hesitated. *Is that enough time? If I were able to get back to the ship in the next day? Kim, I feel really... not good.*

I know. I'm sorry.

Sorry that I feel bad or sorry because four days is too long?

Sorry this happened to you. I'm not sure if four days is too long. It depends on the strength of your immune system.

Oh, hell, I'll be dead within the hour.

If you're still walking, I'm sure you haven't deteriorated that far yet.

Actually, Zee is carrying me.

Just encourage Rache to finish the mission as quickly as possible. Don't worry about the gate and solving humanity's problems right now, all right? Do whatever you need to do to get out of there alive. If we need to, once we get you to the ship, we can cryonically freeze you for the trip.

Ugh, so basically you'd kill me, hope you can bring me back to life on the station, and then hope there's time to tinker with my mitochondria?

Don't give up on us, Casmir, or do anything drastic. Cryonics is an established science. Reviving you shouldn't be a problem. Assuming he wasn't too far gone when they prepared his body for freezing. That would lower his odds a lot.

She swallowed and dashed away the moisture leaking from her eyes with a frustrated hand.

Don't sell your soul to that woman to become a loaded droid, Kim added. *If all else fails, there should be time for us to do that for you on Tiamat Station.*

All right. Thank you for the information.

Wait! What for, she didn't know, but she was afraid to let him go, afraid he would, in a fevered and possibly delirious state, do something foolish, something he would regret.

Yes?

Then she remembered what she'd been wondering before. *Find out if Rache has had the Great Plague.*

I already asked him. He says he thinks he might have had it.

He *might* have *had it?* Kim curled her fingers into a frustrated fist. *Who doesn't know if they had the Great Plague?*

Someone who's afraid his mercenaries will mutiny and take over his ship if he shows weakness. And who is without a doctor. It sounds like this was a long time ago.

Oh. Kim tugged at her ponytail as an image came to mind of young Rache—young David Lichtenberg—sick and alone and maybe afraid for his life. *Well, if he did have it, his blood should hold antibodies toward the virus, and since his blood is essentially a duplicate of yours, Dr. Sikou and I may be able to come up with a way to help you fight it off better.*

Right. We'll try to get back quickly so you can check.

Don't try. Tell Rache. And tell Asger.

Why?

Because you might do something stupid like nobly sacrifice yourself for the mission or some greater good or something else equally ludicrous.

The greater good is ludicrous?

Your perception of it usually is. Promise me you'll tell them that Rache's blood may cure you and to hurry back with it. One of those two will keep your health in mind and try to make sure you live.

One of the two? You're not sure which one?

I think they both *will. I'm just hoping the odds are better if they both know. Promise me?*

When a response didn't come back with its usual lightning speed, Kim frowned.

Casmir?

Yes, sorry. I was just debating if Asger would do something foolish like hit Rache with that weapon, draw his blood while the mercenaries all swarmed him, and then try to run back to you, fight the pilot, and take over the sub single-handedly.

As he described the notion, it seemed a real possibility. To Asger, Rache was an enemy, nothing more. And he was obsessed enough with being heroic that he might find something like that plausible.

Just tell Rache if you think that's possible, Kim said, *but promise me you'll tell at least one of them.*

All right. Kim...?

Yes?

Is it selfish of me to be thinking about myself right now? And how I don't want to die? I wanted to fix things first. All the things I've done wrong, all the things that should be better about the Kingdom, and... I want to ask Oku on a date.

You're not going to die, Casmir. Kim hoped she wasn't lying to him. *Right. Thanks.*

Did he believe her? She couldn't tell. *It's not selfish, Casmir. It's human. I was thinking a lot about my mortality when I thought I was going to die from the pseudo radiation. I was also fantasizing about strangling Rache.*

Hm, would such fantasies help in my situation?

Possibly. But make sure you get his blood before you kill him.

I'll do my best.

And don't let yourself be turned into an android, Casmir.

He hesitated again. *I'll do my best.*

That hesitation scared her. She dropped her head into her lap and lamented how helpless she felt.

Qin peered out the small porthole in the cabin she was sharing with Bonita, wondering if they had reached Xolas Moon yet. She could feel the effects of deceleration mingling with the ship's artificial spin gravity.

Not that their arrival would change much for Qin or Bonita. They had been told to stay in their cabin until the *Eagle* rendezvoused with the *Dragon*—whenever that would be. The last Qin had heard, Viggo was almost to Tiamat Station where he would let the injured civilians off.

A large brown spinning arrowhead of a ship streaked past the porthole. Qin jumped.

"That's a Delgonar Cheetah from System Hind," she said.

"Eh?" Bonita was on the deck, doing some of the knee stretches the doctor had prescribed for her after her procedure.

Qin shifted and peered at another large vessel, a shadowy saucer this time, skimming past above them. "There are ships all over out here."

"At the secret moon where the even more top-secret gate is supposedly hidden?" Bonita didn't sound that concerned.

"I don't think the moon itself is a secret. Just the fact that there's anything there."

Bonita grunted. "Maybe someone will let us out of our cabin and fill us in. But probably not. I get the distinct impression that we're the pesky tagalongs that nobody wants to tell anything to."

"I'm just glad nobody's tried to shoot me." Qin didn't admit that she'd been relieved that their meals had been delivered to them, so she hadn't had to go to the mess hall, where she would have needed to remove her helmet in order to eat. That helmet didn't hide her fangs, but it did hide her pointed ears. "Are you grumpy because Johnny—Bjarke—hasn't visited you?"

"I *am* grumpy about that. From the way he was winking and talking about his toes wanting to spring free, I was sure he'd lure me off for a private meeting."

"And you actually want that?" Qin asked dubiously.

"Just once. I want to see if he's as good as he thinks he is. But now that he's Mr. Important Knight here among his people, I suppose he's got no time for lowly bounty hunters."

Qin didn't know what to say. She'd never thought Bjarke would be a good match for Bonita, whether he was good in bed or not, and she wasn't any more inclined to like him now that he'd revealed his real name. His disapproval of Asger made her feel that the man wasn't fair and also that he didn't know his son well—hadn't made the *time* to know him well.

A quiet tinny knock sounded at the door. Qin strode to answer it, guessing at their visitor's identity from the height the noise had come from. The door slid aside to reveal Scholar Kelsey-Sato.

She hopped in and, without preamble, asked, "Have you heard about what's going on down there?"

"We haven't heard anything." Bonita switched which leg she had stuck out and leaned forward, touching her toes. "About anything."

"My daughter was taken down there for no good reason, and now she and Professor Dabrowski have been kidnapped by the criminal

Tenebris Rache." Kelsey-Sato paced, her tail twitching. "And they're not letting me go down to help."

"How would you help against mercenaries?" Bonita asked.

"Not with them but with the gate, which must be what the mercenaries want. I know even more about it than Beaumont. He's just more trusted by Jager since his family is noble and he has fewer acquaintances outside of the Kingdom. I have done nothing against the crown though. It's frustrating. So what if I know numerous archaeologists from around the systems, and some of them have tried to contact me today? Did you see all the ships out there?" Kelsey-Sato pointed toward the porthole without looking at it herself. "They're mostly research craft. I heard the Fleet warships have been threatening them and telling them to go away, but their captains keep pointing out that the Kingdom has no right to be in this system and certainly no right to warn people away from a free moon."

Bonita grunted in what might have been agreement or indifference. It wasn't as if this had anything to do with her. Or Qin. But Qin was concerned about the kidnapping report. She considered Kim and Casmir friends now—and was Asger down on that mission too? Had he also been kidnapped?

Even though Qin would like to think that Rache wasn't truly a threat to them, she didn't know that. He'd worked with them once, but that had been because he owed Kim a favor. As far as Qin knew, he didn't owe anyone anything now and would be out for his own best interests. Or to thwart the Kingdom's best interests.

"Is there anything we can do?" Qin asked Kelsey-Sato.

Bonita shot her a don't-be-helpful look.

Qin shrugged back. "Maybe when Viggo finishes up and comes back here, and we have access to your ship again, we could take Scholar Kelsey-Sato down."

"Only if you've got a submarine." Kelsey-Sato kept pacing. "They went under the ice."

"We don't even have a bathtub," Bonita said. "Viggo's people—the designers of the ship—were big into showers and saunas and salt crystals."

"None of that would be helpful," Kelsey-Sato said, "but perhaps if your ship came, we could negotiate from a neutral position. I do wonder… Did you hear about the new president of Tiamat Station? Linh Nguyen? We went on a dig together in System Augeas once, and I still consider her a friend. I wonder…"

Another knock sounded at the door, this time from someone as tall as Qin.

"What now?" Bonita snapped. "Unless you're bringing us the dessert you forgot to add to that loathsome lunch meal, we're not interested in anything you have."

The door slid open, and Bjarke stepped in, clad in Kingdom combat armor, with his helmet under his arm, a pistol at his belt, and a rifle on a strap over his shoulder. He had shaved and trimmed his hair. He still had the tattoos, but he no longer looked like a pirate. He didn't exactly look like a knight, since that wasn't their traditional armor, and he lacked the trademark pertundo, but he did appear far more reputable.

"Not interested in *anything* I have?" Bjarke lifted his eyebrows. "Dear Laser, I'd hoped that absence would make the heart grow fonder, not make the heart forget."

"Where have you been?"

"Being usurped into a mind-numbing hierarchy of Kingdom problems. I regret that I can't make my absence up to you by inviting you to a nice dinner tonight—you say you haven't been getting desserts?—but I'm being ordered to take Professor Beaumont down to the moon to stage a rescue mission and try to get him to the gate."

"You have a submarine?" Kelsey-Sato asked.

"The captain of the *Osprey* has two left. We're shuttling over to head down with his team."

"You should take me," Kelsey-Sato said. "My daughter is down there."

"And me," Qin said. "My friends are down there."

Bjarke regarded them and then Bonita, who was still doing her stretches.

"Don't look at me," she said. "I don't want to pick a fight with astroshamans."

"Viggo would be disappointed if you didn't volunteer to rescue Casmir," Qin pointed out.

Bjarke lifted a hand. "I'm afraid I'm not taking volunteers. I'm not in charge of the mission."

"Then what are you doing here?" Kelsey-Sato crossed her arms and glared up at him.

"I came to see Laser."

"Who?" Kelsey-Sato asked.

"That's me. And I'd prefer it if you not point out how unlikely a nickname that is for an old lady doing stretches on the floor."

"You're not old," Bjarke said before Kelsey-Sato spoke. "And it's clear that you're doing those stretches for me. So that you'll be limber when we... compare toes."

"If you'd wanted to compare toes, you could have visited last night. Or the night before."

"I was dragged into meetings. And I had roommates." He quirked an eyebrow at Kelsey-Sato. "As did you." He extended a hand toward Qin. "Perhaps we shouldn't have let that sergeant figure out the accommodations."

"I'm a perfectly acceptable roommate," Kelsey-Sato said.

"You don't sleep. Neither does Beaumont. You share snippets of what you're reading with each other aloud."

"So? We're academics."

"You share snippets of what you're reading with each other aloud *all night*. And giggle about it."

"I'm certain that's more civilized than whatever you and *Laser* would have been doing all night."

"Bjarke..." Qin wasn't sure if she should call him that since he hadn't invited her to use his first name—or real name—but she refused to *sir knight* him. "I'm a good fighter. You should take me. We heard some of our friends were kidnapped. I'd like to help retrieve them. I'm as useful to have along as any Kingdom soldiers. I'm sure of it. And I could keep an eye on Scholar Kelsey-Sato if she goes."

"I don't need anyone keeping an eye on me. I'm much older than I look, I'll have you know."

"I meant to protect you."

"Like a bodyguard?" Kelsey-Sato looked Qin up and down.

"Yes."

"I've never had a bodyguard. I accept your offer."

Bjarke pushed his hand through his hair. "Laser..."

"What do you want me to do?"

"Tell them they're not coming."

"You can take them with you, or when the *Dragon* gets here, we can randomly show up and get in the way of your mission." This time, Bonita didn't point out the lack of a submarine in the freighter.

"I don't have the authority…" Bjarke started.

"Sure you do. You're a knight, right? Just walk up with them at your side, say they're your assistant squires and there to hold your weapons. You're taking more than *that* to deal with Rache, aren't you?" Bonita waved at his rifle and pistol. "He's cybernetically enhanced."

"You can't have a monkey for a squire. Or a, a—" Bjarke waved at Qin, and she folded her arms over her chest, waiting for the descriptor he would settle on. "*Girl.*"

"No girls or monkeys allowed?" Bonita asked. "How ever is the Kingdom going to get past its primitive backward ways if only male humans can become squires?"

"May I speak with you alone? I only came to say goodbye to you in case your ship arrived and you left before I'm done down there."

"You can speak with me alone if you agree to take them." Bonita smiled sweetly at him and shifted into a new stretch that managed to thrust her breasts outward. Impressive, considering they were leg stretches.

Judging by the direction his eyes shifted, Bjarke noticed. "I'm not in charge."

"Squires, my dear pirate." Bonita pushed herself to her feet and offered her hand. "Tell anyone who objects that they're along to carry your weapons."

"My weapons aren't that heavy." Bjarke walked forward and accepted her hand.

"No? Don't disappoint me before I've even seen your armory." She headed for the door next to the built-in chest of drawers.

"Where are we going?"

"You wanted to speak in private. I'm taking you to the only private place in this cabin large enough to fit you."

They stepped into the lavatory together, and the door closed.

"I'm going to pack a few things. You should too." Qin waved to Kelsey-Sato, who wore no clothes, and realized she probably didn't need personal items. Or even hygiene items. "Whatever you'll need to work on the gate."

"You think he's going to let us go after they have sex?" Kelsey-Sato asked.

"I don't think they're going to have sex. I think they'll kiss now, then he'll agree to take us, and then they'll have sex when we all come back alive."

Kelsey-Sato eyed the door. "How can you be so sure?"

"Well, I've been in that lavatory. It's very compact. Isn't yours?"

"I don't know. Androids don't use the lavatory."

"Handy."

"I've found it to be so."

Several minutes passed, long enough for Qin to gather her meager belongings and wonder if they *were* having sex. When the door opened and they walked out, Bonita wore a playful smirk and Bjarke a determined expression.

"Come, squires," he said and strode to the corridor. "I'll see if I can talk the captain of the *Osprey* into sending you down with us."

Bonita patted Qin on the shoulder before she walked out. "Good luck. Don't feel bad about shooting Rache if you get the chance."

"Thank you. I'm just going to worry about protecting Kelsey-Sato and finding our friends."

"Nothing wrong with shooting people while you do that."

"You give such quality advice, Captain."

"It's because I'm mature and wise."

As Qin and Kelsey-Sato followed Bjarke into the corridor, Kelsey-Sato said, "We don't really have to carry his weapons for him, do we? I'm strong but not large. I find long things unwieldy."

"I'll carry his weapons if you polish his armor," Qin said.

"Polish what?"

"It's one of the duties of squires. I've read a number of books about knights." Admittedly, they had been fairy tales, most of them taking place in centuries long past. "We'll also need to fetch his meals and remove his boots at the end of the day."

Qin doubted a modern knight would truly wish that, but it was a task that would allow her to give an answer to the toe question Bonita was so curious about.

Kelsey-Sato pursed her lips. "I hope my daughter appreciates what I'm going through to help her."

"I thought you were going down to help with the gate."

"Yes, but it would also please me to make sure my daughter is safe."

"She will be," Bjarke said from ahead of them. "If I have to strangle Rache with my bare hands, she will be. We'll recover all of the kidnap victims."

Qin didn't say anything, but she thought about how many people on her side were gunning for Rache and wondered what Casmir would think. She also wondered if they would end up so busy fighting Rache's mercenaries that the astroshamans would take advantage and kill them all.

CHAPTER 17

A S FAINT VIBRATIONS EMANATED THROUGH THE SUBMARINE FROM explosives detonating somewhere in the compound, Yas paced and doubted himself. He'd been asked if he wanted to go along with the incursion team, and he'd opted to stay behind. Had Rache been disappointed? It hadn't been possible to tell through the mask, but now that he'd had time to think about it, Yas was disappointed in himself.

With all those explosions going off, it seemed impossible that the men weren't being injured—or worse. And what was he doing? Nothing. All of his years of education and experience, and he was back here looking at the whales painted on the ceiling.

Fear had kept him here, fear and a certainty that he, as a non-combat specialist, would get himself shot out there. But Rache would have protected him if he'd gone. He would have done his best. And Yas might have kept men alive. That was his job, not twiddling his thumbs and—

"Yas." Kim leaned out of her seat, glanced toward the pilot and corporal in navigation, and waved for him to come join her. She scooted over to the next seat to make room.

"Are you feeling as useless as I am?" he asked.

"Yes. I've been considering if there's anything I can do to improve Casmir's chances of living long enough to get back to the ship for treatment."

"If he doesn't get a blood sample from Rache—"

"I told him to ask for one. If Rache doesn't want me to punch him in the nose next time we meet, he'll give one."

Yas started to smile at the idea, but he remembered that Kim was capable and had fighting experience. Maybe she *could* get a punch in.

"You told Casmir? You're able to communicate with him?"

"We had one quick conversation." Her tone turned dry. "He hacked my chip and turned it on."

"He's on their network, then?"

"Wreaking havoc, I gather."

"I'll hope the men are doing better than I thought then. I've been worried that I shouldn't have stayed behind. I should have gone to help Rache, the men, Casmir… everybody in need of a doctor."

Kim eyed him. "I'm a little surprised you didn't stay on Tiamat Station. You don't seem to be the head-into-battle-with-shrapnel-flying-everywhere type."

"I'm not. But I owe Rache. I'm surprised *you* didn't stay on Odin. You don't seem the trail-along-with-the-military-and-follow-orders type."

"I'm not, but Royal Intelligence insisted I go." Kim turned in her seat to face him squarely. "And as long as I'm down here, I want to do something."

"What?"

She glanced toward navigation again, and wariness crept over Yas. Why did he suspect those two men wouldn't approve of whatever she had in mind?

"Time is of the essence," Kim said, "and the most direct way out of here isn't going to be the way we came. It took hours of travel to get here."

Yas lifted his gaze toward the ceiling and all the ice above them. "Are you thinking *up?*"

"Yes. If we could break open a hole in the ice above us, the Kingdom ships might be able to get reinforcements down here to help them and retrieve us more easily. At the least, we might be able to get comm messages out."

"Are you planning to break up the ice with bacteria?"

She snorted. "I wish. In my lab back home, we do have a couple of strains of photosynthetic bacteria from the *Phormidesmis* genus that decreases the albedo of ice and transfers more solar power into it so it melts faster, but even if I could alter them to thrive in the atmosphere up there, it would take decades for them to worry a hole in a sheet of ice that thick. I have a more direct and more prosaic method in mind."

"Explosives?"

"Yes. Any idea how many torpedoes are left on this sub?"

"No, and Kim… You can't start detonating explosives above the base when our men are *inside*. What happens if the ice plummets down and crushes them?"

"Not above it. Adjacent to it. We'd need to convince the pilot to move us out of the harbor here, or step aside so we can move the sub out ourselves, and then we'd also need to have enough torpedoes. Gravity would be against us firing from this side of the ice, but I assume they shoot out with enough force that they would lodge up in there before exploding. Don't you think so?"

"*No.*" When the pilot glanced back, Yas forced himself to lower his voice. "I don't know about that, but this is a bad idea. And what do you mean *we*? I'm just the doctor."

"Well, I might need a little help. Those men aren't going to do anything I suggest. I'm their prisoner." Her lips twisted, conveying how she felt about that.

Yas leaned his head against the seat. He *did* owe her for providing the vials for the cyborg-nerve-targeting weapon. But she wanted to communicate with the Kingdom ships, not the *Fedallah*, and if marines came down en masse, they would try to capture—or kill—Rache's men. Yas could understand why she wanted to facilitate getting Casmir out of here as quickly as possible, but he feared any help he gave would backfire on Rache and the men.

Not that Rache couldn't take care of himself. He might not even be perturbed by extra marines wandering around the base. He could probably use them to his advantage as distractions.

And Yas also didn't want to see Casmir die. He was the goofy friendly version of Rache, and it wasn't fair that as many people—and viruses—were gunning for him as they were for Rache.

"What do you want that won't get me in trouble with Rache or hanged by all of his mercenaries?" Yas asked quietly.

"Is there any chance you outrank those men and can order them to do it?"

"I don't outrank the fungus growing in the ship's lavatory."

"Ew."

"Tell me about it. It's some kind of mutation that resists cleaning agents. Or so the privates say."

"How about a sedative?"

"For the fungus?"

"For the *men*."

"Those are trained combat specialists. Even if I ambled up casually and managed to prick one with a jet injector, the other would pummel me into submission—or death—before I could get near his skin."

"I can block one for a few seconds. Long enough for you to inject the other. But why not tell them you're testing them for the Great Plague to make sure they have the mitochondrial modification?"

"That... might work, but they'll realize when they wake up that I lied to them."

"With luck, we'll be done by then."

"That won't stop them from killing me. Or telling Rache."

"You can tell Rache I forced you to help me by threatening to unleash deadly bacteria on the sub if you didn't. He knows I'm pissed about Casmir. He might believe I went to that length."

"Lies, lies, and more lies. I'm not very good at them."

"Neither am I." Kim shrugged.

"That's good to hear from the person masterminding this plan."

"Go prepare a couple of sedatives in sickbay. Let me see if I can send them back to you in a way that neither of us has to lie."

Yas raised his eyebrows.

"We could also stun them if there are stunners around. They're not wearing their helmets."

"I haven't noticed that Rache's men tote stunners that many places." Yas couldn't even remember seeing one on the ship. "They're more into dealing with enemies in a more permanent fashion."

"Charming." Kim pressed her lips together and radiated disapproval.

Yas hoped he wasn't hurting Rache's chances of getting the date he seemed to be angling for. He also hoped he wasn't agreeing to anything that would get Rache in trouble.

If Kim started communicating with one of the Kingdom warships, Amergin would be able to intercept it, wouldn't he? He'd been monitoring the Fleet and had caught other messages, like the one he'd shown Kim. Of course, Yas could comm the *Fedallah* preemptively and try to get them to pick up Casmir. He could help Casmir as easily as a Kingdom doctor could, so long as he had use of the sickbay lab up there.

"Go get ready, please," Kim said, her eyes intent.

"Right."

Yas headed back to sickbay, but Kim stepped into the aisle and called after him.

"You're sure I'm all right?" Her voice was loud enough that both mercenaries peered back.

Yas realized she was setting something up but wasn't sure what the appropriate response was. "Yes," he guessed. "I checked twice."

She gave a minute head nod. "Thank you, Doctor."

She headed up to navigation. Yas slipped into the sickbay nook but stayed by the open hatch, listening curiously.

"Any word yet from the teams?" she asked, her voice just making it back to Yas.

"Nope. Comms are still off."

"I guess it's good that we're isolated so the virus can't spread."

"Virus? What virus?"

"The Great Plague. Rache didn't tell you?"

"The Great— *What?*" It hadn't taken long for the pilot's voice to escalate to worry.

Remembering his role, Yas hurried to prepare two jet injectors with sedatives.

"We're probably all fine," Kim said. "Almost everybody is these days, thanks to our ancestors undergoing genetic modifications that make humans unpalatable to the virus."

"*Almost* everybody? How'd it get here if we're unpala— unpal— that thing?"

"Unfortunately, my friend's ancestors didn't undergo the transformation." Kim did not have to, Yas was sure, feign the distress in her voice. "He's very contagious and getting sicker by the minute. That's why I was angry that Rache dragged him into that mess." She paused to let that sink in, then added, "Have you two boys been checked for the modification?"

"Uhm."

"Can the doc do that?"

"Yes," Kim said. "I just had him check me to make sure. I was feeling a little hot."

"It is hot in here. Is it hot in here, Needles?"

"Uhm, maybe?"

Kim returned to her seat to sit down. Yas pulled out a scanner and attempted to look busy. A few seconds later, the two men appeared at the hatchway.

"Doc? Is there really a plague?"

Yas lowered his scanner. He also didn't have to feign distress—or graveness. "So far, it's only affected one person that we know of."

"But you're sure it's a plague. The *Great* Plague?"

"I'm sure."

"Can you check us for the thing that makes us not taste good?"

"Yes, that's easy enough."

Yas waved them forward, trying not to notice how large they were in their armor. And how much bone-crunching force that would give any punches they threw at him.

His hands shook as he pulled out the jet injectors. Even non-medically-inclined individuals might realize he was plugging something into them rather than removing blood.

He cleared his throat and glanced at their armored upper bodies. "Do you want to take your armor off? Or I can test at your necks if you want." Where they would be even more likely to notice the full vials in his injector. "But arms are handier."

"This is fine, Doc. Just get it done, eh?" One man leaned in, showing Yas the side of his neck.

Yas didn't let himself hesitate. He pressed the injector to the man's skin.

"Thanks, Doc." The mercenary stepped out to make room for the pilot, who was frowning. He'd been watching the injection.

He stepped into sickbay but pointed at Yas's hand.

"Don't you need to *take* blood to look for stuff in it? What's that?"

"I did take blood." Yas smiled and struggled to come off nonchalant. *Why* was he doing this? "These new injectors work both ways. Here."

Yas reached up, but the pilot caught his wrist. "There's something already in there. Are you—"

An arm snaked around the man's neck, and Kim sprang onto his back, pulling his chin back.

Yas was so startled he almost dropped the injector.

The mercenary cursed, reaching for her arm as he sprang backward, ramming her into the bulkhead behind him.

Yas cursed and rushed in with the injector. The pilot's head was still back, his neck exposed, but Kim grunted with pain. Yas found skin and tapped the button. The injector hissed. He ducked as the pilot tried to backhand him. A fist whistled over his head.

Kim jumped off the man's back before he could ram her into the bulkhead again.

"Grab them, Corporal!" the pilot snarled.

But the corporal had already passed out, crumpling in the aisle.

The pilot roared at Yas, hands raised, but he must have deemed Kim the true threat for he sprang up the aisle at her. She'd backed away, but his armor-enhanced legs carried him toward her in an instant.

Somehow, she anticipated his speed and got a side kick up in time, planting her boot in his torso. Yas had almost forgotten that she also wore armor. The pilot rocketed back so fast that Yas was almost bowled over. He stumbled back into sickbay as the man flew past the hatchway. A meaty thud sounded when he hit the back.

"Shit," Kim whispered and rushed after him.

When Yas leaned out, the pilot was out, lying atop his buddy. Kim jogged back and knelt, her hand in the air, looking like she didn't know if she should check his pulse or pry open an eyelid.

"I'm sure the sedative kicked in," Yas said, "and that he'll be fine."

"It's my first time wearing armor. I knew it enhanced strength, but I never *kicked* someone before while..." Kim looked back, her eyes wide and concerned.

It was the most emotion he'd seen on her face.

Yas came out and patted her on the shoulder. "They throw each other around like that all the time. Trust me. I'll check him, but I'm sure it was the sedative that knocked him out."

"All right." Kim sounded uncertain, but she rose and gave him her spot.

"Just promise me I haven't assisted you in doing something that's going to get any of Rache's men killed or captured."

"I just want to get Casmir out of here, not get anyone killed."

"I know, but sometimes, there are unforeseen consequences to pursuing what one wants."

The emotion vanished from her face as she donned a mask as effective as Rache's more literal one. "I'm aware of that. If anything goes wrong, I'll do my best to make it right. But Rache has been outsmarting the Kingdom for the last ten years. I'm sure he can handle them now."

Yes, but Rache was busy inside the base. He wasn't here. Yas hoped he hadn't made a mistake.

Asger walked beside Zee, who carried Casmir, near the back of the group of mercenaries. The distant explosions had grown less frequent, but the ice continued to snap and crack over their heads, and nobody was speaking, only glancing toward the noises and fingering weapons, as if rifle fire could save them if the millions of tons of ice above them collapsed.

Or was it more likely that the frozen white floor would break away and they would plummet into the depths of the ocean? It was Asger's first ice base. He didn't know how such structures worked.

Rache continued on and on, not hesitating when he came to intersections or tubes that looked like they could carry one higher or lower into the complex on a jet of air. He occasionally glanced at the scanner he held, but he seemed to have made up his mind beforehand and was only referencing it to double-check his route. His men followed him without questioning him.

Asger was tempted to question him, but if Rache was choosing routes at random, he wasn't sure he wanted to know. He decided to believe the mercenary had found a map of the base before they arrived. Though that supposition made him uneasy, because Asger didn't think the Kingdom men had been as assiduous or capable with their homework.

Casmir muttered to himself now and then, his chin tucked to his chest, his helmet comm off so, as he'd said, nobody would have to listen to his mindless babble. Asger doubted it was mindless, but he did worry his friend was experiencing moments of delirium. At least Zee was carrying him in front now, with his arms under Casmir's shoulders and knees, like one might tote a child to bed. Before, Casmir had been slung over his shoulder. Asger had finally pointed out that he might not be comfortable with all of his blood rushing to his head, and Zee had promptly rearranged him.

The mercenaries ahead of them parted and let Rache through so that he could walk on Zee's other side. He looked at Casmir, at Asger, and finally at Zee, who ignored him. Casmir didn't appear to be aware of him. It was hard to tell if he was awake.

"Casmir, you look like a damsel in distress being rescued from a tower," Rache said.

Asger ground his teeth, irritated at the callousness. "Better than like the villain who killed her father and locked her there."

"Her? You agree Casmir is looking feminine and damselly today?"

"Damselly?" Casmir muttered, flicking his comm back on. "I'm telling Kim you made up a word."

"Does she not approve of creative vocabulary?"

"She approves of proper vocabulary. She corrects me when I make up words."

"She might find it quirky and appealing when I do it," Rache said.

"No."

"Damn." Rache thumped one of Casmir's armored calves.

This earned him a flat look from nanny Zee. Zee didn't exactly have eyes, more the vague amorphous suggestion of them, but Asger could still tell it was a peeved look.

"Sir?" someone called back. "There's light up ahead."

"Summon some strength, Casmir," Rache said. "We're about to need you."

"Haven't you been needing me all along?"

"It's true, and you've been doing a good job—for an invalid. If you worked for me, I'd give you a bonus."

"What about letting me talk about silly topics?"

"Let's see if you can fix up this gate, and then we'll negotiate." Rache trotted forward to resume his position ahead of his men.

Asger was tall enough to see past a few of them, though most of the mercenaries were also big men, and he spotted where the tunnel opened into a large chamber, the walls still made of ice.

As the mercenaries flowed out of the tunnel, weapons fired. Asger whipped up his pertundo, tempted to race forward to help, but he was reluctant to leave Casmir.

At the noise, Casmir grumbled and shifted in Zee's grip. "Let me down, please, Zee."

"I will do so if you agree to stay behind me, Casmir Dabrowski."

"How will I see anything then?"

Zee set Casmir down behind him. "You may crouch and look between my legs. I must protect you from the threat ahead. I detect unfamiliar life forms."

Asger jogged to the opening of the tunnel—Rache and the mercenaries were fanning out, taking cover behind more of the omnipresent pillars as well as stacks of crates and rolling tool chests. A few androids and men with noticeable cyborg parts crouched behind pillars farther into the chamber and in front of the—

Asger's breath caught. It was the gate.

It was still in hundreds of pieces, the long curving metal sections stacked ten high in the cavernous chamber. They were toward the back of the vast space.

Countless hulking robot defenders similar to the ones back at the harbor dotted the chamber, but they weren't attacking. They were as inert as the other ones they'd passed. Only the androids and cyborgs were firing.

Some of those cyborgs weren't wearing armor. They should be susceptible to Kim's vials. Unfortunately, they were staying behind the pillars to shoot, and many of them only had small patches of flesh visible among their machine parts. Asger had a limited number of vials, and he couldn't waste them.

"Are you responsible for these dead robots, Casmir?" Asger called back as a mercenary darted forward, crouching to use one for cover.

"Yes." Casmir peeked around Zee. "But they're only temporarily offline, not dead. When Moonrazor gets less distracted, she could override my interference and turn them back on."

"Then I hope you'll forgive me for this."

Asger stuck his pertundo in its holder and slung the shell gun off his shoulder. Staying in the mouth of the tunnel for as much cover as it would give him, he fired at the robots closest to the android and cyborg defenders. The round exploded when it hit. His target didn't blow up completely, as he'd hoped, but a chunk of the side did blast apart. Smoke and flames filled the air, and metal shards flew toward a couple of their enemies.

Rache's men took advantage of the distraction and stormed across the chamber toward the defenders.

Asger itched to join the fray, since his pertundo would be more effective against androids and armored foes than many weapons, but he put more of the robot defenders out of commission first. The last thing they needed was for those monstrosities to come to life and attack them.

He felt cowardly standing back and picking off unmoving enemies, but he doubted he could talk Casmir into doing this. He and Zee had moved up behind him, and Casmir was gaping at the carnage, probably just as disturbed at the destruction of the robots as he would be by the deaths of the human defenders.

One of Rache's black-armored mercs flew across the chamber and slammed into a pillar with a thunderous crack, and Asger realized the defenders might not fall easily. The astroshamans had likely been chosen to defend the gate because they were good.

"She knows we've breached the gate room," Casmir said, gasping and pressing a hand against the wall. "She's trying to override me and activate these robots. Get the rest of them, Asger. Hurry."

He jerked his other hand up to his helmet near his temple—his chip.

"Is she hurting you somehow?" Asger kept firing, loading shells as rapidly as possible. He'd destroyed at least ten of the robots, but there were dozens of the monoliths out there.

Casmir shook his head. It could have meant yes or no.

"Rache," Asger yelled. "The robots might come to life soon."

Even as he focused on another one, yellow power indicators flared to life, and its weapon-arms all came up. They fanned out and fired without hesitation, white flashes of light that Asger thought were DEW-Tek bolts, but when they struck their targets, they exploded. A mercenary in full armor flew into the air as one slammed into his helmet. The explosion tore off his head.

One of the robots spun toward the corridor where Asger crouched, still firing and trying to eliminate as many of the threats as possible. Several of those arms came up, pointing in their direction.

"Get back!" Asger yelled.

He fired at the robot as he scrambled backward himself. Zee sprinted past him, bumping Asger's shoulder as he ran into the chamber.

Casmir flattened himself against the wall in the tunnel, out of the robot's line of sight. Asger's round went off, but when it exploded, it only took out one corner of the robot. The weapon-arms fired.

He expected the white bolts to ricochet down the tunnel, and he tried to block Casmir's body with his own. Several of the bolts zipped toward

Zee as he raced for the robot. He leaped and twisted in the air, but one caught him in the shoulder. It exploded, and Asger saw some of his tarry black bits fly in a dozen directions before two energy bolts slammed into the walls of their tunnel.

Ice exploded, pelting his armor. A crack ripped through the air, and the ceiling collapsed atop Asger and Casmir.

Asger's armor protected him, and he barely felt the glacial chunks raining down on them, but they buried him, regardless.

He snarled and shoved pieces away, determined to unbury himself— and hoping only a small amount of the tunnel had collapsed, not tons and tons.

The shouts of men and firing of weapons continued, muffled by the ice. Asger cleared enough space to get his pertundo out, and he switched to that, using it as an axe to cut the big slabs of ice that had collapsed on them, then shove them away. He bumped against Casmir's armored elbow and was careful not to hit him with the weapon.

Finally, Asger's head came free, and he clawed himself to the top of the pile. The tunnel was only partially blocked. The team could still escape if they needed to. Good.

He spotted Casmir's helmet and hurried to dig him out of the ice, throwing glances over his shoulder toward the fight. He couldn't see much from inside the half-collapsed tunnel, what remained of it, but he could hear the battle raging. Rache's voice remained calm as he gave orders. His men roared like bears as they complied.

"Trying to... get them... back offline," Casmir gritted out as Asger pulled him from the ice. "But I've got... her full attention... now."

"Keep trying." Asger patted him and pulled the shell gun out, knowing there were more enemies, and also knowing he might have to tell Casmir that Zee had been destroyed.

Abruptly, the sounds of battle stopped.

Asger rushed out of the tunnel, weapons in hand. The mercenaries, easy to pick out in their black armor, faced piles of rubble and still-standing robots that had stopped moving again, their weapon-arms back at their sides. Eight of them remained standing amid dozens of piles of metal that represented the destroyed robots.

Asger swallowed at how close one of the still-standing robots was to the tunnel. Less than five steps away. It looked like it had been on the way to annihilate him—or, more likely, Casmir. The person causing Moonrazor the most trouble.

"Most of the defenders are down," Rache said. "Two androids got away. We'll chase them down later. Let's finish off these robots."

Rache stood amid piles of wreckage—and bodies—in the back, as if he'd singlehandedly downed most of the cyborgs and androids. Asger felt a twinge of guilt for not having done more. Even if he'd destroyed a bunch of the robots, it hadn't been the same as facing enemies and battling them head on.

Some of his men were pausing to look around, seeing the towering stacks of gate sections for the first time. None of the pieces appeared to have been damaged in the battle, though shrapnel littered the floor all around them.

To Asger's surprise, Zee stood atop the wreckage of a nearby robot, one that had also been angling for the tunnel. Even though he'd had his shoulder blown off, he was back to his usual self. Asger had forgotten about his ability to suck his bits back together and re-form.

"I have defeated this inferior robot," he announced, looking toward Asger.

No, toward Casmir. Casmir had crept up to the mouth of the tunnel and stood just behind Asger.

"Hurry and defeat the rest, please," Casmir said, his voice strained. He gripped his helmet with one hand and wore the expression of a man with the worst headache in the universe.

"You heard him," Rache barked. "Blow every nut and screw out of these while they're turned off."

His mercenaries focused on the still-standing robots, all save the one in front of the tunnel. Asger lifted his shell gun to take care of it as Casmir gazed sadly around the chamber, no doubt wishing he could have subverted the mechanical creations instead of ordering them destroyed.

A second before Asger pulled the trigger, the robot's power indicators flared to life, far more intense than they had been before. They strobed irritating flashes of light at the tunnel. Maybe the thing was already about to explode.

Asger fired, happy to help that along. His round took it high in the torso and blew the neck off. The lights stopped flashing.

But next to him, Casmir crumpled.

Startled and afraid he'd been struck by shrapnel or an attack, Asger grabbed him and pulled him back into the tunnel, though he couldn't go far with the collapsed ceiling half filling it.

"Casmir?" Asger asked uncertainly.

His legs and arms were twitching, as if his armor was on the fritz. Only then did the truth dawn on Asger. He'd heard about but hadn't seen one of Casmir's seizures yet.

"Shit, what am I supposed to do, Casmir?"

Footsteps thundered, and Asger raised his weapon, afraid some enemy approached. But it was Zee and Rache running toward them.

"Is he all right?" Rache asked.

"I will protect Casmir Dabrowski." Zee stopped beside Casmir to stand protectively above him. "I did not observe him being shot, so I deduce there is a ninety-seven percent probability that he is experiencing a seizure."

"No shit," Rache said. "Sergeant Cabrera, get over here with your med-kit."

"Do we hold his head or something?" Asger wanted to help but was afraid to touch him. Casmir's helmet rocked about as his legs continued to twitch.

"His armor should insulate him well enough." Rache crouched and turned Casmir onto his side. "As long as he doesn't puke in his helmet."

As the mercenary with the first-aid kit arrived, the seizure thankfully wound down. Asger didn't trust a combat medic to have experience with something like this. He wished Kim were here. Even if she wasn't a medical doctor, he believed she would know what to do.

Rache barked a handful of names and said, "Get the Stellar Drill set up. Fast. Moonrazor is still alive somewhere in the compound and probably turning her attention on us." He waved at Casmir. "That was no random robot malfunction. She targeted his weakness directly."

"Wonderful," Asger muttered, watching Casmir through his faceplate.

His limbs had stopped twitching, but his eyes were moving behind his lids, his lashes flickering. Asger bit his lip, willing those eyes to open. Normally, he would assume Casmir would wake up and pull through, but with the virus and everything else going on…

What if he didn't?

"Boss," the medic said, "we lost Tango. His head was blown off. There's nothing I can do."

"I know," Rache said. "Funeral later. Do you have anything that can wake Dabrowski up? We need him to deactivate the gate, or we'll frag everything on the ship by bringing it aboard."

Asger glared at Rache, furious that all he cared about was the stupid gate. And furious that it was all Jager cared about too. Casmir was an engineer, not an elite soldier. He shouldn't have been sent down here.

"Uh, I can check his blood sugar and electrolytes if we get his helmet off. It's a chronic condition, right?" The medic waved at Casmir's undamaged helmet. "Not from a head trauma? He should wake up on his own."

Mercenaries with packs on their shoulders rushed off to an open area in the chamber. Asger had no idea what the Stellar Drill was and didn't care. He was on the verge of carrying Casmir back to the submarine so Kim and a real doctor could care for him—and so he could be someplace relatively safe.

But it had taken them hours to walk all the way back here. Even if Asger ran all the way to the harbor and didn't take any wrong turns, would it be fast enough to help?

And would Rache let him take Casmir?

Asger eyed Rache, remembering their last fight. And that he'd been losing it when help had jumped in. He might have to send Zee back with Casmir instead. Surely, Zee could run faster than Asger and never get tired, and Asger could keep Rache and his men from impeding him.

"Casmir?" Rache reached past Zee to pat his chest. "Are you going to wake up, man? What'd that bitch do to you?"

Asger jerked at the realization that Moonrazor might have done more than order the robot to flash that light. Earlier, she had been attacking his chip. What if she'd found some way to harm his brain through it? It wasn't supposed to be possible, but she was some hacker extraordinaire. Who knew what was possible for her?

"Zee." Asger stood and faced Rache. "Take Casmir back to the submarine as fast as you can so Kim can help him."

Rache rose to his feet and gripped Zee's arm. "No. Casmir is here to deactivate the gate. Once he does that, you can take him back."

Zee looked down at Rache's hand.

"He can't deactivate anything right now," Asger growled. "He's not waking up."

"Give him a few minutes."

"He could be dying."

"It's just a seizure."

"He has the *Great Plague*, asshole."

Zee plucked Rache's hand from his arm.

Rache barely seemed to notice. He faced Asger fully, his hands curled into fists. "Which won't change if he's taken back to the sub."

"It will if Kim gets him back to the *Osprey* and off this forsaken moon." Asger watched those fists and watched Rache, almost wanting him to take a swing, so he would have an excuse to fight back.

Why was Zee still here? He ought to take Casmir and go.

"You don't know that," Rache said. "He would rather do something meaningful before the end. I know I would."

"This isn't meaningful." Asger flung a hand toward the stacks of behemoth hunks of metal. "He doesn't care about the gate. He never did. He's only here because Jager ordered it."

"Jager can shove his head up his ass—further than it already is."

"Zee," Asger ordered. "Take Casmir back to the sub now, for his own good. Your job is to protect him, so protect him."

Zee bent to gather Casmir in his arms, but Rache lunged forward, reaching for the crusher.

Asger sprang and punched him in the chest, knocking Rache back into the chamber.

Rache twisted in the air, landing on his feet in a crouch and facing Asger. A pistol had appeared in his hand, and he pointed it at Asger's chest.

Asger might have scoffed, but ten of his men rushed forward to stand beside their boss, and far greater weapons came to bear on him. His armor couldn't withstand all of them. And there was a chance that Casmir would be hit.

"Get him out of here, Zee." Asger stepped forward to block Zee's retreat from the mercenaries' sights.

He wondered if it was the last thing he would ever do.

CHAPTER 18

AS KIM EASED THE SUBMARINE OUT OF ITS improvised docking spot next to a pillar, she did her best not to bump it.

Well aware of the other two submarines in the underwater harbor, she didn't want to draw any attention. A vain hope, perhaps. Unless the pilots inside them were sleeping, there was little chance they wouldn't see *Bubbles 3* scooting back the way it had come.

Would the other submarines give chase? She hoped not. With the mandated comm silence, they couldn't question her, so she hoped they would assume the pilot knew something they didn't know, not that he was drooling on the deck in the back.

"Do you know what you're doing?" Yas waved at the control panel from the hatchway to navigation.

She held up an instruction book she'd found, open to the *Quick and Dirty Navigation Tips for Tour Operators (aquatic license required)* section.

Yas shook his head. "I knew I was insane to go along with this."

Maybe she should have simply said *yes*. But as she'd so recently told him, she hated lying.

"I spent several minutes reading that and familiarizing myself with the controls," Kim said. "I've also played *Sub Saviors* with Casmir."

"And that is what?"

"A video game where you navigate your submarine through the oceans of Odin, shooting the mutant creatures that mad scientist invaders drop from orbit to attack the planet's harbors." Kim didn't mention that she'd only let Casmir talk her into playing a couple of times. She always had work to do, work that she *preferred* doing to playing games. But whenever they'd both been busy and barely seen each other for weeks, she agreed to spending bonding time engaged in "fun" activities, as he assured her they were.

A lump formed in her throat as the memories surfaced, and she bit her lip hard enough to give her mind something else to focus on. She was doing this for Casmir. And she thought he might even approve. Stealing a submarine and steering it off to blow things up after spending ten minutes reading a technical manual was exactly the kind of thing he would do.

Except that he had a great aptitude for anything mechanical, and he could get away with studying something for a few minutes and then operating it proficiently. She, on the other hand...

"We're not going far," she said, as much to reassure herself as Yas. "Just far enough that the explosions and breaking the ice won't threaten the integrity of the base."

She glanced back and caught a worried expression on his face. That made her wish she hadn't looked back.

She'd been surprised he had agreed to go along with this and wasn't sure if it was because he felt he owed her a favor or because he wasn't that loyal to the mercenaries. She wouldn't ask, lest he have reason to rethink his cooperation, go back and get another injector of sedative, and stab her in the neck while she was piloting.

"The tunnel was long and winding from what I saw," Yas said.

"I know. I'm going slowly."

"Did you figure out how many torpedoes there are?"

"Eight left. More than I thought."

"Enough to blow through a kilometer of ice?"

Kim hesitated. She'd played around with a few equations, but she was missing too many variables to solve them—she had no idea what the thickness of the ice was or the explosive potential of the torpedoes—so she was operating on a best guess. She was also hoping that the bombs that had been going off in the base had weakened the overall ice shelf above this area of the ocean.

"If it doesn't work, we won't have lost anything," Kim said. "We were just twiddling our thumbs. If nothing else, a few more explosives going off near the base might distract our common enemy."

"We might lose our lives if the mercs wake up before we're done," Yas pointed out.

"How long will they be out?"

"An hour or so."

Kim grimaced. That wasn't much time. They might have to figure out how to get the men out of their armor and lock them in one of the cabins. Would that be enough to contain them? They might have cybernetic enhancements that increased their strength.

Yas sighed. "I can dose them again if we need it."

"Thank you."

She narrowly missed a pillar as she slid them out of the harbor and into the tunnel. Fortunately, she was going slowly and had time to correct, but as she soon found out, the tunnel wasn't a uniform depth underwater, and she had to tinker with the ballast tanks to raise and lower them slightly. Which promptly made her wonder how much air the submarine had to work with.

At least the other vessels weren't moving to follow them, not yet. Would they if *Bubbles 3* didn't return? They probably knew that she— Rache's prisoner—was here, but she doubted they would guess she'd managed to overcome the two men and Yas.

Time bled past as she ponderously navigated the submarine through the tunnel, hoping none of those creatures showed up. She knew they'd attacked the men as they entered those doors, and that the mercenaries had killed a bunch of them. She didn't know if they had killed all of them, but the pilot had reported they'd disappeared after the explosions had started. Kim hoped that meant they'd been scared away.

"This looks like a good spot," she said as their tunnel opened up into the sea, a uniform white-blue ceiling of ice stretching as far as the lights reached.

"Next question: what happens to us when we start shooting torpedoes over our heads?" Yas eyed that ice ceiling. "You'll have to fire from straight below if you want them to hit vertically and blow upward, right?"

"They're guided torpedoes, so, no." Kim tapped the improvised control box that Rache's men had wired into the navigation console. "But it's just ice above us."

"A kilometer of ice is still going to be heavy."

"Not heavier than the water."

"Oh." Yas digested that. "I see. It's going to have to blow downward though, at least to some extent, right?"

"I'm honestly not sure what's going to happen, Yas. I can't access the network to download information about demolitions, and I suspect this is a pretty unique scenario, regardless. We'll shoot from a ways down and off to the side." Kim took the sub down as she spoke, empty black water all around them, and she wondered if Casmir truly would approve of this, or if he would think she was taking an unnecessary risk.

No, it was a *necessary* risk. She didn't know how much time he had, and she feared it wouldn't be enough. She couldn't lose her best friend, not if there was something she could do.

"Programming the first torpedo," Kim said.

"Grabbing my wang."

She threw him a startled look.

Yas raised his eyebrows. "Is that not an expression in the Kingdom?"

"I think not in reference to torpedoes… or nonsexual activities."

"Oh. It means I'm bracing myself."

"And your wang."

"A man's most important appendage."

Kim wondered if her erudite doctor had been around the mercenaries too long. Poor Yas. Honor bound to continue to serve Rache, whether he wanted to or not.

"Thank you for your help in this," Kim said. "And for risking Rache's ire."

"I'm more worried about the ire of those two back there, but you're welcome. If this works, will you do me a favor?"

"What?"

"I want to help a friend—you met her. Chief Jess Khonsari. She's in a lot of pain, but she won't come in for an exam."

"This seems to be a theme on your ship."

"You noticed."

"No, you told me."

Kim got the submarine into a spot deep enough that they shouldn't be in danger from debris that might drop down—or the force of the shockwave itself—and she picked her spot on the ice ceiling, tapping the coordinates into the torpedo launcher. She was nervous about damaging the submarine but reminded herself that numerous torpedoes had gone off near them during the skirmish earlier, and they'd survived. The more legitimate concern was likely that they would do nothing rather than do something horribly destructive that wrecked their craft. If only she had scientific equipment that could measure the density of the ice and suggest a weak spot.

"I'd like to help her overcome the addiction she tells me she doesn't have and, more than that, come up with a way to take away her pain. I don't know if it's from her cybernetic implants or if it's less physical and more from the loss of her family and the stress and guilt of being a survivor. Your bacteria seem so versatile, and I'm aware that intestinal microflora play a role in several mood-stabilizing neurotransmitters and neuromodulators that work on the brain. Is there anything you or your research corporation have that might help? I think she might be more amenable to taking some probiotic concoction that a female friend gave her rather than something her doctor prescribed."

"Probiotic concoction, really, Dr. Peshlakai. You make it sound like we make yogurt."

"Sorry, but you know what I mean."

Kim fired the first torpedo. It zipped outward, then arced up toward the ice.

"I might be able to customize something for her," she said. "Trauma can vastly alter the landscape of the gut. A fecal sample would give me insight into her current species and strains of intestinal bacteria, and it's very possible that some tweaking could have a positive impact on her ability to cope. But it would be good for her to have a full exam to check for more obvious issues. Although..."

Kim paused to watch her torpedo hit via the submarine's limited scanners that, according to instructions on a plaque, were designed more to help tour guides find aquatic wildlife for their passengers to view than anything else. The tip of the torpedo, even with all the power propelling it, only appeared to burrow in inches. A foot at the most. When it exploded, the shockwave barely disturbed the submarine.

She frowned at the scanner, not picking up much in the way of ice knocked away. There was a divot that hadn't been there before, but it was laughable compared to the overall thickness of the glacial mass.

Kim fired another torpedo, but her hopes were already sinking. And she was feeling foolish. Even if demolitions were far from her area of expertise, she should have guessed that the sheer thickness of the ice would make this next to impossible. Rache's people must have used a long, sustained blast from the ship's energy weapons to melt their entry hole.

"Although?" Yas prompted.

"Sorry. I was going to say that she might be more likely to go to another doctor. Maybe suggest a woman who has no relation to you or your ship and won't report any issues that are found to Rache."

"There's no reason why she should prefer a female doctor to… Oh, Rache. I hadn't thought about that. Do you think she's worried that I'd declare her unfit for duty if something came up? I mean, I'm confidential to a point with people's medical records, but it's not like a hospital setting. Your allegiance is to the captain and you have to make sure to report if anyone is a danger to the crew or the ship." Yas drummed his fingers on the back of the nearest seat. "I'd like to scoff and say that Rache wouldn't care if Jess had a few… flaws come up, but is that true? His men aren't all geniuses, but he does select people who are very good at what they do, even if killing people is their only specialty. Jess is smart and her specialty is engineering, but if she's struggling, and her brain isn't working as well as it should be—hell, there was an incident right before I left where she was in so much pain she could barely keep going. Damn it. Rache might take her off the job if he knew how much she was enduring. Or he could demote her and put someone else in charge. I'm sure she wouldn't appreciate that."

Kim listened as he muttered to himself, but she was focused on the ice. Her second and third torpedoes made the hole larger, but she reluctantly accepted that her plan was laughable. This wasn't going to work.

Nonetheless, she fired a fourth torpedo. Even if all she managed was to form a crack that went to the surface… wasn't it possible that might be enough for a signal to get through? A very, very focused signal perhaps.

"I guess I need to find a nice doctor who isn't me or related to the ship to send her to," Yas said after a reflective pause. "If she'll go."

"Don't forget my fecal sample."

"I'll see if she's willing to part with one."

"Most people aren't that attached to them."

Yas snorted. "Maybe I should have said, 'I'll see if she's willing to collect one.'"

"And ship it to me. Assuming those two men don't throttle me and Rache lets me off this moon after I waste all of his torpedoes."

She fired again. There were only three left. There was probably no point in carrying on, but she wasn't sure there was any point in reserving any either. So far, the only enemies they'd encountered had been too fast for the weapons.

"It's not working, is it?" Yas asked.

"No. I'm sorry you sedated those men for nothing."

"We'll be really sorry when they wake up."

"Don't forget to blame me," Kim said. "I forced you to do it."

"They're not going to believe that."

"The one I side-kicked across the submarine might."

After Kim fired the last torpedo, she settled back in the pilot's seat and gripped her chin. There was a sizable crater in the bottom of the ice, but it was nothing compared to the ice still above it. And she hadn't created the crack she had hoped for, not that the scanner could detect.

Was there anything else she could try? She dreaded the idea of taking the vessel back to the harbor and having to deal with the mercenaries when they woke up. Unfortunately, the submarine didn't have the kind of DEW-Tek energy weapon that the *Fedallah* had likely used.

"We could go back to the original entry point and try to comm people," Yas said.

"That was hours away."

"If the submarine has mapped our location, we could send the coordinates up to the *Fedallah*. If they knew where under the ice the base was, maybe they could—"

A beep came from the scanner, and Kim leaned forward, hoping it would tell her that a fissure had formed after all. It had just taken a while for the ice to shift and…

No, it was reading a life form. In the ice.

"What is it?" Yas asked.

"Either our explosions woke up a giant whale sleeping in the ice or…"

"There's no life on this moon," Yas said, "aside from the astroshamans' pets."

"Or there's some other heat source that the scanner is reading and being confused by."

"What kind of heat source would there be?"

Kim was tempted to take the submarine up closer so they could look at the crater through the porthole, but it might be safer to keep their distance.

No sooner had the thought surfaced than a massive red beam of light burst through the crater.

She jumped, cracking her knee on the console. An alarm wailed. The water ahead of them was boiling.

Kim lunged for the controls. They weren't close, but fear of that much raw energy blazing within sight filled her with urgency.

But before she could move the sub back, the beam disappeared. The alarm fell silent, as did the scanner that thought it had detected life.

For the first time since they'd entered the water, light filtered down from above. Not a lot, but it was noticeable after the black depths of the sea.

"Did one of the spaceships do that?" Yas asked.

"It must have." Kim checked the scanner and confirmed that there was now a hole in the ice all the way to the surface. It was eight feet wide, not large enough for a submarine to be lifted through, but she trusted it could be made wider. With that thought in mind, she took them a little closer, hoping they could get a comm through now.

"Yours or ours?"

"Let's find out." Kim flicked on the comm panel, hoping the astroshamans were too busy to target them, especially now that they'd left the base.

She also hoped it was one of the Kingdom ships up there and not the *Fedallah* or some other potential enemy vessel. She couldn't imagine who else would be flying around above the icy surface of this barren moon, but someone was up there and detected their torpedoes detonating.

It was only a few seconds before the comm panel beeped.

"Captain Rache," a man said. "Captain Rache, please report. Do you need backup?"

Kim grimaced. It wasn't the Kingdom. Nor was it anyone she could ask for help, not when she'd stolen Rache's submarine and knocked out his men.

"Any chance they'll go away if we don't answer?" she whispered.

Yas gave her an odd look. Right, these were his allies. It was probably who he'd *wanted* to comm them.

But Kim needed Dr. Sikou and the *Osprey*, someone who would care about helping Casmir.

"We're close enough to the hole that they're probably going to pick us up," Yas pointed out.

"Can you talk to them?"

"Me?"

"You are the highest-ranking man from your ship here."

"I'm the only one conscious."

"Exactly."

"I don't think—"

"Captain Rache?" The comm officer's voice took on a suspicious note.

"Maybe the Kingdom got him," someone said in the background. "We could drop a couple of bombs down that hole."

Yas's eyebrows flew up. He lunged in and hit the reply button. "Neimanhaus? This is Dr. Peshlakai. I'm down here and would appreciate it if you didn't drop any bombs."

"Doc!" That was the speaker who'd been in the background, the one suggesting bombing. He sounded relieved to hear Yas.

Kim relaxed an iota. Maybe Yas was more popular among the mercenaries than she would have guessed, and he was her ticket to safety.

"Remember that funky mole you removed?" the speaker added. "That spot is itching a lot. Is that normal?"

Yas dropped his forehead into his hand. "Some itching as a wound heals isn't atypical, but I can look at it when I get back up there. Can you fellows widen this hole so you can extract the submarines when the captain is ready? We're close to the astroshaman base."

"Where *is* the captain?" the first speaker asked, the more suspicious one.

"He took most of the men inside. He hasn't updated us for several hours, but there are lots of explosions going off. I assume he's going to want a closer backdoor out once he's ready to leave."

"You're not trying to leave without him, are you?"

Yas grimaced. "No, if I wanted to part ways from his delightful personality, I would have stayed on Tiamat Station. We're going back into the harbor to wait for him now. I wanted to make contact and arrange a pickup for when we're all ready to get out of here."

"Why are *you* doing that, Doc? Where are the team leaders? Which sub are you on? Where's Hocking?"

Yas and Kim looked toward the unconscious men in the back.

"He wouldn't have gone in to fight," the speaker added.

"He's indisposed. The astroshamans figured out how to attack those of us with cybernetic implants. I'm the only one on the sub who wasn't affected."

The speaker swore. Kim couldn't tell if it was because he was terrified of the idea or if he thought Yas was lying.

"You better not come back without the captain, Doctor," someone else said, the male voice cool. "You should have been at his side down there."

The channel closed, and Yas sighed.

"It's hard to win the love of mercenaries," he said.

"Unless they have itchy moles?"

"Yes."

The alarm on the console blared again. The mercenary beam weapon had started up, increasing the size of the hole.

Kim watched bleakly. As long as the *Fedallah* was right above them, she wasn't going to be able to get a message out to the *Osprey*. For all she knew, the Kingdom ships weren't even on the same side of the moon as the base.

And with the mercenaries suspicious of Yas, she doubted she would find safety on the *Fedallah*, even if she somehow managed to retrieve Casmir and a sample of Rache's blood. She needed Rache to survive too.

Casmir came to, groggy and with ice picks stabbing at his brain behind his eyes. He knew right away he'd had a seizure. What took longer for him to remember was where he was. And why he was dangling above the floor instead of being in a bed. Or even on the floor itself.

Back when he'd been a kid and the seizures had occurred more frequently, he'd had one when his parents hadn't been around, and he'd woken up on the floor. But usually, his mother and father had been there, gathering him in their arms and telling him they would go back to the doctor and keep trying medications until they found one that worked.

Angry voices reached his awareness. He had the distinct impression that everyone and everything was not all right, but he struggled to focus his thoughts. And his eyes. They were open, but all he saw was white, like the inside of an old freezer in need of defrosting. There was a blinking red alert on his contact, but everything was so blurry. He couldn't read, couldn't think.

"Don't do this Asger. I don't have a quarrel with you, but I'm not letting you take him."

That voice was familiar. But it wasn't his mother or father. Where was he?

"Zee is taking him, not me. And good luck stopping him. One of those robots blew him up, and he's back in one piece again."

Zee. The crusher's amorphous facial features formed in Casmir's mind. Zee. His buddy Zee.

More recent memories trickled into his conscious. The crushers chasing him. The flight from Odin. Meeting his clone brother, Rache. That had been his voice. And the other voice… It was familiar too. A knight. A knight he knew. Asger.

"Casmir Dabrowski is awake," Zee stated from right above him. "If he orders me to remove him from here, I will do so."

Ah, that was why he was dangling. Zee was carrying him like a baby. Casmir was disappointed that his parents weren't here, or someone else who cared for him as much as they did, but he was glad for Zee.

"Casmir?" Asger asked, the back of his helmeted head easing into Casmir's view. "Are you all right?"

"Just tired," Casmir said, though the words came out slurred, and he didn't know if anyone would understand them. He was nauseated, too, and hoped he didn't throw up. "So tired."

Why did he feel so bad? This was worse than any seizure he could remember. He wanted to be somewhere else. Anywhere else.

"What did he say?" Rache asked.

The blinking warning on his contact finally came into focus. OFFLINE. Why was his chip offline?

Then the memory of fighting with Moonrazor through the network returned. The rest of his memories unfurled slowly, the mission, the submarines, the gate, that robot with its deliberate strobe light.

He grimaced and closed his eyes, realizing that his new enemy—she must have realized by now that he wouldn't say yes and join her—knew his weaknesses and had no problem exploiting them.

"Wonderful," Casmir muttered.

"Put your halberd down, Asger," Rache said, his voice closer this time.

"Screw you. All you care about is him being able to work on that stupid gate, a gate that you can't possibly have any use for as a mercenary. Your thugs aren't going to use it to explore the galaxy. You're just going to sell it to the highest bidder, you traitorous ass."

"Easy, Asger. You might say something that will hurt my feelings, and then I'll have to challenge you to a duel."

"Gladly," Asger snarled.

"Step aside," Rache said, his voice icy. "Or I might remember that you punched me."

"Come any closer, and *I* might remember that you've killed hundreds if not thousands of Kingdom soldiers."

Casmir was still groggy and confused, but even he could recognize the tension crackling in the air. "Stop," he mumbled, and then repeated himself, focusing to make the word come out clearly. "*Stop.*"

The arguing halted, but he feared his order wasn't enough to make that last. He patted Zee's shoulder. "Put me down, please."

Zee lowered him carefully to the floor but kept his hands on him for support. Which he needed. He teetered and only found his balance with Zee's help, but he was able to look at Rache and Asger, who were less than two feet away from each other, glaring like mortal enemies.

Casmir wobbled forward and spread his arms. "My friends," he said, putting an arm around Asger's shoulders and stretching so he could do the same to Rache. "There's no time for fighting. I have a plan."

Did he? The words sounded honest, but he couldn't think of what his plan might be.

Then he spotted the gate, hundreds of pieces looming in high stacks in the back of the chamber, almost tottering—or maybe that was his perception, which was skewed in the aftermath of the seizure. It didn't matter. He didn't need to climb the stacks. He hoped. Just figure out how to deactivate the security system.

Ah, yes. He remembered that now. The reason he was here surrounded by all of this ice.

Ten of Rache's men were lined up, rifles pointed toward his group, and he remembered the other reason he was here, with these mercenaries instead of with the Kingdom troops.

It didn't matter. His plan could work no matter who had brought him here.

"What plan?" Rache asked.

"I will demo— *demon...strate.*" Casmir grimaced at how difficult enunciation was. "After everyone stops fighting with each other and lets me go to that gate. That's my job, yes?"

A job he would have found daunting even if he hadn't been postictal.

Neither Rache nor Asger pulled away from Casmir's hug. Asger gripped his pertundo, but he lowered it to his side. Rache lowered his pistol.

"Good friends." He patted them both on the shoulder, though he doubted that would do much. He needed to do what they had both brought him here for, and he needed to do it before Moonrazor showed up with more people and robots. Especially since his chip was offline until he could figure out why. She must have gotten through with one of her viruses, and it had shut itself down as a defensive measure. "Good friends. Help me over there, 'kay?"

"Casmir," Asger said. "I don't think you can do your job right now. You need to rest."

"But no time for rest, Asger. That way, go."

Rache shifted to guide him toward the gate. Asger either had to let go—Casmir still had an arm slung around his shoulder—or walk with them. He grumbled something under his breath, but he went along, supporting Casmir from the other side. Which was good, because his muscles were as stiff as if he'd been sleeping all night on that ice floor.

Casmir ached to be healthy and to have all the pain go away, to not need to lean on others. He stumbled as he abruptly remembered *why* he felt so much worse than usual after a seizure. The Plague.

Rache's and Asger's grips tightened, and they kept him upright. Casmir made his legs work and kept walking, even though fear burrowed its way back into his belly.

He remembered Kim's words, that there might be hope. Rache's blood might help him. He needed to tell Rache about that. And he needed to fix the gate so he could leave and get the help he needed. But how could he make his plan work?

Casmir paused as they passed another group of Rache's men. They were assembling a large tool, and he remembered his earlier suspicions.

"Ah, you are going to drill." Casmir thumped Rache's armored shoulder. "Good, good. A hole straight up? So we can lift the gate out?"

We. Rache and the Kingdom, and dare he hope more? He smiled to himself. His plan.

"Yes," Rache said, continuing past the big tool.

It was almost assembled, a Stellar Drill. Good. Casmir just had to figure out the gate. There was hope.

His helmet display warned him of an energy field ahead, between them and the stacked pieces.

"What is that?" Asger must have gotten the same warning.

"They've rigged a high-powered magnetic field around the gate," Rache said. "I ran through it during the fight and half my systems went offline."

"What for?" Asger asked.

"Protection." Casmir nodded his approval. "Against the pseudo radiation." He grimaced, knowing he'd mangled those words, but Rache and Asger both seemed to understand. "Stay outside, and you won't be affected. Until we drop it to move the gate pieces."

He peered around, looking for whatever generator was creating the field. There, in the back, a dark case hummed softly against a wall. There was a DEW-Tek bolt hole in the corner. Casmir hoped the stray shot hadn't damaged anything.

"It's right here." Rache stopped, waving ahead of them, though nothing was visible.

Casmir could feel the magnetic field through his suit. He halted and placed a hand on Asger's torso.

"You have to stay on this side. If you go in there, you'll be exposed." Casmir waved at the gate. The closest piece was by itself, and several sections were translucent, showing what lay under its housing. Strange. What had the astroshamans done?

Even though he felt lousy, he looked forward to investigating it. He wished there had been time to learn more before coming.

"I understand," Asger said. "I'll stay out here and keep our enemies away."

"I will go in with Casmir Dabrowski and protect him," Zee stated.

"Good," Asger said.

"I need my tools," Casmir said. "And a painkiller. And caffeine if you have it."

"Is that wise?" Rache asked. "Could it give you another seizure?"

"It'll be fine. I need it. Maybe ten shots of Kim's espresso will do."

Rache snorted. "I'll get some wake-tabs and your tools." He jogged back toward the tunnel where the ceiling had collapsed and started digging.

"Sorry," Casmir said. "I think I dropped my tool satchel when that fell on us. I was so busy trying to keep the robots offline."

"Casmir." Asger put hands on both of his shoulders. "You don't have to apologize because the enemy attacked us."

"I just don't want to incon… inconven… bother anyone." That word was hard too. He willed his speech to return to normal. Maybe the wake-tabs would help. They sounded like something that might be equivalent to ten shots of Kim's espresso.

Kim. Had anyone been able to check in on the submarine?

"Is Kim all right?" Casmir asked.

"We haven't been in contact with the sub since we left. You ordered that, remember? For us to keep chips and comms offline."

"Right. I remember." Casmir had been the last one to contact Kim. But his chip was still blinking OFFLINE. He couldn't contact anyone until he fixed it.

The buzz of the magnetic field bothered his ears and made his stomach queasy—queasier. Casmir sighed with the realization that he was probably going to have to find somewhere to throw up to feel well enough to focus on the gate. He commanded his helmet to unlock, bracing himself for the frigid air, and lifted his hands to remove it. They were still shaking. Using his fine motor skills on the gate, if required, would be a delight.

Rache returned with his tool satchel and the tabs from his medic's kit. Bangs and thumps sounded as the final pieces of the Stellar Drill were locked together.

"Make sure they're careful and don't bring down the ceiling in such a way that it could compromise the field," Casmir said.

"I will," Rache said.

"And if all the ice up there starts melting, be careful about the generator over there." Casmir pointed.

"We will. Here, take these and get to work." Rache held out the tabs.

Asger stirred at the command, looking again like he wanted to punch Rache. Casmir patted Asger on the chest. It would be fine.

"I will. I just need a moment." His stomach continued to churn. He'd hoped the icy air might calm it, but it didn't look promising.

"We don't have a lot of moments, Casmir," Rache said. "You hear that?"

Casmir didn't hear anything except the buzz of the field. He wasn't even sure it was truly there and not his ears playing tricks on him.

"The explosions from the other side of the base have stopped. The rest of the submarines—yours and mine—and their crews might be dead. Leaving Moonrazor and all of her resources on the way to deal with us."

"I understand. I'm not trying to dawdle. I just need…" Realizing it was inevitable, he walked a few steps away from them, his hand on his stomach.

"To pause for dramatic tension?" Asger asked.

Casmir threw up.

"Or that," Asger said.

Rache waited for Casmir to finish and return before holding out the tabs again. "I'm glad I don't have your genes, you know."

"Everyone is, yes." Casmir didn't bother washing out his mouth, just stuck the tabs under his tongue, grabbed his satchel and headed toward the gate.

He tried to find some zen calm in his beleaguered mind that had to live in his even more beleaguered body. He didn't let himself think about how maybe he should have given more consideration to Moonrazor's offer. If it hadn't meant abandoning his comrades and betraying his friends...

No, this was the only route ahead. And he prayed he could navigate the obstacles blocking it.

CHAPTER 19

THE *EAGLE* RENDEZVOUSED WITH THE *OSPREY* IN LOW orbit, and Qin, Kelsey-Sato, Beaumont, and Bjarke—an unlikely-looking group, if the startled glances from the soldiers they passed were an indication—transferred to the familiar warship via a long airlock tube. Qin had never been aboard, but she'd seen the exterior several times now, and she knew Asger, Casmir, and Kim had all flown on it recently.

She was surprised to learn they were all down on the moon trying to infiltrate the astroshaman compound and retrieve the gate.

A thrum went through the deck as soon as they entered what turned out to be a shuttle bay, and Qin sensed the *Osprey* already accelerating away.

"The Kingdom is in the middle of hunting for Rache's warship," Bjarke said when Qin looked at him. "That's why the *Eagle* was delayed in its mission to escort the *Machu Picchu* safely from the gate when they entered the system. Someone will get in trouble over that. All of the Kingdom ships are hunting for Rache now—they hope to blow up his ship or at least disable it so the mercenaries can't make off with the gate. Rache and his men are down in the moon base, too, and I heard they've been nettlesome."

A nearby soldier who was prepping a shuttle said, "Nettlesome isn't nearly a powerful enough word to describe Rache and his thugs, Sir Asger."

Qin whirled, looking for Asger before her brain caught up to her reflexes. The man meant Bjarke. *Her* Asger wasn't here, but if she went along, maybe she would see him. Maybe they would fight together again.

Bjarke walked up to the open hatch with his crew. "Is this the one taking the submarine down? We're ready to board."

The soldier frowned at Qin. "It's only supposed to be you and Professor Beaumont, sir."

"I brought reinforcements."

The soldier's frown shifted down to Kelsey-Sato.

"Don't dismiss her, Sergeant," Bjarke said, "or she'll bite your knee."

"Sir Knight," Kelsey-Sato said, "I am a respected archaeologist with hundreds of papers published in scholarly journals. I do not bite people."

"Would you smack him in the nuts with your tail?" Bjarke asked.

"If the occasion demanded it, certainly."

"You better let us in, Sergeant."

"Sorry, sir. You need to talk to the captain first, so he changes my orders. He's on the bridge."

"Time is of the essence."

"Yes, sir. The turbo-C lift goes up to the bridge nice and quick."

Bjarke's jaw clenched, and Qin thought he might try to bully or force his way onto the shuttle, but he said, "Put yourself and your things on board, Professor Beaumont. We'll be right back."

The soldier didn't object, and Bjarke strode off, Qin and Kelsey-Sato following. Qin wondered what would happen to her if the captain refused to let her go along. She would be stuck on this ship and wouldn't even have Bonita, who had remained on the *Eagle*, to speak with. Would Viggo and the *Dragon* be allowed to dock and pick up Qin when it returned? Or would the *Osprey* be too busy hunting for Rache's ship?

The lift did get them to the bridge quickly, and they walked out to the crackling static of a poor comm connection.

"...tried everything, sir," a man was saying over the speaker, pain lacing his voice. "Lost all the subs... Lost Simonek... troops trapped... trying to dig out."

A dark-haired man sat in the command chair in the center of the bridge, his elbow on his thigh, his face in his hand. It took Qin a moment to recognize him as the gruff officer whom Casmir had sniped with over the comm months earlier about robotics camp. Captain Ishii.

Several officers at stations around the bridge were looking at him, as if they expected him to spout brilliance that would improve the situation. Bjarke walked up to his chair.

Qin trailed behind, not getting too close. She'd kept her helmet on, so her features would be less noticeable, but the captain might want to see her face and know who she was. *If* he acknowledged them. Bjarke had stopped at his chair, but Ishii hadn't lifted his head yet.

"The first communication we get in over eight hours, and it's to say they've failed utterly," Ishii groaned into his hand, then lifted his head, his bronze skin flushed with anger. "Lamar, if you don't find a trace of that merc ship and blow it out of the sky, I'm going to—" He stopped, noticing Bjarke. "Who are you?"

"Sir Bjarke Asger."

"You're supposed to be on the shuttle and already out the door. Someone needs to get down there and…" Ishii's gaze trailed to the comm station, the weak static still spitting out, though the words had stopped. "Hell, I don't know. Maybe there's no point now."

"Is Asger down there?" Bjarke asked quietly. "William Asger."

Ishii squinted at him, and a light sparked in his dark eyes as he seemed to make the connection for the first time. "He was kidnapped with Sato and Dabrowski."

"Does Rache still have them?" Kelsey-Sato asked.

Ishii looked over at her with a frown. Qin couldn't tell if he knew she was related to Kim.

"The astroshamans could have them now. I don't know. The commander thinks they're dead. They were taken almost a day ago, and it's been chaotic and crazy since then."

Kelsey-Sato grew corpse still.

Bjarke clenched a fist, his face going rigid.

"That's the first report that's gotten through the ice," Ishii continued. "There are explosives going off down there, and they've created fissures. If we're right over them, we can get comm signals."

"If bombs are going off, they're still fighting." Bjarke sounded like he was trying to convince himself. "Send me down. I want to take Kelsey-Sato and Qin along with me."

"Who is Qin?"

"That's Qin." Bjarke pointed at her. "She can break a mercenary or astroshaman in half with her bare hands. She helped me get the scholars off the *Machu Picchu.*"

The static ended abruptly, the channel going dead.

"Are you sure we should send anyone else down there, Captain?" a graying officer asked from another station. "We may simply have to report that the mission was impossible."

Ishii sighed. "We need to at least try to retrieve the survivors. If there are any. And stay here to blow Rache's ship out of the sky if it tries to pull the gate out of that mess down there."

Qin closed her eyes, fearing they were too late. What if Asger was already dead? And Kim and Casmir? Was it possible? And she'd missed it all because she'd been off on her own personal quest? If she'd been with them, would it have changed anything?

"It seems unlikely," the other officer said, "that he would succeed where four Kingdom warships failed."

"The warships aren't the problem. It's that we're limited to those damn rent-a-subs." Ishii sneered. "If we determine that our men are all dead, I'm dropping a nuke in the middle of the seismic activity down there. Right on that astroshaman base. Those pricks had no right coming to our system to steal our gate."

"You can't blow up the gate," Kelsey-Sato protested.

"I'm ready to blow up this whole moon."

"Let us go down and look first, Captain," Bjarke said.

"Another comm coming in, sir," an officer said. "It's the *Falcon*. They're still flying down above the surface, trying to find sign of the base and Rache's ship. They're receiving a message from one of the subs and are relaying it to us."

Ishii lifted his head. "Which sub? Did someone on our team make it?"

"It's one of Rache's subs."

Ishii slumped back in his chair. "I don't want to hear from *them*."

"Uhm, sending it through, sir."

"This is Kim Sato, temporarily in charge of the, ah, I think this is *Bubbles 3*."

"Kim!" Qin blurted before she could catch herself. "Are you all right? Is Casmir with you?" She glanced at Bjarke. "What about Asger? Oh, and this is Qin. We're in your system now on the *Osprey*."

"Kim," Kelsey-Sato spoke up, hopping onto the console next to the comm officer so she would be heard—the man jerked back in surprise, lifting his hands as if she might contaminate him with monkey-droid germs. "It's your mother. I am here aboard the *Osprey* as well."

Ishii cleared his throat. "I'll handle the comm if you don't mind." He snapped his fingers at Bjarke, as if he should be minding his wayward charges.

Bjarke looked at Qin, but he didn't say anything or make any silencing gestures. *He* probably wanted to know about Asger too.

Assuming he cared and didn't consider his son a disgrace he'd be better off without. Qin clenched her jaw.

"Greetings, Mother," Kim said without detectable emotion in her voice. "Captain, Rache kidnapped the three of us. He took Asger and Casmir into the base with his team hours ago. The astroshamans are able to attack and plant viruses through the comms and our chips, so I haven't communicated with them recently." Her voice turned grim. "I don't know if they're alive or not."

"At least there's hope," Ishii whispered.

"That body, Captain," Kim said. "Did Dr. Sikou autopsy it?"

Qin frowned at Bjarke and Kelsey-Sato in bewilderment, but neither of them looked like they knew what she was talking about either.

"Yes," Ishii said. "We tried to warn you, but the ice was either interfering or you'd already turned off your comms."

"The dead woman had the Great Plague," Kim said.

Ishii gaped. "How did you know?"

"Casmir has it now."

Ishii swore and dropped his face into his palm again.

Qin's heart sank. Not Casmir.

"Sir," the comm officer said, "the *Falcon's* scanners picked up a reading of something flying near a hole in the ice, a newly formed hole. They fired and hit what they think could be Rache's ship. They're in pursuit."

"Good," Ishii said. "Tell Captain Malcolm that I'll send a bottle of my best sake over if he nails that bastard."

Qin clenched and unclenched her fists. She didn't care about Rache's ship, not now. She cared about Asger and Casmir. Poor Casmir. Was Rache forcing him to work on that stupid gate when he was dying of a horrible plague?

"Kim," Kelsey-Sato said, "what's the status of the gate? Professor Beaumont, a loaded android gate specialist, is here with me. He was asked to assist in finding out a way to deactivate the defenses so humans can work on it without danger. I invited myself along."

"I don't know if they've located it yet," Kim said, "but I know Casmir was daunted and would gladly accept your help."

Kelsey-Sato spun toward Ishii and Bjarke. "We have to get down there."

"That's what I came up here to tell the captain," Bjarke observed mildly.

"Go." Ishii stood again. "Go, all of you. Take more men to help. Take the sub through—" Ishii spun toward the comm station. "*Falcon*, you said there's a new hole?"

"Yes, sir. It's next to where there's been a surge of seismic activity, likely explosives going off. We think it's the location of the base."

"Is the hole large enough to lower a sub down?"

"Yes, sir. It looks like someone had exactly that in mind. Or to take the other subs out through it."

"Tell Captain Malcolm to keep that area clear for us. I'm sending a team down."

"Yes, sir. Uh, do we shoot at the civilian ships too?"

Ishii scowled. "Did they break orbit and go down?"

It was one of his own officers that answered. "Yes, sir. There are more ships in orbit than there were an hour ago, and more than two dozen are down running searches along the ice. Some are in the vicinity of the *Falcon*'s chase."

Ishii lifted his gaze toward the ceiling. "Why, why are all the *kami* against us on this mission?"

Maybe because it isn't your system and you don't have the right to be here, Qin thought, but she didn't speak aloud. She wanted the captain to agree to send her, now more than ever. Casmir and Asger needed her. She was sure of it.

"Don't shoot any civilian ships on purpose," Ishii said, "but if they get in the way, don't let them keep you from targeting Rache's ship."

"Tell your team to bring my sake," a gruff voice said. The *Falcon*'s captain?

"You need to show me dead mercenaries first," Ishii said.

The man grunted and closed the comm.

Ishii pointed at Bjarke. "Go. Keep them alive and get that gate for the Kingdom."

Bjarke bowed and ran to the lift. Qin raced after him, assuming that meant that Ishii didn't care if she helped. Kelsey-Sato sprang through the doors just in time to avoid getting her tail caught.

"I'm looking forward to another meeting with that gate," she said. "Hopefully without astroshamans ripping my head off this time."

"We'll protect you," Bjarke said.

Qin agreed. She just hoped they weren't too late.

Asger paced in front of the magnetic field as Casmir worked inside, his tools and monitors spread next to a single gate piece that had already been pulled off the stack. Wires ran from a section in the middle to a bank of computers along one wall. Casmir had already checked out those computers. Asger didn't know if he'd found anything.

It looked like the astroshamans, or some impervious androids of theirs, had already been working on the gate. Trying to do in days what Casmir now had minutes to do? Asger assumed that they hadn't succeeded, since the protective field was still up.

"I can confirm that it's emitting the pseudo radiation right now," Casmir said over his shoulder, waving a handheld device that appeared homemade rather than factory-produced.

His words came out slurred, but they were clearer than they had been earlier. Asger tried to find that reassuring.

"I thought we didn't know how to detect that," Rache said.

He wasn't pacing, merely standing with his arms folded over his chest as he alternately watched one group of his men, who were burning a hole in the ice ceiling with the special drill, and the others, who were monitoring the three entrances into the chamber.

"We didn't. On the way here, I borrowed some of Kim's bacteria to come up with something." Casmir lifted a device as if that would clarify everything. Asger imagined bacteria with legs running on little treadmills inside to power it. "Since *they* could sense the radiation."

Asger wanted to tell Casmir to stop talking and save his energy, but it seemed to be part of how he thought. He occasionally said things to them, but mostly he spoke to himself, muttering as he poked through everything. Zee trailed him faithfully, staying close enough to protect him if some hidden attack appeared—or catch him if he collapsed.

One of the mercenaries jogged up to Rache. He was also holding a device, though Asger recognized it as the life-form detector Rache had been carrying earlier.

"Trouble coming, sir." The man pointed to the display. "We've got some humans or mostly humans heading our way. They've got a winding route through some tunnels, it looks like, but they're coming fast. Might be on transportation of some kind. Or riding their robots."

Rache only nodded. "We expected another fight."

"Any chance of getting their robots knocked offline again?" The man looked hopefully toward Casmir.

"Our robot wrangler is on another mission. We'll have to deal with this. Tell Dark Tom's team to stay and guard those tunnels while we make sure nothing comes out of this one." Rache pointed to the one in the direction of the new threat.

"Yes, sir."

While his man conveyed the message, Rache ran over to check on the drill team. A small waterfall flowed out of the hole they were making, pooling around the piles of broken robot debris on the floor.

Asger couldn't tell how far up their hole went yet. Was Rache's ship up there waiting for them to break through? Asger would be irked if the Kingdom ships couldn't detect it and swoop down and chase off the *Fedallah*. If Rache got away with the gate from right under their noses…

No, that wasn't going to happen. Asger wasn't going to fail at his mission again. He would get comm messages out once that hole was complete and warn the *Osprey* about what was going on. Then he would do his best to stop Rache all by himself, if he had to.

"Casmir." Rache ran through the magnetic field, startling Asger until he remembered he was also immune.

A surge of bitterness washed through him as he realized Rache was not only immune to the gate but also wasn't showing signs that he'd caught the Plague. He should have been as susceptible to that as Casmir. It wasn't fair that friendly and caring Casmir would be struck down while a heartless mercenary killer went unscathed.

"Casmir." Rache poked him, startling him. "There's a threat coming."

"I know," Casmir said without looking up. "Moonrazor has turned her attention to us and is sending a team."

"I'm taking Asger and a group of my men to stop it."

Asger scowled at the presumption. "You're *taking* me?"

"You've still got the vial gun, right?" Rache waved at it strapped to Asger's back.

Asger had almost forgotten about it. Was Rache annoyed that he hadn't used it during the first fight? Asger had deemed those robots a larger threat than the cyborgs, at least then.

"I have it," Asger said.

"Then you're coming."

"You're an annoying prick, Rache."

"If we survive this, maybe I'll let you punch me again."

"If you two wouldn't mind leaving the flirting until later," Casmir said, studying one of the strangely translucent panels—or what lay under it, "I'm busy, and your machismo is distracting."

Rache grunted. "I assume Zee will stay with you?"

"Yes."

"I will never leave Casmir Dabrowski's side," Zee announced. "He is going to make me a mate."

"That's not at all alarming," Rache muttered, then gripped Casmir's shoulder briefly. "You need anything? That team over there and the men at the drill will be the backup if anything happens to us and the astroshamans get through. If I don't make it, do something creative with the gate, eh?"

Casmir threw a startled look over his shoulder.

"Like not giving it to Jager," Rache added.

"That's not creative; that's recalcitrant."

"You can creatively not give it to him."

Asger shook his head, not appreciating the suggestion, though he was positive Casmir had already thought of it. Instead of answering, Casmir gazed up at the ice ceiling.

Rache patted him on the back and headed toward Asger and the men gathering by the exit.

Asger didn't want to run off and fight at Rache's side, but if the astroshamans had defeated the Kingdom troops, he had little choice but to work with who was left and buy Casmir the time he needed. Later, he could figure out how to get the gate into the Kingdom's hands. Maybe the warships were up there pummeling Rache's ship right now.

A nice thought, but Asger couldn't bring himself to believe it. So far, Rache had been more prepared and was doing a far better job here than Ishii and the other captains. Asger hated to admit it, but the Kingdom had rushed into this mess out of fear of losing out and had never been in that strong of a position.

"Wait, Rache?" Casmir looked back.

Rache stopped. "Yes?"

"I almost forgot. Uhm, I hacked into Kim's chip earlier so I could communicate with her about something."

"She allows you to do that but she doesn't allow you to make up words?"

"Our relationship works. Don't judge us." Casmir smiled, but the words sounded exhausted rather than joking. *He* sounded exhausted.

Rache must have thought the same thing because he got to the point instead of throwing out more banter. "What did she say?"

"That if you truly had the Great Plague and survived, your blood might be able to help me fight it off. She can't do anything on the sub, but she said if we could get a sample, she and the doctor on our ship might be able to come up with something." Casmir turned his palm toward the ceiling, as if he wouldn't normally ask and didn't want to inconvenience anyone… "I don't suppose you'd be willing to leave a sample in case something happens and you can't get back here?"

In case Rache and Asger got themselves killed battling the astroshamans was what he meant. A distinct possibility.

Asger eyed Rache, expecting him to refuse or dangle the blood sample as a reward Casmir could have only if he fixed the gate. If he did, Asger would be tempted to cleave open Rache's armor with his pertundo and collect a vial of blood while it leaked out through a gash. Even if it meant the rest of the mercenaries would jump him.

Rache tugged off his helmet and walked over to the medic.

"Cabrera, you still have your med-kit handy?"

"I'd be an idiot to put it away here, sir."

"Good. I need you to take a blood draw."

"Yes, sir. From who?"

"Whom. And me." Rache pushed his hood up enough to reveal his neck.

"From the jugular, sir?" his man asked and withdrew a syringe.

"Yeah, you know I hate to take my top off when there aren't any ladies present."

Casmir snorted. "I guess my damsel status was short-lived."

"Are you disappointed?" Asger said.

"I don't know. It was nice being carried." Casmir was on his knees by his tools, but he reached out and patted Zee's sturdy leg.

Zee plopped a hand onto his head. "Do you wish to be carried again, Casmir Dabrowski?"

"Not currently, but thank you for the offer. If I can't figure this out, I may need to be hauled out unconscious and taken… somewhere."

"Are you making any progress?" Asger shouldn't have asked—it hadn't been that long—but he couldn't help himself. Was this something that was even possible? Or were they risking their lives for nothing?

Casmir hesitated. "Not yet. This is so alien. I mean, not truly *alien*, but I'm almost positive computers made it instead of humans, and they created a bunch of their own tech and programming languages before they did. It's definitely not just a more advanced version of the kinds of systems humans make. I sure wish I had access to the Zamek University archaeology database and all previous gate studies right now. Actually, I wish I had a few AIs from Verloren Moon here that could be bribed to help me. Even though they haven't existed long enough to have been involved in making these old gates, they are essentially the second evolution of computers that could."

"Yeah." Asger didn't admit that the words were going over his head. *Alien* seemed right to him. Even the computer banks along the back wall looked alien to him.

"Asger?" Casmir gazed at him sadly, making Asger miss the goofy, cheerful Casmir he'd first met on the *Stellar Dragon.* "Please be careful. I've had a few chats with Moonrazor, at her insistence, not mine, and the last thing we talked about before I had my seizure and my chip went offline was that she was assuming I was rejecting her offer, since I hadn't replied in a timely manner. That irritated her more than I expected, considering I'm not the one blowing up her base. I don't know why she made the offer or why she wanted me, but she said none of us would ever leave this moon."

"What offer?"

"To make me an astroshaman and give me an android body in case…" He waved to his human body. His frail, sick human body.

Asger shook his head bleakly. It wasn't *that* bad yet, was it? Casmir wasn't that far along… They just had to get him back to the ship, and surely, the doctor could do something. Especially if—

Rache returned with the vial of blood and handed it to Casmir. "Once you deactivate the gate, let the men know, and then go back to the submarine with Zee. My men won't stop you. Tell the pilot there the code is nebula-three-seven-dash-fourteen and that I said for him to take you up to the surface. You'll probably end up back on the *Fedallah* with Yas and Kim, since it's not like the Kingdom will come and pick up one of my subs, but I'm sure they can do as well as a Fleet doctor."

"That code will make him listen to me?" Casmir asked.

"It should. If he doesn't, you and Kim can feel free to find a creative way to overcome him. I have a feeling Yas will help. Or stand back and hold Kim's tools while she comes up with a bacterial concoction to waylay him."

"All right. Thanks." Casmir tucked the vial into an insulated pouch in his toolkit. "But I'm afraid you'll be back before I can figure this out. And that I'll have had time to regret turning down Moonrazor."

"So long as you're thinking positive." Rache clapped him on the shoulder. "Come on, Asger."

Asger hated trailing along after the mercenary or following his orders, but he had no choice. He strode off with Rache, the last man he ever thought he'd go into battle with, his pertundo in one hand and the vial gun in the other.

A *clack-clank* came from the corridor they entered.

"Let's do this," Asger muttered.

CHAPTER 20

QIN WATCHED OUT THE PORTHOLE AS THE SUBMARINE descended toward a recently made hole in the ice—it was still smoking. No, that had to be steam. A combat shuttle was lowering them, and in the distance, she could make out the *Osprey* and a second Kingdom warship firing at what appeared to be empty sky. Rache's camouflaged vessel?

The shuttle lowered their submarine farther, and the strange scene disappeared from view. Soon, nothing but slick, shiny walls of ice surrounded them.

"I don't read any submarines or anything else directly below us," the Kingdom pilot said from the front. "But I'm getting all sorts of readings from a couple of miles to the west. Under the ice. It's coming through even more as we descend. Different kinds of energy, and... Sir Knight!" The pilot's voice rose with excitement. "I'm reading the signature output the gates exude."

"Good," Bjarke said quietly. He was leaning against the hatch and watching the pilot.

Qin wished Bonita were here to navigate the craft, even if she had no familiarity with submarines. Qin knew what to expect from her and that she would be a brilliant shot with the torpedoes. She had no idea what to expect from the fifteen Kingdom marines in the submarine with her, Bjarke, and the two android scholars. Even though she had her helmet up, the marines kept glancing at her.

The submarine wobbled as they reached the water, and the marines forgot about her, instead muttering amongst themselves. A clank came from above as the shuttle detached and flew away. The submarine descended, water darkening the view of the white-blue ice all around them.

As soon as they reached the bottom of the hole, they headed west. Toward the base.

Qin fingered her weapons, anticipation and worry mingling in her gut. She looked forward to a battle but kept fearing they were too late.

"There's a tunnel in the ice," the pilot announced. "It looks like the entrance to… *something*."

"Go in," Bjarke said. "Let's hope it's not a maze since Scholar Sato didn't stick around to guide us."

"Because she was *kidnapped*." Kelsey-Sato stood rather than sat on a seat near navigation. "We're lucky she was able to escape long enough to send a message. I hope she hasn't been recaptured and harmed."

"We'll retrieve her," Bjarke said.

Qin tapped a rhythm on her Brockinger as the submarine twisted through the icy tunnel, eventually reaching two giant open doors leading into a lagoon or underwater harbor.

"There are three submarines lying in wait in there," the pilot said. "One is turning toward us and arming torpedoes. Do we turn back?"

Bjarke leaned into navigation, looking at some display. "They're all Rache's subs. Go in and return fire at will."

"Kim might be in one of those." Kelsey-Sato looked like she would spring into navigation to stop them, but Professor Beaumont, who sat in the seat next to her, gripped her shoulder.

"Let the combat specialists handle the combat," he urged.

The words made Qin realize she'd unfastened her harness and surged to her feet. *She* was one of those specialists. But she couldn't do anything against torpedoes, not from inside the submarine. She envisioned herself swimming out, tearing open the hatch on an enemy submarine, and darting in to deal with the crew. Could that work? She had no experience with underwater battles.

Something flashed outside of the porthole, and their submarine rocked viciously. Qin widened her stance and kept her balance.

"Were we hit?" someone asked.

"Not exactly," the pilot said. "Our torpedo hit theirs, and they both exploded in the middle. Ice is raining down on the harbor—there's air up there, a surface, and is that a dock?"

"Fire again," Bjarke said. "Wait, what's that middle sub doing?"

"It's heading toward the one that just fired. And, uh, huh. It just crashed into the side of it."

"They *are* all Rache's, right?" Bjarke sounded doubtful now.

"Yes," the pilot said.

"Kim must be in there," Kelsey-Sato blurted. "She has command. She's piloting the sub." After a pause—everyone seemed too skeptical to speak—she added, "Where did she learn how to do that?"

"It's backing up and... ramming them again," the pilot said. "The third sub is turning toward us."

"Shoot that one instead," Bjarke said. "Before they can target us."

"Firing."

Qin left her seat and came up behind Bjarke to peer through the much larger porthole in navigation. The pale blue light coming from the pillars out there made it possible to see the scene the pilot had been describing. And it was exactly as crazy as it had sounded.

Their torpedo fired a second before the enemy submarine could fire, and it struck the craft straight on. The water muffled the explosion, but the nose of the submarine blew open impressively.

"That one is out of commission," the pilot said. "The, uh, helper sub has the other one pinned against the dock pillars. It's not going to be able to target us from that position."

"Take us in," Bjarke said.

In less than a minute, they surfaced next to the dock. The submarine rose and bobbed in water rocking from the explosions.

"Everyone out who's coming with me." Bjarke jogged back to the overhead hatch.

Qin shouldered a marine aside to go out after him, worried that Kim might be in trouble. If the other mercenaries hadn't known she'd somehow gotten control of that submarine... they would know now. And just because their vessels were inoperable didn't mean there weren't troops capable of retaliating.

Bjarke sprang from the ladder rungs of the hatchway to a strange black dock. He was firing at something before Qin climbed out of the submarine. Two men in black combat armor—Rache's men—had jumped from their craft to the dock ahead of them.

One got close enough to grapple with Bjarke and tried to tear his rifle away.

Qin could have fired, but Bjarke was in the way. She lowered her shoulder and slammed into the second mercenary like a battering ram. He flew over the submarine and landed in the water. She aimed her Brockinger and fired at him.

The mercenary's helmet dipped under the surface an instant before her round hit. When it exploded, she didn't know if it had harmed him or not, but he didn't come back up. Maybe he realized he was outnumbered and should hide, for the rest of Bjarke's marines were streaming out now.

One helped Bjarke tear open the armor of his opponent and knock his weapon away. The mercenary stopped fighting and spread his hands.

The rest of the marines rushed to the two enemy submarines, leaping into the open hatches. Rifle fire and shouts came from the one the torpedo had struck.

"This one's empty," someone called out.

Bjarke looked around. "Rache may have only left a couple of men behind in each one to wait."

"What about that one?" A marine pointed toward the still-closed hatch on the third craft, the one that had been helping them.

Qin sprang for it, wanting Kim to see a friendly face first if she was in there. And if she wasn't, or she was wounded, Qin would deal with whoever else she found.

The hatch opened as she was reaching for it. A helmeted head that she didn't recognize—the man had wide fearful eyes—rose slowly, then jerked back down. Qin kept herself from firing.

"They're your people," a man whispered from below. "*You* go first."

"I was planning on it." The dry voice that answered belonged to Kim. Qin grinned. "Kim? We brought your mother. And some people to help."

"Good." There was little inflection in Kim's voice, as if she'd expected nothing less, but she gave Qin a friendly pat on the arm when she climbed out. She wore combat armor, but not the black gear the mercenaries favored. It was blue Kingdom Fleet armor she must have been lent.

Kelsey-Sato and Beaumont scrambled across their submarine toward the dock.

"Kim," her mother said. "It is excellent that you are alive."

"Thank you, Mother," Kim said when she reached the dock.

They looked at each other but didn't hug, as Qin would have expected. Kim bowed her head slightly. Her mother lifted a hand in a wave of acknowledgment.

"I'm here to help with the gate," Kelsey-Sato said.

"I am the Kingdom-sent *official* gate expert," Beaumont said.

"Meaning the king finds his friends more acceptable than mine," Kelsey-Sato said, "not that he knows more than I do."

Beaumont sniffed. "My memory banks are just as packed with pertinent information as yours, I assure everyone."

Kim pointed toward a tunnel in a wall of ice beyond a beach full of unmoving robots on treads. "Casmir, Asger, and the mercenaries went that way."

Qin glanced at Bjarke, wondering if he would react at the mention of Asger, but his face was blank in his helmet. Qin wondered if Asger knew Bjarke was coming. She hoped that father and son would have a warmer reunion than Kim and her mother had displayed, but given the disapproval Bjarke had expressed the one time he spoke of Asger, that didn't seem likely.

"Let's go," was all Bjarke said and strode off.

It was too hard.

No, that wasn't it, but there was too much to learn, too much to study, and in too short a time. Casmir had fixed his chip, since that had been a far more familiar task, and was accessing the files he'd downloaded before coming, known information about the gate and about the technology and programming languages the artificial intelligences on Verloren Moon used.

There were clues in all of it, but fitting them together to understand the enigma before him was eluding him. He reminded himself that he only had to grasp the security measures and deactivate them, not gain full knowledge of how the gate worked, but that was akin to trying to understand a page in a book without understanding the language it was written in. He felt he had to master the language first.

How goes it, Professor?

Moonrazor.

His fevered body shivered. Would he have to take his chip offline again to avoid some new attack? Why was she speaking with him?

Wasn't she *busy*? Hadn't Asger and Rache reached her and started a fresh fight?

It's an intriguing problem. Casmir was tempted to ignore her, but her people had been studying the problem already, so it was possible she had useful information. *I wish I were examining the gate under other circumstances.*

Such as when your soldiers weren't obliterating my people?

Such as when your robots weren't giving me seizures.

You are more of a danger than any of the others, she messaged. *I would be foolish not to nullify the greatest threat.*

I'm fevered, puking, and dying. I can't possibly be the greatest threat. Casmir kept working while he spoke to her, combining a program that archaeologists used for deciphering old forgotten languages with another the military used for cryptography and cracking codes.

You are because you don't want to steal my gate; you want to share it. Or so you say. Is it odd that I believe you? It could be because two of the ships in orbit have tried to contact us about acquiring a piece of the gate for study, and they offered to trade for it. I suspect your hand at work.

Huh. Casmir hadn't spoken to any of those captains or crews up there, but it was possible the message had trickled through to them. But he wasn't sure what Moonrazor was angling for or if he should confess to his role.

Two weeks ago, nobody knew it was here. It seems that, in addition to the Kingdom and those mercenaries, an awful lot of scientists are here now, expressing intellectual curiosity.

Is that something you approve of? Intellectual curiosity?

Don't you?

Of course.

You don't belong in the Kingdom, Professor.

Because I'm curious?

Because you'd rather make friends with me than put a bullet through my head.

Casmir didn't see the conversations they'd been having as indicative of a friendship being forged, but maybe she perceived their sparring in a different light. *Then the Kingdom is exactly where I should be. If that's the perception of it out here, it must need more people like me.*

She didn't answer right away, and he waited in anticipation of a biting retort about how he was weak instead of strong, something he'd heard so often from his peers as he'd grown up. One day, he'd learn not to make himself vulnerable in front of his enemies. Or maybe he wouldn't. People tended to be more receptive to him when he was vulnerable. Maybe later, he'd have a seizure at her feet, and Moonrazor would be moved enough to accept the deal he was offering.

You are trying to deactivate the security system that spits an undetectable radiation when humans approach? Moonrazor asked, sidestepping his last comment.

That was better than her mocking him for it.

Yes. Casmir saw little point in denying it. She was probably watching him through a surveillance camera.

I lost a whole team of my best people to it before we understood the threat.

I know. I saw their bodies on that cargo ship. And then I saw what you did to Tork-57. Was that out of anger?

Frustration at his failure, yes, but also to intrigue your people into taking him aboard. Then the android could destroy you, and you couldn't come after the gate. It seems I've been underestimating you all along. Of course, I did not know of you personally until recently.

We robotics professors keep a low profile.

How is it that you are alive? I myself haven't been able to go through the magnetic field and study the gate since I still have biological elements.

I'm immune. I have old unaltered genes. The gate doesn't see me as a threat.

I wondered if it might be something like that. You were cloned from Admiral Mikita?

Does everybody outside of the Kingdom know that?

Everybody who's opened a history book and seen a picture. Also, I have a file on him. One of his closest officers was wounded horribly in battle, had half his insides replaced with cybernetics, and became an astroshaman leader after the Kingdom finished its conquering.

I didn't know that. I would be curious to see that file. As soon as he sent the words, Casmir worried it had been a mistake to admit that, to possibly give her another bargaining chip to use against him in their ongoing dance.

Deactivate the gate, and I'll give it to you.

Now that she knew what he was doing, she might want him to have the opportunity to finish, especially if the androids she'd had working on the problem—or had they been loaded droids?—hadn't figured it out yet. That potentially gave *him* a bargaining chip. Maybe the active security system was the only reason the gate was down here in this base instead of already on a ship heading to its destination system.

I'm doing my best to deactivate it, but it would be easier if your people and robots stopped attacking us.

Would it? I thought these mercenaries kidnapped you and that I would be doing you a favor to get rid of them.

Casmir assumed she was being flippant, but he wasn't positive. Maybe now that he was trying to deactivate the gate, she no longer wished to impede him. Maybe she thought if she got rid of Rache's men, she could come advise him herself. And be poised to snag the gate as soon as the security system was deactivated...

One of my friends, who was also kidnapped, is fighting with them because he believes he has no choice, Casmir told her. *I would work better if I wasn't worried about his life.*

Is that so?

Laughter couldn't come across the text messages of the chip, but he had the sense of her chuckling.

I'm afraid I must deal with them, she continued. *They have no interest in sharing the gate with me, and in truth, I still hope to retain it all for myself. Do keep me updated on your progress with its defenses, will you?*

Bring me an orange fizzop, and I'll show you the checks in my bullet journal.

You are delightful, Professor. If you want to change your mind and join my side, you've got about... three minutes.

Casmir grimaced, now more worried for Asger instead of less.

On the other side of the chamber, Rache's team of men let out a few triumphant whoops—they'd successfully drilled their hole through the ice and would now work on widening it.

That only made Casmir feel more pressure to figure out his problem. If ships started sending teams down, hoping to snag a piece, and the gate's security system was still activated, all the people he'd encouraged to come would be in danger of dying.

CHAPTER 21

A SGER WALKED BESIDE RACHE, WHO INSISTED THAT HE lead his mercenaries through the tunnel rather than letting them go first. If Asger tried to pull a half a step ahead, that dark mask turned in his direction, conveying a glare as well as eyes could. Asger glared back.

Their little game did not last long. The tunnel ended at a cavernous atrium full of shrubbery and birds. Asger couldn't tell if they were mechanical or real, but their chirps sounded programmed as they flew from potted tree to potted tree, trunks reaching up toward an icy ceiling that glowed with simulated sunlight. Here and there, empty tables, some still with cups on them, rested under the branches. At the back of the chamber, a counter with bar seats opened into an empty kitchen.

The place looked more like a square at a university campus than some underground enemy base.

"People behind the trees," Rache warned.

"Robots in that tunnel over there," someone added.

Movement behind one of the trees drew Asger's eye, and he fired the vial-gun as soon as he glimpsed human hair.

A grenade whistled through the air toward them. Rache shot it out of its trajectory, and it exploded with a boom that shook the trees.

Asger thought Qin would be disappointed if she were here, but then mercenaries started streaming past him into the atrium, and there wasn't time to think of anything but staying alive and picking targets. Even as those targets were targeting *him*.

He let the mercenaries take the brunt of their ire and stayed in the mouth of the tunnel. Even if he felt cowardly doing so, he could more easily play the role of sniper if he wasn't in the middle of the fray.

The first person he'd shot lay on the ground, twitching. Asger felt triumphant—the liquid-filled darts actually did something. A mercenary ran past and shot the man in the head. He stopped twitching after that, and Asger grimaced, realizing he would only be immobilizing people so they would be easy targets.

But what choice did he have? He saw far more cyborgs and androids leaning out from behind the trees than there were Rache's people. And they wanted to kill him.

More enemies, some in armor and some not, streamed into the atrium. Asger targeted those with necks showing, only realizing after he fired a couple of vials that some were androids. He took more care, trying to spot human—or mostly human—eyes before firing. But with the astroshamans, it was frequently hard to tell *what* they were.

One woman pointed a weapon toward Asger that looked more like a slingshot than a pistol. A high-tech mechanical slingshot. When it fired, a ball of blue light whirled toward him.

Even though his armor should be able to take numerous hits, Asger jumped back into the tunnel to avoid the projectile. But the ball turned in the air like a guided missile and zipped after him. It slammed into his shoulder as he tried to dodge.

A charge of electricity crackled in the air all around him, more like a stunner nimbus than a DEW-Tek blast. Somehow, it affected him through his armor. Pain lit up every nerve in his body, and he bit back a howl of agony.

His armor went rigid all over. Asger pitched against the wall, unable to move as his protective suit turned into a tomb.

Shouts and cries of pain came from the atrium, and Asger could hear the grinding and whirring of robots advancing into the fray. He could see and look around, but his frozen suit allowed no other movement. A stun for his armor. He'd never encountered such a thing, and he feared he was out of the fight permanently.

An explosion roared in the atrium. Out of the corner of his eye, he saw leaves flutter down. A mercenary in black combat armor skidded across the floor on his butt. He sprang up with a roar and ran back toward some assailant Asger couldn't see.

"Get the woman with the slingshot!" someone yelled.

No kidding.

Just as Asger was lamenting that this would be his fate, his armor unlocked. He was able to move his fingers, then his arms, and finally his legs.

He spotted the vial-gun where he'd dropped it and snatched it back up. He loaded more vials and crept back into the mouth of the tunnel.

He got two shots off, vials bursting against the chests of semi-human foes, before a rumble to the side startled him. A giant robot rolling along the wall almost knocked his head off with an arm holding a built-in circular saw on the end.

Asger ducked, sprang farther back into the tunnel, and yanked the shell gun off his back. He fired before the robot rolled out of sight. He expected to blow it up, as he had the others, but a tiny red beam shot out of its head. The shell exploded before it reached its target, and the shockwave blew Asger back down the tunnel.

"Annoying when the enemy learns from its mistakes," he muttered, jumping back to his feet.

The robot rolled back across the tunnel exit, as if to taunt him. Asger growled, slung the shell gun back over his shoulder, and pulled out his pertundo. He charged for the exit as the robot rolled out of view, and he leaped after it.

He dodged a swipe from the whirring saw, darted behind his metal foe, and rammed the point of his weapon into the back of the robot's carapace. It crunched, sinking in, and lightning similar to what had come from that ball arced around the metal monster.

Asger had a split second to wonder if the astroshamans had stolen the knights' technology—or vice versa. Then the robot reversed its treads and roared back toward him, bringing the saws to bear again.

He yanked his weapon free, readjusted his grip in an oft-practiced move, and slammed the blade down on the saw arm. It cleaved through with another burst of blue electricity. The robot seemed impervious to the energy attack but not to the blade itself, and the end of its arm sheared off.

The saw spun away, almost clipping his armor before cutting into the ice wall and sticking there. Asger cleaved off the second saw arm before the robot could attack him again, then slammed his blade into the thing's torso, hoping to find some vital motor that would stop its charge.

Something slammed into Asger's back, knocking him into the robot. He recovered and sprang free, keeping his pertundo in hand. Two huge men who appeared more machine than human had him surrounded.

Worse, the robot rotated and kept coming, trying to run him over even though he'd deprived it of its weapons.

Asger rammed the shaft of his pertundo backward to take one foe in the armored chest and keep him from getting close. He kicked toward the other one, but the big man was far faster than he looked. He caught Asger's foot before he retracted it. Asger's leg was pulled back and shoved upward with muscle-tearing force. He would have been flipped onto his back, but Asger spun in the air, jerking his leg free, and came down on his feet.

Unfortunately, he landed hard and off-balance. The robot slammed into him before he could recover.

Asger skidded sideways, again struggling to keep his feet under him. That didn't keep him from stabbing and slashing with his pertundo. He managed to keep his attackers back, but two more charged in.

One fired a rifle, and Asger had nowhere to dodge. The bolt ricocheted off his armor, but more followed it. An alarm flashed on his heads-up display, warning of a possible resource overload as his liquid armor shifted and morphed, trying to keep a breach from forming.

Asger roared and tried to spring out of the fray—how had he let himself get surrounded?—but one of the impossibly fast cyborgs lunged in and wrapped an arm around his neck from behind. Asger twisted and rammed the point of his pertundo at his assailant. It caught and tore into metal and flesh, but the grip around his neck didn't loosen. Whatever held him was more machine than man and didn't seem to feel pain.

More bolts fired into his back, and his armor struggled to compensate, to bounce them away instead of letting them through. Asger twisted further and jerked his helmet out of the man's grip. *Finally.*

But the cursed robot rammed into him again, shoving him toward another enhanced assailant.

A punch like a railgun crashed into the side of his helmet. Asger saw stars as the hard material crunched, but he didn't let himself fall down. He channeled his pain into anger and whirled, swinging his pertundo with all of his strength.

He clipped another enemy with his backswing, but it barely slowed the momentum of the blade. It cleaved through the cybernetic neck of his assailant, and the cyborg's helmet and head flew off. They clattered across the ice, the banging of the head sounding more machine than human.

A roar came from a few feet away. Asger spun, expecting another attack, but a giant foe looming nearby was hefted into the air and hurled into a potted tree. The pot cracked, and the tree pitched down on top of the cyborg.

A black-armored mercenary stood where he'd been and barked, "Look out!"

Asger's rear camera caught the threat at the same time, and he flipped his pertundo, jamming the point behind him. His attacker impaled himself on it.

The mercenary—that had been Rache's voice—rolled a grenade across the floor toward the robot, the metal behemoth *still* trying to roll over Asger and crush him.

"Out of the way," Rache said and ran to the side.

Asger expected the robot's beam to shoot out again, but maybe it had taken too much damage. As he ran, the grenade blew up, taking the robot with it.

"Shoot the humans with the vials." Rache waved a hand at two cyborgs rushing toward them, then rolled a second grenade across the floor at another robot rumbling in their direction. This one also didn't shoot the incoming threat. Rache must have discovered that they didn't recognize projectiles that came at them from the floor.

Asger, annoyed that Rache had discovered that and he hadn't, couldn't keep from a disgruntled retort. "I was *trying* to do that when the robot came to lop my head off."

Rache was too busy fighting an opponent twice his size to respond.

Asger looked for exposed skin on the cyborgs, finding it hard to believe there was any humanity left in those bodies, but he spotted a patch of flesh. Both cyborgs leaped toward trees for cover—they must have learned that the little vials were a threat—but Asger fired first. The vial missed the skin and shattered on the cyborg's chest. Asger realized that was just fine, as long as he inhaled the gas.

Rache pulled Asger behind another tree and switched from grenades to his rifle, laying down fire to cover the retreat of his men. "We're going to have to head back to the tunnel and fight there where they can only come at us a couple at a time."

It took long seconds for the cyborg Asger had shot to react to the gas, but then he pitched sideways and thrashed on the floor. Rache focused on the robots, trying to blow off their saw arms and damage their treads.

There were more of them than there were people and androids—and they did a lot of damage.

The second cyborg leaned out from behind a tree to fire at Asger. He was ready and fired first, then ducked back.

The potted tree Asger and Rache were behind exploded under the cyborg's fire. Shards of ceramic and wood slammed into his and Rache's armor.

"Substandard cover in an atrium," Rache said blandly, not sounding fazed.

Asger started to run for another tree to use for cover, but he must have hit the cyborg. The man pitched onto his back, arms and legs twitching, as if he were having one of Casmir's seizures. Rache targeted him while he was down, holding down his trigger for sustained fire.

Normally, Asger would have objected to attacking someone who was already down, but they were outnumbered, and they had to buy Casmir the time he needed.

The cyborg stopped moving, smoke wafting from a hole drilled into his armor. Asger turned to find the next threat, but the atrium had grown quiet. Because the robots had stopped moving. There were more than thirty of them still standing in the chamber undamaged, but they'd all halted, their saws included.

A couple of men and androids leaped over the counter and into kitchen. Someone fired at them, but they ducked and disappeared through a back door. Asger thought he glimpsed bronze skin and short white hair. Had that been Moonrazor?

"We were losing," Rache said. "What happened?"

"Casmir?" Even as Asger suggested it, he doubted it. Casmir would be too busy with the gate to monitor them.

"Or a trap," Rache said grimly.

"Is it all right if I would prefer it was Casmir?"

Rache looked at him, hopefully not like he was an idiot. Who could tell?

Asger knew he should thank Rache for helping him out, but he couldn't bring himself to thank the man who'd murdered so many Kingdom soldiers. If he'd helped Asger, it had only been because Asger still had the vial-gun.

"I'm going to find the leader." Rache pointed toward that exit leading out of the kitchen. "It's time to take care of her. The rest won't put up as much of a fight once she's gone."

"You want help?" Asger asked, though his gut flinched away from the idea of *taking care* of a woman. Even one who was a criminal.

"No." Rache took the vial-gun from Asger.

"You're going to risk using that when it can affect you?" Asger waved toward the now-dead cyborg who'd been twitching like a frog in a science experiment.

"To get her? Yes."

Rache jogged toward the kitchen, issuing a few orders to his men along the way. One of them trotted out from behind a tree and joined him. They hopped over the counter and disappeared through the doorway the fleeing astroshamans had used.

Asger clenched his jaw, offended that Rache had chosen one of his brain-dead minions over him. It wasn't as if he'd embarrassed himself in that fight. He'd been outnumbered and surrounded, but he'd taken down a lot of them before they'd overpowered him.

"Which still almost ended with you getting killed," he muttered to himself, then stalked off with his pertundo to make sure those robots didn't wake up again and make trouble.

The man who'd briefly introduced himself as Sir Bjarke Asger—Kim had never seen a knight with tattoos on his face before—set a fast pace, at least until he came to the first intersection, where three icy tunnels offered themselves as options, all heading away from the harbor. The soldiers trotting along behind him stopped, waiting for him to make the choice. Qin was taking up the rear, regularly looking back to make sure those robots didn't wake up and give chase.

Bjarke looked back at Kim. "Any idea which way they went?"

"We didn't leave the submarine until you got here," she said, wondering if Yas knew more.

If so, it was too late to ask. He'd opted to stay behind, artfully feigning unconsciousness so that when the mercenaries woke up, he could tell them that Kim had forced him to drug them and then knocked him out with his own medicine. Whether they believed him or not, she hoped they wouldn't be stupid enough to hurt their own doctor.

"Perhaps our instruments may help." Professor Beaumont opened a bag and drew out a scanner. "I read the gate energy in… that direction." He pointed at the wall between two of the tunnel options.

"Helpful." Bjarke crouched and touched the icy floor.

It was textured, so not too slippery, but Kim couldn't imagine it holding footprints.

She risked turning on her chip, hoping Casmir had left a message—or a map—but if he'd had something important to share, he would have overridden her offline status again.

"This way." Bjarke sounded certain as he chose one of the tunnels.

Kim looked at her mother and the professor, wondering if they were about to be led into a maze they would never escape. She'd hoped for another chance to spend time with her mother, and have a more meaningful conversation than they'd shared on their last visit, but not here, lost in a labyrinth in an enemy base.

"We will need to *arrive* at the gate in order to work on it," her mother informed Bjarke.

"They went this way," Bjarke said without explaining how he knew.

Kim sighed but followed along, struggling to keep up with his fast pace. She had lost track of when she'd last slept, but she was positive it had been more than a full day and a night. Weariness weighed down her muscles.

Kim? A message from Casmir popped up. *You've mistakenly left your chip online.*

It wasn't a mistake. Knowing that he was alive gave her fresh energy, and she willed her legs to move faster. *I was aching for your company.*

Really? It's rather poor company right now, but I'll find your proclamation heartening. I see you're incursioning into the ice palace. I'll send a map.

Incursioning isn't a word, but I'll take the map. Kim wondered how he'd known they were coming when they were all offline. Or had been.

No? What's the verb? Incur doesn't mean the right thing.

There is no verb. We could be foraying *into the enemy base. Where's my map?*

Foraying doesn't sound as epic. The map is coming.

Kim examined the image that popped up, struggling to place themselves on the incomplete tangle of tunnels. At most of the intersections, there was no hint as to where the side passages went. They simply ended in stubs.

This looks like a six-year-old drew it with ketchup.

Try a thirty-three-year-old with a paint program on his chip while he was being carried by a crusher.

I wonder who that could have been. Kim found their current location. *Huh. Old Asger chose right.*

Old Asger?

Our Asger's father, it seems. I haven't gotten the whole story yet. I only met him twenty minutes ago.

"Non-combatants, stay back," Bjarke ordered, then ran forward.

Qin sprinted past Kim as she pressed her back to the wall. Clearly considering herself a combatant, Qin elbowed slower marines aside as she rushed to join Bjarke in the front.

Kim couldn't see over the heads of the taller men to glimpse what was happening, but nobody had given her a weapon, so she didn't mind staying out of the fray.

As her mother and Beaumont joined her, the rumble of a vehicle reached their ears. Weapons fired, and Kim hoped her armor was up to taking a few shots. The long ice tunnel offered no hiding places, no place to take cover.

Kim tried to use her armor to shield Beaumont and her mother. Their android bodies could probably survive some fire, but bolts wouldn't ricochet off like with armor.

"Cyborgs," one of the marines yelled.

"Take 'em down, boys," Bjarke hollered.

Further words were lost in a clamor of weapons and the grinding rumbles of some robot or machine.

Kim eyed the top of her mother's head, wondering if she should say something. Such as if they didn't make it out of here, it had been good to see her again. But they had barely spoken yet. It would feel strange to start out with some dramatic outpouring of the heart. Kim searched for some witty bonding words she could start with, words that they would both understand meant something more.

"You're standing on my tail, Kim."

"Sorry. It's long."

"Yes, it is. I chose it myself. For balance and whimsy."

Metal clattered, and shots fired. One missed its target and zipped down the corridor, tearing out a chunk of ice when it struck scant feet away.

"Do you consider yourself a whimsical person?" Kim knew this was a stupid place for an inane conversation, but she couldn't bring herself to say the more meaningful words she wanted to get out.

"Certainly. I tried to fit in when I was younger, but it was terribly wearying. Walking around as a monkey announces my disinterest in even attempting to do so these days."

"So it's a statement of a sort?"

"A statement of whimsy. Also, tails are handy."

"And you get into the museums for the children's rate," Beaumont said, an approximation of fondness on his android face.

"Yes. I've occasionally been asked if I'm a service animal and should get in for free, but that seems a little insulting, so I say no."

Kim watched another red bolt streak past inches from her faceplate. She should have been afraid, but this whole experience was too surreal. She was far more worried for Casmir than herself. The Great Plague was more real and tangible than cyborgs shooting at them in a tunnel—and experiencing this with the mother she'd barely seen in the last twenty years.

There was a momentary gap in between the armored bodies, and Kim was able to see a pair of cyborgs on the floor, unmoving. Two of the Kingdom men were also down, one writhing and grabbing an obliterated shoulder seam in his armor. A long snake-like vehicle made for zipping through the tunnels was backing away, two enemies riding it, ducking and firing from behind cover.

"Get that vehicle!" Kim yelled, realizing that Bjarke, Qin, and the others were focused on the enemies on the ground. If they got it, they could find Casmir and the others more quickly.

Qin glanced back, nodded once, then charged up the tunnel. The two cyborgs on board it fired at her, bolts splashing off her armor. Kim winced, hoping her blurted suggestion wouldn't get Qin in trouble.

"I don't believe the vehicle is a threat, dear," her mother said.

"We can get you to the gate faster if we can ride."

"Oh, indeed. These marines don't run as quickly as androids." Her mother raised her voice. "Get that vehicle!"

Qin sprang over the front of it, landing between the two cyborgs. The vehicle shuddered to a stop as she intentionally or accidentally struck the controls. She threw one man off, his back slamming into the tunnel wall, but the second was faster than a typical human, as fast as Qin, and had time to grab her from behind.

She dipped down, thrusting her hip into his gut and throwing him over her shoulder. The move was only halfway successful, since he didn't let go, and they dropped down out of Kim's sight.

Bjarke and his marines were busy fighting men on the ground. The cyborg that Qin had hurled away rose, recovering quickly, and sprang back aboard the vehicle.

Qin needed help.

Afraid her mother would try to stop her, Kim didn't announce her intent. She raced around the fighting men, taking the butt of a rifle in her armored side, and ran for the vehicle. Even if she didn't have a weapon, she had her fists, fists enhanced by her armor. She could help.

A man screamed in pain and flew upward, hitting the ceiling above the vehicle. Qin surged to her feet and back into view, and Kim thought she might not need help after all—she slammed her palm into the cyborg as he tumbled back down, the blow hurling him the length of the vehicle and across the tunnel floor. But the second cyborg grabbed her leg and flung her against the wall, as she'd done to him.

Then he started the vehicle and backed it up. Trying to escape? Would he run over his own ally?

But as Qin scrambled to her feet, he threw the vehicle into forward again. He drove it straight at her.

Qin saw it coming and leaped up. One of the cyborgs who'd been knocked to the ground by the marines was watching the battle, and he twisted and fired at her. An explosive round struck Qin's back and went off as she grabbed her cyborg and tried to throw him off the vehicle again.

A boom rattled the walls, and smoke stole both combatants from sight.

Kim ran straight into the smoke, afraid the explosion would have ruptured Qin's armor—and her.

When she scrambled onto the vehicle, the metal almost as slick as the ice, she found Qin pinning a cyborg to the seats, his helmet smashed against them, but another man loomed behind her. She was trying to kick him away as she kept her pinned foe from escaping.

Remembering the power of her kick on the submarine, Kim growled and slammed her heel into the cyborg's back. He tumbled over Qin's head—she ducked in time—and off the back of the vehicle.

The craft lurched backward, and Kim scrambled for balance. What now?

Her mother had followed her and was pushing a pedal. She cackled and drove the vehicle backward. It crunched as it ran over the armor—and the cyborg—that Kim had kicked.

Qin, now dealing with only one opponent, hefted him to his feet and punched him in the face. His nose didn't splatter like a typical human one would, but he groaned, his metallic silver eyes crossing. Qin flung him off the back of the vehicle.

Kim's mother sped up, and again armor crunched like the carapace of a bug under a boot.

"Oops," she said cheerfully.

"I thought you might object to me joining in the battle," Kim said.

"No, I'd object if you got yourself killed. I've done that. *Highly* unrecommended."

Her mother swished her tail as she poked around at more controls. There appeared to be a dome that could slide out over the passenger compartment. A warning indicator flashed at them for traveling without putting their harnesses on.

"Nice kick, Kim." Qin waved from her spot farther back on the vehicle.

"Wait for us," Bjarke called.

He and his men ran down the tunnel, leaving their fallen enemies behind. Unfortunately, several of the marines had fallen, or at least been injured, and were being carried by the others. Professor Beaumont hefted two men over his shoulders, proving he was fully android—and a lot stronger than he'd been as a human.

"You'll have to run faster," Kim's mother called. "The gate awaits."

Kim frowned, wondering if this was a demonstration of her whimsy, and pushed the pedal to slow them down. "I would suggest this event is creating an excessive norepinephrine release for you and stimulating endorphins, but you don't have hormones anymore."

"Are you suggesting my glee is unnatural?"

"I'm not sure androids themselves qualify as natural, though Casmir might disagree. Here, let me drive. I have a map."

Bjarke was in the middle of climbing in behind them and asked, "Where did you get a map?"

"Casmir sent some scribbles."

"This is the other civilian advisor who was kidnapped?"

"Yes."

"He doesn't sound very kidnapped."

A twinge of concern went through Kim. She didn't know Bjarke at all, so she didn't know if he would report to his superiors if Casmir and Rache appeared too chummy. "Rache snatched him to work on deactivating the gate. He's probably got a gun to his head right now."

"We'll see."

Casmir? Kim messaged as the vehicle sped through the tunnels, its body flexing to go around bends. Her chip was offline again, so it shouldn't have gone through, but none of her earlier messages should have gone through earlier. *Are you still monitoring me?*

I'm working on the gate, but I have a program to alert me if there's activity on your chip, he replied.

I'm on the way with my mother and an android professor with gate expertise.

Thank God!

Kim winced, afraid that meant his attempts to deactivate it or understand it at all were going poorly. She hadn't forgotten that the only reason he had been dragged down to this moon was because she'd suggested to Ishii that he might be capable of the task. And now he was dying...

We'll be there soon—we've acquired a fast tunnel vehicle—but is there any chance Rache is standing there with a gun to your head?

Uh, no. He and Asger went off to keep the astroshamans from coming and putting guns to my head.

Well, don't look too independent. A new knight is leading us, and I think he may get suspicious if you don't seem duly kidnapped.

Maybe his suspicions will be dulled if he sees me looking extremely weak and pitiful with a puddle of vomit next to my tool satchel.

I don't think you need to go to that extreme to appear weak.

Too late.

Stay safe. We're coming.

CHAPTER 22

HOW AM I SUPPOSED TO KNOW HOW MUCH the gate pieces weigh?" one of the mercenaries at the drill responded to some comm message. "They're *big*… But the hole is big now too. Get your asses down here and drop the maglock cable so you can start hauling them up."

"The boss isn't here. He's fighting."

"You, gate boy." The voice increased in volume as its owner turned toward Casmir.

He forced himself to lift his head and look over, though all he wanted was to lie down on the gate piece he was working on and go to sleep. He was so very tired. But what if he went to sleep and didn't wake up again? He had to fix this for everyone before sleeping. Or dying. Definitely before dying.

"I'm talking to you, puke-breath. Is it safe to haul that thing out yet, or what?"

When had they regained comm access? Oh, right. The big hole in the ice ceiling, which was now much larger than the last time Casmir had looked, had to be letting a signal through.

One of the other mercenaries knocked his fist against the speaker's armor. "Don't be an ass. He's half-dead."

"What do I care? He's a Kingdom snot."

"He gave me a fizzop. I like him."

"I'm sure the boss will be pleased to learn how easy you are to win over."

"He knows. How do you think he got me?"

Casmir cleared his throat. "It's not safe yet, no. I'm sorry. I'm working on it. I—"

A rumble emanated from the tunnel the group had originally come in from. Casmir's first thought was that Moonrazor had woken up the robots he'd taken offline back at the harbor, but then he remembered Kim's message. They were coming.

The mercenaries—Rache had left more than a dozen in the chamber—swung their rifles toward the mouth of the tunnel.

"Shit." Casmir lurched to his feet, almost blacking out. He gasped, gripped his knees, and struggled to stay upright.

Kim had told him about the knight, and he should have assumed troops too. Kim was coming with *enemies* to the mercenaries.

"Wait." Casmir held up his hands and staggered away from the gate, toward the tunnel entrance, his shambling gait painfully slow. "Help is coming. They're from the Kingdom, but there are two android experts to help me with the gate."

"Where are you going, Casmir Dabrowski?" Zee trotted after him.

"The Kingdom!" one mercenary blurted.

"Rache didn't say anything about that."

A strange worm-like vehicle sped out of the tunnel with ten men in Kingdom armor, and Casmir spotted Kelsey-Sato and Kim, but he was too terrified that a firefight would break out to do more than wave his hands. The Kingdom troops were already swinging rifles toward the mercenaries.

"Don't shoot," Casmir cried, stopping in between the two groups.

Zee leaped to place himself between him and the mercenaries, but he also watched the Kingdom troops, perhaps fearing they were also a threat to Casmir. Maybe they were.

Casmir swallowed, his mouth painfully dry. "We need to work together, or we'll never get out of here alive."

That made them pause. Thank God. Casmir wasn't sure his words were true, since Moonrazor now wanted him to deactivate the gate, but it might be. She might be poised to attack them all as soon as he finished.

Kim sprang down from the vehicle and ran toward him. She also waved her hands. "We brought help that you need. Let our scholars assist him."

Casmir was horrified when Kim joined him, also putting herself in the middle of all those rifles. *He* was dying, so it hardly mattered if they shot him. She was not.

"What are you *doing*?" she blurted, wrapping her arms around him.

"Are you *hugging* me? Do I look that bad?" Casmir had his helmet off again—breathing the frigid air seemed so much better than suffocating inside that turtle shell—so his splotchy face was on full display.

"I'm keeping them from *shooting* you." Her arms were spread protectively more than actually grabbing him.

"Well, don't do that. I'm more expendable than you."

"Not right now, you aren't, kid." Kelsey-Sato trotted past, heading straight into the magnetic field with a toolkit. "Get your butt back in here and help."

Neither the mercenaries nor Kingdom marines had lowered their rifles, but they did stare at the monkey droid with puzzlement rather than hostility.

An android in spectacles trotted after Kelsey-Sato. Qin lowered her rifle, spread her arms, and also came over to stand protectively in front of Casmir.

A big armored Kingdom man hopped off the vehicle, holding a hand up toward his men, then taking a few steps toward the group of mercenaries.

"Who's in charge there?" he asked.

"Me, Lieutenant Killian." It was the man who'd enjoyed Casmir's fizzop—and admitted it. Maybe there was hope he'd be more reasonable than some of the others… "Who are you?"

"Asger, the leader of these men."

Even with Kim's warning, the name was strange to hear applied to someone else. If he was truly a knight, he didn't look it. He was wearing the same combat armor as the marines from the *Osprey*, and he hadn't introduced himself as *Sir* Asger. Maybe because he thought the mercenaries would be more likely to fight a knight?

"Move aside, Casmir." Kim tried to muscle Casmir out of the way. "You're in the middle of everyone's line of fire."

"I know. I was thinking my innocent and charming presence would keep them from shooting."

"Think again. Also, you have puke on your chest."

"Sorry. A man can't hit the mark every time."

"Tell me about it. I share a bathroom with you."

A bathroom in a house that he might never see again. Casmir had been doing fine working on the gate, but with his best friend back and the reminder of what he might lose, he struggled to keep from breaking out in tears. He *did* hug Kim. He needed it.

Kim hugged him back. "Casmir, you're going to be all right."

Zee loomed close, protective, as always. "You must step out of the line of fire, Casmir Dabrowski. I might not be able to block you from all assailants."

"I know, Zee. Thanks."

"Did you get some of Rache's blood?" Kim asked, ignoring the crusher.

"Yeah." Casmir feared the disease was too far advanced for his body to recover even with whatever help could be synthesized from it, but maybe if they could get out of here soon enough...

He looked up at the great hole in the ceiling, the dim light filtering down from the distant sun, and he wished he could simply leave now.

"Is he all right?" Qin whispered. "He doesn't look like himself."

"Because he's not." Kim gripped Casmir's arm. "You take care of their stupid gate, and I'll figure out a way to get you picked up." She lowered her voice. "Whether the gate is fixable or not."

"Casmir," Kelsey-Sato said. "Come show me what you've done. I pray you haven't gotten any fizzop stains on the circuitry."

One of the mercenaries snickered. His lieutenant.

"I haven't, ma'am." Casmir released Kim and shambled back to help.

Qin crouched behind the stopped vehicle along with the Kingdom troops, ready to fire at the mercenaries if necessary. She hoped it wouldn't be necessary. Nearly twenty minutes had passed without anyone opening fire, but both groups kept fingering their rifles and eyeing each other.

Casmir, Kelsey-Sato, and Beaumont were tinkering at various points along one of the massive gate pieces. Stacks of hundreds more rose up behind them like great metal bluffs, and Qin wondered if this chamber had existed before or if the astroshamans had carved it out to make room for their find. Even though she had traveled through the systems' gates numerous times, she hadn't realized how large they were.

One of the mercenaries kept glancing toward a wide hole in the ceiling with a lake of melted and then refrozen ice underneath it.

She heard him muttering back and forth to his ship, listened intently, and then shared the words with those who had less sensitive ears. "The Kingdom ships are up there chasing Rache's camouflaged ship around," she reported. "It's taken some damage. They say they need to talk to their boss—Rache—because they need to get out of here now. But he and his other men went off to fight the astroshamans, and they can't get through to him."

"Good," Bjarke said. "Let's hope he doesn't give any of his people the freedom to make decisions on their own. And that he's dead."

Qin used the excuse of having to eavesdrop not to answer. She didn't want to wish ill on Rache, mostly because Asger was with him. She also wasn't sure how to handle Bjarke-in-command-mode rather than the flippant snarky Bjarke who'd flirted with Bonita. Which was the real man?

"Brace yourselves," one of the mercenaries yelled, pointing up at the hole. "Someone's dropping explosives."

"What?" Beaumont jerked his head up. "They risk disrupting the magnetic field and exposing you all to the gate radiation."

"Not to mention dropping the ceiling on us," Kelsey-Sato pointed out.

Casmir was too focused to comment or even react.

"Who's dropping explosives?" Bjarke demanded loudly, apparently not caring if the mercenaries knew they were eavesdropping. "Rache? The Kingdom warships?"

"It's one of the other ships," the mercenary lieutenant said. "A trio of them. It's—"

The first bomb hit far above. The explosion was distant and muffled, but the floor shuddered, and ice directly overhead snapped ominously.

"The other ships are *all* coming down from orbit," the lieutenant reported. "They must have picked up the gate's energy signature. And they all want it. Or a piece of it."

Qin caught Kim looking at Casmir, and for the first time, he lifted his head, returning the long look. But neither of them said anything. Casmir bent his head and went back to work.

"He's giving me an idea," Kelsey-Sato murmured and waved Beaumont down to an exposed panel.

An idea? All they had was an idea at this point? Qin grimaced as the ice chunks fell from the ceiling.

She had the urge to run in and grab Casmir and Kim's mom and carry them to safety—or at least out from under the target of the bombers.

"...Just tell them to protect the hole," Bjarke was saying, and Qin realized he'd gotten a comm message through too. To Captain Ishii? "We're *right* under it, and they're still trying to fix the gate."

The muffled din of weapons fire echoed down from above. Qin flexed her hands, feeling useless.

She spotted movement at the mouth of a different tunnel and spun toward it. Asger—*her* Asger—strode out in his silver liquid armor, with his pertundo fully extended.

Qin almost rushed to greet him, but a number of black-armored mercenaries walked out after him. It didn't look like he was a prisoner. It looked like he was *with* them, or even leading them.

"What the hell?" Bjarke blurted.

Asger jerked in surprise and looked over, his eyes going wide behind his faceplate.

He mouthed but did not speak, "Father?"

"Kingdom!" one of the mercenaries with Asger roared, pointing at Qin's group.

"Truce," Casmir blurted, lunging to his feet and wobbling. Zee steadied him by the shoulder. "We're having a truce!" Casmir yelled. "If any of us are to get a piece of the gate, we need to finish disarming its security system before those idiots blow the roof in."

As he thrust a hand upward, another explosion landed. All the mercenaries and all the marines, who'd once again been pointing their rifles at each other, stared at Casmir, as if they hadn't realized the roof caving in was a possibility.

That bomb must have dropped right above them, for the ceiling quaked visibly. Chunks of ice plummeted down, smashing and breaking on the hard floor. One clunked a mercenary in the shoulder, and he pointed his rifle upward, as if *that* would help.

"This might not be the best place to loiter," Kim murmured, though she was looking from Casmir to the ceiling and back, not over her own head.

Casmir wasn't even wearing his helmet.

"William! Come *here*." Bjarke pointed his rifle at the floor in front of him. "Without your... captors."

Those captors didn't look like they'd had any intention of keeping Asger from walking away. He strode over, his chin up, and his eyes blazing with determination. Or embarrassment at being called out like a child? It was hard to tell through his helmet.

Asger glanced at Qin, but he looked away before she could lift a hand in greeting. Embarrassment, she decided.

"What are you doing here, sir?" Asger didn't sound excited to see his father. "This is *my* mission."

"They sent me to check on you. Last I heard, you were kidnapped by mercenaries. But it looks more like you're *cavorting* with them."

"Is that different from cavorting with pirates?" Qin asked.

She knew this was none of her business, but she didn't like seeing Asger being belittled. He didn't deserve it.

Bjarke ignored her.

Asger glanced at her but focused on his father and answered. "I've been working with them to defeat the astroshamans. We have a common goal. For now."

"What happened to all of the Kingdom troops you were sent down here with?"

Asger hesitated. Some of the marines behind Bjarke stirred, glancing at the groups of mercenaries again.

"I don't know, sir. I went with Casmir and Kim when they were kidnapped from our original submarine, and I haven't seen them since."

"They're dead. All of the Kingdom submarines were destroyed while these mercenaries took advantage of the distraction they provided. Maybe they could have used a trained knight to help them."

Or maybe Asger would be dead, too, if he'd stayed with them...

Qin knew she should be watching the mercenaries instead of this exchange between father and son, so she wrenched her gaze away. Since the new group of mercenaries had returned with Asger, Rache's men outnumbered the Kingdom troops two to one. Now, they were murmuring quietly to each other over their comms.

She heard the words, "...can take them."

Another said, "We can't *all* have the gate."

"I think they're going to attack," Qin whispered. "Can you two finish your reunion later? Also, it's nice to see you again, Asger."

He jerked his gaze from his father's face and bowed deeply to her.

Before he spoke, the boom of another explosive dropping on the ice above them drowned it out. Several men jumped, and someone's twitchy finger fired.

The marines cursed and shot at the mercenaries. The mercenaries shot back. Soon, DEW-Tek bolts streaked across the chamber from both sides.

"Watch out for the civilians!" Bjarke yelled, waving for his men to stay behind the vehicle for protection.

"No, no," Casmir shouted from the gate piece they were studying, even as Zee pulled him back behind a stack for safety. "We're almost there. So close. Stop shooting!"

But only Qin seemed to hear him. The mercenaries fired from two different positions, pinning down the Kingdom troops.

Qin was debating charging into the closest group, hoping to discombobulate them and force them into hand-to-hand combat before her armor took too many hits. Then Asger roared, a primal roar of frustration and anger. He hefted his pertundo and sprinted toward the mercenaries he'd just left.

Qin gaped after him, startled. Had Bjarke ordered him to rush over and fight with them? Or worse, was he trying to prove something to his father?

She shook her head and ran after him. They'd fought together before, back to back and outnumbered, and they could do so again. But Qin worried that the ceiling would collapse and none of this would matter in the end.

CHAPTER 23

CASMIR, WITH KELSEY-SATO'S HELP, HAD FOUND THE CONTROLS for the gate's security system, and he was close to figuring out how to turn it off, but Zee had him by the scruff of his neck and wouldn't let him rush back to his work. They were hunkered behind a stack of gate pieces, staring helplessly as the mercenaries and marines shot at each other.

Casmir had tried so hard to keep the situation from devolving into this. Why did everyone insist on killing each other over the gate? Yes, it was the archeological find of the millennium, but it couldn't be worth *dying* for.

Kelsey-Sato and Beaumont had also taken cover—a stray energy bolt had blasted a hole through Beaumont's shoulder. The android felt no pain, and had expressed more indignation about the wound to his garment than to himself, but if shots kept coming this way, they might damage the gate. Irreparably.

Huge chunks of ice kept tumbling from the ceiling, threatening further damage—and to bury everyone.

For some reason, Qin and Asger were out in the middle of the fray, battling mercenaries in close quarters. A boulder of ice slammed down inches from Asger's heels. He was too busy cutting a mercenary's rifle in half with his pertundo to notice. Another mercenary sprang for his back, but Qin launched a punch like a pile driver and knocked the man on his ass.

The rest of the combatants fired at each other from behind cover, the marines behind that strange vehicle and the mercenaries behind pillars.

Another thunderous snap came from above. Casmir envisioned the entire ceiling collapsing and killing everybody—even combat armor wouldn't protect people from that much weight.

"Zee," Casmir said, "I need you to grab *that* mercenary and *that* one." He pointed at the pair of Rache's men who were shouting orders. "If we can take them out of the fight, maybe the others will calm down."

Casmir glanced toward the tunnel Asger and the second group of mercenaries had exited. He was tempted to send Zee to find Rache. *He could calm these idiots down with a word.*

"I cannot leave you unprotected, Casmir Dabrowski," Zee said.

"I won't need protection if you stop that fight." Casmir patted his looming guardian on the arm. "I'm very close to accomplishing the mission. I just need a few more minutes over there working on that gate piece."

"You are my mission. I cannot leave you."

"I'll hide behind Kelsey-Sato if someone starts shooting this way."

Zee looked down at the monkey-droid who only rose halfway up his leg and then back at Casmir. "She is not sufficiently large to use as cover."

"It was a joke. Please, Zee, go stop—"

Someone screamed in fear, the cry echoing from the ice walls, and the noise was cut off abruptly. Casmir looked in time to see a decapitated head still inside of its helmet go bouncing across the floor. He winced, wishing he hadn't looked. It was one of the mercenaries, and Asger had landed the killing blow with his wicked halberd. Rache was going to kill him.

If they all didn't kill each *other*.

The vehicle blew up in a fiery explosion that hurled huge shards of metal across the chamber. Casmir gaped as pieces skidded all the way to the gate.

The rest of the Kingdom men, with nothing to hide behind for cover, ran out to join Asger and Qin in close quarters.

The rumble of a ship's engine echoed down the hole from above. Casmir wished he had a way to ask those ships to wait a half hour before continuing—or to back off altogether. He was the reason they were here. He had to fix it.

"The gate first," he whispered.

But Zee still gripped him, refusing to let him move back into the open. Held captive by his own bodyguard.

"Zee, I *order* you to let me go, and go get those men I pointed out." Casmir snapped off his instinct to add please. It had to be an order.

Zee looked down at him, and for a moment, Casmir feared he wouldn't obey. He hoped it was only in his imagination that Zee seemed stung by the cold treatment. Either way, Zee released him and charged out after the mercenaries.

Casmir raced out from behind the stack, almost diving to get back to his work. He'd been so close. A few more minutes…

An alert popped up on his contact—Rache requesting permission to message him. Casmir would have laughed if he hadn't been so miserable and frazzled. Had they never spoken chip-to-chip before?

He accepted the request.

Moonrazor is heading your way, Rache said. *Watch out. Chaplain and I have been hunting her, and we took out a bunch of her bodyguards, but she slipped away, and I think she's circling back toward the gate chamber.*

Can you come back here and order your men to stop trying to kill the Kingdom troops that brought me help? Casmir worked as he talked, keeping his head low. More men were down, but that only made the remaining ones desperate. Energy bolts kept ricocheting off armor and going all over the place.

What help? Rache didn't answer the more pertinent question.

Scholar Kelsey-Sato and another android professor.

Kelsey-Sato? Kim's mother?

Yes. Realizing that might motivate Rache more than a desperate plea for peace, Casmir added, *She would probably be grateful if her mother didn't get filled with holes.*

Kim is there too?

Yes.

I'm coming.

Rumbles sounded in the nearest tunnel before Casmir could repeat that all Rache needed to do was order his men to stop fighting.

Casmir glanced up and spotted the headlights of a huge robot on studded metal wheels heading toward the chamber—heading right toward him. It was different from the others he'd seen, more tank than robot, with a large opaque dome on the top and rotating turrets mounted on all of its flat surfaces.

"Look out," Casmir shouted. "More robots are coming."

A shuttle-sized chunk of ice tumbled from the ceiling, crashing down in front of the approaching robot-tank. It shattered into a broken mound and blocked the tunnel exit. Casmir would have laughed at the timing and the placement, but the robot-tank started firing immediately, cutting the mound into pieces manageable enough to drive over.

The software program Casmir had running, one he'd altered to understand the special operating system and language of the gate, found a digital ON/OFF switch deep inside the security system. Was that it? What he'd been looking for?

With a quick command, he flicked it to off, then held his breath as a fresh batch of energy bolts flew around the chamber. Another great snap came from above, and ice ground as it shifted overhead.

Wincing, and afraid the ceiling would come down any second, Casmir yanked out the scanner he'd modified to read the pseudo radiation. Had he successfully turned off the defenses? He held his breath, waiting for a reading to come back.

The robot-tank finished cutting the blockage into pieces and crunched over the remains. It rumbled straight toward Casmir.

He scrambled away from the gate piece. A tremor went through the floor under him, and something ground deep within it—was there more machinery down there?

The robot-tank drove several feet, passing through the magnetic field, and stopped. The opaque dome started to lift.

Casmir glanced around, looking for Zee. He imagined androids or cyborgs spewing out of the robot-tank and springing straight at him.

"Zee!" Casmir wasn't sure where he'd gone—boulders littered the floor and blocked most of his view of the battle. "I need help."

This was what he got for sending his bodyguard away.

Only one person hopped out of the robot-tank, someone in green combat armor with a clear faceplate. Casmir squinted. It was a woman with short white hair. Moonrazor.

She carried two rifles and strode toward Casmir. But she lifted her hands instead of the weapons and pointed at his homemade scanner.

"What does that say?"

Casmir risked glancing at it. The scan had completed. "It worked," he blurted with relief. "The radiation is gone."

She kept walking toward him, as if she wanted to see for herself.

Casmir, his relief short-lived, held his hands out. Should he run? She wasn't aiming anything at him, but he worried this was a trap. Maybe she would snatch him, drag him into her tank, and take him off to hold hostage. As if someone would pay ransom money for him. She would be disappointed when he ended up dying before she could send a request.

Moonrazor stopped in front of him and flipped up her faceplate. Yes, that was definitely the woman he'd seen in the holographic picture in the *Osprey's* briefing room. She appeared much younger than the long career listed in her bio would have suggested.

She peered at the scanner display. "Excellent." She pointed at his tool satchel and the tools scattered around it. "Pick those up."

"Are we going somewhere?"

Moonrazor looked up as another snap emanated from the ice above and more chunks rained down. One landed a foot away, making Casmir jump. There hadn't even been an explosion. Maybe they'd passed the tipping point and the ice would inevitably come down on its own now. Soon.

Casmir scrambled to put his tools away and sling his satchel over his shoulder. He spotted Kelsey-Sato and Beaumont watching from behind a stack, but he didn't do anything to draw attention to them. Maybe Moonrazor hadn't noticed them yet.

"The tunnels are reinforced." Moonrazor pointed toward the one she'd exited.

Casmir took a few steps in that direction with her, more because he thought the robot-tank looked sturdy and good to hide under than because he wanted to go with her.

They were halfway to it when a black-armored man came into sight, springing over the mounds of ice. A second larger man ran out of the tunnel after him.

"Rache!" Casmir blurted.

Moonrazor swore and grabbed Casmir. He struggled to pull away, but the Plague made him weak, even with his armor, and she had enhancements that would have made her a match for Zee. She easily spun him, not to grab his throat or threaten him but so he faced her, his back toward Rache, who'd been in the process of raising a rifle. Thankfully, Rache didn't fire.

Casmir glimpsed Zee clambering over another pile of ice off to the side. He carried two writhing mercenaries over his shoulders, each peeled out of his armor. If Casmir could buy a few seconds…

But hundreds of meters of ice chose that moment to fall. The frozen boulders tumbled around the gate and smashed the equipment the mercenaries had used to drill the first hole. Casmir gawked as the sky became visible far above, along with ships flying all around the now much larger hole. One of the Kingdom warships was among them, but there had to be dozens of different craft from who knew where.

They were all jockeying for position and lowering high-tech grappling hooks or maglockers capable of lifting pieces of the gate from the pile.

"Stop!" Moonrazor barked, pulling Casmir closer and raising her hand. She was looking at Rache, not the new skylight.

Rache had been advancing, but Moonrazor showed him a tiny device in her grip. A weapon? It looked like a remote control for a detonator.

Rache must not have known what it was, for he paused. His man started angling to circle around them, but the robot-tank started up, blocking his path as it headed toward Moonrazor and Casmir.

Hell, she *was* going to kidnap him.

"What are your orders, Casmir Dabrowski?" Zee called, dropping his captured men. "If I approach, she may harm you."

Casmir opened his mouth to tell him to risk it, but Moonrazor smirked and pressed a finger to his lips.

"What are you doing?" he blurted.

"Thanking you." She smiled and kissed him soundly on the mouth, startling him so much that he almost missed her pressing the button on that tiny remote control.

"Casmir!" Rache barked, rushing toward them. "Get away from her so I can shoot."

Ice cracked and the floor heaved. Moonrazor shoved Casmir hard, so that he tumbled backward. She'd meant for him to smash into Rache as she sprinted toward her robot-tank, maybe knocking both of them down, but Rache caught Casmir.

The floor moved under their feet. It didn't tremble, like it had before, but it moved sideways. What was *happening*?

Moonrazor sprang into her robot-tank. Rache pointed his rifle over Casmir's shoulder and fired, but his bolts bounced off her armor. The dome came down over the driving compartment, sealing Moonrazor inside, and it proved even more impervious to DEW-Tek bolts.

Rache swore and backed toward the tunnel, pulling Casmir with him. Zee ran after them.

Casmir wanted to struggle—he was tired of being pushed and pulled around—but nausea clenched his stomach again, and all he wanted was to collapse somewhere.

"I am a damsel," he groaned to himself.

"Maybe getting some of my manly blood into you will help." Rache had a hand clamped on his shoulder but was looking out on the chaos.

"I don't think it works that way."

"Try the gym too."

"Now you're just picking on the sick man."

All other sounds of battle had stopped, save for a few mercenaries firing at the hooks and beams snatching up pieces of the gate. One managed to hit a chain, but whatever metal it was made from had no trouble deflecting the attack.

As soon as Casmir and Rache—and Zee—reached the tunnel, a couple of mercenaries skidding into it for protection from the ice that continued to fall, the floor in the chamber finished sliding aside.

Casmir stared in bewilderment. His first thought was that it was breaking apart because of all the weight that had fallen from above, but…

"It's a door," he blurted.

Massive sliding doors under the ice—and under the gate pieces. As they opened, the stacks that remained fell into water below. No, it wasn't water. They *thunked* down instead of splashing down.

Casmir rose on his tiptoes, trying to see. Was there another chamber down there?

He almost laughed as the truth struck him. Not a chamber, a ship. Moonrazor had docked a ship down there. Something capable of maneuvering underwater as well as flying up into space? Had she known all along she might have to get away quickly with the gate pieces? And only been waiting until the security system was deactivated?

Her robot-tank bounded over the ice and to the massive opening, then jumped through the great open doors. Someone fired half-heartedly at it before it disappeared, but the bolt was no more effective than Rache's had been.

Casmir shook his head as half of the gate pieces disappeared into Moonrazor's hold and half disappeared upward into the holds of whatever ships had been able to find a position and snag at least one.

"Did you orchestrate all this?" Rache waved at the last of the gate pieces flying upward.

"Uh, can we say *you* did?" Casmir couldn't imagine what report would eventually end up getting back to King Jager. As focused as he'd been on his task, he hadn't missed the two Asgers facing off. Asger's dad sounded like someone who would reveal… far too much when he reported in.

Rache laughed. Casmir had heard it so seldom that it startled him.

"I don't care what you tell the king," Rache said.

"Thanks," Casmir mumbled, though he doubted he had it in him to lie. Even if he was capable of it, he suspected there were too many eyes here for falsehoods to stand for long.

The massive ice-covered doors slid shut.

"Did you orchestrate *that* too?" Rache pointed at them. "That freakish cult leader kissed you. What the hell, Casmir?"

"What, damsels can't get kissed?"

"Not by *other* damsels. Not in the Kingdom."

Casmir snorted. "We're a long way from the Kingdom. And Moonrazor isn't very damselly."

"See, that's a good word, isn't it?"

Casmir slumped as a wave of weariness washed over him. His knees might have buckled if not for the support of his leg armor. He leaned against the wall as darkness crept into the edge of his vision.

He swallowed, fear returning now that he had time for it. He worried he would pass out—and wouldn't wake up again.

"You all right?" Rache asked.

He wanted to be tough and say a definitive *yes*. What came out was a worried, "I don't think so."

Kim, Qin, and Asger appeared, climbing over the rubble.

"Casmir?" Kim rushed toward him.

Rache stepped back, letting them take over holding him upright. Kim shot him a dirty look.

Was she still angry because Rache had taken Casmir out of the submarine? Or because Casmir had been willing to go? The hard look seemed to be for Rache, not Casmir, but maybe only because nobody glared at a dying man.

Casmir had an abrupt fear that he would come between them. He didn't want them to *be* a *them*, but if they were going to be… he didn't want to get in the way. He searched for a way to get Kim to forgive Rache before he passed out.

He patted Kim's arm. "Rache helped me. He gave me his blood. It's going to make me manly."

Kim's expression grew more bewildered than forgiving.

"You better get him up to your ship," Rache said quietly. "He's delirious."

Casmir moaned. "Does that mean I'm always going to be a damsel?"

"We'll take care of him." Kim glanced back. "Asger, tell Ishii to get a shuttle down here."

"Please," Casmir whispered.

"What?" Kim asked.

"You have to say please to people and robots. It's a rule." He looked over at Zee. "I'm sorry I didn't say *please* before, Zee."

"I forgive you, Casmir Dabrowski."

"Thank you."

Kim squinted at him. "I'm not sure if you're genuinely delirious, or you're just being you."

"Yeah." Casmir forced a smile, though he wasn't sure it worked.

He was aware of Beaumont and Kelsey-Sato walking up and was glad they hadn't fallen into Moonrazor's hold when the doors opened. Elsewhere, the dead lay amid the icy rubble. Casmir's last thought before the darkness took him was that it all could have been much easier—much less deadly—if everyone had agreed to share the gate from the beginning.

CHAPTER 24

KIM PACED OUTSIDE OF CASMIR'S LITTLE ROOM IN sickbay until she was too tired to pace, and then she sat in a chair next to his bunk. Machines beeped softly behind him, and his eyes were closed. His face was pale, his skin blotchy with the telltale signs of the Plague rash. He'd been in and out of consciousness all evening after sleeping fitfully throughout the day cycle. It scared her that he hadn't woken earlier when the nurse had come in to change his IV. A part of her wanted to shake him to make sure he still *could* be woken, but if it turned out he couldn't, what then?

She wiped her eyes for the hundredth time that day, relieved nobody was around to see, but sad that Casmir's parents and long-time friends back home weren't here to be with him. The *Osprey* continued to orbit Xolas Moon while Ishii's men searched the mess down below, trying to find survivors from the other submarine teams. It would be days before they left and reached the gate, weeks before they reached Odin and home. Casmir would either be better by then… or he wouldn't have made it.

Kim closed her eyes, tears trickling down her cheeks, not wanting to contemplate that option.

Earlier, she and Dr. Sikou had injected him with the antibodies from Rache's blood. They had confirmed that he'd had the Great Plague at some previous date. The injection they'd given Casmir *should* help, but his immune system still had to have the strength to fight off the virus. After all he'd been through these past days—these past weeks—Kim was afraid to gamble on that.

She wished they were flying to Tiamat Station instead of orbiting this stupid moon that she hoped she never saw again. At least there, he could have undergone the mitochondria treatment. Dr. Sikou had confirmed that the *Osprey* didn't have the equipment for that. But Tiamat Station was three days away. Even with all the advancements to drive technology over the centuries, everything was still so far apart out here in space.

"Casmir, is there anything I can do for you?" Kim whispered, though she knew he wasn't awake.

Zee, his constant companion who stood in the shadows near the head of the bed, looked at her but didn't speak. Kim was glad he was there. She hadn't forgotten that the odious Ambassador Romano was on board somewhere. Since Rache had found that locator beacon and destroyed it, there was no reason to barter a life for it, but Romano probably still wanted Casmir to die, since he'd messed up his plans at Tiamat Station—and again with the gate.

Though it was possible Rache would get the blame for that. The last she'd heard, Ishii believed he'd masterminded all those ships showing up to get a piece. But Kim well knew that had been Casmir's vision for weeks, and she would be shocked if it turned out he wasn't responsible, at least in some part. She wouldn't say a word though. Let Rache take the heat. He wouldn't care. He would be delighted to have Jager blame him.

"If you want me to find some comic books, just let me know," Kim said. "I don't think there's a bookstore, or any kind of store, on the ship, but I'm sure some of the privates share your tastes. The *younger* privates." She smiled and smoothed his blanket, wishing he would wake up and banter with her, argue the literary merits of his beloved superhero adventures.

Unfortunately, he did not.

She looked around the silent sickbay, everybody gone save for a nurse on the nightshift. The nurse came in and checked now and then but didn't say much. Asger, Qin, and even Ishii had been by earlier, spending the evening speaking quietly while Casmir slept. Asger and Ishii had talked about what they would do when they got home—both seemed to feel that getting drunk sounded appealing. Qin had told Kim about her new acquaintance, Sir Bjarke Asger, who also went by Johnny Twelve Toes and was possibly having a romance with Bonita.

Another time, Kim would have been curious about the knight and Qin's recent adventures, but she had a hard time holding a conversation or being a good listener. A part of her kept trying to solve the problem before her, wanting to work on some experimental strain of bacteria that could help Casmir. If she'd had months, or even weeks, instead of days, maybe she could have, but she was afraid the only thing she could do was sit here and be supportive. Which seemed like utter bullshit.

"I know what I'll do, Casmir. I'm going to compose a letter to Oku. I'll apologize that I haven't had a chance to work on her bees, and then I'll let her know about some of the heroic things you've been doing lately. Is there anything in particular you'd like me to throw in? I suppose I better be careful since Royal Intelligence probably reads her messages. You're wise to only send videos of robots and dogs back and forth." She looked at Zee. "You never did get Zee to roll on his back for the camera, did you? Maybe he'll do it for me."

She didn't expect Zee to deign to respond.

He looked over solemnly. "If this type of frivolity would further Casmir Dabrowski's chances of surviving his illness and securing me a mate, I would consider such an activity."

"Thank you, Zee. I know he would appreciate that."

"Do you believe he will recover from his illness?"

"I hope so." Kim wished she had a more affirmative answer.

"He had a seizure in the base, and I did not know how to fix it. I have read your medical databases. The procedures for assisting a person having a seizure are inadequate."

"You're not wrong. We're better at prevention than at stopping them once they start. But traveling all over the Twelve Systems and being thrust into stressful life-threatening situations isn't conducive to prevention either."

Zee looked down at Casmir and then at her. "If Casmir Dabrowski dies, I will have failed."

"There's nothing you could have done before, and nothing you can do now."

"My duty is to protect him, to keep him from dying."

"I know." She wiped her eyes again.

"If he is gone, I will have only Kim Sato to protect."

She looked bleakly at him, not able to find words to respond. She didn't know if the idea of Zee being around when Casmir was gone was reassuring or depressing. It would be something of him, but it would also be a constant reminder that they had *all* failed him.

Why hadn't she asked to see that woman's body? To see the face? She'd assumed the obvious dagger wounds were the cause of death. If Casmir hadn't ridden down in the submarine that had contained the virus, maybe he never would have caught it.

"Kim?"

Kim had heard the voice so seldom in recent years that it took her a moment to recognize it. She took a deep breath before she responded, to steady her voice *and* her feelings. She didn't know if she wanted company now or not, or if this was the company she would choose.

"Over here, Mother," she said.

Her mother walked in, and Kim pulled a seat around to Casmir's bed. She wasn't sure if her mother would stay, but she should invite her to. They'd barely spoken the last time they'd been on a ship together—or in the last ten years, period. Kim's attempt at starting a meaningful conversation in the base had only resulted in her mother's proclamation that she was standing on her tail.

Once she hopped up onto the seat, her mother could see Casmir. "I hope he pulls through. I've forgiven him for the egregious fizzop stains he left on my coffee table."

"That's large of you," Kim murmured, though she wasn't in the mood to banter, not with anyone except Casmir.

"I strive to be large, but that's an elusive goal now."

"Yeah."

Kim wondered if they should leave the room, if they might be disturbing Casmir's rest. But she had a feeling he would prefer to have people around him rather than being alone. *Kim* preferred being alone, but he'd always seen it as more of a punishment, a sign that he'd failed in some social way to acquire friends who would be present whenever he needed them.

"Your friend was surprisingly sharp down there," her mother said, "given how advanced his illness was."

"What did he do?"

"To the best of my ability to discern, he was teaching himself the language of the gate builders, so that he could interact with the operating system at the base level. I'm not sure how. We—we in the archaeology field who have studied the gates from the outside for centuries—had no knowledge of that. It's not anything I was able to share with him. I believe he was surfing around, intuiting and teaching himself."

"The gate builders were the original humans from Old Earth, weren't they?"

"Mm, that's one hypothesis, but I believe the artificial intelligences originally built by those humans on Old Earth evolved into something more technologically advanced and sophisticated and that *they* were the ones to invent the gates and establish the gate network. We may never know what happened to them, or why humans were the ones to settle these systems, and only with a modest level of computer sophistication." She tilted her head. "Maybe that's why the astroshamans hadn't cracked the code yet. For all their technology, they are still humans that all or partially turned themselves into machines, rather than machines that were never anything else and always thought like machines."

"Ah." Another time, Kim might have cared. She couldn't muster the interest now.

"You should marry him."

Kim blinked. "What?"

"If he lives, he would make a good mate. You would likely have very intelligent babies."

"He's my best friend, not anyone I'm romantically interested in." Rache's face—his real face, not the damn mask—popped into her mind.

Her mother waved a dismissive hand. "Best friends are better than hunky males that make your heart zing. For women like us, especially. If you're like me, you'll prefer a logical choice, someone with whom you share common interests."

Since Kim didn't want to bring up Rache—like everyone else, her mother would be horrified at the prospect of him as a romantic interest—she steered the conversation toward a different topic.

"Is that what you had with my father? Common interests?"

"No, and it's why it didn't last. I'd never been that interested in physical relationships, you see, but he chose me, and he wasn't unappealing. He's handsome and has that enigmatic *shinshoku* way of his. I'd always been quiet and bookish—yes, I can see your shock—and his attention was flattering. I do not regret the relationship, but I think it would have made more sense for me to marry someone who shared a few of my passions, so we would have something to discuss when we grew bored with sex."

Kim glanced warily at Casmir, half-expecting him to have woken up to hear her mother talk about her sex life. She could envision him noshing on popcorn and listening with fascination. But he remained asleep—or unconscious.

"Oh," Kim said, sure she should say something, but she had no idea what. As odd as it seemed, they'd never had a discussion like this. She remembered her mother visiting when she had been about thirteen and suggesting a book that explained human sexual practices and the dangers of sexually transmitted diseases. The experience had been thankfully brief but horrifying nonetheless.

"Can't you meet someone who makes your heart zing and with whom you have shared interests?" Kim wasn't sure what interests she shared with Rache except for literature, but the fact that he'd actually read her novels—the novels *nobody* had read—made her believe they could find things to talk about for many years, even if she didn't know if she had it in her to zing at any man's touch.

"I'm sure that happens for many people, but not for ladies like us. We're scientists, Kim, rational beings. Pleasures of the flesh are— Tell me truthfully, for I've never seen you with a man, do you even care about such things?"

"Not... much."

"Find a mate you can talk with and who knows when to leave you to your own devices. That is true happiness, my girl." Her mother patted her hand, gave something between a wave and a salute to the slumbering Casmir, and hopped down and left.

Kim didn't know what to make of the talk, and found the idea that she and her mother were essentially the same to be disconcerting, but Kim was glad she had come by. Their last meeting had been so abbreviated. It felt right that they'd spoken of something consequential, even if Kim had kept her true thoughts to herself.

A text message popped up on her contact. *Kim? It's Qin. The* Stellar Dragon *just docked, and Bonita has something for you. Technically, it's for Casmir.*

I'm still in sickbay. Kim doubted Bonita could have anything useful for Casmir—Viggo had probably ordered some souvenir at Tiamat Station or wherever the ship had been—but everybody who wanted to see Casmir should be able to. She just wished he were awake and aware of the people coming by to give him pats and well wishes.

We'll be there shortly.

"Bonita is coming to see you, Casmir." Kim smiled. "You better get well. I bet Viggo has something for you to fix."

When Qin and Bonita arrived, an armed soldier trailing after them, as if they were extremely suspicious guests, Bonita was indeed carrying something that Viggo must have sent. It was one of the robot vacuums that vroomed around the *Dragon* picking up microscopic pieces of lint.

"Don't ask," Bonita said as soon as she met Kim's gaze.

She walked up and set the vacuum on a foldout tray holding Casmir's glass of water.

"I don't think he's going to be up to fixing anything tonight," Kim said.

"Viggo made me promise to bring one over to keep Casmir company. It doesn't need fixing. Though I'm sure there's room for tweaking if he wakes up and is bored." Bonita raised her eyebrows, as if to ask if he *would* wake up.

Kim shrugged, not trusting her voice to speak.

"Casmir Dabrowski will not be bored when he wakes up," Zee stated. "I am here, and I have numerous games, puzzles, and videos downloaded that I can share with him."

"Yes," Bonita murmured. "Who *wouldn't* be entertained by a six-and-a-half-foot killer robot bodyguard with a media library?"

"Nobody," Zee said.

Qin nudged Bonita and tilted her head toward the entrance to sickbay. Bonita leaned out of Casmir's little room. Their guard must have retreated.

"There's something else I have to give you," Bonita said quietly. "Imagine my surprise when Viggo arranged for a new cargo all by himself before he left Tiamat Station and, when he showed up at the *Eagle* to bring me over to the *Osprey* to get Qin, admitted that a visitor had docked with our freighter recently."

Kim had no idea what visitor might have gone to the *Dragon,* especially if the crew hadn't been aboard.

Bonita slipped a large vial out of a pouch on the belt of her galaxy suit and handed it to Kim.

A simple label called it *ImmunoBooster,* which Kim wouldn't have thought much of, but her breath caught when she read the source. Tyrex Labs on Jotunheim Station. They put out some of the most advanced and most effective anti-aging treatments known to man and were also famous for creating the best immune-system-enhancing cocktails. Not the vague "supplements" that so many hucksters sold.

But how? The station was more than two weeks away.

"It's for Casmir, I'm told," Bonita said. "To help him recover."

Suddenly aware of her fingers shaking, Kim cradled the vial with both hands. "I'll get Dr. Sikou to check it out, just to be sure, and to administer it." She wanted to rush out right away, since every minute might count with Casmir, but she paused to ask, "Who was your visitor?"

Anything from Tyrex Labs cost a fortune. She would be shocked if the vial she held sold for less than fifty thousand crowns. The only person she could imagine having that much money and knowing how badly Casmir needed it was—

"A certain mercenary who knew he'd be shot and his gift destroyed if he tried to deliver it directly to a Kingdom warship," Bonita said.

"I... thank you," Kim said.

"I'm just the delivery lady."

Kim waved and ran off to find Dr. Sikou.

Later, she would write a message for Rache. And the one she'd promised to send Oku. While she waited for Casmir to recover, she would have time to write several heartfelt messages.

Asger found Qin on the *Stellar Dragon,* which was attached to the *Osprey* via an airlock tube. The gate pieces the Kingdom had claimed for itself were loaded onto one of the other warships and already heading out of the system. Soon, the *Osprey* would follow, and Asger would return home to report in and face any punishment his superiors had in mind for his less than ideal results on the missions he'd been assigned.

A part of him wished he could board the *Dragon* for more than a brief visit and go off with Qin to find criminals to turn in. Asger didn't think he could take commands from a grumpy bounty hunter captain, but if he were to dedicate his life to collecting bad guys and bringing them to justice, it wouldn't be that different from what he did as a knight. And his chain-of-command would be much shorter, so there would be little to no politics.

And he could keep fighting side by side with Qin.

A few months ago, such a thought would have horrified him, but when she walked into the cargo hold to greet him, he grinned and waved, pleased to see her.

She had removed her combat armor, and her hair hung down in dark waves that fell around the pointed ears that stuck up through it. Her lack of armor made him aware that she had feminine curves, and even though he should have also been aware of their pronounced differences, like the fur coating the backs of her hands and running up under her sleeves, they didn't seem that important anymore. What he mostly saw was the young woman who'd run through the branches of the park in Zamek City and hugged a tree just because it was there.

"Hi, Asger. Did Bonita send you for something? She stayed on the *Osprey* after we delivered a vial that's supposed to help Casmir."

"I didn't see her, but that's good. The vial, I mean. Casmir wasn't awake when I visited earlier. He looked like he needed something."

"Yeah." Qin shook her head sadly and dropped her gaze.

Asger stepped forward and clasped her hands, wanting to comfort her. The soft light fur covering her skin was strange but soft and not unappealing. Even if his Kingdom upbringing told him it should be. Her palms were warmer than he expected but free of fur and similar to human palms. No paw pads. But the retractable claws, currently painted forest green and dotted with tiny yellow suns with smiley faces, were definitely not like fingernails.

Qin looked up, her expression a little wary, her eyes easy to read even though they, too, were as much feline as human. Maybe she was worried about what he thought about her hands. And her. It wasn't as if he'd gotten off to the best start with her. Guilt swarmed him as he remembered attacking her because he'd mistaken her for another of her kin.

He rubbed the backs of her hands, and her claws flexed a little. Was that appreciation? An involuntary reflex? He imagined them scraping through his hair and teasing his scalp, and a weird little shiver went through him.

"I hope Bonita delivered my robot," came Viggo's voice from the speakers, "and that it will share good cheer with him."

Asger released Qin's hands with a start as he realized they weren't alone. Did Viggo have *eyes*? The ship had cameras, and he could presumably parse the video data, so… yes.

Heat flushed Asger's cheeks, and he hoped Qin didn't know where his thoughts had strayed. She would think he was strange. Or like those pirates who'd slept with her because it was thrilling and exotic or just because they felt they owned her and they could.

"I didn't know vacuums were capable of delivering cheer," Qin said, seemingly unaware of Asger's thoughts. Good.

"Robotic vacuums are," Viggo said. "To those who know how to appreciate robots."

"Why did you come?" Qin clasped her hands behind her back. To make them unavailable for holding? Or because she didn't want him to continue to examine their differences?

"Over here?" Asger waved at the airlock. "To see you."

"Oh?" Did she look puzzled? Or intrigued?

He couldn't tell. "We didn't get to exchange more than a few words down on that moon. Shoot that. Watch out. Don't let the ceiling fall on you."

"It is hard to have long chats while in combat."

"I wanted to let you know that I… appreciated fighting alongside you more than I did with Rache."

"So I'm better than an infamous villain?"

"Much more so, yes."

"I'm relieved. But I'm a little sad that the fighting was mostly over by the time I got there." Her ears rotated and the tips drooped slightly. "It sounded like you saw a lot more."

"Maybe we'll get to fight together again sometime soon. A longer battle. Against determinedly bad, bad guys." After the way things had ended, Asger wasn't positive he considered the astroshamans bad. They'd been competitors after the same goal. A goal that was now flying off in dozens of directions with everyone happy, or maybe everyone equally unhappy. He didn't know.

"I'd like that." Qin smiled shyly and looked at his chest instead of his eyes. "But you're going back to Odin now, and we're going… I don't even know yet. To deliver that cargo Viggo picked up, I guess."

"The cargo is heading to Sultan Shayban in System Stymphalia," Viggo announced. "It's full of food and medical supplies. Perhaps the sultan believes a war is coming, which would mean plenty of opportunities to fight."

"Yes, but Bonita wouldn't sign us up for someone else's war."

"Unless Johnny Twelve Toes entices her to," Viggo said. "I assume she is having coitus with him presently, since she hasn't returned to the ship."

"Who?" Asger didn't know anybody by that name, certainly nobody that would be on the *Osprey*.

"Er, that's the name he first gave us," Qin said. "He was undercover working for the Drucker pirates. Didn't he tell you the story?"

Asger almost asked who again, but his spine stiffened before his conscious brain caught up. His body and gut knew first. Bjarke Asger. His father.

"No, we haven't spoken except for what you saw down on the moon. We're not—" Asger shrugged, "—close."

"I kind of gathered that." Qin drew her hands out from behind her back and reached toward him, but she glanced at her claws and lowered her hands to her side instead.

He frowned. She wasn't ashamed of those claws, was she? She decorated them. They seemed a source of pride or at least something she wanted to show off. Or maybe that was her way of making her friends believe they were more innocuous than they were?

Maybe he hadn't helped anything by jerking his hands away earlier. He'd been surprised by the reminder of Viggo's presence, not by her claws.

He reached down and clasped both of her hands. Her eyebrows rose, her gaze meeting his briefly before she lowered it again, but she didn't object to the grip.

"Whatever he said, it wasn't true. I mean, it probably *was* true, but it was stuff from when I was younger. Younger and angrier and before I started reading philosophy and psychology and trying to figure out what it really means to be a knight. And why I can't stop thinking about things and *rethinking* about them, and just live a normal life instead of always being wrapped up in my own head."

This time, her eyebrows drew together in a frown—or maybe that was confusion. Probably the latter. Hell, he'd confused himself.

"So there *is* a calendar out there of sixteen-year-old you? Naked in all of the photos?"

Asger groaned. His father had told her *that*?

Her eyes crinkled, and she smiled, the expression very human and mischievous.

"My mother was dead, my father was always gone, and there was nobody around to talk to except the grumpy knight who only grudgingly took me on as a squire as a favor to my father. All he ever did was judge me. I was just... I don't know. I wanted *someone* to want me. And maybe to show off a bit, since I was starting to look like a real bodybuilder about then, and see if it would help me lose my—uhm, get women." He released one of her hands to rub his face, hardly able to believe he was talking about this with her. "It was a long time ago. Eight years."

"But you still do calendars. Do you still need to be wanted?"

He snorted. "More than ever."

"Really?" She tilted her head curiously.

"I mean, not by women. I can get that. Them." Why were his cheeks so hot? Was the ship's temperature set too high? "Random women anyway. But not proper noblewomen, since there was some scandal around those early calendars, and I've got a reputation around the capital now. The women who want me mostly just want to see what it's like to have sex with a knight."

Sex. Coitus. Viggo's words returned to his mind. Was Bonita having sex with his *father*?

Asger might have fallen over if he hadn't been gripping Qin's hands. That was so... disgusting. They were both *old*. And she was a bounty hunter, and he was supposed to be a nobleman, but who knew what he was with those garish tattoos? How was it even possible that Asger was the embarrassing one in the family? Was his father going to show up back on Odin like that? And with Bonita in his lap?

"You look really distressed about that," Qin said.

"Sorry, no." What had he been saying? "I was thinking about something else. Just ignore me. I'm whining anyway. At least I had a family when I was growing up. I know you had... well, I don't know exactly what you had. If you want to talk about it, you can."

"Thanks, but I'm more curious about you. I'm enjoying this sharing." Her eyes crinkled again.

"You *are*?" He was embarrassed by his babbling. He never talked about these things to anyone. Who would he tell?

"And curious about that original calendar."

He snorted. "Why? You want to see me naked?"

She looked down at their clasped hands, or maybe the deck. "Not if you think that's weird. Or *I'm* weird. It's not like I'm some lady a knight is supposed to protect and…"

The gentle hum of the ship's vents and engines grew noticeable in the silence, and it slowly dawned on Asger that Qin *liked* him. Even though he'd attacked her and called her a freak when they first met.

He swallowed, not sure what to do with that information. It wasn't as if they could have a relationship, go back to Odin, get married, and have kids. He almost choked at the thought. But some animalistic part of him couldn't help but imagine what having sex with a woman with claws and fangs would be like. Exhilarating, he was sure.

No, damn it; he would never be like those pirates. He wouldn't have sex with someone just because it might be different and interesting. If they had sex, it should be because she was Qin, and he liked Qin. And he *did* like her. But he didn't think he liked her in a romantic way. Until a few minutes ago, he hadn't even considered… whatever it was he was considering now.

Only when she looked up warily did he realize how silent he was being and how many seconds—minutes?—had passed since she'd trailed off.

"You don't have to answer that." She squeezed his hands and smiled, even though it was a sad I-know-I'm-not-good-enough smile that made his heart ache and made him want to fix things for her. "Never mind. It wasn't even a question. And we probably aren't going to even see each other again, at least not anytime soon. But I'm glad I met you. A real knight." Her smile grew warmer. "And for what it's worth, I think you're a *much* better knight than your father."

Those words stunned him—nobody had *ever* said that—and as they sank in, like the warmth of the sun after a long winter, he stepped forward and kissed Qin.

She was startled at first and stood there like a stick, and he feared he'd misjudged her signals—misjudged everything—but then she returned the kiss with enthusiasm. She wrapped her arms around him with strength that he'd never known in a woman, but the soft breasts pressing against his chest left no doubt as to her sex. He slid his arms around her back and then down, exploring her curves. Yes, she was all woman.

William, a message popped up on his contact from a man who hadn't sent a message to his chip in years. *Come to Ishii's office. We have new orders. War has broken out in System Lion, and we can't go home.*

Asger wanted to ignore the message and keep doing exactly what he was doing, and he might have if not for that last sentence. He pulled back from Qin, stunned, and re-read it to make sure he'd gotten it right.

War. War at *home*? In their own system?

There had been talk of it for months, but nobody had thought someone would attack the Kingdom in System Lion. It had always been assumed that Jager was the aggressor, that Jager would act, sending the Fleet out elsewhere to conquer and acquire new domains for the Kingdom.

"I have to go." Asger released Qin and stepped back, half turning before he realized she might think he was rejecting her. "Not because of you," he blurted to her surprised expression. "My father said we have new orders. That war broke out. I have to find out what's going on."

Qin blinked, looking as startled as he, but nodded. "I understand."

Asger ran back to the *Osprey*, wondering if he would see her again.

EPILOGUE

CASMIR WOKE UP AND FELT ABOUT AS REFRESHED as roadkill on the mag-rails back home, but he was in his bunk in his cabin and not in sickbay, so he decided that made his morning lovely, no matter that his eyelashes were crusted with hard gunk and his head throbbed. The only thing better would have been waking up in his house on Odin with the sun beaming in the window. But something almost as good greeted him: a puzzle.

The puzzle was in the form of Zee standing next to his bed with three purple flowers in his hand, a blue-and-green plaid beanie on his head, and a gold tie that Casmir was fairly certain had been improvised from a soldier's dress uniform sash.

"This is not your usual uniform, Zee," Casmir said, his voice cracking. He found the water bottle in its holder attached to the wall by the bunk and took a sip while considering the flowers. They appeared to be real and freshly cut.

"I do not have a usual uniform, Casmir Dabrowski. You made me naked."

"Yes, I thought crushers should come into the world—the universe—the same way that people do."

"This is logical. Also, clothes would make it difficult when I shift forms."

"Yes. But you've decided to don some… clothes today. What's the reason?"

"Now that we are heading home, you will soon make me a mate."

Casmir wasn't sure that solved the puzzle of the flowers and clothing, but he smiled, reminded that they *were* going home. He couldn't wait to give everybody a hug.

His family would be bewildered since they, if he had his way, wouldn't hear about his Great Plague experience until he told them. *If* he told them. By the time the weeks of travel were over, he should be feeling much better, and he hoped his splotches would be gone so Oku wouldn't think he looked weirder than usual. Should he be lucky enough to wrangle an in-person meeting with her. After all the videos they had exchanged, he *thought* she would agree to a coffee date without the pretext of him carrying Kim's specimen case as the three of them met to speak about bees.

"So you're practicing being romantic for her? Do you want a *her*? Tork is a male android, and you're rather ambiguous, but we could attempt to give her female attributes when she's in her natural state." Casmir imagined the military researchers he'd worked with to create the original crushers, and could envision expressions of horror at a version of their killer robot with boobs.

"It is not important that my mate have a sex or gender. Neither the biological reproductive need nor the human social construct applies to crushers."

"This is true."

"Also, I am here with the flowers for you. More specifically, for your future mate."

"*My* future mate?" Casmir touched his chest.

"The female with the dog videos that you showed me. Many times."

"Ohhh. Princess Oku. She's not my—I mean, I'd like to ask her on a date, but I'm still trying to figure out… We've technically only met twice, you know." Casmir decided he couldn't count the various messages and videos that they'd sent back and forth, their number sadly lessened by the time lag of communicating between different star systems, as *meetings*.

"She is your future mate," Zee stated.

"You have faith in my ability to woo a woman?" Casmir was positive he hadn't programmed such faith into Zee, and even though Zee had the ability to learn, Casmir couldn't imagine he'd done anything to *teach* him that he had lady-wooing abilities.

"You turned the female humans President Nguyen and High Shaman Moonrazor from enemies to allies. Is this not indicative of your ability as a male to attract a female?"

"Uhm, not really. The president is married, and Moonrazor is... er, leads a cult. And is old."

"She kissed you."

"That wasn't a sign of affection. It was..."

Hell, he didn't know what it had been. Mostly a way to block Rache so he couldn't shoot her, and maybe a bit of a game-well-played gesture. His own mother would have found him too disgusting to kiss down there, after he'd thrown up and been sweating all over the place. He'd been told the rash on his face had been worse then too.

"Just don't tell anyone about that kiss, please. Not Oku. Or my mother. *Especially* not my mother. She doesn't want to put pressure on me, as she states frequently, but she would also love any kids I have to be good Jewish grandchildren. So I'd have to marry someone of my faith. Which Moonrazor definitely is not. She started her own faith. That's not allowed in my religion."

"Is Princess Oku of your faith?"

"Uhm. Probably... not. The royal family has always been Catholic, at least officially, though sometimes, people who marry into it start out as something else, like Queen Iku might have. And I think Jager is down somewhere as being an atheist, but he participates in the various religious holidays since it's expected. Princess Oku is probably... I should ask. Shinto, maybe? That's what Kim's family is. But Kim thinks religion is a mass delusion used to manipulate populaces into moral and legal compliance through fear, so I don't ask her opinions on, er, anything in that realm." Casmir nibbled on his lip. "My mother might not object to a *princess*, simply on the grounds of that being pretty special. Nobility, you know? And I'm also getting older. She might be happy if I just found *someone*. Maybe I should tell her about the cult-leader possibility to make anyone else seem like a relief. Do you think so? Though maybe Oku would consider converting. It's not that big of a deal for women. There's not as much mandatory reading and testing as there is for men. No pesky circumcision to deal with... Maybe... I should see if she is willing to go out on a date with me first."

Casmir gazed at Zee, as if he might have great wisdom in this area.

"That is a logical first step," Zee said, "and why I have come so attired. Kim has suggested that you compose poetry for the princess and that it would be *cute* if I delivered it. While holding flowers."

"Kim suggested I compose poetry?"

"Yes, but she also said it was unlikely you would do so, and as an alternative, suggested that math theorems or ancient poems translated into a programming language might win the heart of a science-minded princess."

Casmir wrinkled his nose. "I was thinking of sending her a list of comic books with dramatic protagonists who are scientists. I woke up to a few videos from her, and she mentioned seeing *Elder Seeds from Elder Earth*, and the villain who screwed everything up and almost ruined Odin was a crazy botanist. She took exception to that and pointed out all of the mad scientists portrayed as villains in literature, and noted how deplorable the trope is."

The door chime rang before Zee could answer. Perhaps that was just as well.

"Come in," Casmir called.

Kim strolled in with two coffee mugs.

"Good morning, Casmir. You look horrific, but there's color in your cheeks." She set a coffee mug down on his bedside table, then sat at the desk chair with hers.

"Horrific? Is that your professional medical assessment?"

"It is."

"Do you have some bacteria that could fix me?"

Her gaze drifted up past his forehead. "Part of the problem is that you slept with your head stuffed under a pillow, and your hair is sticking out in all directions."

"And there's no bacteria for that? Disappointing."

"Have you looked in the mirror?"

"No. I woke up and looked at Zee, and then I got distracted."

Kim eyed Zee's beanie and smiled. "I can see why. Make sure you flatten that nest—" she waved at his hair, "—before you record any videos for Oku."

"How did you know I was thinking of that?" Then he remembered Zee's attire had been her suggestion. And poetry, ugh.

"You're always thinking of that. How many have you recorded now?"

"Not more than… seventeen."

"How many has she sent back?"

He smiled a little smugly. "Sixteen."

Kim arched her eyebrows. "Really? That's promising."

"You think so? I just got the last batch she sent, since I've been so busy—and sick—but the time stamp on the most recent one is over a week old. I was a little worried she'd... grown bored. But sometimes, the courier ships aren't that reliable about jumping through the gates every day."

"Sixteen indicates some interest," Kim said. "I was concerned she might have only sent a couple and that you were..."

"Harassing her? Wasting her time? Making her wonder why she didn't punt me out of the courtyard the first time I walked into the castle?"

"On a vain quest."

"I'm not questing. I'm establishing a rapport."

"Casmir Dabrowski has expressed concern that Princess Oku is not of the proper faith," Zee announced.

"I didn't say that," Casmir blurted. "And my faith isn't *proper*; it's just what my family follows. And someone's religion doesn't matter to *me*, so long as they aren't a cult leader doing morally questionable or outright illegal things. I was just thinking aloud that my mother might want her to convert if we were ever to... make babies."

"Maybe you should ask her on a date first," Kim said.

"Exactly my plan. As soon as I get back. Which will be soon. I'm looking forward to it, even if I'm slightly terrified of my inevitable chat with King Jager and Royal Intelligence."

Kim frowned pensively into her mug.

"You think they'll let me see my parents before questioning and/ or torturing me, don't you? And Oku... I offered to make her a high-powered robotic composter that could collect its own raw materials from the chicken coop behind the castle kitchen. She seemed very interested."

"Mm." Definitely pensive.

Maybe he should change the subject.

"Do you know how Rache escaped with his mercenaries and his ship?" Casmir asked. "And if he got any pieces of the gate for himself? I know the Kingdom ships were on the *Fedallah's* tail at the end."

"I haven't spoken to him, and I don't know the details of his escape or what he managed to pull out of there, but I wouldn't be surprised if he finagled some of the gate pieces somehow."

"Are you still angry with him for kidnapping us?"

Her lips pressed together. "I wasn't pleased to be kidnapped, but since the *Waddler* and its crew didn't make it..."

"Ah, right." Casmir grimaced. He should have changed the subject to something less bleak.

It saddened him to think of how many people had died on this mission. He didn't believe it had needed to go that way.

Kim's expression remained pensive, so he did his best to smile and assume a light tone. "Dr. Sikou said Rache sent me some humongously expensive vial of immune-improving stuff that he'd probably been saving in a special vault for himself. Is that true? Please tell me I don't owe him my life, Kim."

"He also gave you the blood sample that contained the antibodies that helped your immune system fight off the Plague," Kim murmured.

"Then I *do* owe him my life. That's awful. I mean, I'm glad to be alive, but he's the *last* person I want to owe anything. What if he comes collecting?" Casmir's eye blinked. It seemed improved immunity wasn't going to do anything for his physical tics. Too bad. "Do you think I can just get him a gift when we get home? What gift says *thanks for the blood*? Not underwear again. You can only give underwear once. How about luggage? He travels all the time. Do mercenaries use luggage?"

Kim took a deep breath. "Something's up, Casmir."

"What do you mean?" He didn't like that solemn, concerned expression she wore.

Usually, she inhaled the aroma of her coffee often and smiled contentedly as she consumed it. Not today.

"Nobody has officially told me anything, but I've heard a few rumors from the sickbay staff. There may be trouble at home."

Casmir sank back against his pillows. "No. No more trouble is allowed. Kim, we *solved* the trouble. Or at least, the trouble was resolved in a way that may or most likely may not please the king. But either way, it's resolved. The gate is divvied up and headed off in dozens of directions." He extended his hand toward the outer wall. "And we resolved the trouble at Tiamat Station too. There shouldn't be any more trouble. We've exceeded our quota."

"I don't disagree." She sipped from her mug.

Casmir let his chin droop, new worry forming in a tight ball in his chest. Trouble at *home*, she'd said. Something going on back on Odin? More terrorists? What?

The door chimed again.

"I don't want to answer that," Casmir said. "I don't want to invite the trouble in."

"It's not in this system," Kim said.

Zee walked to the door and opened it. Asger walked in.

"Nice hat, Zee." His tone was flat, tired.

Casmir had a premonition that he knew about the trouble too. They were going to tell him, and he hadn't decided if he wanted to know.

"I am dressed to read poetry to a lady," Zee announced.

"That's good. Ladies like men who dress well. I have news, friends." Asger looked around at the dearth of seating—Kim had the only chair—and then sank down on the end of the bunk. "How are you feeling, Casmir?"

Not wanting to hear his news, Casmir opted for a flippant response. "I'm feeling better, but Kim informs me that my hair is woeful. And she doesn't have a bacterial concoction to fix it."

"Among the nobility, we use a new invention called shampoo. And if your hair is especially fine and full of lush locks—" Asger ran a hand down his shoulder-length locks, though his smile didn't reach his eyes, "—you might try conditioner too."

"Are my locks lush and in need of that?" Casmir looked at Kim for an opinion.

"The shampoo is probably enough," she said.

"That's disappointing."

"You might try some volumizer," Asger suggested.

"It's strange that you know what that is," Kim said.

"Yeah." Asger grimaced. "Don't tell my father."

"His locks are lush. He probably knows what it is too."

Asger looked aggrieved. "*Especially* don't tell him you've noticed his hair."

Kim wriggled a couple of fingers in agreement. "What's your news?"

"No," Casmir said. "I don't want to hear the news. I've been sick. Sick people are supposed to recover and not experience stress. Let's keep talking about silly things. You can even pick on my hair."

Asger smiled sadly at him, then faced Kim. "I was up most of the night in a meeting with Ishii, the three other Fleet captains who were on the comm, Ambassador Romano, a gruff marine commander, and the tattooed formerly-undercover Sir Bjarke Asger."

"Had I known you'd spent hours enduring that company," Kim said, "I would have also brought you a mug of coffee. With extra shots of espresso."

"I'd need it to have extra shots of whiskey to help." Asger scraped his fingers through his hair, artfully mussing his locks. Kim did not accuse him of turning them into a nest. "While we've been busy here, an invasion force entered System Lion. It consists of a new alliance, including several mercenary outfits and ships from two of the Miners' Union families. The Dubashis are one. They've blockaded our gate so nobody can get in or out, at least not easily. Four couriers got themselves killed trying to run the blockade and get the news out. The fifth made it through. Barely."

Casmir closed his eyes, worried for his parents and all his friends and students and everyone he knew back home.

"The captains and I—and my father—got similar orders," Asger said. "Since we can't return to System Lion without running the blockade— where, if there's enough firepower, we might be destroyed—we're to divert to System Stymphalia."

"Stymphalia?" Casmir had heard the system mentioned a few times lately and tried to remember why.

"Prince Jorg got stranded there," Asger said.

Casmir slumped deeper into his pillows. Now, he remembered. Moonrazor had said her people had control of that gate—or maybe that they were in a position to take control when they needed it. They couldn't have control yet, or the Fleet wouldn't have been ordered to go there.

"Jorg went to Stymphalia to announce a betrothal to a Miners' Union princess, but she apparently decided she didn't want to marry him. He was on his way back when the war broke out. We're to go to Stymphalia and unite with Jorg and follow whatever orders he has." Asger grimaced.

Casmir didn't know Jager's eldest son well, just that he was about thirty and had been unwilling to follow the royal family tradition of serving as an officer in the military for a term. Casmir could imagine Asger and the captains not being pleased to have to follow his orders.

"From the conversation, it sounded like *Jorg's* orders are to call in as many allies as he can, gather a huge fleet, and return home to retake the gate, if the System Lion Fleet hasn't managed to do so yet on its own. From there, our combined forces will drive out any remaining invaders in our system."

"And what are *our* orders?" Kim pointed at herself and at Casmir. "As civilian advisors."

"Nobody mentioned you. If you're smart, you'll stay out of the way and keep a low profile, especially since Romano may still be gunning for you." Asger gazed at Casmir. His expression was knowing, as if he didn't truly expect Casmir to do either of those things.

Kim was giving him a similar look.

Casmir lifted his hands. "I'm too sick to get in the way. I'll be in my cabin, hugging my pillows, and hoping Jorg knows what he's doing."

Asger sighed and stood. "Me too, my friend. Me too."

He lifted a hand in parting and walked out.

"What are you *really* going to do?" Kim asked.

"I don't know. I'm tired. I need to think about it. I don't honestly know what I *can* do."

"I'm sure you'll think of some way to be…"

"Brilliant? Integral? Heroic?"

"Meddlesome."

"Ah. Quite."

THE END

Made in the USA
Monee, IL
13 February 2020